First, Tell No Lies

Clare Josa

© Clare Josa, 2018
www.ClareJosa.com

Published by Beyond Alchemy Publishing, UK, 2018
For bulk orders and book club resources, contact hello@beyond-alchemy.com

A CIP catalogue record for this title is available from the British Library.

Paperback ISBN 978-1-908854-91-9
eBook ISBN 978-1-908854-92-6

The right of Clare Josa to be identified as the Author of the Work has been asserted by her, in accordance with the Copyright, Designs and Patent Act 1988.

All rights reserved. No part of this publication may be reproduced, stored in a retrieval system, or transmitted, in any form or by any means, without the prior written permission of the Author.

Cover design by Rocío Martín Osuna
Image credits: Ibrandify and Freepik, freepik.com

This is a work of fiction. Any similarity between the characters and situations within its pages and places or persons, living or dead, is unintentional and co-incidental.

Join the Readers' Club:

www.clarejosa.com/firsttellnolies/club

Members get full access to:

Exclusive deleted scenes
Interviews with the author
Book 2 ½ of the Denucci Deception series

Join free now:
www.clarejosa.com/firsttellnolies/club

Dedication:

To the readers of You Take Yourself With You who told the world it was 'unputdownable'. You know who you are! Thank you for making my dream come true. I hope you love this next instalment.

And to my family, for your unwavering support of the creative process and all its quirks.

Also by Clare Josa:

Fiction:

You Take Yourself With You – Book one of the Denucci Deception series

Non-Fiction:

Dare To Dream Bigger
52 Mindful Moments
A Year Full Of Gratitude
The Little Book Of Daily Sunshine
28 Day Meditation Challenge

Clare's books are all available to order in your favourite bookstore or from online retailer.

Previously

Sophie

Stuart's face contorted with anger, but I was only just getting started. "Look, I'm not taking any more of this from you! You're not better than me. The only reason you're senior to me is because you're Harry's best mate from Uni; because he owns the company and did you a favour. And I won't take you putting me down any more." His eyes were like arrow slits. "We both know I can do this job standing on my head." He was now an unsubtle shade of puce, hungry to retaliate, but I didn't give him a chance, "I've had enough of you putting me down and making me look bad in front of Harry. You have broken so many laws with your behaviour."

I had to pause to breathe, which gave him a chance to butt in. After five months of taking his abuse, I had finally cracked.

"What about your reference, Sophie? You'll never get a new job if I give you a bad one. Remember the *offer* I made you?" *He's trying to make me give up. I won't. I'm worth more than this.*

"Fuck that, Stuart! And, no, I won't ever fuck you, no matter how hard you try to blackmail me into it. You repulse me."

I was yelling by now. Harry's office door was ajar. Everyone had stopped working to listen.

"I don't need a reference from you!"

He looked like he wanted to explode. His whole body was

quivering. Everyone was staring. I wasn't sure we had ever had entertainment like this in the office before.

"And we both know I know you've been fiddling your expenses, which is why you had to leave your last job, because they caught you out. Just fuck off and leave me alone!"

Stuart stared at me in stunned silence as we both saw Harry standing in the doorway. He had heard every word.

I mentally picked up what remained of my dignity and walked back to my desk. "Morning, Harry! I wonder if you might have a minute for a chat later?" I smiled on my way out.

Christof

Luca was itching for news, so I headed straight back to the office after my train got in to Milan, despite my late night stake-out in Naples meaning my body was screaming for sleep.

"Great! I saw him. Watched him in action. I got the videos. The Client will be able to tell who it was and we should be able to trace the transactions to that computer terminal, now we know when it was used."

Luca grinned. "A complete success!" he laughed, looking happy and relieved, "I knew I could rely on you, Christof."

His smile dropped as he looked at my face. He knew there was something I wasn't telling him.

"What is it? What went wrong, Christof? Were you seen?"

"Maybe." I conceded, holding my hands still in my lap, trying not to let my nerves show with fidgeting.

"Walk me through exactly what happened. Don't miss out a thing."

I took him through the whole evening, up to the point where I had thought my bag was missing, but it wasn't, and then got back to the hotel, following procedure by locking the camera in my room safe, before treating myself to a nerve-calming whisky or three. He didn't mind that bit.

"So, what's the problem?" I still wished I knew the answer to that question. I had been racking my brain on it for the whole 4½ hours on the train. Something didn't feel right.

"I don't know. Nothing, most likely. Just something feels off. I was even more cautious than usual for the stake-out, given the raised dangers on this project," we both knew I was talking about the corpse count.

I must have sounded defensive, because Luca rushed to reassure me.

"I know you were careful, Christof. It's just that we can't afford to take any risks. I don't want to blow this project and I don't want you hurt." Genuine concern showed in his face.

"Let's look at the videos," he said, changing the subject and giving us both something practical to focus on.

I pulled out the camera that had been untouched, safe in my jacket pocket for the whole of the journey. I couldn't risk watching the videos on the train. It's always exciting – that moment of slight stress as you hope the camera did its job and wonder what you'll see.

I pressed the play button and nothing happened. I wanted to shake it, like a child frustrated by a Christmas toy that doesn't work without its batteries. I resisted. The screen was telling me that the memory card was empty. There were no videos on the camera.

"Shit! The stupid thing didn't work?" Luca was almost yelling with frustration.

"No, that can't be right. I did the usual test video before I left the hotel. It should be there. I watched it a bit last night before I went to the bar, to make sure the camera had worked." I pulled the camera back from him and desperately searched for at least the test video. It wasn't there.

"Are you telling me that the memory card wiped itself while you were asleep? You must have messed up the settings."

Luca tends to accuse without thinking when he's stressed. I was half a step ahead as I pulled my phone out of my pocket to find the back-up photos.

"Don't worry. I took the back-up shots on my phone, as per procedure. They won't be as good, but they should still be enough to identify our inside man."

I used my thumb to unlock the phone and scrolled through the recent photos in the viewing app. I'm careful to delete old photos as soon as they have been backed up. They can munch up storage space and you never know when you might need to record something important. The last thing I want is for my phone to tell me it's full at a critical moment.

The only photos in there should have been from last night's stake-out, plus one of a weird pattern I saw in the lighting over my platform at Milano Centrale station yesterday, which appealed to my love of abstract designs. I quickly found that, but it was the only photo on my camera.

That couldn't be right, could it?

Luca saw the dread in my eyes and instantly jumped to the right conclusion.

"Gone, too?"

My silent nod confirmed his fears.

"Not even you, distracted as you are these days, would screw up both cameras. What else happened last night that you haven't told me about?"

I felt a sick cold rush through me. I didn't want to have to tell him the truth, but I knew I had no choice. I told him the briefest overview I dared of what had happened in the bar, but not about the events when I took her back to my room. That was private.

"Yes," I said, thinking back, scene by scene through my evening, "I checked the videos had worked last night, before I locked the camera and the phone in my safe. The camera had worked."

"What aren't you telling me about last night, Christof?" Reluctantly I gave in and told him.

"For fuck's sake, Christof! That's the oldest trick in the book! How did you fall for it?"

I felt really stupid. A prize idiot. He was right. How did I manage to miss it? It should have been so obvious.

"I've never done anything like that before," I mumbled. It didn't help. Luca was on a steam train with his anger by this point. Rightly so.

"So... you were so drunk and tired that you slept through the beep of your safe being opened by the room key you no doubt left on your bedside table? And you left your thumb print lying around, so she could get into your phone?"

I stared at my shoes.

"And she followed you to your hotel, without you noticing?" Yes, probably.

"How am I going to break this one to the client?"

I shook my head, glad that wasn't my job.

"Look, it's not all lost. You'll be able to identify the person from the personnel records and you can still remember the name of the person whose desk they used?"

I nodded, still not knowing what to say.

"We'll have our man and we'll be able to trace the transactions, but we've lost our evidence. We can't prove anything, unless you testify in Court, which means Denucci will link you with the case and you would be at risk of taking a swim in a cement bath. Didn't you think?" He was spitting with rage. I had no answers to give him. "We had to show that guy doing it, other- wise they could claim that someone stole their work ID. And you and I both know that's the last time Denucci will use the pattern he's followed for the past few months. Whoever that woman was will have tipped him off. There's no chance of another stake-out."

I wanted the ground to open up beneath me. I couldn't believe I had been so stupid. Luca pointed out what I already knew: "We've missed our chance to catch him in the act. And that means we've missed our chance to convince the police to take this seriously. Denucci is likely to get away with it – again! – all because you let your guard down. I'm disappointed in you, Christof. I hope she was worth it."

June

Discovered

a sunlit sparkle
the thrill of discovery
riches in the rocks

I was feeling irritable; I had been drowning in cherries all week with the festival... the heat; the smell; the sun; the crowds... so many strangers. I was longing to get back to the farm for a few days. Even going back to the stress of my 'real' job in Milan would feel relaxing after this.

I'd had to smile at so many people that my cheeks felt tired, like a bridegroom at his wedding reception. Strangers' faces blurred into one and it was getting harder to be polite to each person who asked for yet another 'free taster'.

Then there was the crumpled petrol station receipt I had found on the floor of my flat earlier this morning, from Naples. The thought of it made my heart race and the hairs on the back of my neck prickle. I looked around instinctively, with that eerie feeling that I was being watched. But there was no one there. I shrugged off my paranoia and allowed my feet to steer me through the empty streets. There were fewer people in this part of town –almost enough air to breathe, though I would have given half my crop for a fresh breeze. I had been forcing myself to pay attention as I walked up the cobbled steps; they were old and irregular and it would have been easy to misjudge them, falling flat on my face and providing an excited tourist with their next Instagram hit.

Ouch! A random tourist had her head half in her bag, as she stumbled into me in the empty street. It was a wonder she hadn't fallen and broken her neck on these old steps. I wanted to yell and ask her why she wasn't looking where she was going. I bit my tongue. It wasn't her fault I was fed up.

"*Sta bene?*" I asked. No response. I tried English; always a good second guess.

"Are you okay?" The traces of recent sunburn on her arms made it a likely bet that she was a tourist from somewhere cooler. She was loaded with bags that made it clear that she was either arriving or leaving – a rucksack and a scruffy holdall. Not exactly *Italian flair*, but also not *American-traveller chic*... more like *Backpacker Brit*.

She had dropped her floppy straw hat when we bumped into each other. I bent down to pick it up for her, a reflex reaction. I didn't notice that she was bending down, too. *Bang.* Heads collided. *Ahia!* Ouch. Again. I reached out and picked up the hat, handing it to her, rubbing my forehead with my free hand.

"Your hat," I said in English, still hopeful it might be a language she spoke. Then I hoped it wasn't, because I just sounded like a complete prat. Of course it was her hat! Who else's would it have been? She pulled it back on, catching her long hair messily under it, to give space for a breeze on the back of her neck. Now I was grumpy *and* an idiot – great first impression. I'd really had enough of this festival. I was glad the street was empty, so there was no one to tease me about this later.

She was rubbing her head where we bumped, totally preoccupied. She still hadn't spoken. Maybe I could still get away with this. *Time to leave. I'll forget about a 'thank you' if I can escape with some dignity intact.*

I was still half-crouching as she started to walk away. She turned back and looked at me with confusion in her eyes. Crazy? Drunk? Sunstroke? Concussed? Early thirties – too young for dementia. Her sunglasses reflected my sullen mood back at me.

"Wait!" she shouted, grabbing my shirt sleeve, to stop me from leaving. She was scanning my face with an intensity usually reserved for school nurses with nit combs. *"It's you!"*

The words were out of my mouth before I realised how bonkers they sounded. *"It's you!"* But I couldn't believe it was him. Chestnut eyes... That smile... *Mr Clafoutis!* Then I remembered he would have no idea who I was or how I might know him. He was looking at me, confused. I was grabbing hold of his sleeve. Maybe he didn't speak English? But of course he did — that's why he'd been interviewed by the BBC for the travel show that had lured me to this cherry festival. *Duh!*

I could see cogs whirring as he tried to get his head round my behaviour.

"Ah," he said slowly. "You saw the TV interview?" He had the slightest trace of an Italian accent. I caught myself wondering if he knew how incredibly sexy that was. Then I thanked my lucky stars I hadn't thought that out loud.

"Yes, the travel programme interview... about the festival. It's why I came. I was already coming to Italy and I love cherries so much that I decided I couldn't miss it. My friend Anna – I sleep on her sofa – thought it would be really funny if we met and fell in love and got married and had a family. But I really came for the cherries. And we met once – in Paris – and you let me have the last slice of *clafoutis*!"

That. Was. Out. Loud. Ground, swallow me up. How quickly can I get away from here?

His face made it clear that he had no memory of meeting me in Paris last year. Why should he? We had been in a queue in a *boulangerie* and he let me have the last slice of my favourite treat – *clafoutis*. When I had seen him on the travel programme it had earned him the nickname *Mr Clafoutis* with my flatmate, Anna.

It was clear that my confession had made him even more wary of me and he looked like he was about to walk away. He couldn't have made it more obvious that he had more important things to do. The chill of my disappointment surprised me.

But I was lost and my bags were so heavy, and it was so unbearably hot, and there was no way a taxi would spontaneously show up in these empty streets, so I had to walk. I knew my hotel must be nearby. I was staring at my hiking boots – another stupid decision. I wanted to ask him for help but I felt I had done enough blushing already in the past few minutes. Maybe if I ignored him he would just walk away. Then I could walk purposefully up a side street and hide in the shade until he was gone.

"Well, you'll certainly find plenty of cherries here. You've come to the right place. Me... I've had enough of them for today." *He hasn't run away yet. Why not?*

"I'm Christof," he said, offering me his hand to shake. How very English he seemed when he did that. "I'm afraid I don't remember the *clafoutis*, but I hope you enjoyed it."

Awkward silence. *Oh, yes, it's my turn.*

"Err... yes... It was lovely. Hi... I'm Sophie. I'm from England." I felt like I should follow it, AA style, with a confession about something I was addicted to. Putting my foot in my mouth, perhaps?

"I guessed that," he replied.

"What? That I'm called Sophie? How?"

"No. The England bit."

Really, ground, swallow me up now. Big hole. Gone. Please.

I could feel my cheeks turning as scarlet as the day when I was thirteen and Miss Montague caught me with a poster of Robbie Williams in my school locker, in nothing but his boxer shorts.

"Are you lost? It's just that we don't get many tourists in this part of the town. Can I help you?"

Would he please stop being kind? Can't he tell I just want to run and hide behind the nearest bin until it's dark and I can stop making a fool of myself? Okay, deep breath. I am lost.

He seemed to know this place. *The BBC wouldn't have interviewed him, if he were a psycho, would they?* I wasn't sure that was a good enough metric, but I had no idea where my hotel was and I needed a shower. And to ditch these bags. They had doubled in weight since I got off the train, half an hour ago.

Should I trust him? Hmmm… Trust and men – not two words that normally go together in my world at the moment. But I'm not sure what other options I have right now. I don't speak much Italian. He speaks English and he has offered to help.

"Yes, I'm lost. I'm looking for my hotel." The words made the decision for me as I scrabbled in my pocket, which was where I suddenly remembered I had left the crumpled piece of paper that wasn't in my bag. Hunting for it in my holdall had been the reason I had bumped into *Mr Clafoutis*. I handed the paper to him, with its scribbled and smudged address. *Ooh, I'm making a great impression again: elegant, sophisticated Sophie with her posh luggage and perfect hair…* I hadn't expected to need to make a good first impression on anyone.

"It's just around the corner. Let me help you." He sensed my reluctance. "Please?" He gave me a smile that caught me off-guard, after his distant attitude so far. Its warmth spread crinkling lines around his eyes. I found my annoyance melting with relief at his offer of help, but I really didn't want to add 'weak at the knees' to my current list of unimpressive skills. It must have been the heat… and exhaustion.

I decided that keeping my mouth shut was the best option, so I tried a smile, which felt more like a grimace, and gave him a nod.

"Let me take your rucksack."

He reached for my bag and my anti-theft instincts kicked in. *Not on your nelly, mate!* I clung to my rucksack for dear life. "No!" I yelled, slightly too loudly, my voice echoing around the shady street with its tall terraces of houses. The dark green shutters on a nearby building, closed for the siesta, opened just wide enough for a curious elderly lady to watch the impromptu street theatre.

"Okay, have it your way!" he smiled at me. It was turning into a grin. Now I could add 'ludicrous' to the list of adjectives he would be using to describe me to his friends by the evening. "You can carry the bags, but I can still show you the way."

It wasn't far to my hotel, but I wished I hadn't been so pig-headed about the rucksack. It was all uphill over cobbled steps that looked like they had been there for hundreds of years. They were just the wrong height and length for normal walking with legs as short as mine, and I soon found myself doing a double-walk on one step only to trip up the next one in what must have looked like an incompetent attempt at skipping. I could see he was finding this quietly amusing. *I will NOT allow myself to feel stupid.*

"Breathe deeply, let it go and smile!" Oh, how I wanted to *kick* the woman who had written that book. What the bleep did she know, anyway? It was one of the many that my godmother, Jem, had given me last month when she had stepped in to rescue me from the ocean of self-pity I had been drowning in because my now-ex-boss was a shit. I had thrown that book back at Jem and she was probably the only person on the planet who could get away with telling me that the book had 'pressed my buttons' and I 'wasn't ready for it yet'. Distracted by my thoughts, I hadn't noticed the progress we were making through the streets.

"Here you are," Christof said, pointing at an old wooden

door, faded blue, with my hotel's name above it in white, flaking paint on a sign that had long since given up hope of anyone caring for it enough to repair it. I wasn't sure this boded well, but all I wanted was a shower and I didn't care if the water was stone cold.

"Thank you," I mumbled, as I reached for the door handle, relieved that this was nearly over and I would never have to see this guy again. Eye contact again. I realised I had managed to avoid it after the unfortunate head-banging-hat-picking-up moment. The deepest chestnut brown. *Anna was right. He is a hefty dose of eye candy. Yes, I know I'm not supposed to say that. But he can't hear me.* I reached out to shake his hand and say goodbye, half-expecting him to have already turned his back and be walking away.

But he was still standing there, looking at me, smiling. He didn't notice my hand. I let it fall by my side, pretending I had been using it to swat away a non-existent, annoying fly. He looked at his watch. "Would you like a coffee?"

"No! I'd like a shower!" I blurted, heartfelt, before I could edit. A hint of disappointment flashed across his face. "Oh. Okay. Well, enjoy your holiday… and the cherries." He started to turn to walk away.

Hang on, I like this guy. He was lovely on the telly and he's even better in real life and he just asked me for a coffee and I have no idea where the nearest café is. I'm turning him down. Why?

I sensed I had only a microsecond to fix this before he walked out of my life forever. Again. My gut told me I didn't want that.

"I mean, I've been travelling for hours and I just want to get showered and changed. If you know anywhere good for a coffee, I could be ready in about half an hour. But I'd prefer an ice cream."

His face lit up. "I know the perfect place. You'll love it. I'll see you back out here in half an hour. Enjoy your shower!"

I couldn't decide if he was being polite or creepy, as I turned to the hotel door and entered the stiflingly hot lobby. I didn't look back.

Well, that was a surprise. I couldn't put it down as one of my best ever first impressions, but the fact that Sophie had agreed to meet me for ice cream showed it hadn't been as bad as I thought. I needed the distraction and she seemed interesting. It wasn't often I found an English woman roaming the streets of this town on her own, and I was curious to find out more.

But first I had to phone my solicitor, to make sure everything was still on for 3 p.m., when we were due to meet with Francesco, to save the farm from his disastrous loan. It felt like an anti-climax, now I was so close to sorting out the mess, after months of lying awake all night, worrying that we would lose the farm. I had given up pulling out the new grey hairs.

Francesco is the cousin of Pietro, who manages our cherry farm. Shortly before the car crash that killed Dad, which I survived, Dad had taken out a massive loan to go into business with Francesco, to open a hardware shop in the quietest part of our town. No payments had been made for over a year and I only found out about the loan when the bank threatened to repossess the farm. Finding out about that last month had been a real shock.

To make things even more interesting, the title deeds for the shop only showed Francesco's name and there was no way of proving that Dad had provided the finance. My work in Milan meant I was used to finding hidden tracks left by money transfers, but I couldn't prove anything other than that Dad had gifted the money to Pietro, who had then given it to Francesco. I couldn't find any agreement to go into business as partners or to split the profits.

Through the miracle of Nonna's – my grandmother's - networks, she had persuaded Francesco's mother, Marisa, a woman who had always looked on Nonna as an 'honorary aunt', to apply pressure and force him to come back to town today, to sign documents handing the shop premises over to the farm and confirming the agreement he and Dad had made. This was in return for us legally promising never to press charges of any form. But I was nervous that he might not show. And even once everything was signed, I would still have to find a way to clear the loan. Doing a quick sale on the shop would generate a massive loss in the current market and the farm had no funds to pay next month's loan instalment, unless I could get a good price for the cherry harvest, which I should have sold back in January. Things were not looking great.

So much was hanging on the negotiations I was doing this week. I was grateful for my experience of high-pressure projects at work, tracking down fraud and theft for large businesses. This meant I was able to stay practical and ignore the emotions that were now making my stomach tie itself in knots.

It was vital that Francesco couldn't sense my panic and fear, or he might change his mind about the deal his mother had agreed to. People can always smell desperation.

I looked at my watch: an eighteenth birthday present from Nonna and Dad. I had time for half an hour with Sophie before I had to go to the solicitor at three. I might as well enjoy it.

One seriously cold shower and a fresh change of clothes soon had me feeling human again. I had worn my Italian-train-air-conditioning-defying trousers and top for the journey from Florence, because otherwise I'd have frozen. Good tickets on long-distance trains come with ferocious air-conditioning and you really need it in the Italian summer. It was hot, even for June. Local stopping services often have broken air-conditioning, leaving travellers gasping for air at minuscule windows, which the guard usually keeps locked for some reason that will remain one of the Universe's eternal mysteries, turning everyone into buckets of sweat by the time they limp out of the train at their final destination. For today's four-hour trip from Florence, changing to a chug-along from Milan to the town here, I had chosen the refrigerated option for as far as I could, donning enough clothes to protect me from inevitable freeze.

As a result, having wandered for over half an hour from the station on foot, I was soaked with sweat by the time I had lugged my bags to the hotel, feeling completely overdressed for the weather. It felt such a relief to wear a lightweight summer dress and slip on my sandals again, instead of my hiking boots, which would have tipped the weight of my rucksack into the 'unliftable zone', had I worn my sandals on the train. I would also have risked losing my toes to frostbite.

I was really looking forward to my ice cream and hoping that it wouldn't be too weird enjoying it with a total stranger. I could hear Mum now: "Do you know anything about him?" *No!* "Why are you going to wander through the back streets of an unknown town with him? He could be a rapist! Or a murderer!" *Or a really nice guy.* I guess she sees it as her job to worry.

My room at the hotel was simple, but clean. There was a desk fan instead of air-conditioning and a large window, which probably wouldn't do much other than let the mosquitoes in, given how close the buildings were in this street. But at least my room wasn't facing the extractor fan from the hotel's kitchen, like it was in my last place. I chucked my valuables into the room safe and grabbed my small bag, with enough cash for today and my passport, and I was ready to go.

I wondered what flavours they would have at this ice cream place. I felt so much lighter without my heavy bags that I half-skipped down the hotel stairs. I handed my heavy, antique room key in at reception, dying to ask how they coped without even a desk fan in this tiny, stuffy space, but my Italian wasn't up to it and I figured a game of impromptu *Charades* might take too long. I went outside to wait for Christof, who was already there.

"Great. Let's go, then!"

Not much of a greeting. Maybe small-talk wasn't his thing. But I could always run, once I had guzzled my ice cream, if he turned out to be a weirdo. It wasn't like we were on a date or anything.

He handed me a tourist map of the town and I noticed two routes marked in red. I looked at him, silently asking him what it was for.

"It's the way to the ice cream place. This area is like a rabbit warren and there aren't many signposts, as you've already worked out. I wanted to make sure you can find your way to your hotel afterwards. I've got meetings this afternoon, so I won't be able to escort you back."

"And the second line?"

"Wait and see!" he replied, tension showing on his face. He quickly replaced it with a smile.

"Thank you. That's kind of you," I said, slightly miffed that this not-a-date might only last fifteen minutes.

"How do you know words like 'rabbit warren'?" I asked, intrigued. "That's a bit obscure for Italian schoolboy English, isn't it?" The smile froze.

"English mother, Italian father, lots of Beatrix Potter at bedtime. But I grew up here. This way!" I could feel him changing the subject and my market research experience meant I knew better than to push for more. He was wearing the face that told me to 'let this one rest for now or I'll clam up and the interview is over'. Years of persuading people to tell me their deepest secrets, so I could brief the team in our advertising agency on marketing concepts, had taught me that pushing my way along conversational dead ends meant I would get nothing useful from the interviewee. I risked wasting the client's fee – and getting in trouble with my boss, when they listened to the recording of the interview.

"Tell me, why do you love this ice cream place so much that you'd share it with a visiting Brit?" I asked, noticing relief in his face at me going along with the subject change, and using my hyper-cheery voice.

I realised slightly too late that I had made eye contact with him again. That was a really bad idea. My insides did a pirouette each time he smiled at me and I was *not* interested in men right now. The latest fiasco with my ex – Jamie – had left me doubting my judgement when it came to romance. And with my new job next week – a promotion to be a planner in an advertising agency – starting next week, I didn't want any distractions.

"It does real ice cream, not the powdered stuff most places sell. It was set up by a friend of Nonna, my grandmother, about fifty years ago and the family still uses the traditional recipes. It's the only place in town that does. Plus, I'm biased because they use our cherries in their cherry ice cream. And given that you said you had come here for the cherries, I figured you might like to try it."

"You grow cherries?"

"Yes, my family owns a farm near here. Remember the TV interview?"

I refused to allow myself to blush again.

"Sorry, I shouldn't tease. It's just that you made quite a fuss about that interview when you met me less than an hour ago and I'm not used to strangers grabbing me in the street. It wasn't broadcast out here, thank goodness, or I would never have been able to show my face at work again."

We had moved beyond the treacherous stone steps and were onto a cobbled street. Right and left turns passed me by and I was glad I had my map for later.

"You mean at the farm? Why would they make fun of you?"

"No. The farm belongs to my family. My real job is in Milan. I work for a business consultancy firm. Here we are!" he announced, before I had a chance to ask him any more.

We arrived at a tiny shop that was more of a counter than an ice cream parlour. A handful of colourful bar stools stood, unused, along one side. Christof was greeted with a torrent of friendly Italian by the man behind the counter. Hugs were exchanged, hands were shaken, and I realised he had introduced me.

"*Ciao, Sofia!*" I heard as I, too, got to join in the hug dance, with added double kisses. "*Gelato alla ciliegia? Con le ciliegie di Christof?*"

I looked at him blankly.

"He's asking if you'd like the cherry ice cream that has my farm's cherries in it."

"*Si, per favore,*" I managed, my face producing a display of instant-sunburn red, wondering whether there had been any point in the Italian evening classes I had taken last year. A few moments later a waffle cone with the biggest scoops of cherry ice cream ever was thrust into my hand. Christof had the same.

"On ze house, *bella Sofia!*" sang Christof's friend. He and Christof exchanged a few moments of what sounded like rapid-fire Italian to my struggling ears, there was no way I could keep up, before another round of handshakes and hugs, with more double kisses for me. I moved towards the bar stools.

"No, not inside," said Christof. "There's somewhere else I want to show you." He led me out of the ice cream shop, through another maze of back streets until we found an ornate metal gate, almost hidden by a coral-red honeysuckle, drooping lazily over the iron fence.

"In here," he said, as he opened the creaking gate, revealing a small park that looked like something out of *The Secret Garden*. It took my breath away, full of scented blooms and shady corners. He walked towards an old wooden bench, under the shade of a lilac tree. No one else was here.

"It's a part of the town that tourists never find, because we fought hard to keep it off the tourist map. We had to petition the mayor. That was years ago now, but the exemption is still working. It's just for us, the locals. On a day like today it's empty, because everyone is at the cherry festival. But I wanted you to see it. You're welcome to stay here after I go to my meeting. Just make sure you close the gate behind you."

"Thank you. And wow!" was all I could say.

We sat next to each other on the bench, but not too close, and I licked up the cherry ice cream drips from my cone. He was right. It was good. Really good. Rich and creamy with a strong hint of fresh vanilla; the real thing, not 'essence'. The half-cherries were juicy and not too sweet and there were streaks of thick cherry syrup, like raspberry ripple, laced through the vanilla. It was too good to interrupt with talking.

It felt so easy sitting next to him, not feeling the need to chat – to keep up conversation. I felt my body relax, sitting there in silence, even though we were practically strangers. His company was nearly as delicious as the ice cream.

"So, what do you do, when you're not assaulting accidental TV stars in Italian back streets?" he smiled, in a pause in the silence.

"I'm in market research. I specialise in advertising. I start my new job next week, so I thought I'd take a holiday between jobs. I needed a break. It can get pretty intense in London: lots of late nights with focus groups, asking total strangers about their most intimate secrets. Wine always helps, but there's a bit of skill in there, too." I thought back to the fateful evening with the semi-naked male models and the deodorant campaign last year, in my old job, and decided to leave my answer where it was. I also decided not to mention the drama that had driven me to quit my last job and was relieved when Christof distracted me with another question.

"You know how people tick?" he asked.

"I suppose so. Or at least the people who pay me think I do. I know which questions to ask and how to listen to the meaning *beneath* the answers."

He looked intrigued. "Do you think you could figure *me* out?" It almost felt like a challenge. There was more to that question than he was saying in words. From what I knew of him so far, it was a definite *no*. But there was something about him that made me curious.

"Maybe," I replied, deciding to play it as coy as he was. "But would you want me to?"

He smiled. Then he looked at his knees, as though lost in

thought. *Okay. He wins. I want to figure him out. Right now, I want it even more than cherry ice cream. And that's saying something.*

His phone beeped. He didn't look at it, as though he knew who it was. He checked his watch. "I've got to go now: cherry business. World-changing stuff, obviously. The second red line takes you from here to your hotel. I wanted to give you both options, because I wasn't sure if you might ditch me at the ice cream parlour." He was smiling, but I could sense a fragile tone in his voice, hinting that he had feared rejection.

"But if you don't already have plans, I'd like to take you to dinner tonight. There's a great little place you might enjoy. I could meet you at your hotel at eight?"

I smiled at him but didn't answer. He took it as a yes.

"Eight then," he smiled back, "and you might want to bring a shawl. It can get breezy by the river."

He walked away without looking back, closing the gate behind him, leaving me to finish my cherry ice cream with just the flowers and the birds for company.

What happened there? I had never taken anyone to the garden before, not even Isabella. I tried to kid myself that I had no idea why I'd done it, but secretly I knew it was because I wanted to impress Sophie. I wanted her to notice me. Or maybe I just wanted the distraction? I felt bad about having to rush off to meet my solicitor and the invitation to dinner had surprised even me.

The negotiations for selling the cherry crop weren't going

well. It was the hardest year since I'd first got involved on the sidelines, back in my teens. I missed being able to ask Dad for advice. I wished he had handed the negotiations over to me a few years earlier; let me cut my teeth while he was still around to help. The familiar pang of guilt at surviving the crash that had killed him reminded me how much better a job he would have made of protecting the farm that I was now managing.

Being back at the cherry festival I had visited every summer of my childhood made me miss Dad so much more. But I had to keep bottling up the past year's emotions, or I'd never stay level-headed enough to run the business – or negotiate this afternoon's deal with Francesco. I'd hated this week, with so many people telling me how much they missed Dad, as though the grief was theirs and theirs alone. Of course, it was great that they cared, but every well-meaning comment stabbed at me, threatening to puncture the defences I had so carefully built up.

I had my standard response now: "Thank you," smiling a smile I didn't feel inside. "I think he'd have been proud of the crop this year, don't you?" It seemed to turn the conversation back to business and gave me a reminder to pull myself together. It was autopilot now. Not an emotion in sight.

I was off to see Giovanni this evening. I'd known him for as long as I could remember; for as long as Dad had been bringing me to the cherry festival. He and Dad had been great friends and Giovanni was determined to find me a decent buyer for the crop, now that my usual leads had done a runner. I had no idea why. It would be a great crop, as long as the rains held off for another couple of weeks. And the price we were asking was fair. But I was running out of time. We'd normally have had this sorted months ago, but when the first buyer backed out, things had been heating up with my work in Milan on the Denucci case and I had lost track of time. Not having sold the crop at this late stage didn't count in our favour for price.

Giovanni had texted me while I was in the garden with Sophie to say that he'd got news for me today, but he was cagey on the phone when I called him back and wouldn't tell me what it was, other than that it wasn't an offer yet – something else. He said he had to tell me in person. I had a bad feeling about it. But I also knew that if it was a problem, Giovanni would have answers. I knew I could trust him.

I was glad Sophie was there to distract me, to stop me from fretting or imagining the worst; someone to entertain, to experience. She was quite an experience: confident and shy in equal measure.

I allowed myself to daydream about earlier, sitting on that bench under the lilac tree watching the sun sparkle on her light brown hair like ripples in a rocky stream. Relaxing. Mesmerising. *She's bringing out my long-repressed inner poet. Need to watch that one, before I embarrass myself.*

I was glad she'd be leaving in a few days; she'd be a high-risk adventure otherwise. The way she looked at me when she smiled gave me butterflies, like going too high on a swing. It made me wonder, though, if she were hanging around, where I might land if I jumped. I didn't even know if she had a boyfriend already. I was surprised to find that I cared.

I scuffed my way through the heaving streets, being jostled by oversized bags that people seemed to forget they were carrying, as they squeezed through non-existent gaps. I was dawdling, reluctant to get to the meeting with my solicitor. I walked on autopilot through rows of town houses rose so high that the sun never reached the road between them, except at the very peak of the day. Green shutter after green shutter rested half-closed for the siesta, like a poorly disciplined army. The only difference between them all was the age of the paint.

I took a final left turn and found myself in the street with my solicitor's office, its big, black front door with its gleaming brass knocker reminding the world of the level of fees that stepping through the entrance would require. My insides tightened, knowing how much rested on the next half-hour, having to trust that all would be well. It was in moments like this that I hated being the 'grown-up', running the farm I had never asked to inherit. I longed to go back to being the little boy, hiding up a cherry tree, beating the birds to the ripest fruit. I felt my heart pounding my rib cage and took a deep breath to calm and steady myself, as I lifted the door knocker and waited to step into the meeting that would have to save the jobs of everyone who worked at the farm.

***

I sat for ages in the secret park, shoes off, feet enjoying the deep coolness of the thick green grass where the lilac tree had sheltered it from the burning sun, listening to birds going about their day, mopeds screeching past, praying that their brakes would outlive the steep, cobbled streets, feeling the warmth of the afternoon on my face, thinking about the strange half-Italian who'd just bought me ice cream. I even remembered to do some of the mindfulness stuff Jem had been teaching me before I came to Italy. The sensations of scrunching my toes up in the soft grass, smelling the lilac blooms, and truly hearing the birds were delicious. Time stood still.

After a while I noticed my bum had gone numb; a sure sign that it was time to get moving again. I reluctantly put my sandals on and shifted myself back up to standing, easing the stiffness out of my lower back. I picked up my bag and dawdled back to the overgrown gate, drinking in the honeysuckle's farewell, noticing a trail of blood-red roses tumbling over a wall and a flood of regal purple clematis, as big as handkerchiefs, crawling lazily over a terracotta roof.

The handle on the gate was hot from the sun and the hinges creaked as I let myself out, feeling grateful to Christof for letting me in on the magic of this place. I pulled the gate closed behind me and rummaged Christof's map out of my bag. When I was walking with him, the route had seemed so easy, but now I was alone the streets all looked the same, with the occasional launderette or tobacconist on corners, shutters down for the afternoon siesta, but none of it marked on the map, just like the *Secret Garden*.

Eventually I found a corner with street signs and took the next left, down the hill to the town.

A sparrow caught my eye, as it dug for bugs in a crack between the cobbles, returning my stare as though daring me to a game where we would see which of us had to look away first. I paused and watched him until he decided he'd rather find his snack elsewhere, away from the curious eyes of a tourist, and he fluttered away into another street.

I was in no hurry as my knees and shins told me the downhill was getting steeper. My calves warned me they'd get their revenge on the way back up. As the streets widened I saw the first cars, and the hustle and bustle of the festival intensified, as though someone was turning up the dial on a crackly radio set.

Before long I was in the market square, packed with stalls and people; cherries everywhere. My love affair with cherries had started when I was tiny, trying to race the starlings to the crop on my grandfather's huge old tree in his back garden. I had been so excited when I'd managed to climb up and reach some, balancing on bins and boxes to get high enough to find a branch to sit on. Grandma used to say I was single-handedly responsible for giving her white hair over it. Grandpa said he was proud of me for showing initiative. And he taught me how to tell when the cherries were perfectly ripe, so that Grandma wouldn't have to sit up all night nursing me with tummy ache.

Cherries had become a symbol of adventure and freedom and winning against the odds for me, because the starlings were pretty thorough. They only ever left me with the fruit that was hiding behind the long, jagged green leaves – the cherries you could only see from underneath.

Then, as I got older, it became a 'thing' in our family – like 'received wisdom' or an urban myth reincarnated – that 'Sophie likes cherries', and I happily played along. The thought of cherries in the early summer had got me through many a grey, dull, drizzly British winter. The earliest fruits would arrive in bubble-wrapped boxes from Turkey, around late April or early May. One day I did the maths and worked out the cost per cherry – almost as much as chocolate. But I always knew which I would rather have. Those Turkish cherries felt like an indulgent, forbidden treat, smearing near-black juice over my fingers as I pulled at a stalk and then gently split the cherry in half, tearing it with my fingers, flicking out the stone so I could enjoy the whole cherry, without being distracted by it.

When I was younger, Mum would buy them for me as a special reward. I would sneak to the fridge and steal them when I thought she wasn't looking. Later she would ask me if I knew where the cherries had gone. "Nooooo!" I would reply, shaking my head vehemently. She always smiled back at me and suggested it must have been the pixies. It was only years later that she told me my face had always held tell-tale signs of the purple-black juice. I was grateful to her for playing my game.

Then the French and Spanish cherries would arrive in the shops, less pampered than the Turkish ones, which had seemed like royalty in their careful packaging, leading the summer's procession. Within weeks the first English cherries would arrive, with a raspberry tinge in their redness, very different from the Turkish purple, and often white inside; quite a distinct flavour. As the English summer threatened to turn to rain, the cherries would arrive in bigger and bigger boxes, crammed in tightly like passengers on a budget airline.

Then suddenly they were gone for another year and I would watch the leaves on Grandpa's tree turn brown at the edges, still green in the centre, before they withered and fell to blanket its roots, while it slumbered the winter away, ready to burst with pinky-white blossom again in the spring.

Until the year that it didn't.

It broke my heart when they cut down my cherry tree. It had a fungal infection, they said, or some kind of virus, and it died. Trees shouldn't die. Not my cherry tree. But it was unsafe, they said, too close to the house, and it would look ugly and barebranched in the summer. Better to cut it down and let more light into the kitchen, they said. But I cried. And I stole a twig when they weren't looking, keeping it with me all the way through university, until it got lost in yet another house move.

Grandpa died the following winter and Grandma followed not far behind. Their house was sold. The new owners would never know that beautiful cherry tree.

"*Ciao, bella!*" I was woken from my memories by a friendly old man holding out a plate of deep red fruit, tempting me to try one. I wanted to, but I had no idea how much he would want me to pay and so I shook my head, and gave him a little smile, so he didn't think I was being rude.

"*Un regalo.* A present," he said, holding the plate out to me again. I took one and said thank you. He watched me taste it, full of anticipation, wanting approval, but already knowing how delicious his fruit was. He was right. It was tasty: firm and fresh and sweet with just the right level of juiciness. He pointed to a bucket and I realised that was where he wanted me to spit out the stone. I laughed at his directness. In England, we struggle with cherry stones – and with olive pits. We chew them and swallow the flesh, whilst trying to work out how to dispose of the stone without causing offence. To take it out of your mouth with your fingers is simply not done; to spit it onto a fork risks following it with the flesh of the fruit, which would be horrendously bad manners. I found myself wondering what the correct procedure was back at home, as I gratefully spat my cherry stone into his bucket. Another *grazie* and I moved on, to walk round the other stalls. So much abundance. A family's livelihood in each harvest.

Sun-browned old ladies sat chatting behind their cherry-laden tables, waiting for visitors to decide what to buy, ignoring them until the "*Scusi, signore*" reached a volume that competed with their gossiping.

Beautifully wrapped packets of dried cherries shared table space with cherries in syrup, cherry brandy, cherry tarts and cherries in mascarpone, even cherry panettone, which surely should be waiting for Christmas.

I had met with my new boss shortly before I came on holiday and he had told me one of my first projects was going to be for a company wanting to bring cherry brandy and other products to the UK market. I meandered away my time, hoping to pick up some ideas that would impress the new client with my understanding of their market in our first meeting. It was one of the reasons I had used to justify my impromptu decision to come to the cherry festival, after I heard about it on the TV travel show. But really, I had just come because I love cherries so much.

The atmosphere was relaxed and welcoming, but I didn't feel in the mood for buying. My brain was nagging me to do some more research for my new client. I didn't want to. There was time for that tomorrow. I felt so glad I had come here. My holiday in Italy had been just what I needed to put Stuart's bullying behind me, so far as I could, and to press my inner 'reset' button, so I could go back home and start my new job. Right now, I wanted to soak up the sunshine. I sat on the low wall of a fountain, with statues of cupids frozen in play, enjoying the cool water mist on my face, watching the world go by.

The town clock struck three in the distance and a smart woman in her sixties opened the door, her silver hair was pulled tightly into a bun, as though attempting an impromptu facelift. Her white blouse was perfectly ironed and tucked into a neat, grey pencil skirt. She didn't smile as she gestured me inside.

The thumping of my heart grew louder. I was about to meet Francesco, the man who had conned my Dad into loaning him money, without a contract or any kind of paper trail, for a project he didn't have the guts to see through; the man who held the future of our cherry farm and the livelihood of its workers in his power; the man whose 'yes' could change my life and give me back the ability to sleep without the 3 a.m. sweats that made it hard to concentrate at work the next day.

The secretary glided towards another shiny, black door with sparkling brass fittings and knocked twice with a calm firmness that showed she wasn't to be messed with and small-talk was pointless. "*Entra!*"

She opened the door and gestured to me to go inside, remaining to close it behind me.

The solicitor's office was full of leather-bound books on shelves that started at the floor and reached the ceiling, complete with an old-fashioned, wooden library ladder that I suspected was rarely used; the collection looked like it had taken generations to build and I hoped, at the rates he charged for his time, that my solicitor kept the most important books somewhere more quickly accessible.

"Good afternoon," he said, looking at me over the top of his glasses, barely lifting his glance from the papers on his desk.

"Is he here?" I asked, without taking the time to return his pleasantries, I had been so worried that Francesco might not show.

"They both are."

"Both?" I asked, confused. But before he could answer, the door opened again and a tired, gaunt man who might once have been tall and proud ambled into the room. His hair was greying and years of smoking had aged his face beyond the forty years I had been expecting. He looked at me with a snarl on his lips, letting me know that the deal was not as 'done' as his mother, Marisa, had led Nonna to believe.

Then I noticed another figure: Pietro, our farm manager, walking in behind the 'defendant'. I wasn't fast enough to hide the shock on my face and Pietro at least had the decency to look sheepish.

"What are you doing here?" I half spat at the man I had called an honorary 'uncle' for as long as I could remember, "With *him*?"

"I think we should get started, gentlemen," my solicitor reminded us, indicating to Pietro and Francesco to take the two spare chairs. "Remember, I charge by the hour," he chuckled, reclaiming the power in the room. He had rightly sensed that conflict was about to break out. He gathered together the papers on his desk and picked them up, tapping them on the large leather writing pad to neaten them. I noticed his name embossed in one corner, next to a carefully placed Mont Blanc fountain pen, black with gold highlights, hinting at what happened with his clients' fees. He held the papers out to Francesco, who made a point of ignoring them, so my solicitor placed them on the desk in front of him.

"I think you'll find it's all in there, as agreed. You confirm that you were lent money to buy the shop as part of a business partnership and the cherry farm was collateral. You had agreed to make the loan repayments, but these ceased after the second payment. By signing this document, you are agreeing to sign the title deeds of the shop and any remaining stock over to my client and, in return, he will not pursue you for damages."

Nonna had been told by Marisa that Francesco had agreed to all this, but the Thor-like thunder in his expression made it clear that was no longer the case. He stuck out his chin and his black eyes narrowed as he laughed – an ugly sound that carried the gift of killing happiness, not spreading it. My pounding heart nearly stopped in its tracks as I heard him reply, "And what if I *don't* sign?" He pushed the papers back across the desk to my solicitor with an air of laid-back confidence.

This had never occurred to me. I had thought this deal was done and that, as long as we could actually get Francesco to show up, everything would be fine.

"I put months of work into this project and I think I deserve something in return, don't you?" he stated, with a calm confidence that showed he was convinced he was right. My usual cool had long left me as panic flooded my brain and took control of my mouth.

"What you get in return is us not dragging your stinking arse through the courts and telling the whole world what a shit you are; how you cheated my father and kept quiet about it after he died, even though you knew we risked losing the farm, and –"

"I think that's enough, Christof," came the steadying voice of my solicitor, gently resting a hand on my arm. I felt the rage I had been holding back ever since I found out about the loan, desperate to explode, like an overheating pressure cooker. I gritted my teeth so hard it hurt my jaw as I waited for what my solicitor might say next. I had to trust him. I couldn't trust myself any more. My fingernails were close to drawing blood in my clenched fists. He turned to Francesco.

"I think you will find that our offer is a generous one. On this paper," he pulled one from the middle of the pile, "you will find a list of the actions we would be forced to take, should you refuse to sign. I believe that waiving our rights to pursue you for the losses you have caused is more than generous recompense for the time you put into the project."

Francesco held the paper with the tips of his fingers, as though it were distasteful to him, and the grimace slid ever so slowly from his lips. His eyes scanned the document and he glared at me, "You wouldn't dare!" It was a hiss, more than words, and I forced myself to use my best poker face, because I had no idea what was on the piece of paper. Francesco passed it to Pietro who glanced down it, skimming its content.

"Oh, I think you'll find we would," replied my solicitor, the calm in his deep voice adding certainty to the document's threats, "but it's –"

"But that's not how it's done round here!" interrupted Pietro, making me jump as I remembered he was there, siding with the opposition.

"It is now," I found myself replying, fully aware that how I handled this meeting would have implications for my future working relationship with Pietro; I needed him to manage the farm while I was in Milan, but his siding with Francesco in this meeting, having hidden the secret of the loan from me for nearly a year, was a mountainous betrayal of my trust.

Silence serenaded the stalemate as I locked eyes with Francesco. I could see he was a bully; his bravado was a front, but I also knew he held the future of our farm in his hands and I had no idea whether my solicitor's threats were real. Even if they were, maybe they would take too long and the bank would foreclose the loan as they had threatened, repossessing the farm.

"What about your reputation Christof?" Francesco demanded, in a clear attempt to wriggle his way out of the mess he could finally see he was in.

"What about *yours*, Francesco?" A flash of white rage in his eyes told me I had hit home. He knew in an instant that I didn't care about the cost to my reputation of taking him to court. After all, I was a *city boy,* as Pietro would often complain to his friends in local bars. But he also knew that my solicitor wasn't bluffing: we could put together a case that would make sure nobody would ever trust Francesco again, and that would hurt him more than me.

"I'll give you half the shop. I put time and effort into the project. I deserve something back." He was standing up now, his palms planted firmly on the desk's leather surface. Somehow, I knew my solicitor would have the desk thoroughly cleaned after we left.

My solicitor pushed the papers across the desk to touch Francesco's fingertips, making them *unignorable*, and handed him a pen – not the Mont Blanc – pointing to the space for him to sign. With his other hand, he pushed his metal-rimmed glasses up onto the bridge of his nose, reminding Francesco who was in control of the meeting.

I held my breath, waiting for what felt like forever for his decision, feeling the future of the farm perched on the knife-edge of Francesco's choice. He batted away the pen my solicitor was holding out to him. My heart sank. It was over. I felt tears of frustration threatening to win and I sank my head in my hands, my elbows on the desk, despite knowing how such a movement would trash my negotiating position.

"Thank you," I heard my solicitor say, as Francesco pushed the papers towards him, putting his own, battered pen back into his pocket. Before my brain had a chance to catch up, I found myself accepting the offered pen, signing on autopilot where my solicitor was pointing, and giving the papers back to him.

"The locksmith is already waiting at the property and I will call him now to change the keys. Good afternoon, gentlemen. Christof," he looked at me, noticing my trembling hands, "I'd like you to stay for a few minutes. I have something I want to discuss with you."

I couldn't bring myself to shake hands with Francesco or Pietro as they skulked out of the office, back to the sunshine. I felt weak with relief and so angry with Pietro. I couldn't think of any reason why he would have changed sides. But dealing with him would have to wait for another time.

My solicitor closed the door behind them and came to sit next to me, rather than behind his desk. "You now own a shop, Christof," he said, trying to make me pay attention to what had just happened. His voice was a bucket of cold water, bringing me back to my senses.

"Yeah," I responded ungratefully. "One that nobody wanted to buy, which is why Francesco got it so cheap. And it could take months – or years – to sell. It doesn't fix anything. I still have the loan to repay."

"Yes, it does, Christof," my solicitor soothed. I looked up into his pale brown eyes and remembered he had been the one Dad used to turn to for help. I had sat in this very chair, not long after the car crash, asking for advice on death duties and how to keep the farm running after Dad died. Now wasn't the time to be churlish. "I've taken the liberty of making an appointment for you, for ten o'clock tomorrow morning, with the debt manager at the bank. He has provisionally agreed to transfer the security for the loan to be the shop, instead of the farm. It will be subject to a valuation, which can't happen until at least next week, but it is progress. And he has also provisionally agreed to extend the term of the loan, to make the repayments more realistic and manageable."

He was right. This could work! It would buy me time and then, even if we defaulted, we would lose a shop we didn't really want, instead of the farm. But would the valuation be enough?

My solicitor could see the questions racing through my mind. He shook his head and smiled, "There's plenty of time for answers, for decisions," he said as he walked behind his desk, reached for a crystal decanter and poured two glasses of a deep orange-red liquid, handing one to me. "First, we celebrate. It could have gone either way today. I was not aware of his change of heart. But we did it. *Salute*. Your father's cherry brandy. I got it out specially for us today."

I took a sip and felt it burn my throat.

"I would suggest you consider applying to turn the property into flats. Then you can sell them or rent them and that will cover the loan repayments. It will never make much money as a shop. Converting the upper floors should be easy to get permission for, because they were previously accommodation for the old shop owner, about ten years ago. The ground floor may, however, require some *influence*," he said, raising an eyebrow and smiling, to let me know he knew who might be open to being *influenced*. "But we don't have to think about that today."

"I don't know how to thank you," I managed, feeling the enormity of what we had achieved – saving the farm and everyone's jobs – yet realising how far we still had to travel.

"That's easy. Pay my invoice and make sure the farm never ends up in a mess like this again!" he chuckled.

"I promise!" And I meant it. But first I had to find a buyer for the crop – my next job. I was meeting with Giovanni at 7 p.m., before I took Sophie to dinner.

Dinner was in a tiny little restaurant by the river. It was the kind of place it would be easy to miss. There was nothing to see except a subtle sign above what looked like a normal front door. Inside and up a flight of old stone steps, worn by generations of feet, the first floor had just six tables, already bustling with the evening's dinner guests. It looked like the front room of someone's apartment. It probably was.

Christof was greeted enthusiastically with back-clapping hugs and handshakes. I stood nervously, like an uninvited wedding guest, as I was introduced with more double-cheeked kisses and smiles. I felt thoroughly welcomed in this secret restaurant.

We were shown to the only table on the balcony, reserved especially for us, a handwritten card with 'Christof' on it in the middle of the tablecloth, with just enough space for two chairs. They were next to each other on adjacent sides of the small square space, giving us both a beautiful view of the river and the hills beyond it. It was already set with long-stemmed wine glasses and pristine linen napkins on a thick, white linen cloth. In the centre stood a small glass vase with a cluster of red honeysuckle that reminded me of the overgrown gate to this afternoon's secret garden.

The waiter brought us our menus, handwritten with the day's specials. Typed Italian was one thing. Local freestyle was another. I was hoping I wouldn't embarrass myself in front of Christof again by not being able to read it – or by ordering something I couldn't bring myself to eat. There was no way I was getting my dictionary out. Not knowing what I was ordering here made me nervous, reminding me of a school trip to France with a surprise portion of snails.

We were asked about our drinks. We already had water. We agreed on red wine. "The usual?" asked the waiter. Christof smiled and nodded, "*Si, per favore.*"

It made me wonder who else he had brought here… and how often. I reminded myself it was none of my business and that I had no right to feel the pang of jealousy that had just popped up to play. I didn't realise I had fallen into the trap of hoping I might be somehow special.

There were only a handful of dishes to choose from and Christof guided me gallantly through them, describing them like the local that he was, and telling me stories about the fellow farmers who had produced the ingredients. He was funny and interesting, but preoccupied, in a way that he hadn't been earlier. I wondered what had changed. Something in this afternoon's meeting?

The wine flowed. The food was delicious. And it felt wonderful to be with someone who was genuinely interested in me. It dawned on me that Jamie had always been more interested in *Jamie*. How could I not have noticed that he never asked me about me, or my day, or my dreams? Did I sleepwalk my way through that relationship? Probably. I started to wonder why, but was jolted back to Italy, sitting next to Christof, by the arrival of our starters. I *uninvited* Jamie from our dinner date and gave my full attention back to Christof.

I had played it safe with an *insalata tricolore*: locally grown tomatoes with fresh mozzarella cheese, drizzled with homemade pesto, made with basil from a local farm, topped with cracked black pepper. Christof pointed out that the salad included three types of tomatoes, all traditionally grown in this valley. It was early in the season, he said, so they weren't as sweet as they would be. The pesto was such a bright green that it surprised me.

"We have a secret ingredient here," he explained, "to stop it from going brown-green, like the pesto you get in shops – fresh lemon juice from the winter harvest in the south. You don't need much or it spoils the flavour, but it helps the leaves to keep their bright green colour. And this is fresh, not pasteurised like the shop-bought jars, which kills the taste."

I cut a small slice of tomato and mozzarella and added a little of the pesto. Christof watched me, without breathing, as I tasted it. The surprise on my face said it all and he grinned at my approval. Of the recipe? His choice of restaurant? His valley? Of him? I wasn't sure.

We were barely aware of the waiter clearing the plates. I felt as though we were the only people there. I loved watching Christof talk. His eyes lit up and his excitement was contagious. I hadn't really noticed quite how handsome he was before, yet he didn't seem to know. When we first met, I was too busy trying to not die of embarrassment to pay him much attention. Then this afternoon the cherry ice cream had been my main focus. But this evening he was drifting dangerously close to Dream Man territory.

His eyes were soft and kind, but with a sadness about them. His hair was dark Italian brown, at the longer end of 'short', so that he could run his fingers through it, but a long way from a Hugh Grant 'fop'. He skin was tanned and he had a soft crease between his eyebrows – the start of a frown line – as though he had been worrying too much. He was probably about six feet tall and his legs seem to go on forever in his dark blue jeans. He had broad shoulders, but they looked tired, slouching slightly, as though he didn't want to own his height. His hands were smooth and strong; they don't look like he did much of the work at the cherry farm. His long fingers looked like they should belong to a pianist, and the red cherry stains gave away what he has been doing for the past week. I wondered how long the stains would take to disappear.

By the end of the meal we had talked about everything from market research for eco toilet cleaner (don't ask) through to endemic tax fraud in Italian black-market businesses – a staple of the investigations Christof's firm led. The sun was setting and the red sky promised another day of sunshine tomorrow. I was grateful to Christof for suggesting the shawl though, as the disappearing sun made it quite clear that summer wasn't here yet.

Tomorrow was my last full day before going back to London, to Anna's lumpy sofa… and my new job. The thought was like a cold shower, drenching the happy contentment I had been bathing in. I pushed all of that out of my mind and concentrated on being here, now, fully experiencing being with this lovely man, watching this stunning view, and enjoying the delicious food, which I had barely noticed myself eating.

But everything about the evening had been entirely professional, as though we were friendly business colleagues, eating out after a long day of meetings. We were both being reserved; slightly polite; determined not to flirt. It was easy to use the view as an excuse not to look at each other, saving us from putting on too much emotional armour. I was still having to avoid making eye contact with him, so he wouldn't cut straight through my defences.

The wine was divine. Being local, the restaurant owner bought full barrels of it, so it arrived at the table in a simple pottery carafe, lightly chilled from his cellar. We were on the third of these by the time we finished our meal. And, of course, dessert had to have cherries in it.

Except that it shouldn't, the owner told me, as Christof excused himself to take an urgent call on his mobile. The locals were sick of them by this point in the week-long festival, so the restaurant never served them cherries, for fear of a revolt. It was the one week of the season when cherries were *off* the menu. But when Christof had come to book our table for this evening, not only had he insisted on the balcony view and the honeysuckle he had brought with him, but he had also asked the owner to make sure there would be cherries for me to enjoy. I was sworn to secrecy. "He must really like you," said the owner, with a wink, as he cleared yet more plates away before Christof came back.

The thought of a stranger going to so much effort, behind my back, was a new one for me. In fact, having someone making this much effort *at all* was a new experience.

Dessert was poached cherries in red wine with homemade vanilla ice cream. It was so good I could almost have cried. The red wine balanced the cherries' sweetness, giving the dessert more body, and the ice cream was nearly as good as the one from this afternoon.

We had nearly finished it when Christof's phone rang again.

"Sorry," he said, "I wouldn't normally have it with me, but we're at such a delicate stage of the harvest negotiations. It's

Giovanni again. I wouldn't take it otherwise."

I was fine with him going off to take the call. It gave me peace and quiet to really enjoy my dessert.

Christof came back to the table and we finished the wine, as he apologised and said he had to leave. He had some big meeting in the morning and couldn't afford to be tired. He needed to be on top form to get the best deal. But he said he still had plenty of time to walk me back to my hotel.

We said goodbye to the wonderful staff at the restaurant and headed back down those old stone stairs, through the heavy front door and out into the bustling street.

We walked along the riverbank; close, but not touching. Actually, being really careful not to touch. Electricity was flowing between us. I knew it was a cliché, but I could feel it, and I sensed that he could too.

"Your hotel's up this way," he said, as he turned left up a steeply sloping side street. We walked for a while in silence; easy, comfortable, companionable, highly charged silence, charged with what was not being said. I was relieved not to have to talk. I was pretending not to be out of puff. The hill was steeper than it looked. London-living and late-night focus groups had taken their toll on my fitness regime.

The houses were getting closer together. The air was thick with the smells of family mealtimes and a hundred TV shows battling for attention. I found myself looking at the front doors – the only sign of individuality along a row of identical homes. Most looked like they had been turned into flats, with beautiful Italian names handwritten in faded ink on white card under curved plastic covers, next to doorbells and postboxes. The door knockers gave a sense of the personalities within. Some of the steps were spotless. Others held the day's rubbish in black bags, tied up to keep out the local wildlife.

Christof breathed in deeply and murmured my name, almost with a sigh. Then it was as though he realised he had said it out loud and there was an expectation that he would follow it with something.

"I was wondering if you're free tomorrow afternoon? I've got a few hours between meetings and maybe you'd like to go on a picnic?" He paused, half-waiting for an answer. "There's a gorgeous place that's about thirty minutes' walk from here, where you get a great view of the town. I can sort the food and stuff. I could meet you at your hotel at two?"

I realised he had stopped walking. I had been too distracted by my daydreaming to notice. I turned back to face him. He looked nervous, like in the TV interview. I sensed that we were moving into *date* territory and my insides couldn't decide whether to sink or fly. I was due to leave Italy in 36 hours. But we had just spent a wonderful evening together; one of the best I could remember in a very long time. The last thing I needed was to fall for someone in another country. And what was the point in a *date* if you weren't open to it turning into something deeper?

I realised he was waiting for an answer, as I was busy chatting with myself. Did I want to go on a picnic with him tomorrow? I surprised myself with the certainty of my answer. I didn't want him to know that my 'yes' was a no-brainer, so I played it casual, "That would be nice. Thanks."

"Just *nice*?" he asked, his gaze was locked on mine, one eyebrow raised in an expression that got my somersaulting insides throwing around cheerleaders' pompoms. I felt relieved that I couldn't see the depth of the brown in his eyes in the evening light or I'd have been a lost cause. He stepped towards me.

"Really? Just *nice*?" We were standing so close I could feel his breath on my cheek as he whispered the words, almost too quietly to hear. His eyes smiled, as he tried to figure out whether he would get away with teasing me.

I felt scared he might hear the "no, it would be bloody brilliant" conversation, going on in my head.

I closed my eyes as his lips brushed mine, so softly I could barely feel it, but I could still tell that he meant it. Something inside me screamed, "NO! No more men!" But the rest of me melted into a yes.

"Really, just *nice*? Are you sure?" he breathed, as he kissed me again. My heart was doing a tango and I wanted to make the clocks stop.

"Well, maybe a bit more than *nice*," I conceded.

I felt him smile, as we kissed again. I could taste the memory of the fabulous red wine.

"This is your hotel," he said, gesturing behind me. I hadn't noticed us arrive. The shabby sign was unlit and I could have walked past it ten times without noticing it. "I'll meet you in the main square tomorrow at two, by the cupid fountain. Do you think you can find it?"

I smiled and nodded. He smiled back. And faded into the night.

I hadn't meant to kiss her. Three times. It felt so good. Like the first hot chocolate of winter - you don't know how much you have missed it until the time is right and nothing else will do.

Just like I hadn't meant to ask her out for dinner. And I hadn't meant to ask her to join me for a picnic. But I couldn't help myself. When I'm with her, everything else melts away. It's just me and Sophie: no cherry farm; no embezzlement investigations; no worrying about Nonna; no thinking about Dad. The knot in my stomach softens when she's around, like I'm letting go of something. I'm not sure what.

I caught myself walking in time to the song in my head. I hadn't noticed it was there. 'Good Vibrations' by the Beach Boys. Where did that one come from? I don't even own a copy. But it was how I felt; like being with Sophie was lifting the heaviness, the weight I've carried for as long as I can remember.

The song took me back to a lecture on materials science I had taken as an option, one semester at university. Our elderly professor had walked in with a 1980s ghetto blaster, waited until we were all seated and proudly pressed play. He made us listen to the whole track before he would tell us why. He got our attention alright. The rest of the lecture was on some horrendously tricky maths you could – allegedly – use to predict whether hitting something would just cause it to wobble and come to rest, or if it would trigger it to vibrate itself to bits. He told us how it had been used in computer modelling for skyscrapers, before they built them, to work out whether freak winds would cause them to fall apart.

I was still walking in time to the music. I wondered which track would pop into my head next, as I allowed myself to daydream about Sophie and pushed aside the worries and stresses that were vying for attention.

Neither of us had made the greatest of first impressions today, but it didn't seem to matter. Watching her totally absorbed by eating cherry ice cream under the lilac tree had thawed something inside me that I had forgotten had frozen, decades ago, perhaps as far back as when Mum left.

I wasn't sure I was ready for unfreezing yet. It had come as a bit of a shock.

I was on autopilot, walking through the streets in the oldest part of town, my feet knowing which turns to take, heading towards our family apartment. Mum and Dad had bought it when they first got married and we'd kept it ever since, even though we rarely used it. But it was useful for doing business in town and the annual cherry festival. And we let friends and family use it, when they were in town. I was still hoping that was how the petrol receipt from Naples had got onto my kitchen floor.

Ever since the stake-out-that-went-wrong back in April I had jumped every time I saw the word "*Napoli*" – Naples. Someone had known I was going to be there that night, but Luca, my boss, and I still had no idea how. I had been watching my back ever since, even though Luca had taken me off the case, so finding a one-week-old receipt from Naples in the apartment, in front of the larder I rarely used, rang major alarm bells. I had meant to visit my neighbour this afternoon, to ask her if anyone had been staying in the apartment last week, but meeting Sophie had taken up my spare time. Maybe I didn't really want to know the answer.

Giovanni had tipped me off this evening about Signor Perillo. That was what his cryptic message had been about. Perillo had come up from the south, the Naples area. *Napoli*. My heart had skipped a beat as I remembered that receipt again. He had come to the cherry festival circuit, looking for farms to buy. And apparently someone had told him ours was a good bet. With Dad gone, Nonna well beyond retirement and me travelling so much with work, he'd been tipped off that we would be open to *an offer*. It wouldn't be the first time. About ten years ago, when we had a terrible summer that almost ruined our cherry crop, people had assumed we were about to fold and would take whatever we could for the land. They had misjudged us then and they were doing the same now.

But Giovanni said Signor Perillo didn't play his game above board. He'd been going around the buyers, warning them that he had inside intelligence on the quality of our harvest that it wasn't as good as usual, because we didn't know the tricks that Dad used to use; the trees were dying; that Dad didn't pass his secrets on to us. Obviously, none of that was true. Pietro had worked with Dad for decades and he knew the closely guarded secrets that made our crop thrive, but it was why the usual buyers had pulled out, back at the end of the winter, and I still couldn't get anyone else interested. And it was why I'd been left, empty bowl in hand, begging for whatever Giovanni's last-minute buyers might offer.

Perillo was trying to make sure no one wanted our crop, so that we were on our knees with gratitude when we finally met and he offered me a pittance for the land. I wasn't supposed to know any of this. Giovanni was risking more than his reputation by telling me – he only did so because he and Dad went back so many years and he didn't want to see us being bullied into giving up.

Giovanni had told me about a farm down in Umbria which wouldn't accept his offer, where the orchard burned down in the middle of the night, in a 'heat wave'. There was nothing they could do to save the trees. Perillo went back and offered them a quarter of what he had offered before, and they had been forced to accept.

I shuddered at the thought of it, of Nonna and Pietro at the farm on their own and what Perillo might try. But I refused to consider it. We would sort something out. Giovanni had promised to call me if he heard anything new.

The old discussions started going around in my head again. Could I manage the farm remotely? It wasn't fair to give any more responsibility to Nonna, especially not now her heart was playing up. Pietro was doing an excellent job of managing the day-to-day running of the place, but strategic decisions were now down to me. And it's hard to find the time to think things through when I'm so busy at work trying to gather invisible evidence of tax fraud from shady business owners who make Signor Perillo look like a fluffy kitten. Giovanni had warned me to be careful. Properly careful. But my gut told me he was overreacting.

I was nearly at the apartment now. And I had the picnic to look forward to tomorrow! I made a mental note to ask Pietro's brother, who runs a deli in town, to put together the picnic basket for us. I could pop by to see him before my meeting with the bank manager in the morning. I was enjoying daydreaming about what the picnic might include; how Sophie might react; what it would feel like to get to spend the whole afternoon with her. It felt so good to imagine it. Like stepping into someone else's world. I was surprised by how much I wanted to make a good impression.

What the...? Out of nowhere, something heavy crunches the back of my head. My kneecaps scream against the cobbles as I land.

A loud grunt from somewhere nearby and then another hit. This time on the side of my head, just above my right eye. A fist. A big one. I hear it a split second before the pain arrives.

I'm dizzy. I fall sideways, arms stretched out to stop myself hitting my face on the ground. Too slow. I'm bleeding. I try to get up, to turn around and see who hit me, maybe even to run? A heavy stick catches the back of my knees and I'm flat on my face again. Then a foot in my stomach. Too quick after the knees for it to be the same person. Wrong angle. The world is spinning. I force down vomit. 'Good Vibrations' fills my brain, like a stereo on full volume in a tiny room, drowning out my thoughts.

Not now! I need to think.

Too winded to cry out for help. How far will they go? They're not looking for my wallet. I'd give it to them in a heartbeat. What weapons do they have? Just fists? Knives? This area's too quiet for them to use a gun. Pain. Screaming pain. My lungs are on fire. It hurts to breathe. Did that kick break a rib?

Is this just a warning? Or is this it*? Ice cold floods my body, despite the stagnant heat. Not now. Please not now. It would finish off Nonna.*

I try to curl up small. I wait for the next hit. Where it will come from? Where it will land? I know I can't escape before it arrives. My heart pounds against my ribs. I hold my breath. I tense up to resist what is coming. I wait. But it doesn't come.

"Ecco, signore," says a deep, strong accent, not from round here. A small white business card floats down next to my face. "Next time you won't be walking away."

Heavy footsteps disappeared into the distance. Two sets of them, I thought, maybe three, but it was hard to tell in the darkness. My body screamed as I reached out to pick up the card. But I already knew whose name would be on it. And then I passed out.

I wasn't out for long and then I managed to make my way back to the apartment. My face was a mess from a cut above my right eye, where they had landed the first punch. My shirt was covered in blood. My head was pounding. My rib hurt every time I moved and my stomach felt bruised. But nothing was broken. Painkillers and ice packs got me so I could function again by this morning.

I had been warned they might come after me, but I hadn't expected them to find me, proving it was right that you could never really hide.

I pushed my worries to the back of my mind. I had other things to think about, including how to persuade the bank to accept the shop as collateral for the loan, when I currently looked like the least trustworthy client imaginable.

I needed to talk to Nonna about the harvest deal, about Francesco, and I had to warn her about Perillo, too. I needed Pietro to be on the lookout for trouble.

I made my usual breakfast substitute – a nice strong coffee – and went down to the entrance hall to collect the newspaper. I don't get to read them usually, so it is always a treat when I am here in town.

At 9 a.m. it was time to call Nonna. She'd have been awake for a while, but we'd always had an unwritten family rule that calls after bedtime or before breakfast meant *bad news*. Like the day Dad died. I shivered and pushed the emotions away, as usual.

Nonna was her natural chatty self, wanting to know about everyone I had met up in town during the festival, what their stalls were like, whose dried sweet cherries were the best, whether Giuliana had used pink or yellow ribbons on her boxes this year, how Giovanni's knees were holding up and whether he was going to get them replaced.

"How did it go with Francesco?" she asked, impatiently.

"All done!" I told her, having already decided not to mention the attempted change of plan or Pietro's betrayal. She didn't need to know that, at least not now. "I've got a meeting in an hour with the debt manager at the bank to see if he'll take the shop as collateral for the loan, instead of the farm. It's subject to a formal valuation next week, but our solicitor seems to think he would agree – for a *fee*." I had to be careful not to breathe too deeply or she'd have noticed the wince in my voice. I couldn't let her find out about last night's attack.

"That's wonderful news! Keep me posted, *carino*." I felt the weight of her trust in me. Renegotiating the loan wasn't something I could finish this week. I would be back at work in Milan before decisions were made and I dreaded asking Luca, my boss, for yet more time off to sign the paperwork that would be required. But it would have to be done.

I steered Nonna on to the harvest negotiations.

"Don't worry," she soothed. "Giovanni always used to help your Dad out. He'll do the same for you. It's time for you to step into your dad's shoes."

We both went quiet for a moment, lost in separate memories. I know she misses Dad as much as I do, in different ways. The hole he left in our lives will never be filled, but perhaps time will help us to find ways to walk round it, rather than drowning in it, whenever his name is mentioned.

"He's got a lead who might buy half the harvest, Nonna, the early picking, but it would leave you and the girls to process the rest over the summer."

"I said don't worry," she replied, meaning it. "If that's how it needs to be, then that's what we'll do. Pietro's daughters are old enough to help out now and it's not so much work. Really. Have you done the figures on what we need to break even this year?"

"Yes, I have." I felt grateful to Dad for handing that side of the business over to me when I graduated from university, even though I was already working in Milan. Those early years of chaotic scrap-paper book-keeping had been hard work, but eventually I had persuaded him to be more organised. He was reluctant at first. "We've never done it that way!" But then I showed him how he was paying too much tax by not keeping proper records and that gave him the incentive to play the game my way.

"What's the point in having an accountant in the family, if he can't save his old dad a few euros?" he would laugh. There was no point in telling him I wasn't an accountant, that my degree was in Business Studies. As far as he was concerned, I did his accounts and that made me his accountant.

"So, what else have you been up to?" asked Nonna; her sixth sense in full swing. Decades of trying to hide secrets from her had taught me that there was no point in lying.

"I went out for dinner last night."

"Ah... went out. I'm guessing that wasn't with Giovanni, then?" she teased.

I told her the barest minimum about Sophie.

"*Una ragazza* inglesa!" she chimed, with a dark emphasis on the 'English' girlfriend, giving the slightest hint of disapproval. Mum was English. Nonna still didn't approve of Dad's choice, even though Mum had been gone more than two decades. Italian mothers know how to hold grudges when their *bambini* got hurt.

"Not a girlfriend, Nonna. Just someone I met in the town. And I didn't want to eat on my own."

"You're not seeing her again?" she retorted, knowing the answer already.

"I'm taking her for a picnic this afternoon."

I heard her smile silently, on the other end of the phone.

"Enjoy it, Christof. You deserve to be happy, even if she is English. You know, Isabella was a long time ago. It's okay to move on."

Like I needed reminding. I didn't want to go there. It was over two years since Isabella and I had split and I still found it hard to imagine trusting someone again, letting them close. With my work in Milan and at the farm, I hardly ever had time for socialising, apart from the occasional business event or office do. The likelihood of me meeting someone special – or having time to grow a relationship – was really, really low.

I didn't tell her that Sophie was leaving tomorrow. For me, that that was the main reason why I could handle this. "I'll call you when I know more about the deal, Nonna," I replied, ignoring her hints, not mentioning my worries about not getting a good enough deal for the harvest and having to make people redundant. But I had to tell her about Perillo.

"There's one more thing you need to know, Nonna."

"Yes, *carino*."

"Signor Perillo. Giovanni says he's come up from the south, near Naples, to buy up farms in this area, getting them as cheaply as he can by bad-mouthing their harvest to the local buyers. That's why our usual contacts haven't come up with offers."

"I did wonder what was going on with that. I didn't think it could all be down to you." She chuckled, so I knew she mean it kindly.

"Well, he's sniffing around and looking to get a good deal once we're nearly bankrupt. He knows how it works: that there are no reserves; that each year's harvest leaves farms on a knife-edge."

"They've tried it before, *carino*, and they'll try it again. But it will never work. Don't you worry."

"But Nonna, this guy isn't nice. They say he's been involved in fires at farms that turned him down. He sends his heavies in to apply pressure to those who say no. People have ended up in hospital." I shuddered at the thought of it. "The police can't prove anything – or *choose* not to." She got my meaning on this. "So, could you ask Pietro to keep an extra eye on the place, to deal with anything unusual?" I knew that it wasn't fair to ask Nonna to manage Pietro, but I was too angry with him to ask him myself just now. And she didn't mind.

She promised she would tell him and did her best to reassure me, signing off with another teasing innuendo about Sophie, forcing me to tell her what she looked like, so she could paint pictures in her mind about her.

"Don't get too excited, please, Nonna. It's just a picnic." But Nonna knew better.

It felt good to have talked to her, to have her advice, her reassurance. I felt lighter and easier knowing she was there.

I allowed myself to look forward to the picnic as I walked into town to order the food at Pietro's brother's deli. I was imagining what the picnic might include; how Sophie might react; what it would feel like to get to spend the whole afternoon with her. It was like stepping into someone else's world. I was surprised by how much I wanted to make a good impression. I was thoroughly enjoying this daydream. The sky was radiant blue and it was going to be a wonderful day.

I was sitting on the fountain wall, letting it cool my skin in the sun, when I saw Christof across the square, chatting with a friend, smiling and laughing, unaware that anyone was watching. I wanted him to be like that with me: natural, unreserved, open. Maybe he would be, once we had spent more time together. We'd got the whole afternoon for the picnic. I smiled a big smile inside, enjoying the prospect of such an unexpected treat.

He was carrying a heavy bag and a picnic blanket as he started to walk across the square towards me. He hadn't seen me yet; I was sitting on the opposite side of the fountain. Then, as though from nowhere, he was there. I stood up to greet him, not sure what to do, having seen so many people hug him over the past few days.

He stepped towards me and gave me a polite double-cheeked kiss. Was that all the welcome I was going to get? It was a stark contrast with his friend just now. Maybe he had been drunk last night when he kissed me. Maybe I'd spent the whole of this morning building this up to be something it wasn't. I stiffened, self-defence mechanisms kicking in.

Maybe he only takes advantage of tourists when they're tipsy. This feels awkward.

Then I noticed the obvious.

"What the hell happened to your face?" I blurted out. A deep cut sat angrily above his right eye, purple bruising around it. He grimaced.

"You don't want to know."

"Yes, I do! Of course I do!"

"I fell over a box on the stall and landed badly on the trestle table."

I wasn't convinced. But I knew I had a choice: to push it and risk him clamming up – or lying to me (that's what Jamie would have done); or to let it go, to accept that it was none of my business, and get on with the afternoon. I was a terminal nosey parker and I loved a good gossip, but I was going to have to overrule my curiosity on this one. I was far too hungry to jeopardise this picnic and the local restaurants had already finished their lunchtime sittings, so I'd be back to the dried crackers in the bottom of my rucksack in my hotel room, probably ground to dust by now, if he walked away.

He was waiting to see if I would drop the subject. I wondered what kinds of emergency stories he was cooking up.

Okay, I'll let it go – for now.

"Where are we going for our picnic?"

He visibly relaxed and smiled again.

"It's about half an hour's walk from here, up on that hill," he pointed into the sunlight. I squinted and pretended to see where he was showing me.

"Let's get started then!"

He gave me the picnic blanket. It was old and blue, with flecks of grey. It felt like a heavy wool. I wondered how many picnics it had seen. He handed me a litre bottle of water. It was heavily chilled and felt slippery with condensation in the afternoon's heat.

"I've got one for each of us. You're going to need it in this weather."

It was a good, solid track up the hill, but after a while we turned right, onto a footpath that looked half-forgotten. The occasional rabbit, startled by our passing, ran away from us. We passed farmers' fields with nearly ripe corn and wheat, with tiny allotments, already bursting with tomatoes and early aubergines, even the occasional proud red pepper, boasting to the world about its precocious early ripening. Some of the plots grew flowers too, with neat rows of marigolds on guard duty over fluffy, green carrot tops.

I watched bees lazing their way between cornflowers and yellow daisies, looking for nectar, their legs heavy with pollen. I remembered asking my A-level physics teacher how a bee actually managed to fly, once it was fully laden. His answer had stuck in my mind: "If I have to explain that to you, my dear, then I have failed in my past two years of teaching you." I remember looking at him, confused and frustrated. "Pure magic, dear girl. They're defying the laws of physics. Now back to the worksheet on page 94, please." He was a gifted eccentric who wore flip flops all year round, except for when it snowed, and he hosted secret parties for his students on the summer solstice. He had ignited my passion for science and maths; for how things worked, which had morphed into a passion for how people worked, once I got past uni. He'd never know the role he had played in my career. I sent him a silent 'thank you' across the waves of time and hoped that it would somehow reach him.

The ground crunched underfoot, with the occasional stone needing to be flicked out of a sandal. My stomach rumbled, telling me it had wanted to eat an hour ago. I hoped Christof wouldn't have noticed. It felt impolite. We didn't talk much, but that didn't seem to matter. The climb was steep in places, so I was grateful not to betray my appalling level of fitness and near-total absence of stamina.

"Not far now," he said, pointing to a solitary tree, about 300 metres away, "under that old oak."

Its deep green leaves and perfectly round shape stood out against the bright blue sky. It had stood through two world wars, I mused, and wondered how many generations of locals had enjoyed its welcome shade.

When we reached it, he was right – the view was beautiful. The whole of the valley was laid out before us, like a life-sized map with perfect rows of houses and a cellophane river running through its centre. You could see for miles. It was so peaceful. A large black bird I didn't recognise soared on thermals in the valley below us. Just for a moment, I felt free from the cares and the worries I had been carrying around with me. I was sure I could pick them up again on our way back down the hill.

Christof laid out the blanket in the perfect spot under the old tree, just shady enough, with a gentle breeze. I sat down and half the view disappeared behind the long summer grass. I wondered whether someone cut it or if it died back in winter. Where did the stalks and seeds go?

He unpacked a picnic from a local deli whose owner he said he knew. I was starving! He had brought local cherry tomatoes that were so juicy they were impossible to eat without them dripping, with the first hint of summer's sweetness coursing through the tart flavour hit. There was an aubergine ratatouille, full of fresh rosemary and thyme, and tomatoes and garlic, with a generous sheen of olive oil over the top. It tasted like sunshine as the flavours exploded in my mouth. We ate it with fresh-baked, crunchy ciabatta, torn into chunks and dipped into the sauce – another perfect opportunity for messy drips. I found myself wondering if Christof had chosen the menu deliberately, as I managed to get ratatouille down my chin and he reached over, wiping it away with his finger tip, which he then licked, as he gave me a massively cheeky grin. I sensed he had decided to relax. I returned the grin, with interest.

Fresh melon slices melted in my mouth, fragrant and almost too sweet. He had brought strawberries that smelled so entrancing I didn't want to spoil them by eating them; deep red and shiny, as though someone had polished them. Sparkling water, chilled with lemon, tickled my tongue as I swallowed it, wiping the slate clean for the next flavour.

The picnic was finished and we lay back on the blanket under that beautiful tree, gazing at the sky for what felt like hours. Time slowed down whenever I was with Christof – in a good way. Maybe it was because our first meeting had been so disastrous that I figured that the only way was up. *Thanks, Yazz. You're in my head now.* I had nothing to lose. I didn't need to pretend to be funny or interesting or clever, or anything else that I would usually do to try to impress a bloke. Frankly, anything I did now would be an improvement on the first impressions I had made.

But I made him laugh. He made me laugh, too. I could tell he liked spending time with me. He at least acted as though I was interesting. I hoped it was real. I didn't feel I had to try hard. It was such a relief. I felt a lightness when I was with him. I could relax. I could let go of wanting or needing to be liked and just be me. And it felt so good.

"I nearly forgot the final treat!" he said with a big grin. I could tell he was trying to impress me. I sat up to see what he was fiddling with in the picnic bag.

He showed me tiny squares of local chocolate, ready to melt the moment I touched them, already halfway there with the heat of the picnic bag. Christof picked one up, risking a tell-tale smudge on yet another white linen shirt, and raised his eyebrow in that way I had now decided should be illegal. I was barely breathing. The air between us was charged, like a thunderstorm.

We were sitting opposite each other, keeping a safe distance, as he reached over and slipped the chocolate into my mouth. I licked his finger and thumb, softly closing my lips around them, before he could escape. But it didn't feel like he wanted to. The deep, dark chocolate started to melt on my tongue. I could smell it as I tasted it. The slightest hint of mint lifted it, stopping it from being too heavy. Very little sweetness. I imagined ancient Aztec cacao rituals, as the flavours forced me to close my eyes. I wanted to block out the sights and the sounds and just lose myself in this.

"Sophie," he whispered, as he drew closer to me. I half-knelt, to move towards him. I reached out and ran my fingers through his hair, gently moving his face towards mine. We kissed, for the first time today.

"You like the chocolate, then?" he asked, in a brief pause between kisses. "It tastes good on you!"

I gave him a playful hit and then returned to the task in hand. My knees were about to give way, but I didn't want to stop kissing Christof. He sensed it and half-guided, half-lifted me to sit on top of him. He tried to hide a wince as he did it; I kept to our deal and pretended not to notice that his injuries must extend beyond the cut on his face. His arms were wrapped around me and both my hands were running through his hair. The floodgates had been opened. Now we had started, we knew we couldn't stop. There was no "taking it slowly".

Christof used a free hand to move the rest of the picnic things off the blanket behind him and pulled me with him as he slowly lay back. *This guy must have some serious abs to be able to do that.* We were lying beneath the oak tree like love-struck teenagers who forget to come up for air. We were both letting go, finally releasing – abandoning ourselves – something that had nothing to do with the two of us; something we had both carried for far too long. And it felt incredible, like a condor soaring above a valley in the Andes; like a waterfall cascading down a mountainside in the Alps; like free-wheeling down a hillside on my bike, when I was a kid.

The sun was much lower in the sky by the time we were ready to return to the festival.

We were wrapped in each other's arms, lying on the blanket with my head resting on Christof's shoulder, both looking somewhat dishevelled. I couldn't stop grinning. His breathing was peaceful, regular, relaxed; just how I felt. I heard the church clock in the valley strike five and Christof jumped up

"Shit!" He knocked me onto my back on the blanket. "I've got to go. Sorry. I'm meeting with Giovanni's business partner at 5:30. I'm only just going to make it. I can't be late for this."

He was bundling the picnic back into its bag and I shook the blanket, starting to fold it.

He was still there, but he was gone, the connection severed by whatever it is that was going on in his head. I tried to talk to him about it as we half-ran down the hill, but I was out of breath and he was being evasive, so I let it go.

By the time we reached the market square, I was feeling hot

and confused. Did this afternoon not happen?

"Look, I'm sorry," and he looked like he meant it. "I've really got to go." He was looking at his watch again. "I don't know what time this meeting will be done, but it's likely to be over by 8:30. Would you let me take you out for dinner again tonight? Then I've got a VIP pass to the end of festival party. If you give me your number, I can call you when I'm finished, so you're not hanging around too long? Maybe you could meet me here?"

It hit me. I was leaving tomorrow morning. This was my last night. A lead weight landed in my stomach and I felt tears prickling. *I. Will. Not. Cry. Not over a man. Not now. Never again.* I wanted to walk away. Christof was standing opposite me, waiting, as patient as a man who was desperately late for a critical business meeting could be.

"I have to see you again, Sophie, please."

I was staring at my feet. Again. I knew if I looked up into his eyes I would say yes. But that would make leaving tomorrow even harder.

He sensed this, crouching down, looking up at me. *Damn. Eye contact. Fatal for my willpower.*

"I want to share this evening with you," he added, holding out his mobile. I typed in my number – neither of us had paper or a pen. He smiled. "Thank you." It was heartfelt. He turned and ran, without looking back.

I only just made it to the meeting. I arrived, dripping in sweat and visibly out of puff. Not the best look for a cool, calm and collected master negotiator.

"What the hell happened to your face?" asked Giovanni, pointing at the angry cut above my right eye. I was grateful he couldn't see the rest of the bruising. I told him the same story I had told Sophie, about tripping over a box on the cherry stall. He was even less convinced than she had been, but he knew me well enough to let it lie. He'd jump to his own conclusions, without any help from me.

Why didn't I phone him when I got home last night, Giovanni wanted to know, like I had promised, when we'd spoken at the restaurant? I hated lying to him. Was it Mark Twain who said that if you never lie, you never have to remember anything? I was getting very forgetful over all of this.

"I think we might have a deal," said Giovanni, but not looking particularly cheerful about it.

"Marco has finished most of his buying for this season, but as a favour, he could take about half of your harvest. I managed to convince him that Signor Perillo has been spreading lies about the family's crop-growing secrets having died with your father. Everyone believed him, forgetting that Pietro – and Nonna – knew everything that was done on the trees each year. The lies were ridiculous, but in the absence of anyone to dispute them, they became the truth. And you know what gossip can be like round here."

"Why didn't Pietro hear about this? He spends enough time in the bars round here. He could have defended us!" I was allowing my anger at Pietro's behaviour with the solicitor to cloud my opinions. "Surely he must have known?"

Giovanni paused and looked at me, as though trying to decide what to say next.

"Tell me!" I commanded.

"Okay, you asked for it," he replied grudgingly. "I know that Pietro has managed the farm for years," he continued. Yes, it had been since not long after Mum left. "But whenever anyone has asked him how the farm has been going recently; he has told them about you *hiding up in the city*, as he puts it, leaving him to do all of the hard work, and that no one has been making the important decisions."

I felt my emotions rising again. If I bumped into Pietro right now, I wouldn't be able to hold back. "So, him complaining about me has been making things worse; helping people to believe Perillo's lies?" My voice was shaking with anger.

Giovanni flinched, again looking like he was considering how much to say. "I don't believe that was his intention, but it will have been the effect."

My fists clenched as I imagined doing to Pietro some of what was done to me last night. Dad had trusted him! They had been best friends since school. Yet he was risking destroying our farm, just to gain sympathy from his drinking pals.

"Anyway," Giovanni interrupted my thoughts, sensing that he needed to get in some better news while I was still capable of listening, "this potential buyer checked out some samples at your stall this afternoon and was impressed. He's offering less than you had hoped for; it's only about half of what you could have got before Perillo started his rumours."

He looked at me, trying to gauge my reaction.

It was a poor deal, but it would keep us afloat. I knew I didn't really have any choice. I let my fists relax.

"Marco wanted me to tell you on my own, because he knew you'd be disappointed. That's why he didn't come this evening. But it's the best he can offer you."

I looked through the figures scribbled on Giovanni's notes from his negotiations. My eyebrows tensed as I tried to do a year's accounting in my head, working out whether or not I could accept this offer. As if I *have* any other option.

"Marco's doing me a favour on this. He knows he could offer less, but he doesn't want to offend the memory of your dad. I have to warn you though: he says he can't do it next year. Next year you're on your own. I don't really see that you have much choice, Christof."

I took a deep breath and sighed loudly.

"You've got a deal, Giovanni."

He grinned and whooped. He loved a 'yes'. He'd been doing this since before I was born. But he didn't understand. This wasn't about selling the cherries: it was about everyone we employed. None of them knew how often I lay awake at night, worrying about whether we could keep them on, whether we could afford to pay the bills, whether we could do the repairs needed on the farm and the outbuildings and machinery. Did Dad feel this way? He had never said anything. I wished he had.

I was taking this offer for them not because it was good, but because it was good *enough*. At work, I'd have refused it and renegotiated. But that wasn't how things worked out here in the countryside. Here, an offer in the hand was worth a thousand in the 'maybe'.

"We still have to sort out Perillo, though, Christof," Giovanni interrupted my thoughts, "Any ideas on that one? My sources say he's a nasty piece of work. You want to watch your back there."

"I've chatted with Nonna and we've got a plan." I said with a bravado I wasn't sure I was feeling. "But I won't let him intimidate me. He's got other festivals to visit and other farmers to scare off and blackmail. He'll be bored of us soon."

"I wouldn't be so sure," Giovanni said, half under his breath.

"Is there something you're not telling me?"

Silence. He was staring at the floor, his reluctance filling the room.

"Please, Gio, for Dad's and Nonna's sakes."

"I'll tell you if I hear anything you need to know – I promise!"

We sealed the deal with the required drinks and chat. But he could see me looking at my watch.

"Got a hot date, eh, Christof, my boy?" he teased. I blushed. "That's a yes, then? Go on, tell Uncle Giovanni who she is. Some buxom brunette from one of the neighbouring cherry stalls? Or a visiting professor from the University of Rome – more your type I reckon. Where are you taking her?"

I didn't want to answer, but it felt churlish not to, after everything Giovanni had done for me.

"I'm taking her for pizza and then off to the party."

"I look forward to seeing you both there. Does she have an older sister?" he joked. He had been single for as long as I could remember, but that didn't stop him enjoying entertaining the ladies, especially those passing through at festivals like this one.

I shook my head, "You know, I don't know!" I replied, realising how very little I knew about Sophie's life.

I was done for the evening. I was still suffering from last night's bruises and I really wanted to go to bed. The deal was agreed in principle. We could wrap things up with the final handshake tomorrow. But I refused to allow myself to feel relief until after the money and the harvest had changed hands. Giovanni would act as the agent, holding on to the money until the buyer had approved the delivery. He would take a healthy cut for setting up the deal. I had worked out that would leave us with just enough to break even for the year, meaning anything we could make from processed cherries would be a bonus. But it would make extra work for Nonna and the girls, and I would have to set up the contracts with the department stores and catalogues. I hoped I would be able to find the contacts I needed in Dad's paperwork. I didn't have the time to start from scratch.

I didn't want to think about all the work that would be involved.

I had an important number to dial and an evening to enjoy. Having wrapped up the Francesco mess and found a buyer for at least some of the crop, I felt like celebrating. But deep down I was blocking out the fact that Sophie was leaving tomorrow.

He called me, as promised, and I half-ran into the town to meet him at 8:30. The number came up as *unavailable* and *international*, so I knew it was him. My heart skipped a beat. I grabbed my shawl, pulled on my shoes and nearly threw the heavy room key at the receptionist as I sprinted out of the hotel door.

On the phone Christof wouldn't tell me how his meeting had gone or where we were going. He wanted it to be a surprise, he said. He was preoccupied, not listening as much as usual.

I was waiting where we had left each other this afternoon and I saw him walking across the crowded town square, carrying a heavy basket. He hadn't noticed me yet. His face looked tense with pain and it looked like he was limping. I really wasn't convinced he'd fallen over last night. Had he been involved in a fight? I realised how little I knew him. Could I even trust him?

"*Ciao, bella Sofia,*" he said, putting down the basket and giving me a publicly appropriate kiss. He looked worried, but he was smiling, so I decided just to go with the flow of the evening.

"Can I give you a hand with anything? What's in the basket?"

"Dinner. Piping hot. You're going to love it. The best pizza in town and we're going to eat it back in your *Secret Garden*. We'll be the only ones there. It's the only way we'll get any peace and quiet in this town tonight. The place is heaving for the celebrations, with people coming in from the whole region. We'll come back down here for the party."

He took out the picnic blanket and a smaller bag for me to carry and we meandered back up through the hilly streets to the honeysuckle gate.

It creaked its welcome as though it had known we'd be back. I laid out the blanket beneath the lilac tree.

He brought out two cardboard boxes of steaming hot pizza, dripping with local cheeses and fresh chillies. One was topped with fresh rocket leaves and the other with last season's black olives and oil-preserved artichoke hearts. They looked and smelled divine.

"This is the best pizza in town. They use the same recipe they used to use when my grandmother was a girl. I hope you enjoy it."

I did. I had to wipe my greasy fingers on the napkins he had brought, between each slice, and it tasted so good there was no space for talking. He poured lightly chilled red wine into small earthenware beakers, pale blue and white, with a hand-painted wildflower pattern.

I picked one up to look at it more closely. It was heavier than I had expected.

"These are beautiful!" I said.

"They belonged to my parents. They were given them as a wedding present and they have always been at the family apartment here in town. They used to be a set of six but now there are only these two left. I don't get to use them very often." A cloud across his face signalled that shutdown again. Forbidden territory. I didn't need my market researcher's vibe to know that asking more about his family would be a bad idea. There was a sudden darkness around him with a neon sign in the middle of it saying, "Don't go there!" I let it rest and turned my attention back to dinner.

The pizzas smelled so good that I hadn't noticed the heaviness of the evening honeysuckle and the very last lilac blooms. They perfumed the air around us with a drunken intensity, swishing oh-so-gently in the breeze.

It was like being in another world where time stood still, just for us.

She looked so beautiful, in her sky-blue summer dress and leather sandals, her golden-brown hair tied back with a red ribbon. Someone should paint her. The way she lost herself in the simple act of eating pizza refreshed my business-weary soul.

For one terrible moment, I thought she might break the spell, by asking about Mum when I stupidly mentioned the beakers, but luckily, she stopped.

The wine was perfectly chilled and it helped me to relax. It had been such an intense few days. My head was raging, throbbing, making me dizzy from yesterday's attack and, although my rib wasn't broken, it still hurt to breathe deeply. Then there was the stress of the deal for the harvest. And I refused to even think about Sophie's imminent departure. I didn't want to grieve in advance.

We had the whole night ahead of us.

I could hear the first band warming up in the distance, ready to welcome the party guests for the end of the cherry festival. We would join them soon.

But first for pudding: fresh cherries from this year's harvest, from our farm. I had saved them from our stall at the festival and kept them in the fridge at the apartment, to stop them over-ripening in the heat.

Her face lit up at the sight of them, their simplicity, their deep purple skin shining as the moon danced between the clouds, so plump and smooth. She picked one up and fed it to me, her fingers resting on my lips for a moment. I licked them and smiled. I wanted to watch her forever. The sweetness of the juice overwhelmed my taste buds.

The bliss of mindfully eating a perfect cherry, staring into the eyes of this wonderful woman, threatened to drive me insane.

It felt like we were the only people in the world, under the lilac tree. There was time to dance later, but for now, it was just the two of us, drinking each other in.

It was time to go to the party. He wanted me to see it, but he also had to go, to represent his farm. It was part of the tradition. I didn't want to leave the Secret Garden. It was a space outside of normal life. I could sense the magic in the air and the history it had shared with generations of locals, escaping the busyness of the town. Christof said it had been there for hundreds of years.

We packed everything carefully into the picnic basket, which he left under a bush. "I'll pick it up tomorrow," he explained. "It'll be safe here."

Tomorrow. I'd be gone then.

A wave of cold dread shivered through me, but I forced it out with the warmth of the evening. I wondered if he was thinking about me leaving. But maybe he'd be too busy to notice. I found myself hoping that he *would* notice when I was gone – more than hoping.

We walked hand in hand towards the market square, the music and laughter and shouting echoing off the buildings in the narrow streets. As we neared the square, the streets opened up more widely. Usually they'd have been busy with cars, but just for tonight they were banned, so we could all enjoy the celebrations without worrying about traffic.

Christof half-dragged me through the moving mass of people. It was overwhelming. People kept shouting hello to him and those back-clapping hugs greeted us on every corner. With each new person we met he introduced me, "*Ecco, Sofia, dall'Inghilterra.*" *This is Sophie, from England.* It felt like he was proud of me. That made me glow inside. He wanted me to meet his friends, who welcomed me with distracted kindness as they, too, made their slow path through the masses to the music.

It was so noisy I could barely hear myself think. Christof kept a tight hold of my hand as he bought us two plastic cups of deep red wine. It was as though he was scared I would disappear if he let go. It wasn't easy to drink it without spilling, but maybe that was part of the fun.

We walked along through the busy square, but there was more space now. People were dancing on the impromptu dance floor and we stood watching them, Christof's hand resting on the small of my back. I felt it burning its memory into my skin. I wanted to pinch myself, to check this was real, as I looked up at the profile of his face, alive with the excitement and atmosphere.

He looked at me. We kissed, lingering, enjoying, oblivious to our audience.

"Come! Let's dance!" He pulled me onto the dance floor.

Even though we were outside, it was hot and sweaty, with so many people not caring about bumping into each other. Laughing. Loving. Celebrating the harvest.

Young children who should long since have been in bed were running wild, high on the fun or the day's sugar-laden cherry delicacies, or both. The wine flowed. No one would let Christof pay for his refills. He was obviously well-loved here. But he only had eyes for me. He barely noticed anyone else. We swirled and waltzed and moved with the music. I felt strangely proud that I hadn't trodden on his toes yet. My heart beat to the rhythms of the band and the music drowned out my thoughts. The air was filled with the sweetness of the cherries, cigarette smoke, wine, beer and sweat and the distant smell of roasting meat and toasting ciabatta.

The church clock stuck midnight. Cinderella's hour.

Boos came from the crowd as the band switched to a slower tempo for its final song. The disappointment was soon replaced by couples swaying gently, wrapped up in each other, shutting out the world, ending the night in happy harmony.

My arms rested around his neck, his around my waist, holding me close to him. He looked tired, but happy. We kissed again. I didn't want it to stop. Nor did he. But it had to. I couldn't bring myself to say it out loud. The lightness in my heart was fading fast as I knew I had to break this spell.

Deep breath.

"Christof," I whispered in his ear, "My flight is at ten. I have to leave my hotel by not long after seven. I don't want to go, but I have to."

I watched his eyes darken. His grip on me tightened and he ignored me, as though pretending I hadn't spoken would make reality go away.

I didn't want the evening to end, but I unravelled my arms from around him and took him by the hand. "Walk with me?"

He followed obediently, without words. The streets were busy with those who didn't want to go home. We soon reached the river. It was quiet there.

He guided me to a wide, old stone wall, where we sat, our feet dangling over the edge, tempting the river to wet our shoes. The stones were still warm from the day's hot sun. The river splashed playfully, ignoring our racing emotions, reminding us that time never rests.

I could smell the stones; their slightly metallic mustiness. I could smell Christof; an earthy mix of coffee, gentle sweat from the dancing and the wine on his breath. His arm was around my waist and I rested my head on his shoulder. His deep, slow breathing calmed me. I could feel his heartbeat, if I moved my head to the top of his chest: strong, powerful, constant. We watched the river flow, paying us no attention, always changing.

I lost track of how long we sat there. He removed his arm from around me and lifted a leg over the wall, so he was straddling it, facing me. I did the same. I moved closer to him. He lifted me up so my legs were resting over his thighs. He pulled me even closer. We kissed. But this time it was tainted by sadness, by separation, by endings.

"I don't want you to take me to the airport, Christof," she said, turning down my offer, pulling away from a kiss I had wanted to last forever.

I didn't want her to say it out loud. Airport. Sophie leaving. I didn't want words to steal these precious moments from us.

"I have to go," she murmured softly, with obvious reluctance, and I knew she was right.

I took my time as I stood up and held out my hand to help her off the wall. We walked the slowest, longest walk, back up the hill to her hotel.

We passed the corner where I had been attacked the night before. I felt myself shudder and I was on high alert, though I didn't think they'd bother me two nights in a row. I had been right about the name on the card. It explained the Naples receipt.

I knew I was going to have to let her go. But not yet.

I guided her a short way up a dark alley, safe from prying eyes, the closest we had had to genuine privacy in the two short days since we'd met. We kissed, slowly, deeply, finally.

"Sophie," I told her, needing to help her to understand, "you are wonderful, brilliant, beautiful, clever. Don't ever let anyone take that away from you."

It felt like a goodbye. It was.

The town's clock struck once.

We walked back to her hotel.

I could feel the seconds running away from us. I didn't know how to stop them.

We were back at my hotel. This was it. I didn't want this to be it. Christof let go of my hand and turned to face me. There was so much unsaid, things we would never say: about how an international relationship wouldn't work; how our careers would get in the way; how this intensity would be exhausted by only seeing each other every few months, stretched too thinly across the miles; how you never knew how often you might find something this special in life; how we barely knew each other yet.

He held my head in his palms and stared into my eyes. My hands were linked around his back. He bent down and kissed me passionately for the last time.

I shouldn't have had to wait until I was thirty-four to be kissed like this! shrieked my Inner Drama Queen. Luckily not out loud. I closed the door on her. This wasn't her time.

He held my hands and I melted in his eyes. Again.

He kissed my forehead, so gently, so tenderly. "You are wonderful," he said, with such feeling, such sadness, as he pulled away. He turned and disappeared silently into the night.

I hadn't expected to cry myself to sleep.

I was sitting on the balcony of my parents' apartment – mine now, I realised, surprised that I hadn't spotted that before – not noticing the beauty of the view as the lights in the village below shone like earthbound stars in the now-moonless night. I looked down at the rusty old chair I was sitting on, with its creaking wooden slats that should have been repainted a decade ago, and noticed how uncomfortable it was. "You need more padding, *carino*," I could hear Nonna laugh. She was always teasing me about being too thin. But she wouldn't be happy if I were fat, either. "I have no problems with that chair!" I imagined her continuing, patting her ample bottom and wrinkling her eyes with a cheeky grin. A pen and old notepad sat on my lap, patiently waiting for me.

The past few days were churning through my brain like the white-water torrents of a glacial river in the spring melt. I knew from experience that I needed to bring my thoughts into some kind of order, if I was going to have a chance of sleeping. I couldn't believe I had just walked away from her.

If I were an artist, I'd draw her, to always have her with me. I'd carry her likeness in the pocket next to my heart like a Victorian romantic. But it wouldn't ease my pain, not right now. It hurt - physically - in my chest; my heart was tight and empty. And I knew there was no chance of me creating any kind of picture of Sophie. I was chucked out of my art classes at school long before the exams counted for anything. My teacher didn't want me bringing down his average.

But I could write. I have always loved mathematical poems, especially pantoums – where the lines repeat in what feels like a random order, though it takes time and care to make them work. If I could capture her in those few lines, maybe she wouldn't be gone. Maybe I would wake up tomorrow and find her still here with me. I'd get a call saying she'd changed her flight.

But she was starting a new job on Monday. She wouldn't change her flight. And she didn't have my number, I realised, with a sudden jolt of panic that made my heart pound. I had to suppress caller display for work, which meant my number would have come up as *unavailable* on her phone when I called her to meet for dinner. For a brief moment, I considered sprinting back to her hotel, waking her up, telling her how I feel. But what would be the point? If she had wanted it, she would have asked for it. I couldn't face the thought of rejection. I had had enough of it, over the years.

I didn't want this to be over, even though I had never wanted it to start. Sophie was only ever meant to be a distraction. But I had to accept that neither of us had talked about the future. This was a holiday romance. I needed to let her go and move on.

I poured myself a brandy – cherry, of course – and enjoyed the sensation as it stung the back of my throat. It was a bottle of ours. Dad would never buy it in. It was from the last batch he ever made, though we had no idea about that at the time. That's the thing, when someone dies, you spend the whole of the next year with 'the first birthday since…', 'the first Christmas since…', 'the first cherry festival since…' and 'the last bottle of cherry brandy…' Each 'first' and 'last' worked like a plough turning over the earth, digging up fresh memories with a potential for pain and the earthquake of emotions that still sometimes catch me unawares, reminding me how much I miss him.

I turned to face the kitchen and held the heavy crystal glass up against the light of the ancient bulb. The liquid glowed golden red, the light catching the ripples as I gently swirled the brandy. It reminded me of Sophie's hair. This wasn't helping. I downed the rest of the glass to drown out the memories and gave myself a coughing fit.

I decided to write it down – how she made me feel – to try a pantoum to exorcise the joy she had brought me. Then I'd burn it, like a cleansing ritual, using the flame from the gas hob. I took my time. There was no rush – I could tell I wasn't going to fall asleep any time soon.

The sweet smell of cherries suffocates the air.
Dancing with abandon, we celebrate the harvest.
Deliciously slow kisses that never want to end.
Children running wild with the sugar and the sunshine.

Dancing with abandon, we celebrate the harvest.
Overflowing baskets feed the hungry crowd.

Children running wild with the sugar and the sunshine.
Feeling so alive.

Overflowing baskets feed the hungry crowd.
So much noise, you lose your sense of taste.
Feeling so alive.
I let down my defences.

The thrill as my hand finds the small of her back.
The sweet smell of cherries suffocates the air.
She has the bluest eyes. We hold hands through the swarming streets.
Deliciously slow kisses that never want to end.

It was done. But she hadn't gone. I knew I'd never burn it. I wasn't even sure that I felt any better; in fact, I thought I felt worse. But it calmed my thoughts. At least now I was certain how much I would miss her. Not much of a consolation. I also knew I didn't have space in my life for that kind of emotional attachment. I made the decision that I wasn't going to go to her hotel and be the Romeo below her balcony.

I tried to fall asleep in the bed I had known since childhood. The white cotton sheets were unwelcoming, as though they were cross with me. The breeze refused to oblige and cool the room, like a petulant toddler wanting to prove to its parent who's boss. A heavy weight in my chest was trying to stop me from breathing and my thoughts didn't have a kind word to say to me. I tortured myself with a scene-by-scene replay of how wonderful my evening with Sophie had been.

I lay in the darkness feeling more alone than I had ever before, as the realisation seeped through the chatter of my exhausted mind – I had lost something irreplaceable tonight.

I woke up with a jolt. That meant I had fallen asleep, which surprised me. I had been dreaming about the attack. It was one of those dreams that feels more real than 'reality'. I looked at the clock. I had overslept. It was nearly ten. I never slept that late. But it must have been 4 a.m. by the time exhaustion took over. Not a problem today, though. We had packed up the festival stall and the team would be driving the lorry back to the farm this morning. I was due to follow later. There was no rush – just the handshake with Marco to do and the festival would be finished for me.

Then it hit me.

10 a.m. Sophie's flight time. She was gone. My practical streak kicked in as usual, to stop me drowning in melancholy.

I made myself a coffee and called Giovanni. All was good. Marco had been in touch with him to arrange details for the deal, so it was full steam ahead with the harvest, once this afternoon's handshake had sealed the deal. It was a relief, but I also knew how much work this would be for our farm team, especially after the festival. I was due back at work in Milan on Monday, so that left me just over a day to help, back at the farm. It was going to be interesting seeing Pietro again, after what had happened at the solicitor's office.

Keeping myself busy was always a great way to blank out thoughts I didn't want to have and I found myself playing music in my head again. Sometimes I wonder if I have a whole radio station in there. I don't normally get to choose the music. This morning I was walking in time to that old Bill Withers classic *'Ain't no sunshine when she's gone'*. That really didn't help.

Maybe I could text her? Say it was lovely to meet her? Ask her how her flight home was? She hates flying. But what point would there be? And what about last night's decision to let her go? But maybe we could be friends? I could feel my resolve weakening.

Where could this possibly go? I decided to put off the decision until after I had been into town. There was no point texting before her flight landed in England, which would be around one, so I'd be back at the apartment and could decide what to do then. It felt good to put it off for a few hours, to escape back to life-before-Sophie for a bit.

I made the tour of friends who would have been offended, had if I left without saying goodbye, and grabbed some breakfast at the baker's. People stared at me as I went by. The bruises on my face and the angry cut above my right eye looked like badly applied stage make-up. I gave the same answer to everyone who asked: I had tripped over a box and landed on the corner of a table.

Town was busy again, with all signs of the festival gone by the time I got down there. Even the dance floor and the stage the band had played on had been cleared away. It was as though the past few days had never happened; as though Sophie had never existed. I was glad I didn't live here. Two short days had created far too many memories for me to be able to be happy here, at least for a while. Being back at the farm and then Milan would be a great way to take my mind off this.

I was putting off collecting last night's picnic basket from what Sophie had nicknamed the *Secret Garden*. I didn't want to be carrying around memories of how wonderful our evening had been for any longer than I had to.

So, I dawdled my way through the Saturday morning market. The market was past the main rush, but stalls were still groaning under the weight of fresh produce. The farmers were relieved that people finally had eyes for something other than cherries again, but the market was quiet for this time of day. Maybe their customers were having a lie-in, getting over last night's celebrations. The intoxicating fragrance of the early melons filled the street between the stalls, along with that distinctive first-off-the-vine tomato scent. Large bunches of parsley stood in big jugs of water, to stop them wilting before they reached their new homes, and the early basil was arranged in jam jars. The stallholders knew that presentation counted in this game, when most people were selling the same thing, at similar quality and prices. The tomatoes were perfectly arranged in their trays. There was a melon sliced in half, with slivers on a plate, so you could taste for yourself how delicious it was. The canopies kept the sun off the produce, or the green beans – *fagioli* – would soon wilt. The early season red onions had been cleaned and almost polished to a shine, with just enough root left on them to prove that they hadn't been out of the ground for more than a day.

I chatted with one of the local farmers, admiring his impressive collection of seven types of tomatoes. They ranged from bright red and lumpy, the size of a small fist, to orange and stripy, to the smallest cherry tomatoes, red as rubies, temptingly bite-sized – the type that Pietro's brother had packed for our picnic.

Memories slapped me.

Okay, this had to stop. I decided I would text Sophie when I got back to the apartment. I wasn't ready to let go of her yet. The farmer waved goodbye and I headed back up the hill, lost in my daydreams, imagining how Sophie might respond to the message. It was one of the habits that made me great at my job – second-guessing people's behaviour and motivations – but it was crap for my love life.

I was half-distracted, browsing my phone's address book, looking for Sophie's number. I had decided to send her a single text with the word 'hi' in it, before I got back to the apartment, so I didn't chicken out of sending the rest of the message when I got there – I knew myself too well. The embarrassment of sending just a single word would force me to send a proper message, ready for when her flight landed.

I was crossing the main street to head up the hill to the apartment when a distracted elderly woman, struggling with too many bags and baskets, bumped into me. I dropped my phone. *Shit*! I wondered if the screen had survived. I started to reach down to pick it up but I was caught in the movement of people crossing the road. A truck drove behind me, impatient, far too close, and I heard the crunch. I knew what I was going to see even before I looked round: my phone, smashed on the road.

Fuck! Fuck! Fuck! Smashed. I don't have a back-up. I risked being run over by grabbing it and I racked my brain. *Yes!* There was a phone-repair shop in town. It closed at twelve on Saturdays, but if I ran, I could probably still make it. The phone was trashed but the SIM should have survived.

Out of puff, I arrived at his door with five minutes to go. "I don't have a back-up," I explained, as he tried to sell me a new phone, "There's a number on here I really need. It's urgent. I don't have it anywhere else." The guy behind the counter expertly prized apart the remains of the phone's case, being careful not to cut himself. Time slowed as I willed him to hurry up; to find the SIM and set it up in a new phone for me. He held the SIM with a pair of tweezers and looked at it, shaking his head. He reached for a magnifying glass to inspect it more closely, tutting now joining the head-shaking.

"Nothing doing," he said, pointing at the SIM, "it's cracked." He showed me a hairline fracture across the card. "Was it a big car that went over it?"

"A lorry." I answered.

"Well, often the SIM will survive a standard car, but lorries are so much heavier. If they catch them the wrong way, the SIM will crack and it won't work any more." He pointed out a piece of metal from the inside of the phone that had snapped and created a knife-like edge, which was probably responsible for the damage to the SIM card.

I refused to accept his answer, insisting we try the SIM in another phone, just in case. Nothing happened. And another. He humoured me by trying a third and then handed me back my SIM card. "I'm sorry, but with that crack, it's unlikely you'll be able to recover the data." He was staring at my injuries, as though shrinking behind his counter, showing me he was scared I might be the aggressive type and had got them in a fight. I knew he was telling the truth. "You really don't have the number backed up?" he asked, trying to look hopeful. I shook my head. I had only had Sophie's number since yesterday and we don't have internet at the apartment – or enough data signal in town to back up a phone. The peace and quiet that brings me is usually something I treasure about being here.

His whole body sighed with relief as I thanked him for his help and took his hints that it was closing time. He could tell I wasn't going to be boosting his takings for the day. I obliged by leaving without drama.

I sat on the wall of the fountain in the town square, fully aware of the irony of the cupids and their arrows that surrounded me. I needed to clear my head.

It worked: I could ask at Sophie's hotel. They would be unlikely to give me her contact details, but they might agree to forward a message to her. The frustration of the past hour gave me extra energy to climb back up the winding roads into the hilly part of town and before long I was outside the tatty blue front door where Sophie had stayed. The reception was dark and musty and far too hot. I had to ring the bell three times to get someone to come out to help me.

A tired-looking man in his sixties grumbled his way to behind the reception desk. He took one look at me and announced, "We're full!" I had forgotten what a mess my face was. I wouldn't have wanted to give me a room either. I had worked out my story as I walked up to this place and launched into an explanation of how I had promised to let Sophie know something important but that my phone had smashed and I didn't have her contact details anywhere else. Could he forward a letter to her for me, if I paid the postage?

He shook his head in silence. In my panic, I started to beg him, to explain how important the message was, to try to convince him what a simple favour this was.

"*Signor*, surely if she is expecting this message and doesn't hear from you, *she* will contact *you*?"

"But she'll call the phone I no longer have!" was my retort. I didn't think that admitting she didn't have my number would help my argument.

"I'm afraid I cannot help you," he replied, turning his back and shuffling paperwork, letting me know the conversation was over.

"Please! You have to! Could you just let me have a piece of paper and I'll even let you read the message, so you know it's okay? You must have her contact details, for the tourist tax. For your email newsletter?"

He shook his head again. "We don't keep a register of our guests and we don't have a newsletter. If people like it here," which I doubted most did, "they contact us to book again." My heart was sinking.

"But surely you still have the tourist registration form?"

"No. We submit those each Friday and we don't keep copies of personal details. They are with the authorities now and there is no way they will let you have a guest's contact details. I suggest you get yourself a new phone and wait for her to call you." He walked to the hotel's door and held it open for me, making it clear the conversation was over.

I had lost Sophie's number. It hit me like running into a glacier that I didn't even know her surname.

Any hope I had of finding her vanished.

I was itching to get back to Milan. I'd had enough of cherries for a while, but I had promised Nonna I'd spend the rest of the weekend at the farm, to update her on how the festival had gone and to agree the plans for the rest of the crop. I had no intention of mentioning anything else that had happened over the past few days.

I got there late on Saturday, having packed up the apartment in town, ready to leave it until someone was next there, which might still be a few months away. I touched the cut above my right eye and winced with pain, realising I hadn't done anything to find out who might have left the Naples receipt in the apartment. But I was already in the car getting ready to drive off, and I knew my neighbour was out. It was too late now. I tried to convince myself it was nothing, but I knew it wasn't. The business card from the heavies proved it was too much of a coincidence.

I eventually pulled up on the gravel parking area in front of the farmhouse. As I got out of the car, it struck me how noisy the countryside could be, after the town. Farm machinery was working overtime to help with the harvest for Marco. At least ten different types of bird were running competing concerts. I heard a distant tractor mowing hay before the summer storms, and a radio – too loud to think to – was keeping the farm team happy in the packing and sorting barn.

We had a couple of crazy weeks ahead of us and then it would be a longer, slower job, to pick the rest of the harvest and preserve it.

Back when Nonno, my grandfather, planted the trees, he chose varieties that ripened at different times, to spread the harvest. That way he could offer cherries at the local markets from June until August. Nowadays most farmers concentrated on a few varieties that gave them one or two harvest points, with a larger bulk. That's what the supermarkets preferred. Dad saw that as a high-risk strategy, which is why he had continued the focus on spreading the crop. He preferred negotiating a deal with a wholesaler to buy the crop as and when it was ready.

Supermarkets could be fickle friends to farmers. They might order the entire crop, only to tell you, after you'd harvested it, that they had over-stocked and were only going to pay a fraction of the price… or that they didn't want your cherries at all anymore. Dad didn't want to play that game and nor did I. When supermarkets worked well, it was much easier, but when they didn't, you could be ruined in a heartbeat, at the whim of someone hundreds of miles away, sitting at a computer, who had never set foot on a farm.

I looked over to the farmhouse and saw Pietro standing statue-still, staring at me. My hands formed involuntary fists, waves of anger threatening to take over. I was hungry to tell him what I thought of him. But I was still sitting in my car and the door was closed. I knew he would have disappeared by the time I could get close enough to shout at him. The fear in his eyes was enough for now. He knew that the repercussions would come; that I would want to know why he had betrayed the farm – and Dad's memory; that we would need to talk about whether I could ever trust him again. But now wasn't the time. I would achieve more by letting him stew and fret than by launching an unprepared attack. I sat and watched as he walked away, back across the field to his family's house, glancing over his shoulder every few steps to make sure I wasn't following.

I looked back to our farmhouse and saw Nonna standing in the doorway, welcoming me with her enormous grin.

"I've got a celebration dinner for you. Well done! It all worked out okay, just like I said it would!" she said, with a cheeky glint in her eye, as she opened her arms for a compulsory and very welcome hug.

Her face clouded over as I walked towards her. She had spotted the cut above my eye and the blue-brown bruising. I couldn't wait until it healed. I didn't want to lie to her, but I couldn't risk telling her the truth.

"Well?" she asked.

"I fell over." Technically it was true.

"Yes, of course you did, *carino*." I held my breath as I waited to see whether she would press me for the truth. She was wise enough to know I wasn't going to tell her more – and I didn't want to lie to her. I gave her a tentative smile, which she returned with a bear hug. I will always remember the day we realised I was as tall as her, when I was about thirteen, and nowadays she joked about hugging my armpits as I was so much taller than she was.

"Glad you showered today, *carino*!" she joked, pretending to sniff the hug. "When did you last eat properly?"

"Last night," I replied, not wanting to give her any more details. It already felt like a dream from someone else's life.

"Then come and help me to make dinner and I'll tell you what's been happening."

"Do you mind if I go for a walk first?" I asked. I felt the need to be alone, just me and the land, before I did any more talking.

"Of course, *carino*, but don't be long. I need your help in the kitchen."

I wandered through the orchards, passing my favourite

climbing tree; an old oak like the one Sophie and I had had our picnic under yesterday. Was it really only yesterday? I used to build tree houses and camp out on hot, breezeless nights in this one... until Mum left. Everything changed after that. The land lost its laughter. Dad got so serious. His temper would flare without warning. No one would talk about her. All traces of her were wiped from the house – and the land. It was like she had never existed, like no one had ever cared about her, except for me. I quickly learned to be quiet and 'good'. Some of the joy went out of life. I never understood why she had gone, or where. I would lie awake at night, trying not to cry, desperate to think of what I could have done differently, wishing I could turn back time to make her stay.

Unwanted emotions were rising up inside me, like old friends whose job it was to force me to go through the middle of the pain, rather than round it, but I still wasn't ready, despite it having been twenty-five years this summer since she'd left. I was still counting. I took the lid of my very own Pandora's box and slammed it closed, locking it tightly shut with its rusty old key. I didn't want to go there today, not with how I was already feeling.

I looked around at the rolling hills, drowning in the evening's golden sunshine. The leaves in the orchards created dappled shade. Some of the orchards had chickens to keep the grasses down. Others were mown. We were heading towards evening and I heard an early owl calling to its friends, rallying them to join it for a night of hunting. A distant owl answered it. It wouldn't be alone tonight. It hadn't let someone insanely special fly away and leave it behind.

I changed the subject in my mind.

I looked at the bounty of crops already growing in the farmhouse kitchen garden, so early in the season. As well as cherries, we grew apples, apricots, plums and peaches, mostly for the local village. We didn't sell those commercially. And there was an acre or two set aside for vegetables. We tried to be as self-sufficient as possible, but it was always a balance between effort and results. Sometimes it was cheaper to buy food at the market than to pay farmhands to grow it for us, now Nonna couldn't manage it on her own.

I heard the distant chime of church bells striking the hour and headed back to the farmhouse where I found the kitchen table groaning under the weight of fresh broad beans, carrots, red onions, the first tomatoes, and early season aubergines and red peppers from the glasshouse.

"You can get shelling," Nonna said, pointing at the beans. It's a good job for mind-numbing and chatting, so I was happy to agree. Nonna often told stories of grandmothers from her childhood, sitting outside their houses in her village with buckets of broad beans in front of them, each removing beans from their pods while they gossiped for hours.

I grabbed a large bowl for the pods and a smaller one for the beans and got started. Nonna chatted away, asking about everyone who had been at the festival, fishing for gossip. We both paused, when we heard the sound of tyres on the gravel driveway, pulling up to the front of the farmhouse. We weren't expecting visitors and being so remote, it always made me nervous when someone showed up, unannounced. Nonna wiped her hands on her floral apron and left the kitchen to open the front door, before the visitors could knock.

"Christof, I think you should come. Now. Please."

Please, God, no. My heart sank. I felt adrenalin kicking in. My hand couldn't help but move to touch the cut above my eye. I flinched with pain. Three large men were dragging themselves out of a smart, black Mercedes van. One held the passenger door open and a wiry man stepped out. He was in his sixties, dressed in black like an undertaker, and he wore an expression that could make a tree wither its leaves and drop its crop.

"Signor Perillo," he said, walking towards me. Neither of us reached a hand out in greeting. "I think it's time to do our little deal, don't you?" One of the gorilla-sized thugs behind him cracked his knuckles as part of this no doubt well-rehearsed routine. My heart was racing. My mouth was dry. I took a deep breath and stood up to my full height, wishing my phone were in my pocket and not smashed and useless, not that there was much point in calling the police. Perillo would be long-gone by the time they reached us.

"There is no deal to be done, Signor Perillo," I said, trying to sound braver than I felt. "I fear you have been misinformed."

He shook his head, with the patronising sympathy a teacher sometimes shows to a young child when they are struggling to understand a new idea. "I have everything I need," he waved a hand at his van, "to make your orchards disappear, if you need more persuasion." He gave his words time to have their full effect. "Or we could sign the deal for me to buy your farm and your crop and consider the matter closed." He reached his right hand into the inside left pocket of his jacket. I tensed and froze. Too many movies had taught me to expect a gun. He pulled out a neatly folded contract.

"Two signatures are all I need. And I'll even give you a week to move out. Of course, though, the price reflects the..." he looked around, disapproval radiating from his eyes, "... state of the farm and the crop." His smile would have frozen ice cream. It was clear he loved ruining people's lives to get his own way.

"We won't sign. We have already sold the crop."

"That can't be! I checked today! Who would have been fool enough to take your mangy cherries at this stage of the year?"

He didn't know about Marco's deal. Giovanni had done us a

favour in managing to keep that one quiet, so it didn't risk affecting next year's deals. Perillo had no idea.

"Your lies didn't work! There's nothing here for you. Please leave. Now."

More knuckle-cracking made it obvious that Perillo didn't like to go down without a fight, even when he was beaten. My mind was racing, trying to work out how many of the farm team might come running if I yelled for them. The answer was none, not at this late hour on a Saturday.

Then Nonna stepped forwards. She had been standing quietly in the doorway. I tried to resist the urge to push her back to safety, to help her understand that these men wouldn't want to leave empty-handed.

Her voice rang out with a strength I had forgotten she had. "So, Perillo, you're from Naples, I believe." It was a statement, not a question. But Perillo nodded, confused by the direction the negotiations were taking. "And I'm guessing you're familiar with how things run down there, when someone insults your *Family*?" The gorilla guards shuffled uncomfortably and looked at their feet. Perillo's expression remained unchanged. "Well, I still have *Family* down there. And if they hear about what you tried to do to us, lying about our harvest and trying to put us out of business, you will regret having ever picked on this farm. Do I make myself clear?"

Again, no response. Nonna stood in silence, staring into Perillo's eyes, wearing an expression of calm indifference that had more effect than shouting or fighting with Perillo's thugs could ever have had.

She pulled her phone out of her apron pocket. "All it takes is one call to the right person and we'll all be sending *white chrysanthemums* to your good lady wife." She paused, letting the emphasis on the funeral flowers make the meaning of her threat clear. "Or you could politely leave and never come near us again and I'd be prepared to write this off as a misunderstanding. Your choice."

I watched Perillo's eyes as he weighed up his options. His bravado was melting like butter left out in the midday sun. He knew we were a lost cause and Nonna's threat meant he wouldn't be taking revenge. His expression told me he was trying to find a way to leave, without losing face with his men. Nonna typed in her code to unlock her phone and held it in front of her, squinting at the screen and preparing to dial a number. I was shocked to realise I didn't know whether or not she was bluffing. Neither did Perillo.

"Remember, Perillo, the police work differently up here from down in Naples and I have already reported your threats to our local police station, so if anything suspicious happens here at the farm they will know exactly who to ask about it."

Perillo made his decision.

He threw the contract onto the ground with a flourish. "My offer still stands. But I won't hold it against you if you don't take it up." He motioned to his guards to open the door of the van for him and I stood rooted to the ground as they pulled away, out of our lives.

I ran over to hug Nonna. "I should have protected you! I'm so sorry. I feel like I've let you down, Nonna! Why wouldn't they listen to me?"

"He wouldn't have taken 'no' for an answer from a youngster like you, *carino*," she said, hugging me warmly, "but these men know when to fight and when to leave well be. Perillo knows not to mess with a nonna."

"How can you be so sure he won't come back?"

"He knows a lost cause when he sees one. And I don't think he'll be taking revenge. He's a grizzly bear with a fluffy bunny inside him. I'd guess he's not so bad, once you get to know him."

I winced at the image that flashed across my mind of a bully like Signor Perillo joining us for Christmas celebrations, like an old friend of the family.

"That's it? All sorted?" I couldn't believe how calmly she was handling this.

"Yes. It will all be fine. Now, tell me what else you got up to in town. I heard some rumours," she smiled. I knew what she was hinting at. Someone had been talking. We weren't exactly discreet at the party last night.

I wasn't ready to tell her anything about Sophie, so I chatted, in general, about who I had seen and who sent their best wishes. She knew I was holding back, but she also knew I would talk to her when I felt ready, so she let it drop.

I was very relieved that Perillo was off the scene, but I wished I had been able to get rid of him – to protect her. She's made of strong stuff but she shouldn't have to be dealing with this kind of thing. Yet again, I missed Dad.

JULY

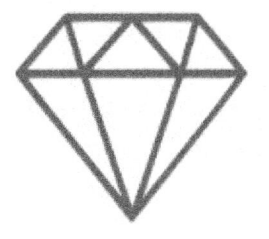

Mined

the volcano's depths
a thousand-tonne explosion
sets the diamonds free

After two fantastic weeks in Italy, I had expected to feel refreshed and excited about starting my new job on Monday. It didn't work out that way.

Somehow, I had managed to get some sleep after my evening with Christof and made it to the airport in time, looking so bleary-eyed that the official checking my hand luggage actually asked me if I was okay. I didn't want to tell her how much I had cried. It felt stupid to be so upset about flying away from someone I had known for just two days, who hadn't even bothered to give me his phone number.

The flight was smooth, so I was spared my usual praying-to-keep-the-plane-in-the-air routine by the crazy priest sitting next to me. He was hilarious, but I don't think he knew it. His rosary rattled round his fingers with his lips moving soundlessly for the entire flight. Each offer of refreshments from the cabin crew was met with a scowl and a reproach of "Don't disturb me. I'm on God's business." And every tannoy announcement had him tutting and eye-rolling. I was grateful to him for distracting me.

I took a cab back to Anna's flat and remembered, with a thud in my stomach, that I was technically 'without home' and living on her goodwill, after my now-former landlord had sold my old flat. I had loved that place. It was so handy for the Tube and had big, sunny windows that let in so much light I could almost pretend I was living in the countryside.

Anna had gone out and I was home alone for once, so I made a cup of tea in one of Anna's comedy mugs. "Good morning? Not until I've had my coffee!" it said in a splash of red on a white background. I caught myself wondering how the mug that so loudly proclaimed its love of coffee felt about being used for tea. I had missed tea in Italy – they just didn't get it. How could it be so hard to make a decent mug of tea? Yet everyone, apart from the Brits (and maybe Indians and Chinese), seemed to struggle with it, like it was quantum physics. *Maybe it is*, commented the part of my brain that always needed to have an opinion on everything. But all you needed was properly hot water, some tea leaves – in a bag if that's your thing – chuck the two together, let them dance for a few minutes, fish out the teabag and add your preferred quantity of milk. I wondered how it was so hard to get right.

I settled down to think about Christof, instantly regretting the choice, sensing that my memories of him had shifted from pleasure to self-torture.

I wanted to see him again, but I had realised on the plane that I didn't have his phone number. I don't know where he works either – he was cagey about that. A heaviness in my stomach told me I had no way of getting in touch with this guy. He was gone, unless he called me. And my Inner Drama Queen would have a field day, as I waited for the call that would probably never come.

We hadn't talked about the future. We had spent two incredible days living in the moment. Was it really only two days? He had never said he'd call. We hadn't discussed seeing each other again. We had packed a lot of falling in love into that time. *In love. No. That's not what I wanted from Italy. But it's where I am. That was more than a holiday romance, wasn't it?* Suddenly I was sobbing, big gulps of air shaking my body, hoping the neighbours couldn't hear me, feeling so glad Anna was out.

"How was your holiday?" she had smirked earlier, when she met me at the front door of her block of flats, grabbing my rucksack and walking up the stairs with me. Funny how I hadn't let Christof carry my bag. I had spent quite a lot of time with someone who I had initially thought might be a psychopath.

Was that how it was going to be now? Everything I thought or said or did reminding me of the wonderful half-Italian I had known for a grand total of two days?

I imagined a whiteboard eraser rubbing through these thoughts, creating enough clear space to think again. I felt slightly calmer.

When she got home, Anna wanted to know everything, so I told her about the Florence adventures – I could write a book on those – and the cherry festival, but I didn't mention Christof. He felt too private. I didn't want to share him. She made quite a fuss about me holding back on something, but I couldn't tell her. She'd have been unbearable, gloating with "I told you so!" comments, given that she was the one who had spotted him giving the TV interview.

I distracted myself by doing the usual after-holiday jobs: unpacking, washing clothes, opening post, checking emails, catching up on the news.

My new job would start on Monday and I needed to be ready to impress.

I was going to be leading the market research team for one of the most innovative advertising agencies in London. They were still quite small, but they had an impressive client roster and my job, as a planner, would be to give their creative team guidance to inspire the ad campaigns and then to check with the audience that the ads worked, before the client busted a seven-figure budget on TV ad slots and full pages in newspapers and glossy magazines or social media campaigns.

I remembered when I had started in this business as a research assistant. I had been reading through a client file my boss had given me, preparing for a client briefing, and I saw some very big numbers on the page. I nearly fell off my chair, yelling in shock at both the figures and the fall. "What's up, Sophie?" my boss had yelled across at me.

"I can't believe a campaign can cost this much! That's crazy money!"

"Yes, it is, isn't it? That's why it's our job to make sure they get a good return on their investment. Better than good."

"But I had no idea it could cost £50,000 for a campaign!" I replied. "You could buy a house for that in some parts of the country!"

He had looked confused then came over to see what I was looking at.

"No, Sophie," he'd said, pointing a finger at a number with some extra zeros on the end, "£50k is the deal we negotiated for a feature in a Sunday paper. *This* is the cost of the full campaign."

I was lost for words. Over £5 million, once you factored in some TV adverts, glossy magazines and posters on the Underground and bus stops.

"No pressure on us to get it right then?" was all I could manage. He had smiled and nodded.

"Luckily that falls on my shoulders, not yours, and I'm here to help you support me. It's a big job we're doing."

I had felt grateful to him for that. He was a good boss, as long as he wasn't stressed, and he got me started on the market research ladder. But tomorrow I'd be wearing his coat, albeit in a different agency. The responsibility for the research that would get everyone making the decisions on the £5 million budgets – and more, these days – would be mine. I hadn't met my team yet, but I was hoping they would already have been trained by someone, so I could get on with settling in. And the research I had done at the cherry festival would give me a great head start with my first new client project: launching a cherry brandy in the UK.

For the first time in my career I found myself wondering what happened if a planner got it wrong. Could they sue me? Would I owe them the £5 million? Would I have to go and hide in some Central American country, drinking cocktails in a backstreet bar for the rest of my life? Did my boss have insurance against my mistakes? What would the excess be on that?

Stoooooopppppppp! Inner Drama Queen bells and alarms going off. This is not a good direction to take my self-talk, today of all days.

When Anna suggested we go out for dinner with the old crew I jumped at the chance to distract myself. Everything would be fine. Christof hadn't happened. My new job would be brilliant.

Sometimes denial and delusion were the only way to go.

Jem, my godmother, is bossy, but almost always right. She called me last night to make sure I was appropriately relaxed and positive about my new job and gave me the pep talk I desperately needed. Jem had helped me to pull myself back together after Stuart-the-perv, my ex-boss, had made my life hell and my landlord had given me notice on my flat. I had been feeling so down I had even been to see my GP for help, without success. Jem had dropped her latest beau and moved in with me for two weeks. She had taken over the packing, dragged me to private yoga classes, force-fed me mindfulness and meditation and generally kicked my backside, every time 'woe is me' had threatened to take over.

And it had been brilliant. After failing every sideways move interview I had gone for, Jem and Lucy (my real ex-boss and best friend – Stuart had been her maternity leave cover) had persuaded me to go for a promotion. And somehow, I'd got it!

I was heading to my new office, dressed in my slightly-too-smart-new-girl clothes with my 'I'm going to rock this' shoes and a shoulder bag that was probably the emptiest it would ever be. It held nothing other than my phone, my wallet, a hairbrush, a pen and a notepad. I was pretty sure that, by the end of the day, it would also be carrying a laptop and several heavy client files. And things would continue that way until whenever I left.

Anna was still asleep when I went out, so I had had to get my clothes out of her wardrobe the night before, leaving them hanging on the back of the kitchen door. I was really hoping this job would mean enough of a pay rise to help me get my own flat again. My old place had been a bargain, compared to the current local rents, even though it was still painfully expensive. But rents went up by 10 or 20 per cent every time a tenant moved out these days. Salaries weren't keeping pace. I had friends who had had to move out of London because they couldn't afford it any more – some as far afield as Newcastle. It was crazy.

Anna had been great, letting me doss at hers, but I couldn't face another flat-share, even if I got my own room. The smells of other people's food, their perfume, their super-fruity shower gels, their late-night TV, rows over the heating bill, someone nicking the last of your milk from the fridge… I was beyond all that. I wanted my own space. But buying wasn't an option unless I moved out of London and condemned myself to a multi-hour commute.

Mum pointed out on the phone yesterday, when she invited me over for lunch on Sunday, that I could get a nice little place near them for less than it would cost to buy a shed in a cluster of tower blocks round here. But I didn't want to live in Essex. And 'nice little place' still meant a cramped studio flat with no view and the trains rumbling past the back of the block every ten minutes.

Today's promotion was a start. I was saving for a deposit for a house, but it seemed like every time I added £500 to my pot, prices had gone up by £1,000. Was I going to be renting forever, living in constant fear of scratching the laminate flooring or daring to hang a picture on the wall, while I pretended that the mould in the bathroom and the leaking roof were okay?

As I walked from the Tube to the building the ad agency shared, I found myself mulling over how strange it was that people got nervous over starting a new job. After all, I'd seen the place three times during the interview process, and I'd met everyone who worked there, even though I didn't know my team by name yet. They seemed friendly. And they had chosen me out of all the other candidates, so they must have thought I was good. After all, who would hire a 'development project candidate' for a key role like this one? So why did I feel scared that they wouldn't like me; that I'd make a bad impression; or that they'd figure out by lunchtime that they had made a terrible mistake?

"Your position comes with a three-month probationary period," said the offer letter, which also included a whacking pay rise. Being on probation made it feel like I was being let off lightly for some crime, rather than starting a new job. "During that time, the notice period is one week." *Wow. If I screw up, I'm gone by Friday. Comforting.*

I arrived at the office five minutes early and the receptionist took me to see the guy who did the security badges. They were expecting me. Well, that was a positive start.

"I'll need a photo," he said, as he picked up a digital camera and manoeuvred me to stand in front of the clinically white wall in his office. I had just a split second to decide how much to smile, flicking my hair into a borderline-acceptable post-commute-frizz style, not wanting him to notice me preening myself, before I was immortalised for the rest of my career in this place on the swipe card that would let me into the offices.

"Smile!" he cried. I obliged. He frowned as he inspected the result. "Possibly not that much," he said, trying again. *Woah, that flash was bright. And I'm sure he's standing too close.* Working with Stuart for the past half year had made me super-sensitive to that kind of thing.

"Great! Job done!" he announced, not even having checked if the photo actually had my face in it. No doubt that was the story he would use to describe me to his friends at lunchtime. "We had this new girl today. Manager she is. Grimaced like the Cheshire Cat when I tried to take the photo for her security pass. Had to get her to calm down before I could take a pic that would be recognised as human."

Photo done, he guided me back to reception, where I was to wait for him to print the pass and then I would be collected by Jeff, my new boss. Jitterbugs were being danced in my stomach, but outside I was a cool professional. Years of focus groups had taught me how to look calm, even if my insides were tying themselves in knots, especially if clients were watching behind a one-way mirror.

Moment of truth.

Here he comes. Big smiles. Handshake. Wow! I'd forgotten how good-looking he is. Now I'm feeling intimidated. Back to being a teenager.

"Welcome, Sophie! It's great to have you join us! How was Italy? Did you get to do that cherry research you mentioned?"

I spent the morning having short meetings with each member of the business, getting to know them, being briefed by them on what was going on and why, what our next steps were, and what they needed from me. It was hugely helpful but also overwhelming. I knew from experience that in a couple of months I'd be sailing through all of this, but right now I was struggling to remember their names.

Then I met with my team, first as a group and then individually.

I had never managed anyone before and I'd never had training in how to do it, so there was going to be some winging-it going on. I knew that first impressions counted, so I couldn't let them see I was nervous or I'd be in for years of hell.

Luckily it went well. I let them do most of the talking and asked them about the projects they were working on, what was going well, what wasn't, what kind of support they needed from me, how I could expect them to help me. I had been thinking about what to ask them when I was in Italy. Okay, when I was in Florence. There hadn't been much thinking about work going on once I met Christof. My insides twisted. *Why hasn't he texted or called me? Yes, I know we didn't agree anything.* I surreptitiously checked that my phone was charged, for the tenth time today, and that it had signal. Double yes. *Niente* – nothing from Italy.

Focus! I asked each team member, on their own, what they *really* thought about my predecessor: the great bits, the bad bits. It was a catch-them-out question and they all fell for it. I made a mental note to be grateful for their honesty and trust, but to watch their gullibility. The question gave me an insight into how the team's relationships had been running, but also the stuff they complained about told me a lot about the kinds of discussions they'd be having about me in their heads and in the pub in a month's time. It also gave me insights into the bits of their jobs they weren't so good at or didn't enjoy: we tend to spot the flaws in others that we don't want to see in ourselves, so the stuff they whinged about, about their old boss, was likely to be stuff they were struggling with inside. Amateur psychology at its best.

I had been scribbling notes during these conversations, but I knew I'd have to burn most of them, once I'd absorbed them. Couldn't have them finding out that I could almost read their mind, even though it was a key part of my job – reading the minds of the people I talked to in my research. And, no, it wasn't New Age Fluff. It was a scientific skill. People say one thing but the language they use, the structure of their sentences, tells you another. The tiny movements they make with their bodies and their facial tics show when they're telling the whole truth – and when they aren't. When you unpick that, you get to the *real* motivators for how they make their buying decisions.

"How did you know?" was something they often said to me in depth interviews.

"Oh, just a hunch!" I would half-lie – a hunch backed up by years of study and practice.

The day went well and I got home without having been fired. But my brain was ready to explode, so I turned down the offer of welcome drinks at the agency's favourite bar and agreed to go out with them on Thursday instead, so they didn't think I was a killjoy.

My first focus groups and depth interviews aren't until next week, as part of the new cherry brandy campaign. Jeff was impressed with my background research. It hadn't taken much effort while I was away, so it was an easy win to get into his good books. There was still a whole week to go through the previous client briefings, design the research protocol and get it signed off. *No pressure then!* But I knew I could do this. Lucy had trained me well. The hardest bit was going to be delegating with my team. After Stuart had taken over from Lucy as my boss I had been used to doing it all myself, with only Siri and Uncle Google for support. Had I ever gone to him with a question or a problem, he'd have used it against me to get me fired. The twisting in my stomach confirmed I was still a long way from being over his behaviour.

I had no idea how much I could trust my new team yet. There were no appraisal records for me to review – my predecessor had felt that was all too formal – so I had no idea what their strengths were yet. I had asked each of them to draw up a training plan request for me to look at next week. It would be interesting to see how good they were at assessing themselves.

And Jeff had been friendly. Enthusiastic. He had been clear about what he expected from me in the next six months, why he'd hired me and he even dropped some not-entirely-professional hints about why he was relieved that his previous planner had left. I was sure I'd get more on that from the other ad agency employees, once I had settled in enough for them to trust me.

I let myself back into the flat. I wanted to go straight to sleep, even though it was only 8 p.m. I had worked pretty late, despite it being my first day. But Anna wasn't back yet and there was no point in going to bed when the sofa I'd be sleeping on was right next to her front door.

I stuck a supermarket macaroni cheese in the oven, flicked on the TV for a mediocre mid-evening drama and slouched around in my pyjamas, waiting for Anna.

Of course, my mind wandered back to Italy. Or rather to Christof. I wondered what he was doing this evening. What was his flat in Milan like? My phone was on the coffee table, fully charged, with plenty of signal. It was ten o'clock before I realised I'd been sitting and waiting, hoping he might call or text me, for the past two hours. Maybe he was too busy. It was his first day back at work too, and he was an hour ahead. He probably didn't want to wake me up.

Still no sign of Anna. Maybe she was staying out tonight. It wasn't like I was her mum; she didn't need to let me know. I threw my bedding over the sofa, turned off the TV and wrapped myself in my duvet, hoping she wouldn't wake me up if she came back, then hoping she would – I didn't want to sleep so heavily that someone could walk through my room without me noticing! I indulged myself by trying to remember the time I had spent with Christof over the past few days, moment by moment, detail by detail. I fell asleep with a big smile on my face, wishing we had arranged to see each other again. We'd never got around to that.

It felt horrible, sitting at home on my own with no one interested in how my first day in my new job had gone. Mum and Dad had said not to bother phoning them as they could find out on Sunday and Jem was away with her latest millionaire. I turned on the TV and looked for a late-night comedy to distract me from how lonely and miserable I felt.

I was back at work after my week 'off', which certainly wasn't a restful one, and my first meeting was a debrief with my boss, Luca. He manages five of us and had been covering my cases while I was away. I had wrapped up as much as I could, so there shouldn't have been too much to do, but things could move fast if we had a breakthrough, so there was no point in me opening my inbox until we had chatted.

"What the hell happened to your face?" was his greeting, before the usual pleasantries about holidays and cherry festivals and whether we had sold the harvest.

"This!" I replied, handing him the business card they had given me. Crisp, thick white card, empty apart from a single name, printed in blood-red ink. No contact details. If you were important enough to need to get in touch with this guy, you'd have the connections to find a way. It was the ultimate statement in 'don't call us, we'll call you'. Although, from my experience with the heavies he'd sent round to say hi to me, I didn't think *calling* was his preferred method of communication.

"Denucci!" Luca's look darkened and his eyebrows furrowed. He would be rubbish at poker. Every thought he had was there in full view. That was why he sent us out to do the fieldwork – there was no way he'd get away with being undercover.

"Damn! We haven't had one of these for at least a couple of years. Do you know how many forms I'm going to have to fill in?" he was half-joking, half-not; trying not to show me how serious this was, like I didn't already know that. "Not good. I assume you're okay?" I nodded. "Tell me what happened. Don't miss anything out."

I took him through the attack. He asked me why I didn't hear them coming. I told him the truth about being distracted, singing in my head, thinking about Sophie. There was no point lying to him, he had an airport-sized radar for when someone was holding back on him. He was silent for a while, thinking this over, working out how it might affect our strategy.

"How did they know where to find you?"

"It was just around the corner from my apartment. They must have been waiting for me. They could have found that address easily by asking around in town. And there's more." I handed him the crumpled receipt from the Naples petrol station that I had found on the floor of my apartment during the festival. Luca started at it with such an intensity I wondered if it might disintegrate. We both knew what it meant. Not only had Denucci's heavies found me in a back street, they had been through my apartment during the festival – though why, I didn't know. Nothing had been taken. They would have left no trace, had one of them not been sloppy with the contents of his pocket.

"Do you think they were following you?"

"No. I'm sure I'd have noticed."

I didn't want to tell him about meandering by the river with Sophie, taking the longest possible route back to her hotel. "Why do you ask? The receipt in my kitchen makes it fairly certain that they knew where to find me."

"I need to know: did they see you with her?"

Panic flooded through me. I had been denying the truth for days now, drowning it out with my frustration over losing Sophie, but there was no running from it any more. I felt the heat drain from my body as twinges of fear took up icy residence in its place. Implicit in this simple question was whether or not Sophie was also now in danger. Why hadn't I thought of this before? It should have been second nature; making sure those closest to me weren't implicated in my cases. I hadn't realised Sophie was in that category as firmly as she was until Luca asked the question. I fast-forwarded through the whole of our final evening, not wanting to miss a single detail. There were too many distractions. I tried not to grin. Then I remembered this was serious. The smile inside me vanished. Was there anywhere where I had felt that I was being watched? Followed? Could they have seen her? It was their favourite way to get to you, to take it out on those you love – or those they thought you loved. They rarely bothered to check. I calmed my breathing. I needed to be rational, objective about this.

"No, they didn't. These guys were the beef, not the brains. If they'd been following me I would have noticed. I'm sure they were staking out the apartment. They knew I'd go back there eventually."

Relief was clear on Luca's face. "That's okay then. We don't need to warn her. Pity you didn't go back to her hotel," he smirked. "They'd have missed you." I blushed, despite knowing that would leave me open to months of teasing. The guy was such a mind-reader.

I didn't want to admit to him that I couldn't warn her, even if I wanted to; that I didn't even know her full name, let alone her number. Luca wouldn't have been impressed. Finding information was part of my job; the kind of information that the country's most secretive people didn't want me to have.

"Was your flat in Milan okay when you got back, Christof?"

I thought back to arriving late last night, so late it was dark, despite being so close to the longest day of the year. Everything had seemed untouched, exactly where I had left it. I hadn't done much besides fall asleep, half-undressed, wake up, shower and grab a coffee, but that had been enough to be sure that no one had been in.

"Yes. No sign of anything. All clear."

"Even so, I want you to be extra careful. It's a long time since we had a direct attack in one of our cases. These guys want to warn us off. Remind me what they said to you, again?"

"Next time you won't be walking away."

"And did it feel like they meant it?"

I pointed at the bruises and the cut on my face, which looked like it would leave an obvious scar. It felt like an answer. I paused and thought back to the attack. There hadn't been much going on in my head at the time, apart from coping with the pain, fear and adrenalin screaming through my body, waiting for the blow that would end it all. But I needed to connect with my instincts, as I heard that threat. Did they mean it?

"Yes, I think they did."

"Not good," Luca shook his head, "but that's enough for me to take action. I'm assuming you didn't call the police?"

I shook my head.

"Good. Of course you didn't. I'm sorry I doubted you there. But someone might have called them on your behalf. That would really mess things up. I had to check." We had handed the fraud investigation over to the police when the perpetrator confessed, despite my evidence being destroyed. We had thought this would get Denucci off my back. And it might have done – this could have been a 'farewell gesture'. The last thing we needed was for the police to start investigating the assault. It would get back to Denucci and make things worse. "I need to talk with The Boss on this one," Luca continued. "You're going to need to give me a few days, but we'll figure something out. In the meantime, light duties only."

I sighed with frustration. I knew this would be the result. It meant I was desk-bound; no more fieldwork. *For my own safety.* I wasn't surprised, but I had been hoping it wouldn't happen. It was protocol, to keep us alive – it sounds so dramatic – and to protect our cases. It took too long to train us up for the company to risk us being out of action, temporarily or permanently. Plus, once one of us had been a target, it meant whoever we were investigating knew we were onto them. Someone must have said something. There was an untrustworthy link somewhere in our informant chain. We already knew that from the night of the stake-out in Naples back in April. I felt myself redden with embarrassment at how my stupid decision to accept the offer of a one-night-stand had cost us our evidence. We still had no idea who could have tipped Denucci off about that evening.

Had I done something stupid? It would be my job to figure that out. It was essential to keep our investigations silent, until we had enough evidence for the police to press criminal charges, otherwise all traces of the fraud or crimes miraculously disappeared – often along with the people who could have testified, who risked ending up in body bags at the bottom of big mountain drops or convenient rivers.

The police had been after Denucci for years, but there had never been enough evidence; there never was with the Camorra; the Naples equivalent of the Mafia. This fraud had been the first thing in years they could pin on Denucci. It was small-fry compared with most of what they suspected he was responsible for, but they were super-keen to proceed, because it might still put him behind bars.

"We need to figure out how your cover got blown, Christof," Luca interrupted my thoughts, "so that's your priority while you're desk-bound. Isabella's a fresh face on this one, isn't she?" My heart sank. Not Isabella. "They won't be expecting a woman. Brief her today, please, and she can take over the fieldwork for you."

"Sure thing, Luca. I'll go and see her now." I knew there was no point in objecting.

"Christof?" he added, as I was walking towards the door of his glass-walled office. "It's not forever. Don't look like that."

He was misreading my expression as being upset about getting stuck in the office, which I was. Isabella and I had 'previous'. I had never told him the reason why we had split up or how frosty things were between us now. Or did he know? It was his job to know everything. Maybe he had decided it shouldn't matter. He was right. But it would.

I put off the Isabella briefing by pretending to be horrendously busy with my emails for the next hour, feeding my coffee addiction with enough espresso to keep an ocean liner afloat.

I smelled her perfume before I saw her. Not overpowering, but the ability of a scent to take you back to memories never ceased to amaze me. Smell was one of my keenest senses, acting on the most primal part of the brain: useful for smelling danger, lies and secrets. Gardenia was Isabella's signature scent. I felt myself tense. Working in the same team for the past two years since we had split up had been hard, but so far I'd managed to be assigned to different projects and she had been based in Paris for most of that time. I didn't want to say anything to Luca. He'd want one of us *reassigned* and I didn't want to force him to have to choose. I was good at what I did, but she was too and, in this job, being a beautiful woman had the element of surprise and advantage when it came to getting information out of reluctant people.

"Nice war wound!" she said, pointing at the cut above my eye. "Luca says you're supposed to brief me on your fieldwork?"

I had been caught red-handed by both of them, avoiding her. She knew why.

"How are you, Isabella?" I replied, as coldly as I could, without sounding rude.

"So you got yourself mugged back in that tiny town of yours and now you're handcuffed to your desk. Poor little Christof."

You wouldn't think it from her behaviour, but it was she who dumped me for some big-name hunk who owned a record company. Maybe today's behaviour was because I had turned her down in May - she knew I'd never trust her again.

I was comparing her with Sophie, in my head, as I looked at her and it struck me how different they are. Isabella is magazine-cover-beautiful, and she knows it. Her clothes are always elegant. She was wearing a cream silk blouse and a deep blue tailored skirt with skin tone heels just high enough to make you catch your breath when you saw her, without forcing her to wobble. And her hair is always perfect, even after 'bedroom exertions'. I remembered when she had first made it clear that she was interested in me. I couldn't understand what she could possibly see in me. But I hadn't hesitated.

Whereas Sophie is so much more real. I don't think she'd ever have the confidence to ask a guy out. And it's clear that she's brilliant at what she does, but she still doubts herself. I had felt a connection with her that I had never felt with anyone before. And for the first time since childhood, since before Mum left, I felt *good enough*; able to show her who I really was. I somehow knew she wouldn't judge me. The way the sun caught the blonde highlights in her hair and her nose twitched when she spoke and the way she smiled with her eyes, just before she teased me (another terrible poker player) meant more to me than all the magazine cover photoshoots in the world.

"Well?"

Bump. Back to reality. Sophie was gone, and Isabella was sitting in front of me, greedily demanding my attention in a way that made it impossible to refuse.

"Let's do lunch," I suggested. I needed to get out of the office, even if I was on desk duties, and sometimes the best place to discuss confidential stuff was somewhere busy and noisy. "I'll email you over my latest update now and then I can fill you in on the next steps."

"I'd love you to fill me in," she purred.

"You and I both know that is never happening again, Isabella." I retorted. She pretended to look sad. "I know I broke your heart," I continued, the sarcasm not lost on her, "but it really is time for you to move on, to put us behind you."

She pretended to look distraught, while still managing to flutter her eyelashes.

"Anyway," she replied, "I hear you've found yourself an English plaything. I hope you enjoy her."

Damn it! Why couldn't we ever have any secrets in this office? But I knew, deep down, that Luca had to brief Isabella with the full picture, especially since I had been attacked.

"Lunch at one, Isabella. I'll meet you at the front entrance."

The conversation was closed. I wasn't sure who had scored the final point. I had calls to make and files to research, so I turned back to my computer, to make it clear to Isabella that we were done.

Sunday lunch at Mum and Dad's always means Yorkshire puddings and roast potatoes to die for. After twenty years, Mum has finally got the hang of me being vegetarian, but I still bring my own gravy with me. "Oh, I didn't think a little bit of goose fat would be a problem, dear!"

I got the train to Shenfield, where Dad picked me up, driving me back to their place in the countryside. They can't understand why I love living in the city.

Jem was there too. 'Jem' is short for Jemima, but she got called 'Puddleduck' at school, so she disowned the name as soon as she was old enough to leave home. She's a hoot. She had never hooked up with a husband (or wife) or having kids of her own, which made her the perfect person to help me through the inevitable teenage angst. I used to love spending weekends with her. She's in her late fifties, like Mum and Dad, but she doesn't look a day older than forty. "That's the advantage of not having children," Mum told me, one day many years ago, when I asked her why Jem looked so young.

"And a loyalty card at the Botox salon," said Dad, half-spitefully, half in support of Mum.

"I don't think she's had anything done, you know," said Mum. "At least, that's what she told me at Christmas." Dad grunted in obvious disbelief. I dropped the subject. Jem had let her hair go gracefully grey and her bright blue eyes were alive with excitement and intelligence, as though they were always on the lookout for amusing distractions. "She never had to do the five years of sleep-deprivation that you and your brother put me through," said Mum, justifying Jem's apparent youth for no particular reason.

Jem dressed with colourful confidence and a radiant smile. Slightly taller than me, she was very active and took great trouble over her appearance, yet she still managed to look chilled out about it all, as though she didn't care what anyone really thought. Today she was wearing a brightly patterned summer dress with an avant-garde cut that Vivienne Westwood would have been proud of. Jem happily matched 'labels' with charity-shop bargains and always pulled it off with an air of effortlessness that left us mere mortals feeling frumpy, even in a frock that cost a month's food budget. But I had never felt her judging anyone on their looks or clothes, so I could be myself around her.

It was wonderful to see her again, full of enthusiasm for life and with her wicked sense of humour. I asked about visiting her for the weekend at some point over the summer. "We haven't done that for ages, *dahling*, we must do it again very soon. I'll get the girls round!"

By 'the girls' she meant her three friends from uni, who were as outrageous as she is. Thirty years on and they were all still inseparable. None of them had had kids and they were all pretty much retiring from their careers, so now they seemed to spend more time on holiday than working. One night, a few years ago, when Jem had drunk more wine than she would have said was good for me, she confessed that they had a name for their little group: The Godmother Club.

"We collect godchildren like other women collect handbags, Sophie," she admitted. "It's so much more fun!" The next morning she was mortified that she had told me and refused to ever utter another word on the subject.

My perfect big brother, Jonathan, arrived late as usual, with his wife, Delilah, and their two kids, both under three and – confession time – of very little interest to me. It's probably because Delilah seems to think that the world would come to an end if she dared to stop giving them her attention for more than a nanosecond or let anyone else near them.

That suits me fine. Is it really terrible that I struggle to remember their names? I always get there in the end, but I definitely have to think about it. I'm really not that into kids. But that's not something I would admit to my parents, whose grandparently expectations are high.

Lunch was lovely and I was interrogated about Italy. I told them all about the mad nuns in Florence and gave them a sanitised version of the cherry festival. Mum and Dad were happy to hear it all. Jonathan and Delilah completely ignored me, too distracted by their own lives, and Jem mouthed at me that she would hear the rest later, which she did when we took Bouncer, Mum and Dad's dog, out for a walk in the nearby woods.

"So, who is he?" she demanded. I feigned innocence.

"I know you too well, young lady. Spill!"

I wasn't sure I wanted to. It had been over a week since I'd left Italy and I still hadn't heard from Christof. My reserves of hope were getting so low they were bordering on self-delusion.

I gave Jem the barest of details, but it was enough for her to jump to the right conclusion.

"The way I see it, dear girl," she announced, after a few minutes of thinking, "is you need to make a decision. Either you want to see this guy or you don't. More fool you for not raising the subject before you left. But if you want to make something of this, you have to contact him. I'd say it's a fair bet that, after eight days, if he hasn't been in touch, he's not interested though."

"Thanks, Jem, that really helps. Not." I replied.

"I could hunt him down for you, if that's what you'd like. I have *people* who could find out where he stands; what's going on."

Jem's network was simultaneously awe-inspiring and fear-inducing. She had a way of *sorting* things and I promised myself, over a decade ago when I first noticed her *helping* me, never to ask her how she did it. It was a *service* she provided for all of her godchildren, apparently.

"You know, I think I'll leave it, Jem. Thanks though." I replied. "You're right. If he wanted to see me again, or even just to be friends, he'd have done something about it by now." I realised that I was giving up hope. That really hurt. But I had to look at the facts: it had been over a week and I hadn't even had a text. I was just a holiday fling that he'd never intended to have.

I felt tears welling up, but I didn't want to cry - not in front of Jem. She was right: I needed to let him go, to move on; to allow time to morph our few days together into a wonderful memory, rather than a searing sense of loss. Easy to say.

I made a fuss of throwing a ball for Bouncer and changed the subject, telling Jem how my new job was going and how useful it had been to be able to background-research the Italian cherry industry at the festival for my new client. She was tactful enough to accept the subject change and to laugh at the story. I loved her for that more than she realised.

In the evening I saw Lucy. I turned up at seven with a bag of takeaway – we had agreed we wouldn't waste time cooking. Her husband, Sam, was away on business, so we'd be juggling our evening around the baby's bedtime, but it should still leave us plenty of time to catch up.

So much has happened in the month since I last saw Lucy, just after I got the offer for my new job. I hadn't met Christof back then, and she hadn't decided whether or not she was going to go back to work, or to stay at home with baby Emma for a bit longer.

"It's a really tough choice," she explained, wobbling her chopsticks as she lifted a piece of slippery sprouting broccoli to her mouth to take a bite, only to have the rest drop back into her bowl, splashing the sauce over her top. She shrugged, "Whether I'm covered in vomit or food, it doesn't bother me anymore." How she has changed. Lucy used to be Little Miss Pristine, everything 'just so'. "It's the first time in a month I have blow-dried my hair or worn make-up."

"I'm honoured!"

"Actually, yes. And I'm grateful. It's easy to lose yourself in the baby when you're a mum." Baby Emma was coming up for six months old and Lucy said that she was even more of a handful now she had started crawling and trying to put everything in her mouth.

"You're going back to work next month - already?" I asked, "Isn't that earlier than planned?"

She nodded, saying yes through closed lips as she munched her broccoli.

"What made you decide that?"

"Easy. Three things: mortgage, motherhood and me."

I laughed, hoping that was the correct response. "Do tell…" I led.

"Well, a London mortgage on just one salary is nearly impossible. And Harry," she mentioned the owner of the agency, "only gave me six months' paid maternity leave. After that, it was down to the Government's minimum level, which doesn't even cover our food bill."

I nodded in what I hoped was an understanding way, even though I had no idea what kinds of figures she was talking about.

"And, much as I adore Emma, I'm going absolutely crazy having my life revolve around nappies and feeds and sick and baby talk. Not many people know this, but I need more than motherhood. I need *me*."

I was grateful to her for her honesty. Personally, I couldn't imagine being stuck in the house with nothing but a baby for company and no hope of salvation apart from mother and toddler groups where they talked about nothing but – wait for it – babies. Even so, I knew women for whom that would be bliss. I had interviewed enough of them for market research projects to know they were being genuine about it.

"The thing is, I can't run focus groups with a baby and a husband who works away so often. And I don't want a live-in nanny; we've got nowhere to put her!" Emma waved an arm to gesture at her overflowing flat with its two tiny bedrooms. "I can hear the old ladies in Waitrose already tutting about 'what's the point in having a child if you're going to put it into childcare?' But I'm done with feeling guilty about that. I need some balance back."

"How are you going to sort it?"

Well, Harry and I discussed Stuart staying on as my deputy but, as you're well aware, he hasn't been the most popular maternity cover ever, so we decided not to try that one. Instead, we're going to recruit an experienced senior researcher who can run the evening focus groups and we'll have a strict rule that I leave on time every night, even if it means working from home once Emma is asleep. That way I can either share someone else's nanny or find a childminder or nursery. I'm looking into options, but it's so expensive!"

"And will you be able to make that work?"

"I'm not sure. Not yet. But I have to try. It was that or quit. I really wish Harry had been more flexible. I asked for four days a week but he told me he wasn't prepared to tell clients he could only have planning meetings with them on certain days. And he didn't want to set a precedent for flexi-working."

I wasn't sure how legal his response was, but he always felt under pressure to offer a quick turnaround for clients. I could see his point of view. On the other hand, Lucy was a superstar at what she did and surely moving her to more of a mentoring role would be good for the business? But that wasn't my problem anymore.

"So, do you have any gossip for me?" I asked. I missed my old friends, but life had to move on.

"Yes! You're going to love this one. I went back in last week for one of my 'contact days' - you know, the handful of working days you're allowed on maternity leave so you don't forget what a laptop looks like, or something."

I nodded, vaguely curious.

"It's about your replacement."

Now I was interested!

"Ooh! Has Stuart groped her yet? Threatened her with dismissal if she won't give him a blow job in the loos?"

"I told you that you should have reported him! What he did was illegal."

"I know, but I didn't want to have it on my record – or in my reference. I figured it was better just to move on." I replied, firmly letting her know that the topic was off-limits.

"Well, Stuart hasn't been groping your replacement. Harry recruited a bloke. Six foot two, neatly manicured bushy beard and so gay he makes Julian Clary look straight."

I laughed. This was truly ironic. Stuart was a Grade-A

homophobe, so having an openly gay guy working for him would have shut him up, big time.

"And how's it working out?"

"Well, Harry is so impressed with him he's thinking of making the two of them swap jobs."

"Oh, I'd love to see that!"

"Anyway, how about you? Love-life? Still hanging around with Jamie?"

I filled her in on the barest details of Italy, and how I had sent Jamie packing, before I went away, after he had given me a box of cherries at work.

"Run a mile from that one, Sophie. He was never any good and he never will be. Too smooth a talker and no substance to back him up. But tell me more about Christof. He sounds much more interesting."

I told her I was ready to give up on him and explained why.

"Don't close the door on him, not yet. You never know what might be going on in his world – in his head. But I wouldn't pine over him either, if I were you. I had a friend once who went on a date with a guy, didn't hear anything for three months, and then they ended up getting married."

It's funny how everyone *has a friend, who once...* when they want to offer advice.

The rest of the evening passed in a blur of gossip and memories. It was really good to see her again, but, true to her motherhood exhaustion, she asked me to leave at nine so she could go to bed.

"How things have changed!" I teased, as I kissed her goodbye.

"Indeed. You'll know all about it yourself, one day."

I didn't reply as I headed for the Tube, relieved to be able to leave the nappies and sleepless nights to someone else.

I stayed in my apartment in town last night, before my 9 a.m. meeting with the architect to discuss options for the shop that my brain still calls *Francesco's*. Being back here triggered me feeling so cross with myself for getting my phone smashed and losing Sophie's number. Now there was no option to stay in touch, I was painfully aware of how much I wanted to. But I also knew I didn't. It was safer to let her go – both for my emotions and her safety. I felt like a coward for being too scared to try to find her, and I felt secretly grateful to Denucci for giving me a plausible excuse.

Luca made me beg to take a day's holiday today for the shop meeting, so I eased my guilt, and drowned out my memories of the cherry festival, by working until I was too tired to type last night. This morning I realised I had forgotten to even bring milk or coffee with me, so I had to leave the apartment early to get to a café before my meeting.

The architect had been recommended by our solicitor and was already waiting for me as I approached the shop, with the shiny new key in my hand, ready to use it for the first time. It felt strange that I hadn't been inside the place yet, but there simply hadn't been time during the festival and this was the first time I had been back in town since then.

With a firm handshake and a relaxed smile, I was surprised by the architect's youth. Maybe it was the fact that my solicitor is approaching retirement that made me expect someone older, but this guy couldn't have been much older than me – perhaps late-thirties.

The key moved easily in the lock and I noticed my stomach

jigging between apprehension and excitement as I pushed the door open, hearing the creak of rarely used hinges. Inside it was dusty and it had that universal smell of a place that hadn't been loved for far too long. Trails of recent footprints swarmed like ants in parallel lines from the front door to a door in the back of the room, which turned out to be an empty store room. The dust-free areas told me that Francesco had cleared out the stock Dad had paid for – which I legally owned – before visiting my solicitor. My jaw clenched as I wondered whether Pietro had helped him. There were two types of shoe sole in the footprints. I wasn't surprised that Francesco had done this, even though our agreement had formally signed the stock over to me. In his world, there was no stock to hand over at the time that he signed, so his conscience was clear.

The architect and I spent half an hour looking over the property, which was a shop, with a store room and toilet downstairs, a small kitchen area, and then a multi-floor apartment upstairs. The windows were large and sound and the roof looked in better condition than I had expected, so any changes we made would be internal, which would make getting permissions easier. The floorboards were in surprisingly good condition, but the plumbing and electrics looked like they hadn't been touched since the fifties.

The architect scribbled notes in a black notebook that had appeared from a jacket pocket, using an old-fashioned wooden pencil. I could see his brain imagining options as he paced out measurements and peered up staircases.

I needed to decide what to do with the building before the next payment on the loan. The cherry harvest down-payment had covered the upcoming instalment but continuing to pay it wouldn't be sustainable for the farm. I wanted to sell it – to get rid of all memory of the mistaken trust Dad had shown; of

Pietro's betrayal of our family when he convinced Dad to go into business with his cousin, without any proof of the loan; of Pietro's lies as he concealed the loan from me after Dad died, destroying the evidence that Francesco had defaulted on the repayments so that we risked losing the farm.

After much pencil-tapping and brow-wrinkling, the architect gave me his assessment.

"I don't recommend selling yet, at least not in this market, in its current condition. You're unlikely to get what Francesco paid for it, because too many people know the story behind the sale." My heart sank as the building became a millstone around my neck. I hadn't realised how deeply I wanted to be free from it. The architect saw my disappointment and tried to add some cheer and hope into his tone as he continued.

"My advice is to separate the upstairs living quarters into two self-contained flats. If you want to sell them as separate properties, then getting planning permission could take forever. But if you rent them out – keeping the building in single ownership – then it should be easier. Plus, selling them would take too long to turn a profit and you need cash now. I'd also suggest keeping the ground floor as retail premises and renting the shop out. The rents for the three should easily cover the loan and in ten years' time you'll have paid it off."

The objections raced through my head. I didn't want to be in Milan adding three tenants to the weight of responsibility that already came from distance-managing the farm, especially now I knew I could no longer trust Pietro as the farm manager.

As though reading my mind, the architect continued, "I can recommend a local agent." My eyebrows must have told him how cynical I was about trusting people these days. "I'd make sure you didn't get ripped off, Christof."

"How much might the conversion cost?"

"I can't tell without getting some quotes, but there's much less to do than you might think. I'd have thought that thirty should cover it. Does the farm have reserves?"

It didn't. I had wiped them out, trying to cover the back-payments of Francesco's defaults on the loan from the past year.

"No, it doesn't. I would have to lend the farm the money." The loan Dad had taken out had been in the farm's name, meaning the shop building was now owned by the farm, not me personally, so I would be lending the business money. This was more complicated than I would have wanted and I also wasn't sure I was prepared to pour more money into this project.

The architect sensed my reluctance and knew exactly the carrot to offer. "In my professional opinion, the work you would be doing would add at least 100,000 to the value of the property, so even if you did decide to sell afterwards, you'd be selling at a profit. And here is a valuation report that takes this into consideration, so the bank will agree to change the loan's collateral from the farm to the shop." He finished writing figures on a form, signed it and handed it to me. This was what I had been waiting for, to be able to take the next steps with the bank.

I needed to think about it, but his advice made sense. And after a mid-morning espresso at a café down the road I went to my meeting with the bank's Debt Manager. We filled in the required forms to start the three-month review process that could mean the farm would be safe, whatever happened.

I wasn't looking forward to my next meeting, but it had to be done. It was time to have it out with Pietro, to find out why he had sided with his cousin instead of his employer – the son of his life-long best friend – at the solicitor's. Knowing how he had hidden the secret of Dad's loan and business agreement with Francesco from me, I wasn't sure he would tell me the truth, but

I needed to at least ask the questions. And we were going to have to have a frank discussion about his position as farm manager if his loyalties lay elsewhere. That's what was crazy about his behaviour: he had put the future of the farm at risk by undermining the deal that Marisa and Nonna had agreed, leaving us with a loan he knew we couldn't repay and risking the farm closing... and his job and family home disappearing. Pietro lived in a cottage on our estate with his wife and two teenage daughters.

I didn't have a Plan B though, if I had to sack Pietro. He and his family had been part of our lives since not long after I was born. If he lost his job, his wife and daughters would also lose their home. I didn't want to do that to them, but it also made it all the more unbelievable that Pietro would risk it.

We had agreed to meet in Sophie's secret garden. Calling it that in my head was like stepping into a metre-deep, freezing cold puddle. How could I miss someone I barely knew? I was walking through the narrow streets towards the garden when I realised I was at the spot where I had been attacked the last time I was here. In bright sunshine it seemed so harmless a place, but it had been a clever spot for them to choose – one of the few where there were no apartments to overhear yells and grunts, with a small cut-through alleyway off to the side, to allow the attackers to escape unnoticed. I shuddered at how well they had planned it.

Luca thought it was probably just a warning and they wouldn't try anything else. There's no reason why they should. But we still couldn't understand why Denucci came after me, or how he'd known I was involved in the first place, as the busting of the Naples stake-out had proved. Luca says he's got a project he wants to talk to me about next week, which will be a relief, now I'm stuck on desk work. I could really do with a fresh challenge to distract me.

Without realising, I had arrived at the creaking metal gate to the garden. The summer blooms were fading already in the midday heat and the fragrances were almost overpowering, with the buzz of insects gathering pollen and nectar and birds' singing drowning out my inner monologue. I had rehearsed this next conversation so often.

I found the bench under the old lilac and went to sit down on it, then stopped myself. It was where Sophie and I had sat. Having a row with Pietro there would feel like dishonouring her memory. Stupid, I knew. I had only suggested meeting here because I didn't want to meet Pietro in public; not anywhere that he might have friends to support him, and I didn't want to meet him at my apartment, because we would both feel like caged animals and it could make things even more difficult. We both knew that meeting at the farm would involve Nonna finding out about what had happened and neither of us wanted that.

I wandered round the garden, trying to admire the beauty and fragrance of its plants, but it wasn't working today. The gate creaked, announcing Pietro's arrival. He looked surly, aggressive, like the day just a few months before when he had first admitted to me that the loan existed and I had forced him to tell me where the money had gone. He walked slowly towards me and almost spat, "Well, *boss*," making it clear what he thought of the concept, "you wanted to see me?"

I allowed my breathing to calm, consciously easing the knot in my stomach and the tension in my jaw. I needed to be calm and grounded for this, so I wouldn't lose my temper. I could sense the resentment I had felt towards Pietro for so long building up into a wave of energy that would be hard to control. The longer I waited, the less confident Pietro seemed; I wanted to time this right.

"Pietro, I was very disappointed by the way you tried to undermine the deal that Marisa and Nonna had agreed with Francesco, at the solicitor's office. You were betraying the farm, betraying Dad, risking us all losing our livelihoods and our homes, and…"

"You wouldn't have lost *your* livelihood or *your* home, though, would you? Yours is tucked away nicely in the city!" he interrupted, with loathing in his eyes. I felt myself reeling inside and put all of my effort into not showing it on the outside. This man, whose knees I had bounced on before I could even walk, hated me, resented me, wanted to hurt me, even if that meant hurting himself. The ferocity of his response shook me.

My instincts told me that defending myself would only make things worse, so I decided to ignore his attack. I paused and then continued, "You knew you were risking us losing the farm and we couldn't make any more repayments on the debt. Why did you do it, Pietro? It doesn't make sense. I need to know I can trust you, if you're going to stay on as farm manager. Why did you do it?"

The colour drained from his face. He hadn't been expecting this option. I could see his eyes searching my face, to see whether I was bluffing. We both knew that I couldn't afford to lose my farm manager now that the main crop was sold and harvesting was well under way. He stuck out his chin with pride, as though concluding he was too important for me to lose.

"I said, why did you do it, Pietro? If you value your job and your home, then you must tell me!"

He flushed with rage as he clenched his hands into fists. The answer he gave me – through gritted teeth – was one I never would have imagined, but now everything made sense.

August

Processed

crushed into pebbles
revealing the priceless hoard
their journey begins

A shock of ice-cold fear pushed me bolt upright in bed. The clock said five. The nagging doubt that had made it so hard to fall asleep had formed into a concrete thought that was now screaming alarm bells in my head. Jake, one of my team, and I had done something last night that was likely not just to get us both fired, but to get us sued by one of the firm's clients.

I have been struggling with learning how to delegate with my team. There are just five of us, and we all take on different roles, but I wanted to make sure I wasn't micro-managing the way Stuart had done with me. So, I have been going to the opposite extreme and drowning them in trust. That's where I had gone wrong last night.

Jake specialised in quantitative research; the kind of thing that gets news presenters talking about how 72 per cent of cat lovers miss their moggie so much that they wish they could take them with them on holiday in their suitcases. He had run a 2,000-respondent survey for an industry-changing new formulation for lipstick from one of Europe's biggest brands. It was a huge trade secret we were testing out and the deadline for getting the final results to their market research manager had been last night, so she could present them to her board meeting this morning. Jake had been feeling the pressure, because he was also in the middle of a study for a different project that had already had its deadline extended by a week, until tomorrow.

Both Jake and I were working on the lipstick report until late last night, but there came a point where our brains had stopped working and I suggested we should go home and Jake could finish it after dinner. It just needed some tidying up of the formatting before being emailed to the client. He knew what needed doing and I left the office feeling relieved that I could delegate the super-late night to someone else, for once.

At 11 p.m. I was reading in bed when my phone pinged with a text from Jake.

Report done. Have sent it to Rob. Sleep well!

I was half-asleep, so I sent back a quick "thank you!" and turned my phone off. But something kept niggling – something we had forgotten. After an hour of tossing and turning, exhaustion took over and the next thing I knew I was sitting up in bed, just before dawn, feeling sick with worry.

I knew what was wrong. It was a stupid, stupid, stupid mistake, but I knew that either of us could have made it, we were so exhausted.

Rob was the market research manager for the man-bun project, not the lipstick. We had sent hugely secret research results to the wrong client. But, what was worse was that the parent company for the man-bun accessory also owned a business that made make-up. We never took on competing clients, but this had been deemed separate enough not to fall under this rule … until last night's mistake.

I paced up and down Anna's lounge for an hour, downing coffee and biting my nails, trying to work out what to do. By six I decided that Jake had had enough sleep and I texted him.

Rob is the other client! The research findings should have gone to Jennifer Hamilton! How do we get the email back?

It produced the desired response: a blurry-voiced phone call within sixty seconds. I had an hour's head start on Jake, so it was me leading the '*Shit! What do we do?*' conversation. First, I made sure he sent the research to the correct client immediately, in time for her board meeting. Then we had to sort out the Rob problem. We decided on the only thing we could do: tell Rob the truth... *ish*. I was pretty sure that Rob didn't check his email before he got to the office – he had told me he refused to let it stress him during his commute – so we were going to have to camp out at his office and insist on him deleting the email before he could open it!

We debated texting him and telling him not to read it, but that would have been like sitting a kid in front of a big, shiny red 'do not push' button, expecting obedience to override curiosity.

Rob's office wasn't in central London. It was about thirty miles away. Jake and I decided we should go together, but soon realised that public transport wouldn't get us there in time and a taxi was likely to get stuck in rush-hour traffic. There was only one thing for it – Jake was going to take us on his motorbike. I couldn't work out if I was more terrified at the thought of that or at the prospect of being fired and sued.

At seven he picked me up from outside Anna's flat, handed me his spare helmet and instructed me to 'hold on tight'.

I screamed as he pulled away. It was unlike anything I had ever done before. As he cranked up to forty miles per hour, once we reached more open roads, I was terrified. I was holding on so tightly I wasn't convinced that Jake could still breathe. The wind hitting my body took me back to sitting in the open doorway of a Cessna, back in my uni days, when I had once had the crazy idea of doing a charity parachute jump. Every ounce of terror that had taken me over back then flooded back to me now, sitting on Jake's bike. He started to swerve through the traffic as rush hour hit. I tried closing my eyes and gripping him harder, but my palms were slippery with sweat against his leather jacket and I struggled to hold on. I clenched my thighs to the sides of the seat and wondered whether it was time to start praying. I tried closing my eyes and counting the seconds, but I soon realised that just made it worse.

Jake slowed down and I looked up from my knees to see we were approaching Rob's office. By eight we were banging on the building's door, but there was no answer. 8:15 and 8:30 passed, still with no one home. Jake and I filled the time by sitting on the building's front steps of the building - my legs were like jelly after the hour of adrenalin - talking ourselves around in circles over how we were going to break it to Rob, to persuade him to let us delete the email and all traces of it from his employer's IT system – and not tell our boss, Jeff.

I was terrified that Jeff would fire me over this – that I'd fail my probation. I couldn't face the thought of job-hunting again; not after last time. And I knew this was a mess-up worthy of dismissal.

Then we saw Rob arriving. He looked confused and suitably surprised, seeing us waiting for him. As his boss, Jake left the talking to me. My voice was shaking and my palms were so clammy with nerves that Rob surreptitiously wiped his hand on his jacket after shaking mine. It was one of the least eloquent speeches I have ever made, but the relief I felt as he agreed to let us delete the email made my legs finally give way. Rob saw the funny side of it all. But we had to refuse to tell him what the research report was really about because it might have changed his decision.

He let us delete the email from his phone and laptop, but when we asked him if IT might have a back-up copy on their server, he dropped the bombshell.

"We'll have to get written consent from the MD to delete the email. Our IT team and servers are off-site."

That meant there would be no way we could hide this from Jeff. Rob's boss was much harder to convince than Rob had been. As a businessman, he could tell there might be something interesting or even advantageous in the report, even though we still refused to tell him which client it was for, but eventually he had to agree. Jake and I spent the rest of the morning driving to the IT server location and looking over the shoulder of the person who reluctantly deleted the evidence of our mistake.

"You owe me one!" Rob's boss had made clear before we left. And I knew it. We had already had to agree to add in some free stuff on their project, owing to having moved their deadline to make space for the extra work we had been doing for another client, and now I could feel more bonus work coming their way.

How was I going to tell Jeff? And what would that mean for my probation? It was Jake's mistake, but my responsibility.

I had been back at work for less than ten minutes when Luca called me into his office, shutting the door behind me as I entered. Never a good sign. He said he wanted 'to talk'.

"You're not enjoying being stuck here, are you?" he opened. *Is it that obvious? I suppose so.* I had been downright frosty with Isabella, partly because it was the easiest way to keep her flirting in check, and partly because I was angry with her for taking over the best bits of my job.

The Denucci investigation was progressing well. There were fresh leads to support the confession from the man I had seen during the stake-out and we thought we were getting close to being able to prove the fraud Denucci had been committing, opening up trails in other companies too. It was an ugly mess, with blackmail and beatings littering the trail, and the occasional – but unprovable – suspected murder. Sometimes key witnesses ended their days in peculiar ways, like the guy who had drowned in a vat of sugar at a jam factory, which everyone was sure was down to Denucci, although the police had found it impossible to prove. Apparently, that particular witness had *slipped* and the railings on the gantry he was walking along just *happened* to fail at precisely the wrong moment. The night watchman who found him was pretty sure he was dead before he hit the sugar, based on the bullet wound in his head, but both the body and the security guard disappeared soon afterwards. *Reassigned* for the guard and *cremated* for the body. *Accident* said the police. I don't remember the last time I heard of someone being cremated, rather than buried, here in Italy, but the police didn't see anything suspicious in this convenient way of making evidence disappear.

Denucci had been using a complex trail to hide his fraud and he was great at destroying proof, even burning down one of his own factories to stop the police from getting too close. Somehow, he'd managed to keep that out of the newspapers and the local police had already dismissed it as an 'electrical fault', so his insurance would pay out. He was winning all round. The guy had contacts to die for, and I'm not just talking metaphorically. His power extended into local government – and beyond. We were playing a dangerous game trying to catch him.

Even if the police found the proof that they needed, I was concerned he'd try to wriggle his way out of a prison sentence like a maggot escaping a fishhook and would end up laughing at us.

Isabella had been kept on the periphery by Luca – he didn't want another one of us getting hurt – but her work had been enough to help us get answers to the remaining questions. We couldn't go to the authorities until our evidence was bullet-proof – literally. Any single witness would be risking too much by going public; we needed as many as possible, to spread the risk.

We knew from experience on the Lake Garda case a couple of years ago that the police witness-protection programme had holes in it.

It was so frustrating only hearing about all of this in team briefings. For the past year I had lived and breathed this case, second-guessing what might happen next, figuring out past motivations, looking for invisible paper trails and it would have been fair to say I knew even more about Denucci's dealings than his wife, though possibly not his mistress, not that we had either of their names.

"Yes, I'm bored," I replied. No point pretending. Luca knew the answer already.

"I've been chatting with *the Boss*," he said mafia-style, smirking. The irony was not lost on me, given Denucci's background leading a Camorra clan. "He's got a proposition for you. Something that will take your mind off things here for a bit, and – the Boss doesn't know about this bit – give you a chance to see that *bella Sofia* you've been pining over."

I started, visibly surprised. I hadn't expected that one.

"What do you mean?"

"Oh, come on, Mister Love-Sick Romeo. Everyone knows you're only half here. Have you seen her again yet?"

"No." I replied. I didn't want to say any more.

"Well, whatever… The Boss is offering you an opportunity that will give you a chance to add to your CV and – though he doesn't know about her - also see your lovely lady."

I raised an eyebrow to save myself the effort of replying.

"The London office is interested in getting into the kind of work we've been doing here. Word of our success has spread. They think it could be a good earner for the business: tax fraud, embezzlement, corporate theft, blackmail – all juicy stuff. But they need guidance on how to get started: the mistakes to avoid;

the shortcuts that put us one step ahead of the person we're chasing. That's where you come in."

I raised the eyebrow slightly higher. I was feeling really fed up and Luca's enthusiasm was jarring.

"London. Six-week placement. Train up their team and show them how it's done. Gets you out of Italy for a bit; tells Denucci's heavies that you've moved on; and gets us some great PR with the Board, as we get to showcase our talents. Then, once Denucci is off your trail, we can get you back on active duties. What do you think?"

I allowed myself a few silent, deep breaths, before I responded – the classic technique to buy valuable seconds of thinking time without showing emotions. It's funny how often people rush into giving an answer to a difficult question, putting their foot in it, in their desperation to fill the silence. Those few breaths are enough to change your response. I sometimes wonder how many wars could have been avoided, had people just paused to think and breathe, rather than responding in anger. There was a good reason why I didn't study philosophy…

"When?" I asked.

"Start of October. Are you up for it?"

"I need to think about it. Nonna and the farm, you know."

"And *bella Sofia*?" he teased, with a sing-song lilt.

I gave him a smile that told him to shut up. "Nonna and the farm. I need to make arrangements now Dad's gone."

"Okay," he said, looking disappointed that I hadn't risen to his bait. But that's why he pays me: to be unreadable and outwardly calm under pressure. "I can give you a week to decide, tops. Then we need an answer."

"Fine. I'll let you know. I'll go back to the farm this weekend to see Nonna and Pietro and see what we can work out. I'll let you know on Monday."

That was four days ago - the clock was ticking and I still hadn't made a decision.

It's strange, but I'd rather go anywhere than London at the moment. Had he offered me New York or Paris or Madrid, I'd have said yes, subject to a phone call with Nonna. But London meant facing up to feelings that were still driving me crazy and taking over my thoughts, all because of two short days in June. Part of me would rather run – hide – get over Sophie. But part of me was also desperate to see her, to find out whether there might be more to this. I was running circles with my thoughts, so I fell back on my usual coping strategy: getting practical and shutting out the emotions. I went to see Nonna, to get her advice… on the career bit, not the love life.

"Who is Christof?" demanded Anna, angrily waving last month's copy of *Marie Claire* at me, before I had even closed the front door.

"Has he called?" I asked, completely betraying myself in those three words.

I hadn't mentioned Christof to Anna. I had wanted to keep him for myself, not dilute those memories by sharing them. But as the days morphed into weeks and I still hadn't heard anything from him, I had kept him to myself because I knew I would look like a love-sick fool, pining for someone I had only known for two days, who didn't care enough to even send a text to make sure I had got home okay. I had hoped we might at least stay friends. But for him I had just been a distraction from the stress of his stupid cherry harvest sale.

It was strange, but I hadn't eaten a single cherry this summer, even though the supermarkets were practically giving them away. I couldn't face them. *That sod has ruined cherries for me!* I was gritting my teeth and frowning. That was better. Anger was like a relief after the 'missing him' month I had just been through.

Work had gone really well. I had been socialising with my new co-workers, as well as working really hard, and my first round of research – the cherry brandy study – was finished. We had great feedback from the client and Jeff had almost forgiven me for the mess-up with Rob. He had taken it well and had been impressed at our dedication to fix the mistake, but he had made sure I knew it was one of my 'three strikes' on my probation, as I trembled my confession in his office that day.

"Well? Who the hell is he?" Anna yelled, bringing me back to the tiny flat we share.

"Did he call?" The anger had melted into desperate hope.

"I'm not telling you until you tell me who he is."

Bitch. Why is she so angry?

But suddenly my heart skipped a beat as I realised he must have called, if she knew who he was! I had been so careful not to say anything about those two days. There was no way she could have known about him otherwise. He had found my home number! How? That didn't matter right now. *He must like me, after all! He didn't even know my full name. How on earth did he find out where I lived?* That was dedication. Or stalking. I was going with dedication. My heart was soaring like that condor over the Andes again and I was so excited I forgot about Anna. I could feel the grin spreading from my mouth to my ears and my eyes as my whole body lit up with the knowledge that Christof had been in touch.

"I'm not telling you until you tell me who he is." Anna

repeated, staccato, her words staccato like metal-tipped high heels across a tiled floor.

"Okay, I'll tell you, but then you have to promise to tell me what he said. And I need a cup of tea first." She nodded her agreement.

So, with a good old English cuppa, we sat on her sofa and I told Anna the briefest details about Christof, rushing the story and missing out the best bits, so that she would tell me what the phone message was as quickly as possible. She was persistent with her questions and there was something tense – annoyed – about her, as she listened to my answers. Normally she would have lapped up this kind of gossip.

"So, are you going to see him again? Are you two a *thing*? Why didn't you tell me?" I answered her as best I could. One, I didn't know; two, I didn't know; three, I didn't know. After twenty tortuous minutes of interrogating me, she seemed satisfied, if grumpy. She shut up for a moment, so I seized my chance.

"Now I've told you everything, what did he say?"

I was trying not to shriek with impatience. Knowing how desperate I was to get the phone message would just make her prolong the torture even longer.

"Can I listen to it on the answerphone or did you talk to him? What did he sound like?"

"You've really not heard from him since Italy, then?"

"No! I told you that. What did he say?"

I was now at the demanding stage. My patience had run out.

"He didn't say anything."

"So, you didn't speak to him?"

"No."

"Did he leave his number on the answering machine?"

"There's no message."

I was confused. This wasn't adding up.

"What's going on, then?"

She held out *Marie Claire*, open on a feature about trendy cocktails, with an accusing look in her eye, as though I was meant to understand.

I gave her my best confused look, taking a deep breath to stop myself from shaking her by the shoulders to get the truth out of her. She pointed at the bottom of the page, where I saw a teenage girl's doodle of a cupid's heart with a name in the middle – Christof.

"This was the issue that came out while just before you went to Italy. You took it with you."

The penny dropped. I must have doodled that in my hotel room. I didn't even remember doing it. I had brought the magazine home and left it on the coffee table in the lounge. I had forgotten all about it.

"You mean he didn't call?" I asked, like a newly rehomed puppy, missing its litter-mates. The truth was sinking in, draining my hope like a river over a waterfall.

"No, he didn't. I saw this."

"Oh."

"Why didn't you tell me?" she demanded, the accusations unspoken but clear from her tone.

I took the magazine from her and wanted to run to my bedroom, craving some privacy to process all of this. I wanted to cry. Again. I felt so empty. This felt so final, like a sign that he would never call. Then I remembered that my bedroom was the sofa I was sitting on and that this was Anna's flat.

I grabbed my coat and bag. "I'm off for a walk."

"Will you be back for dinner?"

"No, I don't think so."

I heard her *huff* as I picked up my keys and headed into the street, with no clear idea of where I was going, feeling overwhelmed by deep disappointment that Christof didn't care. My Inner Drama Queen told me it was time to let him go, to move on: there were plenty more fish in the Thames. But I wasn't interested in them right now. I wanted to sit somewhere quiet and get my head round all of this. I knew, in my heart, that it was time to let go of Christof. I had given him a month now. He was never going to call.

I headed out of Milan in the Friday rush-hour traffic and it took me the usual two hours to get to the farm. Nonna laid on her customary feast, with Pietro and his family invited, to make up for me being malnourished when I'm in the city, as she sees it.

"You're looking so thin!" she lamented as she hugged me when I arrived, even though I wasn't. "Don't they feed you in Milan?"

I survive on adrenalin half of the time with my job, and I often end up grabbing food on the run, even now I am desk-bound, so she was right – I don't cook like an Italian grandmother in my apartment. In fact, my fridge is rarely used, other than chilling an occasional bottle of wine or beer. I can cook – she taught me well – but I don't have time and it's no fun doing it for one. Nonna sees it as her job to *fatten me up*, whenever I go back home.

It was weird to think that this place was mine now. Dad's father had left it to him in his will, with a proviso that Nonna, his wife, could live out her days there, and Dad had to continue to run the business, to avoid inheritance tax arising, which would have forced us to sell the farm. And Dad had left it to me on the same terms, which bound me to running the cherry farm business for at least the next five years. But I still thought of the farmhouse as Dad's and Nonna's, not mine. We were sitting in *my* kitchen at *my* old oak table, which had served meals to three generations of us now. In my head, *my* place was my apartment in Milan, which I had paid for with bonuses from work over the past ten years. The farm was my family's home.

I had been curious about how seeing Pietro again would work out, especially at a family meal, now I knew his secret. It wasn't until I saw him walking into the kitchen that I decided how to play the evening. He barely greeted me – behaviour that was not lost on Nonna – despite the affectionate hugs and kisses I received from his wife and daughters. He was still angry with me, even though I had done nothing wrong. I wasn't surprised.

Nonna had cooked lasagne, followed by steak with an enormous home-grown salad and Pietro's wife, Marta, had brought a peach tart for dessert. The food was delicious and the wine flowed freely and perhaps that was why I was taking bigger risks than I would normally have done.

"Any news on Francesco, Nonna?" I asked, feigning innocence, watching Pietro's face darken with apprehension.

"Oh, he's back with his fancy woman, so Marisa's plan to get him back home didn't work out. But I'm not surprised. I wouldn't want to live with her either!" She laughed. I watched Pietro like a hawk. I saw him worrying about whether I would say anything: about his betrayal; about the secret he had yelled at me, full of anger, in Sophie's Secret Garden.

"Remind me," I continued, knowing I was tip-toeing through a mine field of Pietro's past, "why did her husband leave her?" Marisa's husband, Paolo, had been a distant cousin of Dad's, but

I didn't remember much about him. Marisa had been on her own since Francesco was young.

"Oh, you old gossip, you!" reproached Nonna, but we both knew she would carry on anyway. "Paolo was a bit of a drunk and a gambler and he hung around with a bad crowd. She should have thrown him out the night he threatened to hit her, not long after Francesco was born. She never said why he did it, but we all had our guesses. She was a beautiful woman, back then. Gosh, it must be nearly forty years ago now!" Pietro was slowly turning the same scarlet as the tomatoes in the lasagne's sauce. "They bumbled along for a while, then one night, a good few years later, a gambling partner of his – someone he hadn't seen since around the time that Francesco arrived – showed up and started stirring up the past. Rumour has it that he still had a bee in his bonnet about Francesco maybe not being his son, and the friend wound him up about it again. Paolo went home drunk as a skunk and demanded the truth from Marisa. The neighbours said it got very ugly and they called the police. Marisa told them about a garage full of stolen goods she knew he was handling 'for a friend', somewhere well away from their apartment, and that got him off her back for a while. When he was let out six months later, he knew there was no point in going home. She had made sure he would never show his face in the town again. Marisa never denied the rumours, but she also never confirmed them."

The table sat in stunned silence. I was trying not to grin. Pietro was scarcely breathing, gripping the handle of his fork so hard that it looked like it might shatter, despite being made of stainless steel. "So, Nonna, do you think the rumours about him not being Francesco's father are true?" But I wasn't looking at her. I was staring at Pietro. Neither of us listened to her reply, telling me it was decades-old gossip and of no importance now. In that moment, Pietro knew I would always hold the trump card and wasn't afraid to use it. I knew he would never dare to cross me again. But we would also never be friends again.

After Pietro and his family had left for the night, properly fed, Nonna and I got down to proper talking. I told her about the London placement.

She was excited at the chance for me to try something new, though she would never fully approve of England, not after Mum, her disappearing English daughter-in-law. And Pietro had made it clear over dinner that the hard work of the year was done. It would be quieter now and I knew they would manage without me for six weeks. I would only be a phone call away and, as Nonna reminded me, flying back from London wouldn't take much longer than driving through the Milan rush hour if I was desperately needed.

One excuse gone.

Nonna was sure we had seen the back of Signor Perillo and, as she pointed out with her customary, affectionate directness, I would be no less useful to her in London than I was in Milan if something kicked off.

Another excuse gone.

Why was I still hesitating?

Because I wasn't sure I was ready to be in the same city as Sophie, staring up at the same hazy-blue sky, knowing that she would have moved on by now. She had started her new job. Lots of new people. There was bound to be someone else who was taking her out to dinner and walking her along the river. And there was the small matter of Denucci – the reason I was taking the London placement. Okay, so Luca and I thought I was probably safe, that the attack had just been a warning shot, but surely it was crazy to get romantically involved with someone when I was moving to a new country to avoid crossing paths with the Camorra? As so often happened, I felt torn between doing what felt right and what I wanted. I had spent most of the past year dancing that dance over the cherry farm and my job in Milan, after Dad died. Now I was doing it with my love life and the mafia.

I managed to avoid the subject of my UK placement for most of the weekend, but Nonna knew something was up and she badgered me until I told her. She's older and wiser than I am, but also as blunt as the fist that whacked my head when I had my impromptu date with Denucci's heavies.

"For goodness' sake, *carino*," she said on Sunday morning, as we were sorting through the paperwork from the summer's orders for the many ways we preserve cherries, "do you like this girl or not?"

"Yes, I do."

"Just *like* or something more?"

"Something more," I replied, choosing to be fascinated by a pile of receipts and refusing to look up to catch the wicked glint I knew would be in her eyes.

"Then what are you waiting for? No grandson of mine should be moping around like this," she said, wagging a finger at me. Her compassion was astounding. "The way I see it, you either get in touch with her and find out how she feels, or you need to forget her."

Ouch. She's right.

"But Nonna …"

She could sense my excuses coming. She started to shake her head.

"Sometimes it's doing the very thing that scares us most that brings us the most joy in life."

I stared intently at my shoes.

"No buts. Just do it. Today."

"But I don't know her name or her number and London has millions of people," I objected.

She laughed at me. "So? You work in a team that can find out the inside-leg measurement and preferred colour of underwear of a *mafioso*, just because he *might* be something to do with a case you're working on, but you're telling me you can't find the phone number of a girl you're in love with?"

She had me there. I didn't reply. I realised I had *chosen* not to look for Sophie.

"If she were vital to a case you were working on, how would you trace her?"

I thought it over for a moment, taking a dried sour cherry from the bowl on the table to buy myself thinking time. Its flavour hit my taste buds and whizzed through my brain, somehow clearing my thoughts. I had my answer.

"I know she's a planner for an advertising agency. That's quite a specialised job. And there are a finite number of ad agencies in London. I know she started her job the Monday after she left Italy. I know that this kind of business is likely to have put out a press release, announcing a new senior member of staff: it's good for their brand awareness and a chance to get into the industry magazines. I would check the press releases for that week on the news wire for that sector and look for a *Sophie*. Then I'd go to the company's website and hope that they had profiles of their key staff, which they usually do, and that's how I would find her."

"*Molto bene, carino.*" She smiled, smugly. For the first time in over a month I felt hope – a shiver of excitement. Nonna was right: I needed to know either way, and now I knew how to find Sophie.

"Your laptop's in your bag, *carino*?" She wasn't going to let me escape on this. She knew I'd go back to making excuses if I left it until I got back to the office tomorrow. "You have access to your press wire thing?" She gave me a face that said she didn't really know what it was, but also didn't care. I nodded. "Well, go and look now. I'm making cannelloni for lunch." My stomach rumbled. She knew it was one my favourites. "And you're not eating any until I have seen her photo. Anyone can be found if you put your mind to it."

Her certainty was well founded. She knew we had ways of getting the information we needed at work. And she knew I needed this now. Why didn't I do this back in June? Fear of rejection? Feeling stupid? Pride? Pretending to protect her? I didn't know. I was doing it now. That's what counted. I only hoped I wasn't too late.

Half an hour later and there she was. My heart was racing with excitement and fear, and I could barely think straight. I had found Sophie. Nonna was polite, but unenthusiastic. The photo didn't do her justice: bright white background, badly exposed, too much flash and a nervous, forced smile – the kind you normally see on a security pass or an embarrassing passport photo. Almost unrecognisable from the beautiful woman I had spent those days with in June. But it was her. My insides were singing an aria with the full force of a 20-stone soprano locked in a potting shed.

I checked the company blog to see if she had been writing anything. She had. Last Thursday. She was still there.

"What are you going to do now?" asked Nonna, as I buried my face in her pasta. "Are you going to call her?"

"No," I replied, cringing at the thought of having such an awkward conversation with both of us at work. "I've got a better idea."

I didn't want to tell her what it was. I felt embarrassed, like a teenager going on his first date. Some things needed to stay private, even from Nonna. She sensed this and let it drop. She was just happy I was taking action. I changed the subject.

"I guess I'm going to London then."

"I guess you are, *carino*. Make sure you come and see me again before you go."

"Of course."

I needed to know whether Sophie still cared, or if she had moved on, before I told her about the London placement. Her British politeness meant that talking to her on the phone wasn't the ideal way to do that. She could chat for an hour even if she was secretly trying to get me off the call, while I tied myself in knots, unable to read what she was really thinking.

I needed to find a way to get her to contact me, so that it was her choice whether or not we turned our two days in Italy into something bigger. I couldn't believe how nervous I felt.

I went out into the orchards to find the last fruiting trees, sending Nonno a silent thank you across the years for spreading the ripening of the crop by means of different varieties and planting locations. The harvest was long over, commercially. Only the cherries that were hidden beneath thick clumps of leaves on a late variety would have ripened slowly enough to be spared by the birds at this stage of the season. It took me half an hour, but I found eleven perfectly ripe cherries.

I wrapped them carefully and put them in a box – one of the branded ones we use for selling our glacé cherries in the markets and department stores. And I wrote a note for her, tying it to the box with raffia string – a ribbon would have been too much – written from the heart, without editing; going out on a limb. It sat in the coldest part of the fridge overnight, well out of Nonna's sight, so the cherries would be as chilled as possible before I packed the box in bubble wrap and put it in a shoe-box-sized packing box first thing tomorrow, leaving the farm before seven to head back to the city. I knew I'd be at the post office when it opened first thing in the morning, sending these by priority overnight air mail. She would get them on Tuesday. Then all I needed to do was wait. And hope.

I arrived at the office this morning slightly later than usual. Jeff and I have a deal that I don't have to be in before ten if I've done a late-night focus group the evening before, though we both know I'll always be working by eight typing up notes on my laptop, perched on my sofa bed, while it's all still fresh in my mind. Ok, so Jeff doesn't know about the sofa bed bit. I've kept that one quiet at work because I figured that finding out I was kipping on a friend's sofa, long-term, wouldn't make the best of impressions.

I wanted to get a summary from last night to Jeff by the time he got to his desk early this morning. I'm still trying to impress him, hoping it might make him forget the disaster with Jake sending the research results to the wrong client. Last night's group had been fun: ten men in their early twenties, many with full on-trend beards, obviously gym-addicted, fashion-magazine-readers, giving us feedback on a new accessory to make their 'man-bun' look bigger. You couldn't make this stuff up. It was a doughnut-shaped roll of mid-brown foam that you coiled your own hair round to make your man-bun look more voluptuous. I had no idea how our recruiter had found the attendees. She had done a brilliant job. They were on-brief and – bonus! – drop-dead gorgeous. Normally we would do a range of focus groups, but the client's budget was too tight, so we had agreed on the depth interviews and one extended focus group, which would give good indicators for their wider target audience. That was why it had been so important that the recruiter had done such a good job of getting a great fit of men for the brief. I made a mental note to let Jeff know.

We covered everything from hair-care confessions, to their newly discovered nightmare of split ends, to the awkward in-between phase where their hair was growing to shoulder length and girls thought they were a lentil-munching hippy and assumed they'd got a thing for sandals with socks. I pointed out that I was vegetarian and quite into peace and sandals and stuff and they had the decency to blush.

But we were soon back on track. I needed to understand what had inspired them to grow their hair long and then to want to put it up into a man-bun, even though they knew that might make some people jump to conclusions about their life preferences. I was careful not to call it a "bun" though. The initial depth interviews (one-on-one sessions to help me draw up the plan for the focus groups) had given me clear pointers for the language to use and the topics to avoid, so they wouldn't think I was laughing at them.

It turns out that they suffer from man-bun-envy. I'd never have thought it. They spent hours wondering if theirs was big enough, fat enough, firm enough, shiny enough. Should they wear it on top or at the back? One said he even tried it by the side once, like half a Princess Leia, but that didn't last long. It wasn't cool.

Should they tie it up and then wrap it, or wrap it then tie it? The intricacies of their hair choices opened up new worlds for me. I made a mental note to try out some of the stuff they were attempting, if I could ever get my hair to grow long enough without it turning into flax-coloured straw.

They were generally enthusiastic about the new man-bun

accessory, which they had been allowed to try out for the past week, but they had one main concern – one I would never have guessed: what happened if you were spending the night with someone and you wanted to let your bun down? You couldn't sleep in it; it was too uncomfortable. What did you do with your man-bun-foam-roll, if you were at someone else's house, not your own? It would be mortifying if your date found it. They wouldn't want anyone to know they were *cheating*, but man, did they want to cheat and give themselves the man-bun advantage!

It was hard not to giggle, as I thought about how women stress about morning-after make-up and all the other complexes we have. These guys really weren't so different from us girls. I had to keep a straight face or they would have clammed up and that would have been £3,000 of the client's budget down the drain. Yes, that was what they had paid for this single session. They must have believed they were going to sell a *lot* of these man-bun accessories.

The men could see themselves buying one, but, no, they didn't want a twin-pack; they only had one bun. Did they want it to come in different sizes? They had all been using the 'standard' size for the last week and I had brought 'mini' and 'maxi' samples with me for the research evening. They even let me video them doing it, though some wouldn't let me show their faces.

Then I told them the proposed name and they nearly wet themselves laughing. But after a few minutes of discussion, they really liked it: 'Does my bun look big in this?' It appealed to them in an *ironic* way. The name was just at the idea-stage and the client wanted to know how it might work, before spending time and money on trademarking it. They were a really fun group to work with and most of them, never having met before, went to the pub together afterwards, though I had to remind them that they were sworn to silence until after the product launch.

I was due to pass their feedback on to our creative team and the client at a presentation this afternoon. They would use the information I collected last night to make a final decision on the product's name and to start work on the advertising campaign. But it was priceless to have uncovered the deep-seated 'what if I pulled?' objection. It could have derailed the product launch.

I must have checked my phone a hundred times that morning, going over and over in my head what time the parcel might have arrived, what time she might get to work, whether it would take three days to get through some kind of internal mail system – cue rotten cherries. I had worked out that 10 a.m. was probably the earliest I might hear something, but I also knew there was a strong chance I wouldn't hear from her at all.

I had booked a meeting room to work in for a couple of hours, so I wouldn't be spotted with my compulsive text-checking. I told everyone I needed to focus on getting a report out by midday. That was true… Sort of.

"You've had a parcel delivery. It's on your desk," said Jeff, as I walked into the office, carrying a thermal mug of coffee I had just picked up on the corner café, still too hot to drink. I missed my old *local* with Lucy from my previous job. We used to have half of our meetings in there. "It's got an airmail sticker. Sent priority... From *Italy*. What have you been ordering, dear girl?" I wondered how many of them had been gossiping about it. Jeff was wearing a cheeky grin as he reminded me not to let it distract me from getting ready for this afternoon's client debrief.

I scurried into my office – with its wonderful glass-wall privacy.

What on earth is in that parcel? The twenty metres to my desk seemed to take forever. Everyone was staring, like they had just stopped talking about me. By the time I got there I had convinced myself I must have left something at one of my hotels on holiday and they had taken a month to send it back to me. But then I realised they would have used Anna's address, because that was the one I had given on the tourist registration forms when I'd checked in.

I knew who I was hoping it would be from. But it couldn't be him. He didn't even know my surname, let alone where I worked. It was ridiculous to think he would find me. And anyway, why would he wait so long, especially when he hadn't even texted me?

It was much more likely to be some crazy marketing gimmick from a European market research company, trying to persuade me to listen to their pitch.

I was sitting at my desk, my door pointlessly closed. It was there in front of me. Someone had arranged it neatly in the centre of my workspace. I could sense their curiosity burning holes through the glass.

Time for a focus-group unreadable face. I need to act vaguely curious, but not excited.

I picked the parcel up. It was light for its size. It had been sent by overnight priority airmail. The post office printed label had my name and our business address and the price of the postage. *Ouch. Courier prices!* I thought back to the time in my old job when we'd had to overnight some product samples to Paris for a focus group someone was running for us. We had all forgotten to send them in advance. Harry had been so shocked by the bill he had threatened to take it out of my pay that month. I'd never make that mistake again.

My fingers were shaking as I fumbled with the tape. In my heart I knew it couldn't be from him. I wasn't ready to think his name yet. But I decided to indulge in the hope for a few minutes, enjoying the pleasure it brought me, not caring that disappointment would follow.

I was into the first box and then there was half a tonne of bubble wrap to unwind. Someone wanted whatever this is to arrive in one piece. A sudden thought occurred to me – a shot of adrenalin. I checked it wasn't ticking. *Silent. Phew! Do parcel bombs tick, anyway, or is that just in the films?*

Another thought hit me: was it Anna, taking the mickey again about my *Italian lover*, as she called him? She could have got me a whoopee cushion or something else stupid shipped via Italy, to wind me up. *The cow!* But, no, she wouldn't have gone to the expense of the priority airmail. She'd have had it sent overland, for the element of surprise on the timing.

Unwinding and unwinding, I wasn't sure where to put all of the bubble wrap. Then I had the idea of piling it on my desk, in front of what was now a very small box, so that the others couldn't see what it was as I was opening it. *Yes! That works.* I looked across and saw disappointed faces, rushing to look intently at their computers, pretending they hadn't been watching. I smiled.

It was a small, cream box, made of good quality cardboard,

with a tree embossed in deep green foil in the top left corner. It was tied with raffia and there was an envelope between the ribbon and the box. I decided to prolong the anticipation by opening the box before I read whatever was inside the envelope, where my name was written on it in fountain pen, in deep turquoise ink.

I opened the lid of the box, carefully, slowly. Inside was crumpled off-white tissue paper. I lifted out the top sheet, adding it to the view-blocking mountain on my desk. I didn't want to look in the box. Deep breath. *Smile. They're still watching.* I looked down.

Cherries.

My heart screamed and whooped. My insides trampolined. There was only one person who would send me cherries, wasn't there? Okay, there was Jamie, too, but he would never go to this kind of expense. Eleven perfectly ripe cherries. Deep red. Stalks still attached to keep them fresh, packaged with such care. Still slightly cool, as though they had been chilled before they were shipped. I hadn't had cherries since Italy. I couldn't bear to. I wanted to taste one; to bite into it; to let the sweet, smooth juiciness run riot over my taste buds. But I wanted to read what was in the envelope more.

I tore it open impatiently and unfolded a single sheet of heavy cream paper.

More of that turquoise flowing writing. This wasn't from a market research agency. *Like I ever really thought that.*

Dear Sophie,

I lost your number. My phone got smashed by a truck the morning you left and then I convinced myself you wouldn't want to hear from me. There's too much to explain in a letter.

But I had to find you. I have missed you. I want to see you again. There. I have said it.

If you feel the same way, here's my mobile number. Send me a text. If you don't, that's fine. I'm not about to turn into a stalker. I promise I'll never contact you again.

Christof

P.S. These are the last of the year's harvest at the farm. Whatever you decide, I hope you enjoy them.

That was all. But it was enough. Everything changed in a heartbeat.

I knew what I had to do, before I got distracted by prepping my presentation; before my nerves or Inner Drama Queen could change my mind. Aware of the curious faces on the other side of my office wall, I calmly reached into my bag for my mobile and used my thumbprint to unlock it, wondering whether Apple shared that data with the police. Big Brother knew my every move.

I typed in his number. My heart was racing. It was nearly in my throat. I had no idea what I might be starting here. I was so nervous I could hardly type and I made a mistake in his number twice! I pressed send. One word. It felt like a good place to start.

My phone dinged to let me know there was a text. 11:16. *Grazie.* Thank you.

That was a start. My heart did an impression of a jazz band on a Red Bull high and I felt my grin light up several minor Italian cities. *Sophie doesn't hate me!*

Nonna had been right. There was hope.

September

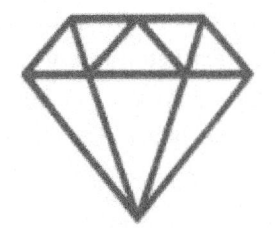

Revealed

acid melts away
the rock to which you're clinging
no longer hiding

I was like a kid with a credit card in Hamley's toy department when Christof suggested meeting up for a weekend in Toulouse.

We had been chatting and messaging most days since I'd received the cherries and I finally felt like I was getting to know him. But I'd be lying if I said I wasn't a bit nervous about seeing him again. I managed to persuade Jeff to give me a couple of days off, so I could make a long weekend of it. Apparently, I wouldn't normally be allowed holiday during my three-month probation period. *How kind! And why on earth not? I'm worn-out!* But since he told me I had passed my probation early, on Monday (a huge relief), I didn't think they could enforce it.

I met up with my Jem for dinner last night and she wanted to know everything. She was excited about Christof, but grumpy that he had taken the initiative to trace me and I hadn't let her help. Typical Jem.

She's a bit like a modern-day matchmaker, cloned from Jane Austen's time, but with a funky hair colour (purple at the moment) and I'm-old-enough-not-to-care-what-you-think-of-me ethnic-print baggy trousers. She's a 'fixer' as well. I have to be careful about telling her my problems or she'll have them sorted for me before I get home. Sometimes a blessing; not always.

Over the past few weeks, since that Sunday lunch at Mum and Dad's, I had told her a bit more about Christof and what had happened in Italy and her conclusion was a simple one:

"For God's sake, you really like this guy. Would you just make sure that the two of you talk about the future before you leave

Toulouse?" she ranted, waving her wine glass to mark her words, yet somehow never spilling a drop, the deep red liquid playing as dangerously close to the rim as an over-confident teenager on a skateboard ramp. "I'm not going to sit through any more of you festering, waiting for him to text you once you get back. Okay?"

"Yes, miss!" I replied, cheekily, knowing she was right.

"People *do* manage long-distance relationships, you know! And Milan really isn't that far. There are direct flights from London. You just need to decide what you want."

That was the thing, wasn't it? What did I actually *want*? It's one thing saying you'd put up with travelling to see each other and only manage it a few times a year, but surely there would come a point in the next few years when I would want to settle down? What would we do then?

"Would you stop trying to predict the future?" she threw at me, knowing from the look on my face that I was trying to be too logical about this.

I told her I'd figure out what I wanted, at least in the short term, by the end of the weekend. She knew that was the best she was going to get and she dug into her starter, vegan dolmades; stuffed pickled vine leaves with rice and vegetables and a delicious sweet-chilli-style dipping sauce. Brilliantly messy finger food and incredibly tasty.

The place was heaving and we were having to shout to make ourselves heard, so I was glad she had let my love life drop. I wasn't enjoying having to screech the details of it – and its potential absence – to the tables around us.

"How are you and your fellow Godmother Club members getting on with that course you're on, Jem?" I asked, changing the subject. "Cobra, or something, wasn't it?"

"Python!" she giggled. "And I told you *not* to mention the name of our group, thank you."

"Okaaayyy!" I said, doing my best rolling-eyed-teenager impression, spoiling it with a friendly grin. "Remind me what that stuff does again?"

"Well, I can't say too much, but we've got some information we want to manage and keep updated and it's a programming language that will help us to do that more easily."

"Can't you pay someone to do that for you?"

"Of course we can, but sometimes you need to play your information cards close to your chest. You never know who you can trust these days"

It was a sufficiently cryptic answer and I sensed it was all I was going to get. Jem was always off somewhere or up to something. Being single and having no kids meant there was no one for her to answer to, but she still had her fair share of romance, usually with a generous dollop of drama.

I remembered back to a couple of years ago when she and the girls spent the winter in Monte Carlo doing heavens-knows-what with some extraordinarily rich business men. She had sent me regular postcards - much more fun than emails, she says, and I agree - telling me the sanitised versions of their adventures. Then she had arrived back in London, out of the blue, one cold January morning with a fabulous tan and the police hot on the heels of one of her friends. All a complete misunderstanding, apparently. It's never dull with Jem around.

"Back to *your* love life, *dahling*," she continued.

"Do we have to?"

"Yes!"

I shrugged and resigned myself to listening to her advice. It was normally good, but I wasn't in the mood.

"I've got two pieces of advice for you. You're obviously loopy about this Christof and that can cloud a girl's judgement. Now, here's one thing I have learned from bitter experience: never make a life-changing decision about a relationship until you have survived your first row."

I looked at her, confused. *She wants us to fight?*

"It's only after you have argued with someone that you see their true colours. You need to know whether or not you can live with the worst of them before you say 'yes' to the best of them."

"I can see your logic, Jem, but I'm hoping we won't fight."

"Oh, you will, eventually. Couples who say they never fight are either lying to their audience or to themselves. Either they're pretending, or they're totally devoid of emotion and passion and I'd never want that for you, my dear."

I nodded, agreeing with her whole-heartedly. My strong emotions and I went back a long way! "And piece number two?"

"You've been pining like a love-sick teenager for nearly two months now. Would you please do us all a favour and just get the guy into bed. Get it over and done with."

I spat the olive I was chewing halfway across the table, drawing even more attention to myself with a coughing fit.

"That's a bit direct, isn't it, Jem? And not really any of your business!"

"Probably not, but when did that ever bother me, Sophie? It's my job, as your godmother, to advise and guide you through life's intricate problems. But there's no point in you putting in months' more effort into a long-distance relationship if he's crap in the sack. The magic is either there or it's not. Yes, you can work at it, but the foundations have to be there. If they're not, then no matter how romantic he is, I advise you to run."

I was blushing as red as Jem's wine.

"I suppose you're going to want me to text you to confirm when the deed is done?" I suggested sarcastically.

"Splendid idea!" she replied. I couldn't tell if she was joking or not. I breathed a sigh of relief when she let us go back to lighthearted small-talk for the rest of the evening. I love spending time with Jem, but even after all these years she still knows how to shock me. The thing is, her advice is always spot on.

God, I'm nervous. I must have been to the loo ten times today. I'm not a great flyer at the best of times, but meeting Christof again was doing my head in.

What if it doesn't feel the same as it did in Italy? What if it was just the cherries, the sunshine and the wine? What if it was just a holiday romance that was meant to end when I flew home? What if what happened in Italy was meant to stay in Italy?

What if he doesn't like me anymore? What if I don't fancy him anymore? What if he's really geeky and awkward, once he's off home territory? What if he gets clingy? Why was I doing this? There were plenty of lovely guys back in London, weren't there? And the last thing my career needed right now was to be distracted by a long-distance – no an *international* – relationship. And he was busy with work, too.

I hate turbulence. It doesn't matter how often I tell myself that it's just like a bumpy bus going around a pot-holed corner, my brain knows the plane has no road beneath it. Those were big potholes today. How does everyone else just carry on chatting when I feel like I have to pick a god to pray to, to make this metal box stay up in the air? I don't mind it so much once we're on the way down; when we're heading towards land I can relax, trusting that the airport must be close enough by then for the pilot to be able to sort things out if something goes wrong.

But today's flight was super-bumpy.

Please keep flying. Please keep flying. Please keep flying. Ouch! Just nearly pulled my earring out. Hadn't realised I was fiddling with it so much. Guess that's the nerves.

That awful smell of slightly stale, super-heated ham croissants being warmed up in the plane's ovens announced that cabin service would soon be with us. I saw the hostess trolley inching towards me, one painfully slow row at a time. Polite voices placed their orders as though they were in some kind of posh restaurant. But the effect was soured by the deafening drone of the engines, which meant everything was half-shouted. Of course, I was happy the engines were working, but it would be days before I could hear properly again.

No, I don't want a bloody coffee or any purchases from the in-flight magazine! Can't you see I'm single-handedly stopping this plane from crashing us all to our deaths with my powers of concentration and worry? Don't distract me! Saying a silent thank you to myself that I didn't just say all of that out loud, I managed to smile courteously and shake my head, then I buried my nose in my book to give everyone the very strong hint that I was not to be disturbed.

"I'll meet your flight," he had said, when I suggested we meet at our hotel. He travelled up from Milan by train so he would be here before me and he had hired a car for the weekend, so I wouldn't have to figure out how to get the bus into the city. He knows this area well and we agreed that our next meeting should be somewhere neutral. I had suggested Milan, but he said he would just get caught up with work, and be dragged back into the office, just because he's around. This way he's officially *away*, so he can switch his work phone off.

I realised I don't even know what he does. 'Consulting' is a big vague. *What is he hiding? And I'm on a plane to meet up with him?*

What would it feel like, to finally see him again? I still remembered how crazily wonderful that final night at the cherry festival had been. If he had asked me to marry him, right there and then, I'd have said yes, which would have been stupid. It was so romantic: the food, the wine, the music, the weather. I was scared it was all so intense that anything else would feel like an anti-climax. But I had to find out. That was why I was on this plane. Two days off work to make it a long weekend in Toulouse. He said he'd drive us into the Pyrenees, to a small town he knew, with a chateau where we could get the most amazing local food.

It was over two months since I'd left Italy. I hadn't let him take me to the airport at the end of my stay. I hadn't wanted to break the spell of our days together by finishing them somewhere so clinical, so perfunctory. So, we hadn't seen see each other again after he kissed me goodbye at my hotel on that final night.

Everything between us had been so magical. I wasn't sure if we could recapture that. I really didn't want this to be a disaster. We'd texted lots and chatted a few times since he sent me the cherries, but that's it. Luckily, I got over the stalking thing. After the initial excitement, it had really freaked me out that he had found me, without even knowing my full name. But he explained how easy it had been and I chilled out a bit more after that. Funny how we think life is private, but actually it's all in the public realm these days.

Oh God, we're nearly there. I'm going to see him again soon. Part of me felt sick with excitement, like a teenage girl on a school trip who had eaten too many sweets in the back row of the coach. Part of me was scared we'd feel like strangers and have a horribly awkward weekend and never want to see each other again.

Once out of the plane, I stood in the passport queue for what felt like hours: two little counters, each with its officious, unsmiling, uniformed officer, deciding whether or not we were allowed to enter France. Surely it was a bit late once we'd arrived? Shouldn't they have checked this before we left, when we had hours to kill at the airport?

The queue moved like an arthritic snake, twenty inches every thirty seconds – the exact space a human body was allowed to take up as we waited for permission to enter the country. We shuffled forwards obligingly, rearranging our hand luggage (aka maximum-sized cabin suitcase) with each step, trying not to stare at anyone or to look suspicious, pretending our backs didn't ache from standing and carrying our bags for so long. It was like the airport was taking silent revenge for us being cheapskates and cramming a lifetime's indispensable possessions into Tardis-like in-flight bags instead of paying to check in a suitcase.

I wondered how long Christof would have been waiting. I wished I had luggage instead of just my carry-on, not just because of my back, but because waiting for it at the carousel would have bought me another fifteen minutes before I had to see him.

I barely know this guy. This is insane. No, that's not the right way to be thinking. Here's the Customs exit. I've got to keep walking or people will trip over me. I want to go home. What if this doesn't work? I shouldn't be thinking this stuff.

I walked through the doors and he was there, smiling. He looked a bit nervous too, which was probably a good thing. He came towards me, arms open for a hug, and I gave him a two-cheeked kiss, like a maiden aunt. He looked confused and took my case. I could feel the weight of my mistake, tipping us into the 'awkward zone'. We weren't even holding hands, as though we were just casual acquaintances, not people who had emptied their diaries and travelled hundreds of miles to see each other.

I looked over at his crisp, white linen shirt and distracted myself by wondering how he could have travelled for hours, just like me, yet it still looked fresh-on, when I felt like an old bag lady, crumpled with too many layers of clothes. I concluded it must be an Italian thing – the *bella figura* you hear about – always showing their best side in public.

We reached the hire car, passing the time with polite small-talk about our journeys, about work, the weather. *What am I doing here? It's all my fault with that double-peck kiss. But somehow, I can't undo it.*

He lifted my bag into the boot, briefly failing to mask his surprise at its weight, and held the passenger door open for me – I had tried to get in the wrong side. *Duh! So now I look like an idiot, as well as frigid. How can he still be smiling at me? Maybe he's pleased to see me?*

He paid the parking and we were off to the hotel. I felt a sudden panic. Should I have offered to pay for the parking? After all, he had come to collect me. The car still had that new-car smell. Someone had once told me they sprayed that inside the car at the end of the production line, because people wanted it to smell that way when they first drove it. I wondered what chemicals that smell had got in it, and whether they were carcinogenic. Anything to stop myself from having to be present and actually experience this.

The hotel was about twenty minutes away. Two nights together: the frigid-idiot-girl and the nervous-smiling-boy.

But hang on, we haven't discussed rooms. Shit! Has he booked us a double? Or a twin? Which would be worse? Oh, I don't know what to do any more. I kept making small-talk, imagining I was warming up the respondents in a focus group. I'm good at small-talk. It feels safe. Years of working in market research had taught me it was a great way to put a nervous interviewee at their ease. I was using my best techniques on myself now.

We're here. It looks lovely. I want to go home. He grabbed both our bags and gave his key to the valet to squirrel the car away in an unparkable space in the underground labyrinth where no guests were allowed. This place was posh.

With a flash of panic, I realised it was too late to change my mind: he was carrying the bag with my passport in. I couldn't run. He was talking to the receptionist in fluent French. I was wishing I had tried harder at school. I wanted to impress him.

Too polite. Distant friends. Business colleagues. The receptionist was handing him a key: a beautiful antique brass key on a huge carved wooden key fob. I wondered how many decades of guests had carried it. Room 227. Christof took it and looked at me, still smiling, gesturing towards the staircase. He lifted up both our bags. A gentleman. *What will it be like? Twin or double? Which would I have booked? I need to take this slowly. I'm scared. Maybe I could book my own room? But what if they're full? Would Christof ever speak to me again?*

The receptionist smiled at me and handed me a key too. Room 228.

My knees wobbled with relief, letting go of the tension, I allowed myself to relax and realised I was about to cry. I stopped myself just in time and allowed myself to hope that this weekend might improve.

Well that was crap. I knew this morning was going to be a bit weird, because we had done so much of our relationship virtually, but I was so excited about seeing Sophie again that I had barely slept last night. It was a complete shock this morning when she went cold on me. At first, I thought she was going to shake my hand! Then she at least upgraded me to a double-cheeked kiss. We spent the whole day walking around

Toulouse not even holding hands, barely looking at each other.

How could I have misjudged it like this? I had really thought she liked me. What on earth has changed? Did I do something wrong?

She was enthusiastic as I pointed out the sights of the city to her. We used to come here when I was a kid, just Dad and I, so I know my way around the place. It's funny the things I remember: Dad would always order room service hot chocolate for us at the end of the day. We always stayed in this hotel. But I started to wonder this afternoon if Sophie had come to Toulouse just for a few days away and I happened to be a convenient tour guide. Surely I couldn't have got her that wrong?

Even over dinner it was still detached friendliness. No romance. No spark. Just shut down. And my defences were up: protecting me from the rejection I secretly feared. I felt so confused. It had been a lovely evening, but it was such an anti-climax. Maybe it was better this way. It would save a lot of stress and life-juggling and the potential heartache of an international relationship. London was a big enough place that I could spend my six weeks there and she would never know.

We walked back to our rooms and I knew it was my final chance to turn this around. I was about to kiss her or at least try to give her a hug when she said, "Goodnight then", and turned to open her room door with its antique key. It was so abrupt and final.

There I was, sitting in my gorgeous room, with its plush upholstered armchair, looking at the lights shining in the city below me, wondering what to do. Should I try to fix this? Go round and ask her what's wrong? The Italian in me would. Or should I accept that she's not interested and leave her in peace; no arguments, no stress. That would be my inner Englishman.

I was feeling pretty sorry for myself – an understatement – so

I picked up the room service menu and flicked through it, more for a distraction than anything else. I came to the page with hot drinks. That was it: hot chocolate with cream. I had a plan. It was the only excuse I could think of to disturb her at this time of night. I wasn't ready to give up yet. I felt like I had got until the end of this evening to sort this out. I needed to know where I stood, one way or another, even if it meant spending the rest of the weekend awkwardly avoiding each other - or even going our separate ways.

I dialled room service and ordered two hot chocolates to be delivered to my room. Ten minutes, they said. I picked up my room key, closed my door behind me and took a deep breath, holding it as I knocked on her door, trying to sound confident.

I was sitting on my bed, on my own. That wasn't what I had expected. I didn't care that the view from my window of the city was breath-taking, that the deep gold damask bed cover looked like it had cost a week's salary, or that the carpet was so luxurious it was one of those you could squish your toes into. I was thinking back to that fantastic final night in Italy where the passions had run so high I had expected someone to tell us to get a room. Where had that energy gone?

It had been a lovely day today, but so *polite*. We hadn't even kissed. It felt awkward, clunky. Christof had been the perfect gentleman, opening doors, listening attentively, pointing out the best bits of the city as we wandered our way through the streets. But the further we got through the day, the more wrong it felt.

Maybe what happened in Italy needed to stay in Italy. Had it been the heat, the holiday or the cherries? I didn't know. Or was it the fact that we knew it could only be a few days, so we had let down our defences? Perhaps it was my fault for that two-cheeked "mwah" welcome I had given him at the airport. It certainly didn't offer him much encouragement. But where had the passion gone?

We had barely made eye contact all day, other than the minimum you would expect out of normal, business-like conversation. It was like we were avoiding it. Why? What were we afraid of? What terrible thing might happen if we allowed ourselves to look at each other again? It hit me: what if he didn't really want to be here, now we had met again?

My stomach was tying itself in hollow knots. I kept fidgeting with my earrings. I didn't want to lose what we had almost had. We had another two days of this. Part of me was wishing I had booked a flexible flight home. But there was another part of me that didn't want to give up yet. Maybe there was something I could do to fix it. But I could hear my stubborn Inner Drama Queen wanting to come out and wreck things. I didn't see her putting in the effort to make this work, when she was already grumpy about how things had changed. She was at risk of digging her heels in and ruining everything, just to prove she was right – *not that I had ever done that before.*

I was about to brush my teeth when there was a knock at the door. "*J'arrive!*" I yelled, wondering what on earth room service or housekeeping might want at this time of night. I knew it was posh here, but it was a bit late even for a turn-down service. I had been getting undressed and had got most of the way through the process, down to just my pants, so I hurriedly pulled on my t-shirt and skirt, before they did that annoying hotel thing of pretending they hadn't heard you and letting themselves in. I wasn't sure I wanted the staff getting a strip show from me.

My t-shirt got stuck going over my head with an elbow through the arm hole. I was stressed and rushing, wrestling with the fabric, determined to win. "*Moment, s'il vous plait!*" I yelled in a panic, hoping to delay the inevitable door opening. *Great, so now they'll think I'm trying to hide my male escort in the wardrobe and remake the bed.*

I opened the door, flustered and out of breath, expecting to have to test out my schoolgirl French with a bemused stranger, only to find Christof standing there. For some reason, it took me by surprise. "Hello." I was less than welcoming.

"I forgot something," he said, "May I come in for a moment?"

I opened the door wider and gestured him into the room. He closed the door softly behind him.

"Couldn't it wait?" I asked, allowing my irritation at how today had gone to show in my tone. *There she goes, my Inner Drama Queen!* But I didn't feel inclined to shut her up. "I've been up since five and I really want to sleep."

"Oh, okay." He shrank visibly and looked with fascination at the dried-flower arrangement on the table between us. "I'll leave you to it then."

"No," I was being a cow, but my mind was yelling abuse at me for weakening, even a fraction, "don't worry. What was it you had forgotten that couldn't wait until tomorrow?" I was still far from friendly.

"It's just that…" He looked nervous again, like he was plucking up courage. "I've just ordered some hot chocolate from room service and I got you one as well, just in case." He looked at me, hoping for some indicator that this was good news. "They're delicious here. I always order them."

That pang of jealousy again. *Always*? Who else had he brought here? When was the last time? My Inner Drama Queen was thinking evil thoughts about long-legged, skinny blondes who spoke fifteen languages and studied for their seventh PhD in their lunch breaks. Why was that any of my business? I didn't want to care, but I did. My blood pressure rose as I wondered what kind of sex they had indulged in and which room they had used. Was that why the receptionist was so friendly? Was she wondering which woman he was bringing with him *this time*? I felt my skin growing cactus spikes and I wanted to make sure he knew it.

"Oh, thank you. Maybe you could ask them to drop it round when they bring yours. That was kind of you." Those cactus prickles were now fully formed and inflicting significant injuries.

He looked crestfallen, his shoulders hunched. He stared at the floor. Silence. Awkward. Again. I sighed, making it clear how bored I was. I could feel myself wanting to hurt him, even though that was crazy, to stop myself from crying.

"Was there anything else?" I tutted, inspecting my fingernails for dirt, like the heroines did in black and white movies when they wanted the man they secretly adored to feel the full force of their indifference.

"There was something else," he added, hesitating, "yes."

"Well?"

He stood up tall and there was a determined look on his face, like a man who had decided he had nothing to lose. "I realised I had forgotten to kiss you hello, and I didn't want to finish the day without doing it. That wouldn't feel right."

My brain took a moment to process this. I slowly worked it out – he had wanted to kiss me at the airport. This was good news. Not Drama Queen good news. She still wasn't happy. I told her to shut up. Butterflies fluttered up and down my spine, fighting with the cactus spikes. *They had better watch their wings.* But I didn't want to jump to conclusions. It might still be a peck on the cheek, like that maiden aunt. Memories of the cherry festival filled the room. Hope was resurfacing.

He lifted his gaze and met my eyes, daring an optimistic smile, possibly feeling more confident because he hadn't had a 'no' or been slapped yet. "May I?" he added.

I stepped towards him, feeling like a teenager on a first date again. Nervous. Excited. I nodded; a tiny movement that he wouldn't have noticed, had he not been hoping for it.

We kissed. Properly. Maiden aunts would not have approved. I smiled.

"Hello, Sophie," he said, staring into my eyes for the first time today, his arms slipping round my waist.

"Hello, Christof," I replied, desperately packing away the cactus spines, before they could do any more damage.

"Could we pretend I'm just collecting you from the airport and I'm getting to show you how much I have missed you… properly? It's what I wanted to do this morning, but I wasn't sure if it was what you wanted. And when you seemed so distant, I lost my nerve. I thought maybe you had come to see Toulouse, not me. But if I allowed us to go to sleep without telling you how I felt, I knew it would be too late. You'd have written me off."

I wanted to deny it and defend myself but he was spot on. I would have given him until I fell asleep to redeem himself or I would have been hell to be around tomorrow.

"Kiss me, then tell me," I replied. "That last one was pretty good, but I think I need to do some quality control. I need a larger sample size."

He laughed and we kissed again. His hand was on the small of my back, pulling me towards him, so I could feel how pleased he was to see me, making me tingle from head to toe. He was running his other hand through my hair. We were kissing with an increasing urgency, betraying the frustration of two months of not being able to admit we were missing each other. My arms were wrapped around his neck. I didn't want to let him go. For once in my life, the commentary in my head shut up as I abandoned myself to the physical sensations of this moment. I loved the way he smelled, the smoothness of his hair, the touch of his hands on my body, the light stubble against my face. We were so close I could almost feel his heart beating. I wondered if it was racing, like mine.

Oh, how I've missed him. And it's wonderfully clear that he has missed me, too.

And we still had the rest of the weekend with no commitments, no meetings, no festivals, no obligations. Just us.

I started to unbutton his shirt, fumbling, rushing, running my fingertips over his chest, noticing the soft curls of his chest hair, sensing the contours of his body. He shivered under my touch. "That tickles!" he said, without stopping kissing me. I giggled and kept going with a firmer touch. He arched his back and groaned with expectation as I finished with the buttons and reached for his belt buckle.

The hand that was running its fingers through my hair was now inside my t-shirt. A thrill of delight rushed up my spine as he reached my breast and caressed it. "No bra?" he asked.

Shit! I don't want him to think I'm a floozy.

"I was getting undressed when you knocked!"

"Perfect timing!" he smiled, cupping my breast in his hand as his thumb gently made my nipple go hard. He paused his kisses and lifted my t-shirt, moving his mouth towards my nipples. I felt like I was about to explode. I wanted this. I closed my eyes in anticipation of his lips, his tongue, his teeth.

"Bzzzzz!"

I jumped as I heard the sound, confused. Christof stopped, too, dropping the front of my t-shirt. Then he realised, "It's my room bell. It must be the hot chocolate!"

Sheepishly he opened my door, pulling his open shirt across his chest, red-faced, half-hiding behind the door, calling across to his door to explain that the hot chocolate now needed to be delivered to this room instead. The silent room service attendant handed him the tray, looking at Christof's shirt and my dishevelled state. His raised-eyebrow-smirk told us he knew exactly what was going on. Christof closed the door behind him as he set the tray down on the desk. We heard the rattling wheels of the room service trolley disappearing down the corridor.

Christof breathed a sigh of relief and gave me a look that said we had been caught out red-handed, like naughty children breaking into the school sweet shop. We both started to laugh; a laugh that released the stresses and tensions of today, of two months of uncertainty, of truths unspoken and hands unheld.

We spent the rest of the night lying in each other's arms, talking in heartfelt whispers, finally having the time and space to get to know each other. There was no rush. It was the first time we had ever had any privacy together. It was blissful, like coming home.

We forgot to drink the chocolate.

We spent a beautiful day driving around the foothills of the Pyrenees, having lunch in a tiny restaurant in a hillside village that Dad and I had discovered over a decade ago which, thankfully, was still there. Being with Sophie was such a joy. She was funny and serious in equal measure, but I scarcely remember what talked about, only how much she made me smile and forget everything else I had to do.

On our way back to the hotel, I pulled up a small track to park and we walked to a nearby clearing, with a stunning view over the valley, sitting on the grass to watch the sun set.

"I've never brought anyone else here before," I told her, opening up about my past for a rare moment, "I used to come here as a kid with Dad and Nonna. And I came back here once when I was at uni, on a field trip to a local aeroplane design company."

"How come you know the hotel so well?" There was a tension in her voice, jarring the peace of the evening.

"We always stayed there." I could feel myself getting defensive.

"And you've never brought anyone else?" I gave her a confused look, genuinely not understanding what she wanted to know. "The hot chocolates?" she continued, "Remember? *'They're delicious here. I always order them.'* Last night?"

"Yes! Dad. Nonna." I felt like I was on trial. "Hang on, are you feeling jealous?"

"Yes! I am!" she spat like a stuttering motorbike exhaust. Then she continued, with a deep sadness, fidgeting with blades of grass, "That's why I was such a cow to you. I'm sorry. I was upset."

"But why? I've never brought anyone else here. But what if I had?" She looked up at me. I could see the threat of tears in her eyes. "They'd be in my past. We both have a past, don't we? Or are you a secret virgin, because you certainly didn't give that impression last night."

She blushed. I felt guilty for embarrassing her.

"I just hate being compared to anyone. I do it to myself all the time." It felt like a confession.

"Sophie, I'm not comparing you to anyone. I'm here, with you. Right now. Anyone else is irrelevant, because I'm not with them anymore, am I? Why do you make yourself miserable about it?" I paused, giving her time to reply, but none came. "I just want to get to know you better, Sophie, to spend time with you. Would that be okay?" She nodded. I moved over to kiss her. She responded with enthusiasm. The sun was nearly down and it was stunningly beautiful, but we ignored it. I wanted to forget everything in the world apart from being with Sophie.

We drove back to the hotel as fast as the curves of the mountain road would allow and I handed the car key to the valet as we almost ran up to Sophie's room. Things quickly got amorous, until I suddenly remembered I had left my wallet, passport and phone in the glove box of my hire car. While I was happy to trust the valet with the car, I wasn't so keen on leaving whoever might go past the keys with access to my credit cards and passport. I shuddered at the memory of what had happened the last time I had left my phone locked away, unsupervised, after the stake-out in April. I couldn't relax until I knew they were safe, which was a bit of a passion-killer, so Sophie gave me her room key and told me to come back as quickly as I could.

I ran down the stairs, through a maze of corridors that led to the entrance to the underground carpark. I had to keep pausing to look at the fire escape route maps on which it was marked. Guests weren't really supposed to find it. It was while looking at one of these that the hairs on the back of my neck told me there was somebody in the shadows nearby, watching me. I tried to ignore the feeling and walked along the corridor with as much confidence as I could manage, until I got to the next fire route sign, at a three-way crossroads. I paused and then turned round, abruptly, asking, "Who's there?"

I held my breath, listening for any sounds. I counted to twenty before I allowed myself to breathe again. Nothing. A wave of fear threatened to make me run. Those hairs were still insisting that I was not alone. I worked out that I was nearer to reception than to the valet's office, so I turned back. And as I retraced my steps, my senses were on high alert. Someone was watching me. I was quite sure of it.

Then something caught my eye - something on the floor, almost hidden up a side corridor, in the shadows. A sky-blue baseball cap. I bent down to pick it up, keeping my back to the wall, being careful not to let my defences down in case it was a ploy to catch me unawares. Still no sound or movement. It was slightly warm, as though it had only just been dropped. And it looked clean, so it hadn't been kicking around on the hotel floor for long.

My heart stood still. Then it started to race. I saw a capital 'N' in white, inside a royal blue circle: the logo for SSC Napoli – the Naples football team. The virtual photo album in my brain screamed at me for attention. It was the same coloured cap the man had been wearing in our local town, when I was sure I was being followed, the day I had first visited Francesco's shop, back in May. I couldn't have seen the logo at that distance, but there was no mistaking its unusual light blue colour on top of his dark brown hair. It was too much of a coincidence.

I froze, trying to work out what to do. Surely I was making this up? Jumping to conclusions? Jumping at my own shadow? I must be going crazy.

In an attempt to do something that felt calm and normal, I decided to give it to reception, to see if they recognised it from a guest. The steam train in my brain was rattling possibilities at me. Surely the only way the cap could have got down here was with a guest or a staff member? The hotel was secure. The receptionist was uninterested, turning it slowly in his hands, as though hoping it might give him an answer, but it didn't. He pointed to a label inside it with the name of the team. "It's an

Italian football team, from the look of this. Are you sure it's not yours, monsieur?" he asked me. I shook my head and he put the cap down, telling me he would take it to lost property, in case someone claimed it. I knew they wouldn't.

I had no idea whether the person I had thought was following me was still in those corridors, so I asked the receptionist to call the valet to the front desk, to could give him my keys and ask him to collect my things from the car glove box. I knew I could trust him to do that. It took him just five minutes, but it felt like forever, as my brain analysed everyone I saw for signs of a recently removed baseball cap.

He gave me my wallet, passport and phone, then wished me good evening and I walked slowly back up to Sophie's room. The shock of what I had just found – and what that might mean – had killed any passion I had been feeling. I wasn't sure how I was going to blot this out of my thoughts and get back to feeling excited to continue where we left off on the hillside. It was with a guilty sense of relief that I found Sophie lying on her bed, sound asleep.

She was naked apart from a spaghetti-strap top – it looked like cream-coloured silk – and matching pants. I knew I should leave her, but I didn't want to be alone after what had just happened. I gently moved the duvet to cover her as she slept. Having spent the night with her last night, I hoped it would be okay to get into bed beside her, so I slipped under the cover, with her back to me, wearing my t-shirt and boxers for decency and I gently wrapped my arms around her.

I loved the smell of her hair, the softness of her skin, the calm rhythm of her breathing. It soothed me, melting away the worries of the past fifteen minutes, reminding me that all might be well.

But where was this going? Was this just a fling? Or could it be something more for her? For me? I hadn't told her about London yet. Even if she got excited about me coming to England, it would only be for six weeks. Where would we take it after that? Neither of us wanted an international relationship, I was fairly certain of that. And we both had jobs that were more than work – they were careers – and we were heading upwards. Would either of us want to sacrifice that for the other? She barely spoke Italian, so she'd drown in my world. Would she learn Italian to be with me?

I felt like I was getting ahead of myself, but part of me wanted to decide whether or not this might work before I opened my heart to her. I had a strong sense that it wouldn't take me long to lose myself in Sophie.

I gently stroked her hair. I feel complete when I'm with her. Accepted. Loved for who I am. Though neither of us had mentioned the L-word yet. That's still a while off. But I wasn't sure I had felt this way before: so captivated; so hungry to be with her.

I kissed Sophie's neck oh so softly.

"Mmmm," she sighed, wrapping her arms around mine and easing herself back towards me. I realised with that early relationship nervousness that there was no hiding how I was feeling, once she was that close. I felt myself blush.

"Sorry. I didn't want to wake you."

"That's okay." She turned to face me and put her arms around me. She was still half-asleep.

"Sleep well," I whispered, as I kissed her forehead, hoping she couldn't tell how much I didn't want her to sleep, now the closeness of her body had reminded me why I had been in such a hurry to get my stuff from the car.

She was waking up. She lifted her face to mine and kissed me. Gently. Sleepily.

I ran fingertips over her skin. She groaned. She stretched and reached out to run her hands over my body too. We were kissing, properly, reminding each other of the pleasure we had begun to discover last night, lazily exploring each other's bodies with fingers, tongues, teeth.

I wanted to know what it felt like to make love to her. But it had been two years, apart from the disaster in Naples, with Denucci's beautiful distraction, which I preferred to pretend hadn't happened. What if I had forgotten how? Was it true it was like riding a bike?

Sod it, my inner dialogue told me. *She's half-asleep. If you're crap, she won't remember.* I laughed.

"What's so funny?" Sophie asked.

"Nothing," I replied, "I was just wondering what it would feel like to make love to you." That took some guts to say. Good old fear of rejection. Even though she was lying in bed with me, hands everywhere. She smiled and kissed me again.

"Do you want to?" she whispered in my ear.

"Of course! Since the moment I first laid eyes on you. Okay, that's a lie. Since the moment I picked you up to take you for ice cream." She gave me a playful punch. We both knew how unsuccessful our initial meeting had been.

"Well, what are you waiting for? I've waited months for this!" she said. I reached into her bedside table drawer and found a packet of condoms, just as I had hoped.

"Oh, I do hate being a foregone conclusion!" I teased.

"How did you know they would be there?" she asked, slightly embarrassed.

"Really? Like I don't have a pack in my own bedside table drawer?" She giggled. We made love, slowly, sleepily, deeply, savouring every moment. It was every bit as wonderful as I had hoped it would be.

October

Chosen

priceless or useless
are you worth the investment
expert eyes decide

Leaving Nonna had been hard this weekend. I knew she'd be fine and she'd got Pietro and the rest of the farm team to support her, but it was still hard to say goodbye to her. I'd be back in six weeks, but that felt like a long time to be this far away. When I was in Milan, even if I was travelling through work, I spoke to her a couple of times a week and saw her at least once a month.

"You've got to get on with your life, *carino*," she said, as I was saying goodbye. "Mine is all about the farm. At the moment, yours isn't. And that's fine. And anyway, you've got your Cherry Girl to see!" She was smiling impishly, relishing the part she had played in getting me to find Sophie. I was grateful to her, but I squirmed when she dropped so many hints. She wanted great-grandchildren, she said, but I had to be clear on that one. They were not currently in my plans and I wasn't going to have them just to keep her happy. I thought that might be going a bit far for a third date with Sophie. Luckily, she agreed.

I'm pretty certain that Pietro would have mutinied over my placement, had I not had my hold over him. I knew Dad would be angry with me for using my joker card, but I no longer trusted Pietro to do his job and I knew he neither liked nor trusted me. That hadn't been a pleasant farewell.

I locked up my flat in Milan – something it was so used to with my work that it didn't object. I didn't have any house plants to wither and die and my fridge was quick to empty. All it took was setting the heating to winter frost settings and turning off the hot-water heating. I was redirecting my post, so that was easy too. And my car would happily sit in the garage beneath my apartment for the six weeks I was away. A friend at work had my spare key in case anything went wrong.

I closed the door and walked down the stairs to my waiting taxi, wondering how much my life might have changed by the time I got back in six weeks' time.

We had done the final briefing meetings at work yesterday. Luca wanted me to stay updated on the Denucci case. All my other projects had been handed over to team members to cover, while I was away. The UK Branch had got a full timetable lined up for me, so I couldn't juggle both jobs.

Isabella was dressed in black yesterday: the grieving widow, apparently heartbroken at me going away. She stopped short of the black veil. She had been a nightmare to work with ever since I'd told Luca that I was still in touch with Sophie. She had even tried to kick up a fuss that would have forced me to cancel my trip to Toulouse to see Sophie, demanding that I couldn't be spared from the office in case she needed to check leads on the Denucci case. Fortunately, Luca had brushed away her pleas.

She had worked her magic on me two years ago and I had drowned in it. I had been devastated when she dumped me, or rather *cheated* on me. She craved attention – and adoration – and she'd try anything to get it. It was going to be a relief to be out of her way for a few weeks.

It was time to get her out of my head; I didn't want to be taking her with me to England. She knew there hadn't been anyone since we'd split up, when I became invisible to her, but now I had moved on she had taken it as a challenge to win back my attention. I knew her well enough to predict that she would get bored with me, if ever she won me back, like a child with a puppy that won't perform tricks on demand.

I turned my focus back to the practical side of things for the next few days. I was going straight to our London office from the airport for initial meetings and to agree our six-week strategy with the guy who would be my temporary boss. We had done some video calls already, so I was fully briefed, but it would be good to meet the key contacts I'll be working with.

I was the ideal candidate for this interim role, with my background in the cases I had led over recent years and being bilingual in Italian and English, thanks to Mum. She and I had always spoken in English, but after she left it was banned at home. I kept it going by reading the books she had left and secretly tuning in to the BBC World Service when Dad and Nonna were out of the house. School wasn't much use. I was stuck going at the same speed as my classmates, who were struggling with the pronunciation and the irregularities in English spelling, while I was so bored I wanted to walk out of the lessons. The one time I tried it, our school principal told Dad, who made sure I never did it again. I could still feel that belt on my backside. Every single English lesson reminded me that Mum had left. I learned to be good at hiding it. Professional even.

My written English didn't really improve until I got to university. My business studies course included two modern languages, so I chose English and French. By the time I had left home I was free to practise whenever I wanted to. But even after all these years, there are idioms I don't quite catch and nuances I mess up. I tend to drop in a ten-year-old's vocabulary in the middle of business meetings or use super-long words in the pub. This visit was to be the first time I had ever been to the UK, which was hard to believe, until I remembered that everything to do with England had been forbidden once Mum left. Before she went, we didn't have the money to travel internationally on holidays. My English-language placement at university had been a six-month internship in New York and my work cases had never taken me to the UK with work. Holidays were so rare, and usually spent at the farm or in the mountains, that I had never felt the need to go somewhere that had the potential to be so grey and rainy. Or maybe I had been making excuses, scared that going 'home' would dredge up too much of the past.

I had been warned that my new colleagues have a welcome night out planned for me tonight. Obviously jet lag wasn't allowed in this team! I was hoping to cut it short so I could head back to my apartment as early as was polite. I knew my head was going to be screaming with the effort of travelling, meeting everyone and being full-time in what was still a foreign language to me. I think in Italian, not English, and it's going to take a while to transition.

All of this kept my brain occupied until the end of airport security. *I'm through. I managed to have the right things in the right bags in the right quantities to keep them happy and be allowed on the plane.* It's second nature for me now, given how often I fly. But families in the queue with me, heading off on hot holidays, had bottles of suntan lotion and shampoo confiscated for being too large. I could see how stressed the parents were and I was grateful I was travelling on my own. There is so much waiting involved with flying these days that I wouldn't want to have to keep children amused for that long.

Sitting on the plane, getting ready to taxi to the runway, I paid half-attention to the safety briefing and then I let myself relax. For the next couple of hours I was going to daydream about Sophie. In the six weeks since Toulouse, we have stayed in touch as much as possible, but this placement will give us a chance to feel what it might be like to have a normal relationship, to live in the same city, even though I know that might never be an option. How often did people end up like Sophie and me, splitting their lives between cities, countries – continents even; trying to make it work?

My flight was smooth and passport control was faster than I had expected, so I was soon in the baggage-collection area, with its slow-moving conveyor belts decorated with brightly coloured suitcases, like slowly moving baubles on a colourful Christmas tree.

Work had given me a UK SIM for my phone and I decided to call Sophie while I was waiting for my suitcase.

"You've landed!" she shouted, excited, making me hold the phone away from my ear.

"Yes, I'm here."

"I can't believe I'm not going to see you until tomorrow! A whole thirty-six hours in the same country before you get around to seeing your girlfriend!" she had teased.

Girlfriend. It felt good to hear her call herself that; made it more *real*; worth putting in the effort to make it work.

"You've got my address?" I asked. She confirmed she did. We were meeting at my new apartment tomorrow, after work. There didn't seem to be any point in going out for dinner. We had other things on our minds, not seen each other for weeks.

"I can't wait to see you." She knew I meant it. "And don't forget to bring your toothbrush!"

The day went well. Hectic, as I had expected. The night out with my new colleagues was low-key, but still went on too long. I finally made it to my apartment after midnight: 1 a.m. by my body clock. Luckily the keys had been sent to work, so I already had them with me. I didn't think the caretaker would have been very impressed, had he had to wait up. My suitcase was already waiting for me in the hallway and the fridge was full of food basics. It was up to me from now on, but I was grateful to whoever had made sure I'd get breakfast and coffee in the morning. I was asleep almost before my head had touched the proverbial pillow.

It wasn't weird at all seeing Christof last night, which was a relief. We had got through that stage in Toulouse. I could hardly wait for the day to pass at work, I was so excited about seeing him. I kept making stupid mistakes while I was preparing a client debrief with Jeff until he finally told me to go home early and get ready to see my *Italian lover*. Not that I had been mentioning his arrival fifteen times a day for the past few weeks.

I turned up at his new apartment exactly on time. I didn't want to be *fashionably late* for once. We had the decency to shut the door before we jumped on each other. We both knew we had to get our frustrations sorted – on a physical level – before there would be much chance of focusing on anything else.

Afterwards, I spent the rest of the evening wearing one of Christof's shirts with my pants and not a lot else, just lazing around his flat, picking at dinner. He had pulled together a salad with chickpeas and a lovely, creamy dressing. He had been exploring his local supermarket and was lamenting everything that was missing compared to Italy, such as truly fresh, seasonal fruit and vegetables. I warned him this was what London city life was like.

Then we curled up on the sofa and just chatted, putting the world to rights, luxuriating in the fact that there was no rush, no deadline; we had the gift of time. Falling asleep in his arms, knowing he would still be there when I got up to go to work the next morning was so fabulously *normal*. We had got six weeks of this and I was taking Christof's advice – he's already spotted I'm a worrier – let's handle the future when we come to it. Easy to say.

I met up with Jem at lunchtime. She had tickets to an art-gallery opening. "Very la-de-dah, *dahling*," she had sung down the phone, when she invited me, "but a girl has to be *seen*, you know, even when you reach my side of fifty." I didn't point out that she should have said sixty.

"In other words, you've got a romantic interest on the go and want to catch his eye?" I teased, grateful that, for once, she could be on the receiving end as we swapped roles. I could almost feel her blushing.

"Just grab a quick sandwich at your desk before you leave to meet me," she had instructed, ignoring my jibe. "There will be canapés, but champagne on an empty stomach can soon get embarrassing and these nibbles are ordered by size-two women whose idea of a decent lunch involves dolls-house-sized portions."

I met her at the Tube station nearest to the gallery. She hadn't wanted to meet me outside the event. "What if you're late, dahling, and they think I'm too nervous to go in? That simply wouldn't do. A terrible first impression!" She was dressed to the nines, with her current favourite designer frock on, heels that would have made Naomi Campbell shudder and just the right amount of make-up to satisfy for a lunchtime event.

"So? Tell me about your new beau!" I commanded, as we walked to the gallery. She carried off the heels as though she had worn them since birth, which she probably had.

"Oh, he's just an *interest*; someone it would be useful – and fun – to nab. But there's nothing happening yet. Every time I see him he's got some nubile eighteen-year-old hanging off his arm, but he always looks a little bored when he listens to them, so I've decided it's time for him to enjoy some more *mature* company. And it adds a certain *frisson* to know that he was recently declared one of the top twenty eligible bachelors in Europe."

"But I thought you were seeing some *Julio* bloke?"

Jem raised an eyebrow, warning me not to mention him again, "We're *on a break, dahling*. Probably permanently, though I haven't broken that to him yet. It seems a girl *can* have too much of a good thing."

"What happened?"

She shuffled her foot, as though stubbing out an invisible cigarette, with a hint of nervousness that was rare to see in her. "He proposed," she spat with the force of a machine gun, "and that kind of behaviour ruins *everything*."

"You're not thinking of settling down then?" I asked, eyebrows riding high.

"Heavens no! That would cramp my style!" she replied with so much conviction that I was far from convinced, "The girls and I have got a bet on."

"The Godmother Club?"

"Shhhh! I told you not to use that name!"

She gave me a look that would have scared an angry lion, but it quickly faded back to her habitual smile.

"It's a bit of a dry period, the months between the Summer Season and Christmas. We're so good at match-making for others that we decided it was time to try it out for ourselves. It has been a while since we've had to. Things normally fall into place quite nicely. But it's not much fun being single at Christmas and New Year, so we've made this competitive, to see who can get the most exciting or exotic Christmas invitation."

"And the winner gets?"

"To go, of course! The prize is, in itself, the prize. And the subject of my attentions at the moment would be quite the prize."

I nodded, pretending to understand half of what she had just said as we reached the gallery. The door was opened for us by a smartly dressed woman in her early twenties, who was openly luxuriating in those years before wrinkles or bags under her eyes showed up to spoil her fun. Her shampoo-advert-shiny hair was swept up into an elegant French-style *chignon* and everything she wore looked so perfect but so understated, as though she didn't want you to notice her, yet that was the very reason no one could ignore her.

"Welcome!" she trilled, holding out a hand not to shake ours, but to be given Jem's invitation. Jem knew the drill. I would have made a complete fool of myself. "Please enjoy our little party," she smiled at us and waved in the direction of the champagne and micro-canapés, as Jem had predicted. Then her smile instantly switched to the next Person-With-Wallet who approached the door. I looked back at her as we walked across the room and my Inner Drama Queen wondered when she had last eaten, evilly telling me I had childhood bookmarks that were fatter than her. I felt out of place, frumpy in my work clothes, twenty sizes too large and a decade too old to be 'staff', but two decades too young to be 'wallet'.

Jem made a beeline for a group of men she seemed to know, digging me in the ribs with her elbow as she hissed under her breath, "That's him!" She was showing me a very handsome man on the other side of the room. Perhaps late fifties, tall, confident, tanned: think Pierce Brosnan in *The Thomas Crown Affair*, but with less confusion over his accent.

"So why are we heading over *this* way?" I asked, innocent as I seemed to be in such things.

"You have to get *him* to see *you* and want to come over to talk to you, Sophie. You don't chase him. He can't know he's in any way important in your world. Don't you know these things yet?"

Obviously not. I was thinking back over my past few romances: chasing Jamie's socialite world and putting up with his shitty behaviour would definitely count as breaking the rules, as far as Jem was concerned. But if I hadn't chased him, I'd have lost him. "Would that have been such a bad thing?" my Inner Benefit-of-Hindsight Guru asked. No. But I'd have been lonely. And I guessed, at some deep level, taking the shit I did from Jamie was the price I'd chosen to pay for not being lonely and for being able to hang out with the 'It crowd', even though they weren't exactly kind to me.

Then there was Christof. I hadn't played hard to get there either. Had I done the right thing? Should I have made him work harder, once he sent the cherries and admitted losing my number? Probably. But surely if someone makes you feel happy, you don't need to play games? Why was it all so confusing? I decided to push it from my mind and focus on trying to be nice to some very rich, fairly unattractive men in extraordinarily expensive suits who were hanging on Jem's every word. They were talking yachts and villas and were unselfconsciously turning nouns into verbs.

"Where are you wintering, *dahling*?" was the current conversation topic. I looked over my shoulder at Drop-Dead Gorgeous and saw that Jem's plan had worked. He was dripping in beautiful women, but they had only part of his attention. Most of it was on Jem, from the stolen looks he kept giving her, when he should have been concentrating on the woman talking to him. And Jem was ignoring every single glance. I was sure she could feel them though. Her system was working.

I told her about his adoring behaviour during a pause in conversation. She was surprised that I was surprised. "But of course, it works. He'll ask me out for dinner tonight. I shall be too busy, but I'm sure I will be able to clear a slot in my diary for later in the week."

I wondered what my life might be like, by the time I got to

Jem's age. Part of me hoped it would be glamorous and exciting, as hers was. But she'd never settled down and I'm not sure I still wanted to be man-hunting at sixty. Wherever life took me, I knew she'd be there for me. She was certainly a mould-breaker when it came to godmothers.

Work has been flying. It feels great to get to be doing something new. Being desk-bound in Milan had been torture. My job would normally have involved meeting people to interview them, to find out everything I could or going undercover to try to find the bits that no one wanted to tell us. Sometimes the client's company ran a formal, public investigation. Other times, the work had to be 'invisible', so that only key members of staff knew we were involved.

The UK team is excited to learn new skills and I know that over the coming six weeks they're going to gain the practical strategies they will be able to draw on over the coming years, when they get out in the field. But I need to start them off gently. This kind of work can get nasty, if you slip up, as I know all too well.

Sophie and I have been seeing each other a few times during the week and spending every weekend together. It feels so strange, getting to be a normal couple. She wants to do the 'tourist thing' with me, so each weekend we spend at least one day of sight-seeing. Apparently, despite having lived here for so long, she's never done it. Most of the amazing sights on her doorstep were totally undiscovered for her, and she says that it's the same for most of her friends.

"London is for tourists," she tried to explain one evening, as we made the most of the privacy my apartment gives us, compared to her sofa bed in Anna's flat. "The rest of us enjoy the bits the tourists don't find."

"But doesn't that mean you miss out?"

"Probably, but we're too busy working, and paying the taxes to build the London that the tourists want. Anyway," she threw back at me, "how often do you visit the *duomo* in Milan?"

She had me there.

I would never go there *just because*; it's always too crowded with tourists. And despite the 600 years the Gothic masterpiece has taken to build so far –it still has uncarved blocks in hidden places – it doesn't do much for me. Yes, it's big, it's extraordinary, it has over 3,000 statues, it has great views of the city from its roof and to describe it as *flamboyant* would be an understatement, but I almost never go there. In fact, the last time I remember being inside it was for some event we were sponsoring at work, at least five years ago.

Sophie and I have now done the London Eye at sunset; we've marvelled over the size of the crown jewels at the Tower of London; we've watched the Changing of the Guard at Buckingham Palace; we've cruised down the Thames on a barge eating dinner by candlelight; and we've sat in raincoats on the top deck of an open-topped bus, with someone barely intelligible giving us life-changing insights about the streets and buildings we passed. We've been to shows, we've managed a red-carpet night at a Leicester Square cinema and we have eaten in more *nearly* Italian restaurants than I can count, each of which made me miss Nonna more than I would admit to Sophie.

The one thing we have never done is to discuss what's next: what happens when my London placement is over. But each time I see Sophie I know I'm one visit closer to us finally having to deal with the elephant in the room – the future of our relationship.

I feel safe here. It has taken a while, but I've finally stopped looking over my shoulder. I haven't had that awful feeling of being watched since the underground car park in Toulouse. I feel guilty about not telling Luca about the baseball cap. He's pretty sure that Denucci has decided to leave me alone, accepting that I'm off the case. I have resisted allowing myself to feel total relief, but I have been able to relax here.

Walking along a street, holding Sophie's hand, I feel so present, so relaxed, as though the worries and stresses of normal life have melted away. And as days tick into weeks and the seesaw of my time in England tips past the first half into the second half, each time that little voice in my head asks me 'what next?' I slam the lid shut again on its invisible box and pretend there are no decisions to be made.

November

Rough cut

the diamond cutter
unlocks your hidden beauty
he plans your future

Sleeping on Anna's sofa was only ever meant to be a temporary arrangement, but finding somewhere nice to live that wouldn't involve a five-hour commute had been really hard. Okay, maybe I hadn't put a huge amount of effort in since Christof arrived, but I had been busy. And I couldn't face spending every waking hour trawling the internet and traipsing round dumps that even druggies would turn their noses up at, behind smarmy estate agents extolling the virtues of the next 'up-and-coming area' or the flat's 'potential to put you mark on it'. And staying with Christof half the time had made living at Anna's much easier.

That said, she'd been really grumpy with me lately and I did wonder if it was time to find a space of my own. Perhaps, despite paying half her rent, I had overstayed my welcome in her tiny pad. I decided to pluck up the courage to talk to her about it one evening when I knew I wouldn't be seeing Christof, because he had gone back to Milan for a few days. I made an effort with dinner as best I could, and even got in a bottle of wine.

Things started off well, but there was a frostiness in the air. I figured asking *the question* couldn't make things much worse, so I took a deep breath, changed the subject and asked her, "Anna, do you want me to move out?"

I had expected to see relief in her face, but instead there was surprise.

"Of course not!" She looked shocked. "What would make you ask that?"

"It's just you seem to be a bit irritable around me at the moment. I wondered if you've had enough of flat-sharing?"

"No. I'm just a bit stressed at work. I like having you here."

"It's a bit cramped, you know."

"But we've made it work, haven't we?"

"Anna, have I done something to upset you?"

There was the classic pregnant pause as Anna decided how to answer. "Well, I haven't exactly seen much of you, since Christof arrived. You're always either with him, or off doing focus groups, or with your other friends. I miss you."

She was right. I hadn't realised. I felt that old friend – guilt – welling up inside. I wasn't sure what to say. I already felt like I was spreading myself too thinly. I wanted to spend time with Christof. He is only in the country for six weeks and who knows what we'll do after that. I didn't want to think about it. And work was work. If I needed to travel for a research project, then that's what I'd do. And Anna wasn't my only friend. We share a flat. We go back a long way. But it wasn't like we were a couple. I hadn't realised she felt this way. She always seemed busy. But maybe she was right. I am hardly ever here at the moment.

"I'm sorry. I'll put in more of an effort." I replied, not knowing what else to say and having even less idea what that effort might be. But Anna smiled and the tension lifted. I had done something right.

"Actually, I've been thinking of moving," Anna said. She spotted the look of panic on my face. "Don't worry," she added quickly. "I was wondering about looking for a two-bedroom place. If we combined our budgets, we could get somewhere nice. What do you reckon? This place was too small even when it was just me." She gestured her arm around the lounge, as though I needed reminding how cramped it was. "Would you be up for it? I could line a few places up to view this weekend?"

She paused, hopeful, waiting. "I can't do this weekend, I'm seeing Christof. It's his last one here." I felt knocked off my feet by the tsunami of sadness I had been keeping at bay since the moment he had arrived, knowing that every time I saw him meant one less time until he left. I had never said it out loud before. The smile slid from Anna's face. I knew I had to work quickly to repair the offence I had just caused.

"I'm sorry. I'm just a bit upset about him going. But flat-hunting together would be a brilliant idea. Thank you! Maybe you could get some details and we could arrange some viewings for the weekend after that? How long is your notice on this place?"

She looked relieved and we spent the next glass of wine imagining what kind of place we might rent together, agreeing what we wanted – for me, a big bath – and bouncing ideas on areas and budgets. Then, out of the blue, as though she had been psyching herself up for it, she changed the subject.

"Tell me, what's going on with Jamie?" She never asks about Christof. They have only met twice. He had tried to be nice to her, but she pretty much ignored him. She had to admit afterwards that he was gorgeous and she could understand why I like him so much, but she shows absolutely no interest in him when I talk about him, so I barely mention him nowadays.

I wasn't surprised that she was curious about Jamie. He had shown up at work last week, out of the blue. I had found him in reception, waiting for me at the end of the day. He wouldn't let the receptionist phone up for me. He just said he'd wait, implying we had arranged to see each other. It was only afterwards that I realised I had never told him where my new job was. Just like Christof. He had invited himself along for drinks with my workmates and I couldn't get rid of him until after they had left. I had to make a big fuss about running late for Christof.

"Do you think he's still in love with you?" asked Anna, squeezing the orange of juicy gossip.

"No way! I'm not sure he ever was. I don't know what he wanted. I've told him to get lost again, that I'm not interested. We'll have to see if he takes the hint."

For much the first half of the year Jamie had been hanging around like the stench from a city drain in the height of summer when the pipes were blocked. I had *nearly* let down my guard, until the evening he had brought me a gift-wrapped box of cherries after work. It had been an epiphany for me, showing me that it was the first kind thing he had ever done for me and making me see how much of a people-pleaser I had been around him. In that moment, I vowed to myself I would never trust him again or fall for his sob stories. He had walked out on me on the night he had hinted he would propose, leaving me sitting on my own in the most expensive restaurant I had ever been to, only finding out the truth via Facebook, while he was chasing the money and the DD cups of some gentrified heiress. Despite never getting an apology from him, and how devastated I had been to be dumped like that, I had felt so low over my ex-boss's bullying, back in the spring, that when he started hanging around again I had even considered taking him back. I hadn't seen him since before Italy, but now it seemed he was back.

"Admit it," said Anna, "you like the attention!"

I denied it, unconvincingly, but she was right. It was flattering to have him following me around, even though I was now with Christof. But he knew I wasn't interested in him. Why wouldn't he leave me alone?

"What does Christof think?"

"He doesn't know. I haven't told him."

"I'd play it carefully if I were you. Christof doesn't strike me as the jealous type, but no guy likes to think his girlfriend is hanging around with her ex, the moment his back is turned, especially not when he's leaving the country in less than a week."

She was right. But surely Jamie was harmless? *Ouch.* Christof leaves so soon! I was fast running out of time to ignore that one. And neither of us had had the guts to raise the question about what would happen next.

When Luca told me he was flying to London to see me I guessed it wouldn't be good news and I was right. He flew in with Alitalia to London City Airport, so I took the Docklands Light Railway to meet him there. He wouldn't tell me what was going on until we were seated in the private dining room of the restaurant his secretary had booked for us.

"So, are you going to tell me what's up?" I asked, half-dying of curiosity, but also scared what it might be. I knew it wasn't about Nonna – he had already told me that much – and I wasn't about to be fired.

"Look," he said, scanning my face for signs of a response to the news he hadn't yet shared, "I'll get straight to the point. The man in Naples who you saw committing the fraud," he phrased it like a question, like I could ever forget the stake-out in April. "Well... he's dead." He let the news sink in. I raised an eyebrow, as my head tried to prioritise the million questions that teemed through my brain. "No, it wasn't natural causes. It was, most likely, though as always unprovably, Denucci."

Silence. Inside and out. He sipped his sparkling water. My thoughts shut up. I didn't know what to say.

"How?" I half-mumbled.

"Faulty brakes on his car." Luca let this sink in. Cogs whirred for attention in my brain, and I blurted, "But he was in the witness-protection scheme!"

Luca nodded silently, "But that wasn't enough. Somehow they found him. The police have no idea how. They suspect it may have been the same mole that knew you were going down to Naples and arranged for your *special rendezvous* in the hotel afterwards." That was code for 'the beautiful woman you slept with who deleted your evidence, you idiot, and we still haven't forgiven you'. Then it hit me. With the perpetrator dead, he could no longer confess in court. Without my video evidence of him in action – the stuff Miss Italy had wiped– we couldn't prove anything. Whirrs turned to clicks and I realised why Luca had come.

"You want me to testify, don't you?" It wasn't really a question. We both knew it was why Luca had travelled all this way to see me. I didn't realise my hands were shaking until I spilled my red wine over the tablecloth as I picked up my glass. "And Denucci will know I'm the only person who can, won't he? My brake pedals are the next in the queue." Luca gave me what was probably intended to be a reassuring smile, but it didn't touch the sides. I was used to the adrenalin rush of fear as I did a stake-out or other fieldwork. I was used to the danger of hiking challenging mountain tracks. I was used to the terror of throwing myself off mountain sides with a parachute on my back, before drifting down into the valley below. But this was the first time in my life I had ever felt really scared. "So, basically, you're saying my life may be at risk, but the police still want me to testify against this known murderer?" He nodded. "Please tell me you have a plan, Luca!" Over our extended lunch, which I barely touched, he explained how it would work.

They would start with an anonymous affidavit, where my name wouldn't be released until a court date had been set. This would give the police the evidence they needed to press charges, while protecting my identity. Our lawyers would try to find out whether my witness statement would suffice, but if not, I had to be prepared to testify in court. It might still be a long way off because the police hadn't managed to locate Denucci yet, which seemed insane, yet was surprisingly common for clan bosses. This fraud was the first thing in over a decade that the police had felt they could pin on him. They were working hard on the case and so we needed to be on standby at any time for things to move quickly. And the Boss had a plan, to keep me out of harm's way while we waited... and waited.

"They want to make your move to London permanent, Christof," Luca explained with a smile that implied he thought I would be happy at the news.

"But I don't want to move to England!" I almost shouted, thinking about my life in Milan and the farm and Nonna, and how hard it had been to be so far away for just six weeks at the quiet time of the year. I didn't want to leave Italy. In that single comment, I felt like I was betraying Sophie. Luca looked confused.

"It doesn't have to be forever. We just have to make it look like it is. You know, taking on the new job, buying a flat, that kind of thing."

"But I don't have the money to buy a flat in England!"

Luca grinned. "We can help with that. If you can find a deposit," he waited for my nod, which said *maybe* rather than *yes*, "then there are ways for us to lend you the rest, interest free, for as long as you want to stay here." He paused, letting this sink in before he launched his final incentive. "And there's always *Signorina Sofia* to consider. You could turn that into something really special." I blushed, my poker face failing me. "Surely she's worth staying for? From what I've heard you two have become quite an item over here."

I said nothing. Yes, we had spent a great few weeks together, but I barely knew Sophie, and I certainly wasn't ready to move country to be with her yet. I was worried that it might freak her out; scare her off. "I'd need to make sure she thinks it's a work thing, not about her and me."

"Whatever. However you want to handle it, Christof. If it's not working, I'll see if we can pull you back, after a year."

"A year!" The feeling of a fist punching my stomach told me that wasn't what I wanted. "Do I have any choice in all of this, Luca?" His look gave me my answer.

"We have some flats lined up for you to look at this afternoon. The first viewing is in about half an hour. Shall we get on our way? I've got a driver booked to take us round them." Why did it not surprise me that my agreement had been assumed?

I had arranged to meet Sophie after work, but the flat viewings meant I was going to be late, so I texted her to apologise and arranged to meet her in a bar near her office, after Luca was on his way back to the airport. I hadn't told her he was coming, so I just made an excuse about a last-minute client meeting. She said she would go for a drink with work colleagues and then we could meet up and go out for dinner.

By the time I reached the pub I had decided there was no way I could tell her about any of what had happened. I had never mentioned Denucci, or much about my work. The scar over my right eye from the heavies at the cherry festival had faded, but when Sophie had mentioned it I told the falling-over-a-box lie again and she'd bought it. Why wouldn't she? I hadn't told her the real reason why I been given this six-week London placement. I wasn't ready to tell her I was going to be moving to the UK or that I had already found a flat. Luca's team had done well. I'd chosen the first one we viewed – with a cherry tree in the garden. Nice touch.

The evening post-work celebrations were in full swing, with crowds out on the pavement, wrapped up in winter coats against the November chill. Shop windows were shifting into Christmas mode and the Oxford Street Christmas lights had already been on for a over a week. We were meeting in a bar, away from the main thoroughfare, which was already heaving with early Christmas shoppers who were behaving like they had to loot the shops in advance of some unannounced festive apocalypse.

Tonight's bar was quieter than most, being hidden in a back street. Its full-height glass windows sent a soft yellow glow into the street, tantalising passers-by with the warmth and laughter being enjoyed inside. And that was when I saw them. Sophie and a man who must have been Jamie, based on a Facebook virtual paper trail I had followed a couple of weeks back. I hadn't mentioned that to Sophie. They were sitting in the window at a high bar table, and I saw them laughing, each with a nearly empty wine glass. There was a bottle of chianti on the table between them. Jamie topped up Sophie's glass, emptying the bottle, and I watched her twiddling her hair in her finger and gazing at him with an affection that made my inner green-eyed monster want to attack. Jamie was much better looking than I had realised. He reached over and touched her hand, stroking it with his fingertips, like a lover. She didn't even notice. She just smiled and listened with rapt attention to whatever story he was telling. She was wearing my favourite black dress – she must have changed after work – and I could see the lacy top of her stockings as she crossed her legs, balancing precariously on the bar stool. She looked so sexy I wanted to drag her back to my place and forget about dinner. But inside I seethed. I realised I didn't trust her. And I felt jealous.

I decided to take the coward's way out. I didn't want to risk her comparing me to Jamie. I hoped I would win, but I didn't want to give him the satisfaction of her looking disappointed to see me. I wasn't sure I could survive feeling that way, especially not after today's decision.

I made a quick phone call to our favourite Italian bistro, whose Italian owner I was on first-name terms with, about ten minutes' walk away, to check they had space for us. They did. Then I texted Sophie.

"So sorry I'm late. Have told the clients I'm already booked for dinner and sent them out to eat on their own. Didn't want to stand you up. Don't really feel like the bar. Just checked with Andrea and he can give us our favourite table in the corner. Could you be there in ten? Can't wait to see you!"

I watched the text arrive, standing in the shadows, frozen with more than cold. It broke Jamie's spell. I watched her eyes scan the screen, her right thumb scrolling down the message. A smile spread across her face as she reached her left hand to her wine glass and finished the last of its contents. She said something to Jamie that looked like a 'sorry I've got to go' and I looked on with a sense of triumph as his disappointment went on public display. Sophie reached for her coat and pulled it on, pecking Jamie on the cheek and making to leave, but he held her arm. She looked surprised as he gave her a hug and tried to kiss her. She turned her head just in time, so he landed on her cheek, not her mouth, then shook her head and smiled back at him, before turning away to leave.

I didn't know what to make of the scene. I felt relief that she had stopped him from kissing her, rage that he had tried, and jealousy from the way she had smiled at him afterwards.

I was still standing on the other side of the street when suddenly I realised Sophie was about to exit the bar and would see me, which would lead to one hell of a scene. Somehow, I had to make it look like I was arriving from work when we met at the restaurant, so I needed to be coming from the opposite direction. That meant the ten-minute walk would be nearer fifteen, so I started to jog, hoping I knew these streets well enough by now. I made it, out of breath and dripping with sweat under my heavy winter coat. She strode towards me, beautiful and slightly tipsy, giving me a welcome kiss that tasted of the wine she had shared with Jamie.

"You're out of puff. Have you been running?" she asked, full of curiosity. I had my story already.

"Yes! I didn't want you to have to wait a minute longer than you already had. Anyway, you can help me to shower it off when we get back to my place." The smile she gave me made me determined not to ruin our evening by asking her about what I had just seen. I put the emotions back into their little box and became the most attentive boyfriend in London.

"What do you think, Sophie?" he asked me, looking uncharacteristically nervous. After a gorgeous meal at Andrea's place, where I had a bit too much wine (I hadn't told Christof I had already had half a bottle), we went back to his place and he broke the news that he had been offered a permanent position in London from February.

What did I think?

He was due to go back to Italy in just a few days and we still hadn't talked about the future. I had refused to think about it. And now it was here, I didn't know what I wanted.

"Wow! That's a surprise! When did you find out?" His eyes

told me it wasn't the response he had been hoping for, as he explained that his boss had flown over from Milan for the day to tell him. I avoided having to give any real answer by bombarding him with questions about where he would live and what he would do about the farm. He said he had negotiated being able to get back to Milan at least once a month to see Nonna and to check on the farm. He would keep his Milan apartment, because it was nicer than a hotel whenever he had to go over there for business. It seemed that everything had been arranged; I hadn't even been asked. I wasn't sure why I felt I should have been.

I spent the night with him, but he was distant, somehow detached; preoccupied. I was glad he hadn't seen me with Jamie. I'm not sure how that would have gone down, given how tense Christof seemed. They hadn't met yet and I wanted to keep it that way. I had only said yes to Jamie because Christof had already stood me up and he was there, waiting for me as I left the office. But it had been good to see him again.

This afternoon Christof took me to see the perfect little flat he has found. He said he didn't want to rent and that his relocation package was going to help him with finding a mortgage and stuff like that. He went into the financials about how it made much more sense but stopped when I glazed over. He was trying to get me excited about his plans to refurbish it. It had been rented out for years but the landlord was emigrating to Australia and didn't want the liability of managing it long-distance, so he was selling up. I thought with a deep sadness about how the tenants must have felt when they got the news that such a lovely home would no longer be theirs.

"Work is going to help me with tradesmen, so once I have the keys, it shouldn't take long to change the bathroom and upgrade the kitchen area. And I'm going to get the whole place painted, to give it a facelift. I'm not convinced that just cleaning would be enough to remove the traces of so many years of tenants. What do you think?"

What did I think? I was still in shock. But why? I loved being with Christof, but I also loved going out with my friends who were complaining how much I had neglected them while Christof was here, because every available evening that wasn't spent at work had been spent with him. I had been looking forward to catching up with them again. I certainly wasn't ready to dive into full-time *coupledom*. I enjoyed being *Sophie* too much – not half of *SophieAndChristof*.

Yet I had also cried myself to sleep a few times at the thought of Christof leaving and not seeing him again for months, knowing that neither of us could really commit to an international relationship; feeling like the last few, precious weeks had been the only time we would ever get.

I smiled the smile I use for focus-group delegates, when my head is telling me that what they are saying is crazy-lady territory, but I can't risk breaking rapport. Christof hadn't noticed that I wasn't listening.

"Sophie? *What do you think?*" His insistent tone broke through my self-talk's defences.

"Oh, yes, lovely! And it has a cherry tree, you said?"

"I meant about Christmas!" he said. The blank look I gave him betrayed my distractedness, proving I hadn't heard a word of what he had said. "Nonna and I would love you to join us at the farm for Christmas and New Year. Will you come?" It suddenly felt terribly serious. Christof hadn't met my parents yet. I could feel my pulse rate rising, like an animal, trapped in a cage, not knowing how to escape. I wasn't ready for this. But for some reason I found my mouth saying, "Yes!" And the look of joy on his face meant I knew I could never disappoint him by changing my mind.

Christmas

Bruting

diamond cuts diamond
removing your hidden flaws
but still you look dull

I was so nervous – again – as I got on the plane to meet Christof at the airport, this time in Milan. I was going to stay at the farm, to meet Nonna and Pietro and everyone Christof had grown up with. He had kept reassuring me how lovely they all were, but I was scared I wouldn't meet their standards. After all, the last girlfriend they had met was Isabella and from what I had heard she was a beauty. Coming to Italy for Christmas felt like such a big statement and I wasn't sure I was ready for this.

It had really upset Mum and Dad telling them I would miss Christmas day for the first time ever. They had dragged me to Shenfield last weekend for a 'family Christmas', which translated as a Sunday lunch with Jonathan and Delilah and the children, who were constantly complaining about what an inconvenience it was.

I managed to catch an evening flight after work on 23rd December, so it was really late by the time I landed, with Italy being an hour ahead of the UK. I hadn't used up any holiday in my new job, apart from my long weekend with Christof in Toulouse, so Jeff had agreed to me having Christmas Eve off and coming back on 2nd January. Christof had explained that it was unusual in Italy to get the full week off between Christmas and New Year, so he would have to work a couple of days, but that I would go with him to his apartment in Milan and could explore the city, which was something I had always wanted to do.

He welcomed me with a bear hug as I exited the Customs gates, and almost dragged me to the car park. "The sooner I get you to the farm and you have said hello to Nonna, the sooner I can show you how much I have missed you!" he promised, as we headed towards the motorway. The feeling was mutual.

But first I had to meet Nonna and I had to admit I felt scared. "Christof, what if Nonna doesn't like me? Surely you need her approval?" He laughed and patted my knee with his free hand, chancing a smile at me. The roads were quiet.

"Don't worry, *bella Sofia*. The first thing she saw of you was your awful security pass photo on your work website. She'll be so pleased to meet the *real* you that you've got nothing to worry about." Apparently, that was supposed to make me feel better.

Driving to the farm took forever. Part of me didn't want the journey to end, as we moved on to winding country lanes that felt like a race track, because Christof was so familiar with their bends, despite the dark. And then we were approaching the golden-lighted windows of a rambling old stone farmhouse.

"Don't look so scared!" Christof soothed, reading my mind. "Nonna will love you. And you're going to get your first ever Italian Christmas!"

He pulled up to park and the front door opened, silhouetting the figure of a tall woman with long hair tied up in a bun, with her arms open wide, shouting with excitement as she walked towards us. Christof walked round to my side of the car and opened the door, intuitively sensing that I was too scared to do it myself.

"Nonna!" he shouted, hugging her tight, "*Ecco Sofia!*" He pulled me out of my seat and soon I was wrapped in Nonna's arms with him, as she welcomed me with all her heart to her family and her home.

Nonna had left some dinner for us, aware that Sophie wouldn't have eaten, and she sat with us in the kitchen as we ate, bombarding me with questions about Sophie. It was fun watching the two of them sizing each other up. If Nonna dropped her dialect, then Sophie could understand some of what she said, but Nonna had never learned English at school, so I was the interpreter.

Sophie was unable to hold back her obvious tiredness and tomorrow was going to be a long day, so Nonna made her excuses and left us to go to bed.

"Well, that wasn't too bad, was it?" I asked when Sophie looked relieved at hearing Nonna's footsteps going up to the bedrooms. "I think she likes you!" I walked over to hug her. She looked too tired to answer. "Let me show you where you're sleeping."

"What do you mean, where *I'm* sleeping?" she yawned, looking confused. That had been an interesting discussion with Nonna. She was forward-thinking when it came to cherry-farming methods, but where girlfriends were concerned, she was a bit of a traditionalist. Plus, she hadn't really forgiven Sophie for being English yet, making her pay for Mum's behaviour. After all, it was only twenty-five years since Mum had left us. I didn't answer Sophie. Instead I walked her to the ground-floor guest room, with its white-washed walls and deep blue curtains with tiny daisy-like flowers on them and a matching deep-blue blanket on the wrought iron-framed double bed. I brought Sophie's suitcase with me.

"Why am I in the spare room? Why aren't I with you?" She

was tired and cross with me. I sat on the bed and gestured her to join me. She refused, with her classic stubbornness. I guess that tenacity is part of what makes her so good at her job.

"This," I said, waving my arm over the bed, "is one reason. Here you have a double bed. Upstairs we'd have had to put up with my teenage single that no one ever thought to upgrade." She didn't look convinced. I could tell she felt annoyed and rejected over this. I decided not to mention that I hadn't had the courage to discuss alternative sleeping arrangements with Nonna. "Then there's the fact that we won't have Nonna on the other side of the bedroom wall. She's in the opposite corner of the farmhouse, so we'll get more privacy." She was starting to soften. I decided to risk it. "And there's the small matter of me not having to take down my teenage posters of scantily clad film stars!" Luckily, she realised I was kidding and aimed a playful punch at my ribs.

It didn't take much unpacking before we were making up for lost time, clothes scattered over the white tiled floor, our bodies telling each other that the past month apart had been too long. As we lay together afterwards, sleepy and happy, I gave a silent thank you for having had the courage to ask Sophie to join us for Christmas. "I'm glad that Nonna couldn't hear that," she giggled, as she reached over to turn out the bedside light. "This lamp is pretty!" she added, running her fingertips over the midnight blue ceramic base and the cream linen lampshade.

I smiled. "Nonna bought it especially for you. This room didn't have a sidelight before. She thought you might like it."

"That was kind of her," Sophie whispered as she snuggled into my shoulder and fell asleep.

I had no idea how beautiful a cherry farm could be in winter. Christmas Eve was full of sunshine and new faces. I met Nonna properly – now I was awake – and, one by one, the rest of the farm team, including Pietro. He and Christof were surprisingly cool with each other. When Pietro had left the room, I whispered in Christof's ear to ask him why, desperate to hear some Italian gossip, but all I got was confirmation that there was a story to tell and a vague promise that I would hear it another time.

The day passed in a whirlwind of helping in the kitchen, walking round the estate, being introduced to friends and sampling Nonna's cherry panettone. Christof had explained to me that in Italy the big celebration was on Christmas Eve, with a family meal and then a trip to the village church. But because he and Nonna didn't have any family nearby any more, they always invited Pietro and his family.

I watched Christof meet the farm team, before lunch, as he handed out the *tredicesima* thank-you envelopes. It seemed a really cool idea, getting a bonus month's pay at Christmas time. Christof told me afterwards how hard it had been last year when he had done it for the first time; a role his dad had always taken, but that this year was easier. I couldn't imagine what it must have been like for Christof, having to step into his father's shoes, taking on responsibility for the farm as well as his own job. He seemed so at ease here in a way I had never seen him be in London. It felt wonderful to be getting to see the *real* Christof.

Nonna and I spent several hours in the kitchen in the afternoon with Pietro's teenage daughters and his wife, Marta, preparing the evening meal. The girls studied English at school and had grown up with American pop music in their blood, so their English was really good. Between us we managed to prepare the pasta, the fish and the side dishes that would make up our evening feast, without any translation disasters.

After a while, Nonna asked me – via the girls – to go and find Christof and to let him know that the meal would be ready in an hour or so. He and Pietro were walking through the orchards, so Pietro could update him on how the trees were. I went to find him, which took me a while. Cherry orchards stretched across the valley for as far as I could see. It blew me away to think that Christof owned all of this. I didn't even own my own flat. In fact, I didn't even rent my own flat; I was still on Anna's sofa. Comparing his life to mine freaked me out a bit. Then I thought back to so many of Jamie's friends, when we were part of the 'It crowd', whose families owned estates that took up major chunks of counties. I would never forget how many of them looked down on the people with less than them; how rare it had been to find one who didn't judge me; based on what I did and where I lived. And I gave a heartfelt thank you that Christof was so grounded and low-key about all this.

Then I saw them in the distance. Or rather I heard them. Christof and Pietro were shouting at each other. I had never heard Christof raise his voice before. The setting sun cast light around them, like actors on a stage. Pietro was waving a fist and stamping a foot. Christof was yelling back, fists clenched, not quite managing to keep himself under control. They looked up and saw me. Pietro said something I didn't understand and then stormed back to the house. Christof looked exhausted.

"What was all that about?" I asked, wishing I spoke better Italian. He sat down under a tree and looked at me, asking me with his eyes to sit down next to him.

"You know, Sophie," he said, his face looking calmer already, with the start of a smile in his eyes as he wrapped his arm around my shoulder and we leaned back against the old cherry tree's trunk, "I'm not used to having anyone to share my life with. I'm used to talking it through with myself. I'm so glad you came along." I couldn't work out if he meant just now or in general. "It has been hard, managing the farm long-distance. Pietro resents it. Dad used to do at least half of the work and the deputy farm manager I asked Pietro to hire is still *in training*, making mistakes, but also challenging Pietro's judgement, which isn't necessarily a bad thing." He ran his fingers through my hair and kissed my forehead. "Do you want to know the story?"

I smiled and nodded. Christof told me about how angry Pietro had been about him Christof accepting the permanent job in London, and how he had just threatened to leave the farm unless Christof stayed in Italy.

A sudden wave of panic broke the happy peace I had been feeling inside, "But you didn't say you'd come back, did you?" I blurted, in that moment realising how much I wanted Christof to move to England. He smiled and shook his head.

"No need to worry. It's all sorted."

"But how?" I asked, genuinely clueless as to how he and Nonna would manage the farm without their farm manager.

"Oh, I have my trump card. I threatened to tell Marta about Francesco and that was enough." And he spent the next fifteen minutes telling me all about last year's loan, the extra dramas that had been going on at the cherry festival, which were all fresh news to me, and how he had worked out Pietro's secret – about Francesco being his son, and how discovering that had made the mess over the loan and the lawyer make sense.

"So, you had all of that going on while I was daydreaming about cherries and pizzas and secret gardens … and you never told me?" I asked, feeling slightly hurt.

"I barely knew you," he laughed, "and I loved how you distracted me from the worry."

"But you never told me afterwards either!"

"There was never a right time – or any need. It never came up. But I've told you now. And I promise to let you in on my gossip if any comes up once I'm in England." I knew he was telling the truth. I could have sat with him under the cherry tree forever, then I remembered the message I had been sent to deliver and we ran back to the farmhouse, to help with the final preparations for dinner.

Sophie had brought Christmas crackers. We had never had them before – they're not an Italian thing – so they were the high point of the meal as she tried to convince us that no self-respecting Brit would eat their Christmas meal without wearing one of the brightly coloured paper hats. As if! We each promised to treasure our tiny cracker presents and I had great fun translating the terrible jokes.

Then we all sat round the Christmas tree, complete with its freshly lit candles. Sophie couldn't believe we would take such a risk. Everyone had a gift under the tree. Sophie had brought beautiful tins of shortbread for Nonna and Marta, pop magazines for the girls and a bottle of whisky for Pietro, which softened his grumpiness.

After the gifts, we had a couple of hours spare before the church service, so Pietro's family went home and Nonna went upstairs to rest. Sophie and I went to the guest bedroom and I pulled out her gift from the back of a drawer under the wardrobe.

"Not tomorrow?" she asked.

"No. Here we do it tonight. *Babbo Natale* must think you have been a good girl this year! Go on!" She gingerly took the box from me. It was wrapped in aqua blue paper and tied with a cream ribbon. She shook it. It didn't rattle. "Good, it's not broken then!" I told her. She carefully untied the ribbon and unfolded the paper. Inside was one of our cherry boxes. The only other time she had seen one of these was the one I had sent her in London, with the last of the season's cherries. She looked at me, raising a questioning eyebrow. "No," I shook my head, "not at this time of year." She opened the box and pulled out a thick cream envelope, carefully opening it and sliding out two tickets, with a gold-embossed crest on them.

"For Giselle at the Royal Ballet?" she asked, grinning, "in *April*?"

Sophie had lived in London for years, but I had discovered during my last few days in London that she had never been to the ballet and I had teased her relentlessly, trying to convince her it was far from boring. I had told her the stories of my favourites, but I wasn't sure she had listened.

We had ticked opera off the list when I had taken her to see *Carmen* at the ENO a few weeks before I left. It had been an incredible performance. She had been fascinated by the story. "Are you trying to tell me something?" she had asked me afterwards, with a cheeky grin, "But instead of being a factory worker distracting a soldier from his duties, I'm a market researcher taking a cherry farmer away from his?" I hadn't thought of the comparison, but she had been right.

"Though obviously I won't be killing you in a fit of jealous rage," I had promised. She feigned relief. "Thank you," she had said, kissing me. "I'm touched."

CHRISTMAS | 221

I was dragged back out of my memories by seeing the start of tears – not the effect I had intended. "It's just a pair of ballet tickets," I tried to reassure her, surprised by her response.

"No, it's not that. It's that you think we'll still be together in April. I'm not used to thinking about the future, to feeling safe like that. Thank you."

And, in that moment, I realised I never wanted to let her go.

On what would have been Boxing Day in the UK, but which would have been a normal working day in Italy, had it not been a Saturday, Christof and I headed up to Milan. We were going to go back to the farm for New Year. I was almost as nervous about meeting Christof's bachelor pad as I had been about meeting Nonna, as though I needed its approval too. I had never seen him in his *natural habitat*. The apartment in London had been rented by his firm fully furnished, and the farmhouse was the joint effort of generations of his family. But the Milan apartment was pure Christof.

It struck me how white it was. How uncluttered. Just the occasional cushion and rug to give it colour. But I approved. I wasn't sure I could live as tidily as this, but that wasn't my problem thankfully. Christof took me out for dinner with his boss, Luca, and his wife, Daniela. They were lovely and seemed to know much more about me than was decent, but it was wonderful to meet them. Christof and I had the whole weekend together and then I spent three days wandering around the city while he was at work. He was taking New Year's Eve off.

Milan didn't disappoint. Aside from the shopping, which had to be window shopping, despite the sales, given the state of my credit card, I took in all the tourist sites. The *duomo* was incredible. I still preferred the Dom in Cologne, but the *duomo* looked like the design had been handed over to a group of kids who had gone crazy with upside-down ice cream cones. It was quiet at this time of year, outside of its services, so I got to spend hours finding as many of its statues as my feet could bear. Christof would come home from work, rustle up some dinner in his pristine kitchen, then we would sit and chat on his sofa, with his favourite local wines, while he rubbed my feet and we enjoyed the luxury of having nothing to do.

We had never had this much time together. I started to become aware of the little things that showed me how much Christof cared. After knowing him for six months, I finally noticed the way he says my name, with the slightest hint of his Italian accent, almost adding an 'a' at the end, making me feel special. Such a contrast from Jamie's 'Soooaaf' that made me sound like the first half of a sofa. I realised how much I was falling for Christof. I had been too busy to allow myself to see it before.

I joined Christof each day for lunch, sometimes with his friends and sometimes just us. It was great to get to meet them all, until the final day in Milan, when we were in a beautiful trattoria near his office, hidden away in an old wine cellar. Christof dropped his fork when he saw her come in. She was with a man so tall, dark and handsome that speaking anything but gibberish in his presence would have been beyond me. She left him to sort out her coat with the waiter and came straight over to us. Christof moved to stand up and say a polite hello, but she gestured him to sit, placing a cold hand on my shoulder. I instantly knew who she was. And she was one of the most beautiful women I had ever seen, with her big brown eyes, her chiselled cheekbones and cascades of dark brown hair.

"Isabella, this is Sophie."

"Oh, I think I worked that out, Christof," she said with a perfect smile that rivalled the White Witch of Narnia's talent for turning everything around her to ice-cold winter. "*Ciao, Sofia! Ti piace Milano?*" Did I like Milan? She was scanning my face for signs of reaction, taking in every detail, no doubt comparing it to her own reflection. "I have heard so much about you!" She let the words work their intended effect, watching me shrink in front of her. I thought I might be sick. What had she heard? "It's funny how different people are when you finally meet them. Christof had told me you were beautiful." Her intonation made it clear it was a question, not a statement. I felt tears prick my eyes and she saw them.

"Isabella, that is not necessary. I think your date is waiting." Christof stood up, looking furious, eye to eye with Isabella. I hadn't noticed how tall she was. She said nothing, smiled a victory smile and then glided across the room to a man who looked ready to hang on her every word.

"I'm so sorry about that, Sophie," Christof apologised, resting his hand on my hand on the table. I was shaking. So *that* was who he was comparing me with. There was no competition. "I had no idea she would come here. She was being unkind. You *are* beautiful. We're leaving tonight. You won't have to see her again."

But I knew I would never forget what she looked like. It didn't matter what Christof said. It didn't matter that they weren't together any more. He saw her every time he came to Milan for work. A little bit of my self-esteem curled up into a ball and gave up the fight.

Seeing Isabella had been a shock, but Sophie and I didn't talk about it again. I didn't want the woman to ruin any more of our time together. We made it back to the farmhouse in time for a New Year's Eve dinner with Nonna, before she excused herself for an early night.

Sophie was leaving tomorrow and I would be taking her to the airport on my way back to Milan for work, so I was grateful to get some final quiet time together. Had we stayed in Milan, then we would have been dragged over to Luca's place for a party, which would have been great, but I wanted to savour every moment with Sophie. I had had enough of sharing her this week. She seemed disappointed to be missing out on New Year's Eve, but I was grateful to her for humouring me.

"Put your coat on!" I told her, once Nonna's bedroom door was closed and her light was off. Sophie looked confused. "Please?" She obliged. I pulled mine on, too. "We're going for a walk. There's something I want to show you."

We held hands along the footpaths between the orchards, a candle lantern lighting our way, until we reached a point that was out of sight of the farmhouse, looking over open fields towards the village and the town beyond. I could just make out their lights, twinkling in the darkness.

Sophie paused and looked around her. "Wow! That's so cool! We can't see the house! It must be strange to own so much land that you can lose sight of your home while you're walking around it!"

I hadn't ever thought of it that way before, but Sophie was right. I felt lucky; more than she could imagine. "Over here!" I pointed towards my favourite tree; one that was too old to produce a decent crop, but which I had begged Nonno and then Dad to let us keep, because it had been my favourite climbing tree as a child. I used to come and sit in it when Mum and Dad argued. Then I would hide in it after she left, secretly reading the English books she had abandoned in her rush to go. Now it had a picnic blanket under it, surrounded by jars with tea lights in them, and a bottle of chilled Prosecco, with two glasses.

Sophie sat down next to me on the blanket and we leaned back against the trunk of my old tree. I told her about its history, about how important it had been to me, about why I would never let anyone cut it down. She told me about the cherry tree she had loved in her grandfather's garden, and how she had felt so sad when they chopped it down. We sipped the Prosecco and I found myself telling her everything: about how Mum had left, out of the blue; how no one would tell me why; how I would to come to this tree to cry, because no one would let me talk about her; how they had all pretended she had never existed; how I had defied their attempts to get me to call Dad '*papa*' after she left; about how many times I had thought about going to look for her, but I was too scared she would reject me again; about how guilty I had felt about surviving the car crash that had killed Dad; about how hard it had been to admit I didn't want to run the farm. Sophie stroked my hair as I lay with my head in her lap, my gaze alternating between the stars and her eyes.

She told me about how hard the past year had been for her; how she had struggled at work with Stuart's abuse; how lonely she had felt; how Jem had helped her turn things around; how scared she had been when she realised she liked me; how she worried about making bad choices in relationships. Under the old cherry tree, we opened up and showed each other who we really were, finally trusting that all would be okay. I had never done that before. I suspected it wasn't common for Sophie either.

We lay on our backs on the blanket, the bottle empty, wrapped in each other's arms, gazing at the heavens. So much had changed since the first time we had done this, under the summer sun and that old oak tree at the cherry festival. This far from the farmhouse there was no light to disturb the infinite light show the sky offered. Time seemed to stand still.

"Christof," Sophie whispered, not moving her gaze from the stars, "make me a promise?"

"Mmmm?" I smiled, looking over at her.

"No more secrets, please?"

I thought about the Denucci case, about the attack during the cherry festival: I had lied to her about the scar above my eye, about the real reasons why I had been given the London placement and then the permanent posting; all things I could never tell her. "Of course, no more secrets." I promised.

The air was cold and I pulled the spare blanket, which had been a pillow against the tree trunk, around us to keep us warm. Sophie nestled her head onto my shoulder. I wanted to drown in this moment, breathing in the softness of her hair, feeling her starting to fall asleep in my arms. "Sophie," I whispered as I gently kissed her forehead.

"Mmm hmmm?" she was so sleepy it was barely audible.

"I love you." I felt her smile and hold me more tightly. The enormity of that simple phrase hit me. I had never felt this way about any girlfriend before. I had never said it to any of them. I had never *allowed* myself to feel this way about them. I had kept them locked out, scared of the childhood pain it might unleash if I allowed myself to feel love. But no more. I felt a wave of surprising gratitude towards Denucci, for forcing me to take the job in London, so I could be closer to this wonderful woman who had already changed my life forever.

February

Blocking

jeweller's first cuts
give you your eternal form
the moment of truth

Leaving Italy was so hard, but Luca and I had agreed I could go home once a month and I'd promised myself that this *permanent* position was only until the Denucci case was over. I couldn't help but contrast my new flat with my Milan apartment. Milan's white walls, shuttered windows and steam-clean floor tiles gave a sense of space and freshness that cooled in hot weather and stayed warm with gentle heating in winter. My place in London was a ground floor flat, in a leafy street in an area that was pretending to be an urban village. Hard-pollarded London plane trees gave cars shelter and blocked views. The carpets told stories of a decade of tenants, with parties and pets and vacuums that never quite got them clean. Before I had bought the place I had lifted a few corners and promised myself that my first job would be to liberate the Victorian floorboards they covered.

The walls were painted in pastels and marred by years of furniture scrapes and bumps of boxes. These too would be redecorated, though Sophie had advised me to opt for a warmer cream, rather than white, which she knew from experience could feel cold and unwelcoming in an English winter.

One thing I loved already, though, was my blue front door. It reminded me of the colour of Sophie's eyes. And the sky of an Italian August.

Despite its failings, I felt a tingle of excitement as I turned the key in its stiff lock, the day I moved in. The front door opened on to what the estate agent had rather grandly termed the 'entrance hall', which the rest of us would more accurately have described as 'a poorly lit corridor with an intrusive coat and shoe rack and mud-splattered walls'. But I didn't care. The coolness of the

Victorian floor tiles took me back to my childhood siestas, when anything but lying on the hard, polished stone floor felt too hot. I suspected I wouldn't have that problem here.

The bathroom was off to the left, but the less said about that, the better. It was cold, damp and cramped, with a radiator that sometimes chose to work, but mostly just dripped dark-orange staining liquid onto the scuffed linoleum flooring. I would have to make friends with the musty smell in there. No amount of cleaning was likely to shift it. I guessed it was a *feature* of the property.

Then, on the right, was my bedroom. It faced onto the street, giving me zero privacy, but I figured I was rarely there during daylight and would have the curtains closed in the evenings. It grudgingly allowed a double bed and a wardrobe, but only just, plus two tiny bedside tables. Most of my bulky bits were stored in boxes, under the bed, mouse-proof, just in case, on Nonna's advice. She had read an article once about London rats and had never stopped worrying since the moment I had told her I was moving here. But, as she said, that was what a nonna was for – to make sure her *nipote* was well looked-after.

The gentle yellow walls helped me to forget it was a north-facing room – something that would have been a bonus back in Italy – bringing back memories of home, of spring sunshine through half-closed blinds. The biggest difference between my room back at home and the one here in London was the thickness of my duvet. I'd never had to keep out the cold at night before. The farmhouse and my flat in Milan were built to handle freezing winters and boiling summers. This seemed to be *new news* to my London home.

At the end of the corridor came the main living space, or rather the *only* living space. Within the first few weeks, the lounge had wooden floorboards again, which Sophie helped me to sand and scrub and seal. That made an incredible mess. They polished up beautifully and gave an extra warmth to the room, once we had sealed up the gaps that let the winter draughts through like fast-moving razor blades of icy-cold air. There was a tiny Victorian fireplace, with an open fire hearth, but I hadn't had the courage to use it yet, in case one of the upstairs neighbours had taken out their part of the chimney and I killed myself with the smoke. This being England, despite having lived here for nearly a month now, I hadn't met any of the fellow occupants of this former Victorian home, now turned into four flats – at least not to talk to and certainly not to ask them about chimneys. Getting someone in to check that was a job for 'later', whenever that might mean.

I bought the lounge a deep red sofa and a friendly armchair. The kitchen and table were in one corner, and that's where I worked, whenever I worked from home. It faced the French doors that opened out onto the sole reason I bought this flat: the garden, with its solitary cherry tree.

The garden was small – very small – though 'generously proportioned' had been the estate-agent's phrase. And compared to most houses round here, he was right. It faced south and it actually got the sun. I had seen the photographic evidence in the sales brochure, but I hadn't been here much in daylight yet, what with working all hours and it still being the end of winter. I was going to have to trust on that one.

I had a small patio area, right outside the kitchen, a lawn the size of a couple of duvets and then my cherry tree. I could just see signs of the first buds forming and I kept catching myself wishing them luck, hoping that spring frosts wouldn't kill the blossoms.

I loved sitting beneath it, with my eyes softly closed, feeling the glossy red-brown bark, smooth under my fingertips; I could almost catch the birdsong, the breezes and the memories of home. My cherry tree. My very own cherry tree.

Dad would have laughed. "A cherry tree? What are you doing having one of those in the middle of London? And what use is a single cherry tree to anyone anyway, except the birds?"

Exactly that. It was a single tree. It was *my* cherry tree. And, in the middle of London, it anchored me,to remind me of who I really was. And, in his funny old way, I think Dad would have understood.

Anna had been nagging me, again, about flat-hunting. I only stay at her place when I'm working late these days and I never bring Christof here. Although she has never said anything, Anna has made it silently clear that he isn't welcome. I barely see her now.

We had looked at a few flats to share after I got back from Italy after Christmas, but there was nothing we could agree on. Considering what we were trading up from, nearly all of them were an improvement, with our double-budget. But I had been too busy to keep up with the viewings, so Anna had started seeing them on her own, dropping grumpy hints whenever our ships passed in the night.

Then, when February came, all my spare time was spent helping Christof to decorate his flat. It looks amazing. He had got people in to do the heavy work and repairs, which left us the fun bits, though it took me a week to get the dust out of my hair, ears and nose after we sanded the floorboards.

On Valentine's Day, while I was at work, I got a text from Lucy with two bits of unexpected news: she was pregnant again and her *husband*, Sam, had proposed, despite me thinking they were already married. I was so excited to find out more that I almost wanted to cancel my Valentine's meal with Christof, but it had to wait until the next day.

We met for lunch, back at our favourite coffee shop. "Tell me everything!" I commanded, before we had even finished our hello hug, as she whisked me to a quiet table in the corner where we wouldn't be overheard. She beamed, but the bags under her eyes told stories of sleepless nights and morning sickness. She wiggled the ring finger on her left hand as she picked up her mug of latte and I was near-blinded by a stunning collection of rubies and diamonds. Her face broke into a Cheshire Cat grin and I could see she had been bursting to tell me her news. I really missed working with her, this coffee shop being where we had held most of our team meetings – just the two of us.

"Baby or proposal? Which do you want first?"

"The proposal! I thought you guys were already married?"

She wiggled the finger again in response and dived into the story of the Vegas wedding that had turned out to be invalid. She and Sam had got married there three years ago and the Chapel that had held their wedding wrote to them just after Christmas to break the news that the Elvis impersonator who officiated their ceremony had also been faking his licence to marry people, so their ceremony was invalid.

Lucy had taken it as 'a sign' and she and Sam had had quite a row about whether or not they should stay together. They had reached a stalemate.

"Why didn't you tell me?" I demanded, indignant that such important gossip had been kept from me.

"Because, frankly, it was embarrassing. We didn't want to talk to people about it. No, not even you. But we're going to do it properly this time."

The ring box had been hidden inside the cornflake packet at breakfast the day before. Lucy told me she had been in the middle of a complaint that she couldn't stomach the idea of cold milk, despite the tray Sam had brought her in bed, complete with a miniature vase of flowers, when Sam got insistent about her "at least trying some cornflakes". That was when the penny dropped and she went along with the game.

Once the ring was on her finger, she decided to tell Sam her news: she was six weeks pregnant. It had been a shock to her, because it was only a year after Emma had been born. But they were both over the moon, despite how unexpected it was – they had struggled for years to conceive before Emma had arrived.

"So, when's the Big Day?"

"Actually, it's Easter Saturday, before my bump gets too big and spoils the line of my dress. Can you come?"

Of course I could. I would move everything out of my diary to be there. The rest of the afternoon disappeared in an excited wave of wedding planning and gossip. Harry, my old boss, had taken the news badly this morning, because Lucy wasn't long back from her maternity leave with Emma, but this time he had promised not to get lecherous, expense-fiddling Stuart back to cover for her.

"How about you and Christof," she asked, in a pause between forkfuls of the delicious warm goats' cheese salad we had both ordered. I did the eyebrow thing again, to force her to be more specific with her leading question. "How are things going? Has he asked you to move in yet? How is Anna taking it all? Are you still flat-hunting with her?"

I updated her on the latest news: Anna was blanking me, livid that we hadn't yet moved to a bigger place; Christof was gorgeous and it was fun being with him; but work was so busy that I usually fell asleep not long after we had eaten. And I was worried I was neglecting my friends, because my weekends had been spent helping Christof with his flat, ever since he'd moved in. Lucy could hear me trying to find objections – reasons not to be happy; reasons to avoid admitting that I was besotted. I felt too scared to say it out loud, in case I jinxed things.

Lucy and Christof had met once during his placement before Christmas and we were all due to go out for dinner together in a couple of weeks' time, so she barely knew him, but she could tell how happy we were and I sensed a Jem-level of match-making brewing, especially now Lucy had a ring on her finger. "You two are good together," she smiled, "and he's certainly an improvement on Jamie!" That wasn't hard. "I'd bet you a small fortune that he asks you to move in with him and proposes by the end of the summer."

I laughed her prediction off and tried to ignore my Inner Drama Queen as she dived into a rant about losing my independence. There was a tiny part of me that thought it would be rather wonderful.

"Talking of Jamie," Lucy interrupted my thoughts, "is he still hanging around after work? Or have you got rid of him yet?"

He was still there, like the fragrance of a pair of last summer's running shoes that had been stuffed into a plastic bag, wet and forgotten at the back of a wardrobe until spring. "He doesn't come to my office any more. I think he got the hint once I got back from Italy at Christmas and spent the whole time talking about Christof and the farm and his apartment in Milan and how wonderful he is. But he still keeps texting and phoning. I refuse to pick up *withheld* calls on my mobile these days, in case it's him. It gets me into trouble when it's work clients I'm ignoring."

"What are you going to do about it?" I shook my head. I didn't know. "You're lucky Christof's not the jealous type."

March

Perfecting

so much could go wrong
as the brillianteer shapes
radiant facets

Nonna sent me three precious packets of tomato seeds from home, probably breaking two hundred European food-hygiene laws in the process. We collect them every year. It's part of living on the land. "Why give the seed companies all that money when Mother Nature gives you everything you need, for free?" I heard Nonna's voice in my memories.

She called me yesterday with my strict instructions for planting her seeds. She said she hadn't bothered sending aubergines or peppers; she knew there was little chance of them ripening, in what she says the English laughingly call *summer*. But she held out hope for the tomatoes, especially if her *nipotino* got them started early.

It was mid-March and the south-facing kitchen windowsill looked slightly confused by its twelve little pots of compost; each hopeful that its three little seeds would sprout and grow. As per Nonna's instructions, I brought in water from the water butt and warmed it on the stove until it was tepid. "Never give them cold water!" she commanded. "It'll send them into shock. How would you feel if I threw a bucket of icy winter water over you, when it was time to wake up?"

Looking back, I was pretty sure she had done that at least once, when I was a kid, asleep under a shady tree when I probably should have been helping, but I resisted arguing the point.

"And make sure you never use tap water. Only rain water... unless there's a river or stream or pond near you?"

"You know there's not, Nonna. This is London. And I can hardly trek to the Thames each time I want to fill up my watering can and the water would probably kill the plants anyway! Though I've heard it's much cleaner than it used to be."

She sniffed in unspoken disapproval, but I detected a loving smile in her voice as she explained, perhaps for the tenth time, that the chemicals in the tap water could hurt the seeds and the good bacteria in the soil, forgetting that my pre-sterilised compost had been bought in a shop, not nurtured on the farm. My seeds lay waiting for the sun to wake them up, silently promising a summer full of abundance.

It was only a couple of weeks until Lucy's and Sam's wedding, when I was planning to ask Sophie if she would move in with me. Sophie and I had been getting on better than I could ever have imagined. She was the silver lining in the cloud of this grey, English winter. And I was about to take the biggest emotional risk of my life. I hoped that by the time these tomatoes were seedlings, there would be two of us to enjoy watching them grow. *God, I'm feeling nervous about this!*

I had been waking up at 3 a.m. every day for the last week, worried that she might say no; that asking her would make her run, or that it was far too soon. But my instincts told me she'd say yes. It felt so right. And I know she loves this place, or she wouldn't have put in so much time helping me to gut it and redecorate.

Sophie is impetuous and always lives life to the full, but this was the craziest thing I had ever done. The few months I had known her had changed me more than she would ever realise. And it felt amazing.

If losing Dad as unexpectedly as we did had taught me anything, it was that there is no point in waiting until the 'right moment'. If something feels right and it fills you with love, with happiness, then forget timing, logic, reasoning; take action to make it happen. And that was how I felt about Sophie.

I knew that Luca would freak out at the news. He would remind me of all the reasons why diving in so deeply with my relationship with Sophie was a stupid idea right now. But we hadn't heard anything from Denucci since I had been beaten up last June. Okay, so I was conveniently ignoring the baseball cap in Toulouse. There was no news on the police finding him or me having to testify. And I was sick of having my life on hold, just in case the Camorra came after me.

But, deep down inside, I hated that I still hadn't told Sophie about any of this; that she didn't know the real reason why I had moved to England. I couldn't tell her. Aside from my legal obligations to keep secrets that didn't belong to me, I knew it would freak her out and she'd run a mile. I didn't want to risk that.

April

Polishing

dazzling sparkling gem
your limitless potential
ready to be set

Lucy's wedding was beautiful. She looked radiant in her cream silk dress and she was accompanied up the aisle at the Register Office by little Emma, just toddling, wearing a floaty pink number that she will probably hate her mother for in a decade's time. Sam and Lucy wanted to keep the event small – especially given that they'd had only had a few weeks to organise it – so twenty of us went to a private dining room at a swanky hotel where we spent the afternoon nibbling from the buffet, drinking more champagne than was decent and dancing to Lucy's favourite nineties classic tracks.

Sam looked like the happiest man alive and Lucy was every inch the beautiful bride. She kept wiggling her ring finger at us and giggling about it finally being 'legal'.

I'd had no idea how amazing Christof could look in a suit. He never wore one to work. He had never met anyone at the wedding besides Lucy and Sam, but he did a great job of getting to know everyone. I felt so proud, *wearing* him on my arm. It made me realise how rarely we got to be together and have fun; how much our jobs had taken over. I promised myself I would put in more effort. But juggling everything – everyone – in my life was hard.

On the way home, still wearing winter coats against the evening chill, after a day blessed with sunshine, though not enough to make it feel like spring, I was holding Christof's hand. I felt like the Queen of Sheba, high on champagne and the day's excitement, revelling in the jealous looks sneaked by passing women who seemed to agree with me that Christof was major eye candy today.

"Sophie," he said, in a tone that stopped my musings in their tracks, "there's something I want to talk to you about." Oh, no. I had that feeling of dread that goes with opening my email inbox when I know I have messed something up and Jeff has just found out. *Balloon popped.*

Christof stopped walking, guiding me to the edge of the pavement, with a look so serious it should have been impossible for someone who had as much to drink as us in the past few hours.

"What is it?" I managed. *What's wrong? I thought we were happy?* My Inner Drama Queen had already launched into a torrent of 'I told you so' lectures.

Silence. He turned to face me. He looked nervous. He was still holding my hand – good sign. He was biting his lip. Half of me wanted to kiss him, to hug him, to tell him it would be okay. But the other half was convinced he was about to dump me.

"Okay," he started, pausing again, psyching himself up for something. "Here goes. Sophie, will you move in with me?" My knees wobbled with relief and Christof managed to reach out his spare hand, just in time to help me keep my balance. His brow furrowed, making it clear that hadn't been the reaction he had hoped for. "I know it's still soon, but it seems crazy for you to be living at Anna's, particularly now you're not getting on so well, and well…" My Inner Drama Queen was ranting that moving in for the sake of convenience wasn't good enough. "Well… you know how much I love you, don't you? I want to wake up with you in my arms every single morning."

That sealed it. I grinned. His face lost ten years as he saw my 'yes'. We kissed to seal the deal before Christof hailed a taxi to take us back to what would soon be *our* home.

I moved in the next weekend. There had been no point in

waiting. Christof and I had agreed just to do it and to work out what to do about furniture and the stuff I had in storage afterwards.

But Anna wasn't impressed. It was late on Easter Monday, at the end of the Bank Holiday weekend before I went back to the flat and broke the news. Actually, 'wasn't impressed' didn't come close to describing the nuclear explosion of anger with which she took the news.

We spent a very awkward week together – Christof was back in Milan and visiting the farm – during which Anna didn't waste a single opportunity to tell me all the reasons why I was making a terrible mistake, and to remind me what a dreadful friend I was for breaking my promise to flat-share with her. I saw no point in defending myself. She was right. But did she really think I would ever choose her over Christof? To try to placate her, I agreed to give her two months' notice, paying her the rent we had agreed, so I wasn't 'leaving her in the lurch', as she claimed, although she had always funded this place herself before I'd moved in. I wasn't sure if our friendship would survive this. I just wished she could be happy for me.

The following Saturday, Christof sent a taxi over to collect me and my oversized suitcases. He and I had agreed it was probably better for Anna not to see him right now. I dropped the key through the letterbox as I left to begin the next chapter of my life.

Christof had cleared out space in the wardrobe and the drawers and the bookcases and even the bathroom cabinet for my things, but I could sense the wave of chaos I was bringing with me. He was used to his pristine all-white apartment in Milan and out of the blue here came Sophie with her noise and colourful clothes and mess.

Living with him, it didn't take me long to notice his crazy

quirks, like tapping his foot in time to the music he was singing in his head, or the way he arranged the plates in perfect size-order in the kitchen cupboard, or the way the labels on the tins all had to face forwards. He hated me leaving my razor in the shower and the way my clothes so often missed the laundry basket when I threw them in that general direction, but we were working it out. It's amazing what you can accept and forgive when you're in love.

Over the next few weeks, we settled into a rhythm that worked for us. He did most of the cooking: Nonna had ruined my cooking for him, I couldn't compare. And I organised our social life. Now we were living together, it freed up time for us to see more of our friends and family, or rather *my* friends and family. It still nagged me that Christof hadn't put any roots down here. His friends and family were in Milan. He rarely talked about work. He didn't socialise with his new colleagues. His life in the UK revolved around me, as though he were only visiting. I wasn't convinced that was a good thing, but I couldn't force him to make new friends.

We had my parents and Jem over for dinner and broke the news. Actually, I had already told Jem, but she advised that telling Mum and Dad would work better in person. She was right. They were pleased, but it was clear they'd have preferred a ring on my finger first. I caught Dad muttering about 'living in sin', when they thought I was too far away to hear them, washing up at the sink just a few metres away. Mum told him off and commented that maybe now she would be in with a chance of grandchildren. I shook my head. Neither marriage nor children were in my plans any time soon. For now, I just wanted to enjoy settling down and having fun with my cherry farmer.

Things have been great with Sophie the past couple of months. This evening she had gone out with Lucy and a few old workmates. Lucy being pregnant again meant it would be a quieter night out for the two of them than usual, with Lucy tired and not able to drink. I wasn't sure where they were going, but I knew Sophie would enjoy it. And I was okay with that, now we were getting to spend better quality time together at home.

This evening I had to go out for a working dinner. I hate being out on Monday nights. It leaves me exhausted for the rest of the week and nowhere is fun on a Monday. At the end of a long day, all I ever want is to go home and have some peace and quiet – or Sophie time. Being out in a noisy restaurant, having to shout to make myself heard, straining to understand the English accents of my dinner companions, always feels like torture for me, draining my energy. Small-talk leaves me cold. I feel like a party-pooper. *Wow. That's a ten-year-old's word.* But I'm not antisocial; something Sophie sometimes accuses me of. I just need to ration out my people-energy and I hadn't expected to be going out tonight. It had been a last-minute decision when a meeting overran and we still hadn't reached answers. It was meant to be just me and three of the guys in our department.

Isabella was over for the day for some project or other – a meeting with the UK's Treasury Department I had been told – and she heard the guys discussing their plans. Of course, no red-blooded male would turn down her request to come with us. She didn't even have to get to the fluttering-eyelashes stage. I had had to put up with her sitting next to me for the whole evening, with the guys looking at me as though I had won the lottery. How little they knew her.

We ploughed our way through our starters and main courses, washing them down with liberal quantities of wine so good it was meant to be savoured, not gulped, all on the client's expense account. We had wrapped up the main decisions from today's meeting and the guys had gone outside for a guilty cigarette or three, before ordering desserts.

Actually, only two of them smoked, but all three had gone outside, deliberately leaving me and Isabella alone for a while, even though they knew about Sophie. Their smirks looked like they thought they were doing me a favour. I wondered what hints she had dropped at the office to make that happen.

She came back from *powdering her nose* to find the guys gone.

"Where are they?" she asked me, slipping back into our shared Italian.

"Outside, smoking."

"They'll be gone for a while?" she asked, walking past the back of my chair.

She was standing behind me, looking over my shoulder at my dessert menu, as though trying to decide what to order; standing too close. Deliberately. I felt the hairs on the back of my neck tense. I could hear her breath in my ear. Gentle. Slow. My heart started beating faster. I didn't want it to. She was breathing softly on the back of my neck, like she used to when we were an item and stuck together at work, when she wanted to remind me of the intimacies of the night before.

I felt her moving closer. "Christof," she whispered, almost inaudibly, her cheek so nearly touching my skin.

Her lips brushed the side of my neck, followed by a more intentional kiss. She moved round to bite my earlobe, teasingly. She knew that would drive me crazy. Time slowed down. Lost in the sensations, I let out a sigh of pleasure. Memories of what it felt like to make love to her flooded through my mind – and my body. "Christof, how much do you want me?"

I turned around to look at her, noticing how the soft fabric of her dress had fallen forward, as she leant over me, and I had a glimpse of a naked breast in the dim light of the restaurant. My mind had grown slow – it being so long since I was out in the field – but a memory flashed up, sending shock waves through my system like an electric bull fence. She was wearing an ankle-length, deep blue silk dress and a long split to the thigh of the left leg. My heart stopped and a cold chill crawled over my skin. I remembered this dress. A dress designed to seduce. But it hadn't been Isabella wearing it. I could see the image clearly, in that split second, of the beautiful woman in my hotel in Naples after the Denucci stake-out last April.

My brain screamed at me as I compared the images in my mind. No. This dress was a different type of blue – much more turquoise – and the straps were completely different. Panic over. But it woke me up. I couldn't trust Isabella any more than I could trust the woman in the bar in Naples. It was the bucket of ice-cold water I had needed to bring me back to my senses.

I pulled away and turned in my chair to face her. My thoughts couldn't keep up with the speed my brain wanted to work. A bottle of expensive red wine was getting in the way of clarity.

"Not at all!" I lied. But it was also not a lie. "I'm living with Sophie. Since April. We've moved in together. Would you please leave me alone or I'll have to report you to Luca!"

For a fraction of a second, she looked like a broken woman. She really hadn't known Sophie and I were that close. This was a shock to her. Luca hadn't told her anything, keeping my secret, even though he had gone crazy when I'd told him, reminding me about all the reasons why I shouldn't be distracted by romance or be putting Sophie at risk by giving Denucci a chance of knowing how much she meant to me.

Isabella's glare showed she had assumed Sophie was just an amusement in London. She had thought she could wrap me round her finger, play with me like a bored cat with a wriggling mouse. Then she recovered herself and brought on the full venom of a woman scorned.

"If you think you can undermine me with Luca then you might as well pack your desk up now," she threatened. "The things I could tell him about you would make his toes curl."

"I'm not trying to undermine you, Isabella, and anyway you've got nothing on me!"

"Maybe, but only you and I know that. And I can be very convincing when I need to be."

"I think you should leave."

"She doesn't know you're here with me this evening, does she?"

I didn't respond. She took it, correctly, as confirmation. It didn't matter that it had been a last-minute arrangement and Sophie was already out with Lucy, so there had been no point in stirring up her jealousy about Isabella, after their accidental meeting in Milan at Christmas. If she found out, she'd hit the roof.

"You're lying to her already. How often do you lie to her? About your work? Your past? About the *real* reason why you moved to London? Does she know *any* of it?"

I gave her an icy look that betrayed my anger, my usual poker face failing under the barrage of thoughts that were drowning out my common sense – that and my fear of what this woman might do. I had never seen her look so cold. So full of hatred. So soulless.

"That's not much of a basis for a relationship, is it?"

Again, I didn't respond. Experience had taught me not to play games I couldn't win, especially with Isabella. I refused to rise to her threats. She sensed that she wasn't going to get the fight she was craving. My well-rehearsed poker face returned, convincingly hiding the turmoil and panic she had kicked off inside me.

"You have to face facts, Isabella! I love Sophie and I don't want to let her go. I don't want to be with you. I want to spend the rest of my life with her. And one day I'll find the courage to ask her to do that." The strength with which I meant what I had just said surprised me. I hadn't really thought about it before – the future; maybe marrying Sophie.

Hatred washed the beauty from Isabella's face and it felt like something had snapped. For the briefest moment I thought she might do something irrational. We stared at each other, both refusing to blink. Then she reached for her bag and her shawl, ready to leave the restaurant.

"Do let me know where you're holding the wedding list and I'll make sure to send something… *appropriate*; something to remember me by." She walked away, dignified and malevolent. I felt the power of her threat to sabotage our relationship and suddenly knew how Sleeping Beauty's father had felt when the evil fairy godmother had shown up at the christening and cursed his family's future.

Let it go, Christof. She's just angry. There's nothing she can do.

May

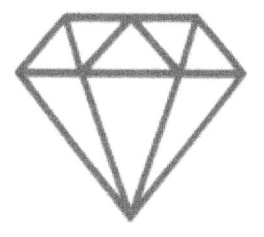

Designing

the perfect setting
exquisite understatement
lets your beauty shine

I got the phone call I had been dreading from Luca on Friday – the one that I knew would turn my life upside down: he told that my name had now been added to my affidavit, because some manager somewhere had ruled that they couldn't justify keeping it off. It hadn't been released to Denucci's lawyer at this stage, but it was no longer anonymous. I hadn't realised until he told me how much I had relaxed, how I had stopped looking over my shoulder for heavies ... how I had started to feel safe.

And sure enough, by the weekend, I was sure I was being watched again. I got off the Tube today and that guy was there again, the one I had seen when Sophie and I went to the Royal Opera House to see *Giselle* last week. He had kept looking away whenever I looked over at him. I had had a bad feeling about him that evening but had put it out of my mind as ridiculous. Even now, I couldn't be certain; it was just a hunch. Nothing worth bothering Luca over yet. Or was it? Was I just putting it off because I knew what Luca would say? Or I thought I did. I was worried he'd pull me out of the UK and ship me somewhere that Denucci's guys wouldn't care about – but nor would I. Or maybe he'd tell me I had to drop Sophie, to protect her. Neither option bore thinking about. That's why I didn't want to admit it. I couldn't *prove* I was being watched, though in my heart, I *knew* I was.

And these feelings couldn't be to do with any of my British cases yet because none of them were advanced enough for anyone involved to want to find me. Most of them were too low-key to have heavies involved. We wanted to start the team off with safer stuff, while they learned the ropes. It wasn't like this was MI5. They hadn't turned into spies. These days most of our investigations were digital, only using fieldwork when we hit a dead end. And the team hadn't got there yet. What they had done so far had been invisible. The people our clients had us investigating didn't know they were under suspicion. That meant that this had to be an Italian case and the only person who would bother following me over here was Denucci.

It made me nervous about Sophie though. I refused to think the word "scared". If they were watching me, how did I know they weren't watching her? I was probably just being paranoid, but I really didn't want Sophie to go out this evening. She had hooked up with Anna, who was only just letting Sophie back into her good books after Sophie had broken her promise about finding a flat with her, and they were off for a classic girls' night out with some of their old friends. It sounded like a hen night without the wedding: too much alcohol and not enough clothes. She had looked drop-dead-gorgeous in her little black dress, but I couldn't help wishing it were a little less 'little', given how many drunk guys she was going to be hanging around tonight. Yes, I was feeling jealous. Part of me was hungry to take that dress off her. Something we hadn't done much of lately.

My stomach tensed. My inner green-eyed monster came out to play whenever I saw Sophie going out without me. I wanted to be with her. But these days I was simply too exhausted. Or craving some downtime. Or maybe wishing she would prioritise the 'two of us' sometimes. I felt the tension in my jaw as I kissed her goodbye, as she left for the evening. She wouldn't be home until long after I was asleep, smelling of booze and her friends' cigarettes, crashing around the bedroom as she got undressed, thinking she was being quiet. And then tomorrow she'd be grumpy and hungover and would try to pick a fight with me.

Sophie thought I was being possessive, trying to stop her from going out all the time. And maybe I was. We'd only been living together for a couple of months and I felt like I hardly saw her. I knew it was partly my fault, with all the travelling for work, but her focus groups happened at least once a week and she didn't get back until after midnight from those. Sometimes they were outside London and she was away for a couple of days. Add in a night out with her friends and we were down to just a couple of evenings a week to spend together.

It's funny, but this might have been easier had we stayed in different countries. We would have made extra effort to see each other once a month and that would have been quality time – just the two of us. But then I'd have been missing the simple joys – normal life – like seeing her smile at me over breakfast, as she scrambled to pack her bag for work. Or the thrill of waking up in the middle of the night with her in my arms, watching her sleeping face in the moonlight through the gap in the curtains, listening to her gentle breathing. Or that amazing feeling of collapsing, exhausted, laughing, after we'd made love when one of us had just returned from a trip away.

I couldn't tell Sophie about my worries. She'd freak out. She'd want me to go to the police. She wouldn't understand how it all worked. It was safer for her if she was able to act normally, to relax and not to look on edge. That would make her a magnet for them, if they were watching her. But how could I keep her safe? And she knew I was hiding something. She had a sixth sense for that. It was why she was so great at her job. I dreaded to think what she was imagining.

I was at home, on my own, catching up on paperwork and promising myself I'd watch a good film later, with a bottle of Italian beer. I still felt homesick for Italy, like I was just a visitor here in London. I longed to go home to Milan – to the farm. But would Sophie come with me?

The cherry tree was helping, though. Its spring blossoms had been beautiful – a miniature version of the orchards I grew up with. On the rare occasions when I was home in daylight I could see the tiny green cherries, dangling on their spindly stems, promising a good harvest come July. It felt like a connection with home, as though my cherry tree here could talk to my cherry trees there. Funny how it still felt weird to think of them as 'mine'. And how much I missed them. And everyone.

Paperwork done, chilled beer bottle in hand, I was about to sit down to leaf through my DVD folder and find something to watch when the doorbell rang. I instantly switched to high alert.

Who on earth can it be at 9 o'clock on a Wednesday? It's late for house-callers. I don't know many people here. My gut says it's not a neighbour asking to borrow some milk or a lost car driver. Adrenalin is raging through my veins, making it hard to think straight.

Attackers don't ring doorbells. Calm down, Christof.

I took a deep, slow breath and walked to the front door, bottle still in my hand, in case I needed it. A young man was standing there, with bushy blonde hair, wearing a courier uniform, smiling hopefully, his motorbike parked on the kerb.

"Parcel for you, sir," he said, rummaging in his deep courier's bag. He pulled out an A4 bubble-wrap envelope. Light brown. Not overly full.

"Name?"

I told him.

"Great. It's for you. 'Ere ya go."

He turned to leave. I had to stop him.

"Hang on! Wait! Don't I have to sign something?" I asked, hoping to delay him so I could think straight and get more information from him.

"Nope. Not one of them kinda jobs. I was told ta drop it off 'ere, mate. Paid cash. Nice tip. In a bit of an 'urry, mind. 'Ad to be by bedtime tonight."

"Thank you," I replied. I still needed to know more. "Do you remember anything about them? Did they give you a name? What did they look like?"

"Didn't see 'em, mate. Dropped it off at the counter and I was the next one free."

"Okay. Thank you. Have a good evening." He waved goodbye and rode off. I made a mental note of the name of the courier company, in case I needed it tomorrow.

I closed my door and headed back to my sofa to open the parcel.

There was no sender name… or course. I hadn't expected there to be.

I wasn't sure about opening it. It was obvious that it wasn't friendly, from the way it had been delivered.

I followed the usual procedure, so before I opened it, I rooted around the back of the cupboard under the sink to find a pair of latex gloves. Thank goodness Sophie was low-key about cleaning and hadn't found my stash. God knows what she'd have thought. I put them on. I didn't want to add any more of my own fingerprints to confuse forensics, if they needed to go through this stuff. And I found my digital camera.

I took photos of the parcel and then opened it carefully, sliding a sharp knife along the tape, and lay the contents out on the table with a large sheet of paper beneath them, to catch anything small that might fall out of the package. I took more photos.

It contained a box. A notecard. An envelope.

The notecard made my heart sink, confirming my deepest fears. I felt sick. I found myself starting to retch and I fought it back. Memories of the attack at last year's cherry festival. *Shit!*

How did this happen? We thought I was in the clear. This is the whole reason I moved to London. Okay, maybe not the whole reason. Isabella was given my case, and I was stuck on 'babysitting' the UK team, banned from field work, to stop this from happening.

The card was A6 size, thick, off-white and high quality. On it were four words and an initial, in the same blood-red ink as the business card I was given at last year's festival by those super-friendly heavies.

Per la tua ragazza. For your girlfriend.

Then there was the now-familiar, elaborate capital 'D'. There was only one person this could be.

I didn't want to think what this might mean. Of course, I knew. But I needed to drown out those thoughts and stay rational.

My hands were trembling as I moved to the box. It was one of our cherry boxes from home, the kind we use to sell glacé cherries at markets and in department stores. Good quality cream card with a deep green foil-embossed tree in the top left-hand corner. I felt sick as I wondered how he had got the box. It was unused, so it wasn't from one of our market stalls. It didn't have our sealing sticker on it or any traces of it having been removed. More photos. The only place we kept unused boxes was at the farm. *Please God, tell me that his heavies haven't been there!*

I wanted to phone Nonna, to check she was okay, then I reminded myself it was past our 10 p.m. deadline and she'd think someone had died. Also, this box would have been in the UK for at least a few days. If something were wrong at the farm, I would already have heard by now. And there was still a chance they had picked one up from our printer, maybe pretending to want a sample to order some of their own. As I forced my adrenalin levels to calm down, I could see this was a more likely option – almost easy for them to do. Even so, I needed to check on security back home. I needed to keep Nonna and the team safe.

I opened the box carefully, very carefully. Inside, nestled in tissue paper, was a small wooden box, beautifully made and highly polished. Not veneer. Lovingly carved from a single piece of wood, from the look of the grain, with a delicate golden hinge at the back and a cutaway at the front to make it easy to open. The kind you would use for a very expensive ring. I took more photos.

I followed protocol and set my camera up on a mini tripod, with the box on the table, and set it to video. I slowly, cautiously opened the box, half-expecting some kind of booby trap. I gasped.

Nestling in a bed of white silk was a ring, with one of the biggest diamonds I had ever seen. It took my breath away, shining brightly as though lit from within. Insanely beautiful. I eased it gently out of the box and held it up to the light to let it sparkle.

Per la tua ragazza. One hell of an engagement ring.

How did they know about Sophie? How on earth did they find me? I was supposed to be off the radar! I was trying hard not to panic. My heart was using my throat as a springboard, trying to get out of my mouth. I put the ring safely back in its beautiful box.

I turned my attention to the third part of the parcel, an A5 Manila envelope. Nothing written on it. The flap wasn't sealed, it was just tucked in so there wouldn't be any DNA on the flap from someone licking it. I took more photos. I opened the envelope and tipped the contents onto the paper on my coffee table.

Four photographs. Black and white. Reportage style, like the ones private detectives use in films. I picked them up and leafed through them, one at a time.

Me. Sophie. Kissing in that quiet side street after the Royal Ballet last week – the tickets from my Christmas present to her. My hand up her skirt. The passion was palpable. My mind flashed back to how we had felt, how we could hardly wait to get home, how amazing the rest of the night had been.

I dropped the photos and sprinted to the bathroom, just in time to aim the contents of my stomach at the loo, rather than the living room floor.

I was dripping in sweat, but shivering with cold. Frozen to the core.

I half-crawled back to the kitchen and poured myself a glass of water from the tap. *Sip it slowly*, I told myself. *Calm down. Get logical. Look at the facts.*

Denucci knew where I lived and he knew I was serious about Sophie. This hugely expensive ring – I didn't want to know who it had last belonged to or how he'd got it; it was bound to have a tainted history – was an offer of payment, a bribe. If I took the ring and dropped the investigation, Sophie would be safe. They would want to see her wearing it, as proof. They would be watching. They also wanted to force me to propose to her so that my future decisions would be tied to her safety.

Clever.

But if I didn't do what they wanted, the photos proved that they knew what she looked like and how to find her. They had been following us. They would know I couldn't always be there to protect her.

I ran to the bathroom and retched again as I realised Sophie was out tonight, unaware of all this. Unprotected. There was nothing more to come up, but it still hurt. I couldn't breathe. *Can I find her? Where did she say she was going?*

Then I remembered they probably knew all of this. It was likely that they had watched her leave before they booked the courier. They wanted me to get the parcel on my own. She would be safe for a few days. They would give me time to make my decision. And, as a fellow Italian, Denucci would expect me to put a bit of planning into the perfect proposal.

How much time does that buy me? A few days? Maybe a week?

Sophie would be visiting her parents this weekend. She'd be safe there. I am supposed to be going with her. I could go to Milan, instead, to see Luca and figure out what we should do. I'd have to find some convincing excuse and Sophie would be livid. But that couldn't be helped. Luca could get the parcel and its contents checked for DNA and fingerprints. It might give us some more leads on the case.

It was late, but I knew I had to tell Luca about this now, not tomorrow. I couldn't pretend I wasn't being followed any more. It was time to come clean. He would go mad at me for not telling him about my suspicions before. But I needed his help on this. I found my mobile and logged into our secure connection. I sent him high-resolution photos of the ring, the card and the photographs. The photographs – my hand up Sophie's skirt – it felt like I was baring my soul.

"These arrived by courier this evening. At my flat. They've been watching me – us. Sophie still not home but assumed safe. Let me know when you can talk. I know it's late."

Sixty seconds later his nickname appeared on my secure message notifications.

"Quite a photo, Casanova. Will call in five. Need to make an excuse to Daniela so she doesn't think I'm calling a mistress!"

A wave of relief rose up from my feet, flooding my body. I didn't have to handle this on my own any more. I didn't have to keep lying. Luca would know what to do.

I caught the red-eye to Milan on Saturday morning and Luca was waiting for me at the airport. We had a lot to get through in just under twenty-four hours, so there was no point in wasting any time.

While I was on the flight, I kept going over the options in my head and it boiled down to two: propose to Sophie and make sure she is seen wearing the ring; or don't - and risk her being seen without it.

I wasn't ready to propose – to get married. This wasn't what I had planned or how I had imagined it would be when I reached that stage of life. Things between us have been a bit too rocky recently, with my travelling and her socialising. We've lost the spark, and we only seem to reconnect with it now when we go away; when it's just the two of us and we aren't so distracted.

If we could get that back, then, yes, I wouldn't ever want to lose her. But I'm not ready to get married. It's such a huge commitment.

The blast of heat hit me as I left the air-conditioned coolness of the airport. A few short months in London with its crisp, dewy late spring mornings had made me forget the rawness of Milan's early summer heat, even in May; the way it pounds your skin and makes your lungs scream for a breeze. And how much I love it.

Back at the office, Luca handed the parcel over to some forensics expert. He was relieved I had followed the procedures correctly. Then he had a vintage jewellery expert on standby to assess and value the ring, so we knew what we were dealing with. He had to invent excuses, because we had agreed that no one but the two of us should know about the ring's connection to Denucci.

In the meantime, he took me to his favourite restaurant to *chat*. Any excuse for getting the company to fund his favourite food, he joked. I pretended to laugh.

It was only a ten-minute walk. The atmosphere was busy enough to let you know it was popular but calm enough to remind you that reserved behaviour was expected and that raucous laughter could head to the bar on the other side of the street, instead. Thick white linen cloths covered round tables holding from two to ten settings, scattered with plenty of space for privacy, funded by the extravagant menu.

An invisible-looking waiter in traditional black and white showed us to Luca's favourite table in the corner, furthest away from any doors or windows. We could talk without being overheard here.

"You haven't brought me here for years, Luca!" I teased him, knowing full well he likes to save this place for entertaining visiting dignitaries or important leads, especially if they were beautiful and female.

"Maybe you've earned it this week," he replied.

The menu was exquisite, with freshly prepared in-season food and price tags that would have made the diamond ring feel quite at home. We decided to pass on wine. We both needed a clear head to work out what to do.

We placed our order and the waiter collected the menus, bringing our mineral water, perfectly chilled. He poured it into each of our glasses with an understated back-hand action. We knew we wouldn't be disturbed for a while now, so Luca turned to me, looking serious.

He didn't say anything. He was staring at me, as though trying to read my mind. After what felt like forever, he said, "Christof, you know how pissed off I was to find out you had moved in with Sophie, after this whole Denucci mess and the *accident* that happened to the fraudster who confessed. To say it was irresponsible of you doesn't even begin to describe the situation." I tried to look defiant, but I hated the thought of Luca being angry with me; of him judging me. "But we are where we are and that's where we need to start with our miracle action plan. We can't pretend that Denucci doesn't know who Sophie is any more. You led him straight to her." He paused for effect. I had barely slept since I'd got the ring, fully aware of this. Sophie's safety had been jeopardised because of me – because I'd put what I wanted ahead of what was right. Luca must have decided I looked suitably chastised, because he shifted back into practical mode. "How likely would you be to ever want to propose to Sophie? Is she a keeper?"

He was direct, as usual. "Yes, it is something I have imagined might lie in our future, but it's not something I'm ready for yet."

"Well, you'd better get ready for it, because you're going to do it. And I suggest tomorrow. It gives her time to think it over and give you a 'yes' before they see her with no ring on her finger and take more *direct* action. You can always break it off later, if that's what you want, once the case is over."

"I couldn't do that. I'd have to mean it, to make this work. I wouldn't want to break her heart like that. And she'll be able to tell if I don't mean it. She's hot like that."

"Then mean it. You've got twenty-four hours. Think about all the reasons why you love her and get daydreaming about the future."

Our main courses arrived and the food would have been as delectable as I remembered from past visits had I been in the mood to enjoy it. Both of us knew there wasn't much more to say and that the decision had been made. I would propose to Sophie, to keep her safe. But I had made a second decision that I wasn't sure Luca was going to like.

"You know I can't testify, don't you?" I asked, badly faking a casual tone, waiting until Luca was mid-mouthful, so he would have time to think before responding. "Double-crossing Denucci would be tantamount to signing my own death warrant. And you know the Camorra would go after Sophie and Nonna first."

Luca shook his head, still chewing, sacrificing manners in his need to reply, "We can find ways to get the message out there that we're pulling the case, secretly keeping Isabella on it, low-key. You *have* to testify. Due to your mess-up, you're the only evidence. And the police will go ballistic if they have to close this case. You know how hard it is to pin anything on someone like Denucci. They have been after him for decades. This is the first evidence they have had in years to actually pin something on him."

"It's not happening, Luca," I interrupted. "Someone, somewhere, has access to information that should be secret and they're letting Denucci treat the police files like Google." He swallowed his mouthful and stared at me.

"And if I ordered you?"

"Do you want me to shout in a place as civilised as this one, Luca?" I asked, feeling rage and confidence rising, like a teenage boy standing up to his father, man-to-man, for the first time. "You need to get your priorities sorted. Surely my life means more to you than this case?"

He said nothing for a while, then sighed in agreement, "I'll get it sorted first thing tomorrow. We'll insist on your affidavit being withdrawn and tell the police you won't be testifying."

The weight I had been carrying since the ring arrived started to lighten. I had been in denial about the risks I was facing; but no more. "Do you know what changed in the case, Luca, to make them come after me now?"

He shook his head. "Nothing, as far as we can see. It doesn't make any sense. The police were still on standby for you to testify, once they located Denucci. But they haven't got him yet, so all of this was still hypothetical. They can't prosecute until they know where he is – and he's still as good as invisible." His use of the past tense on the prosecution reassured me that he knew I meant it; I wasn't going to sacrifice myself to put Denucci behind bars.

When the waiter brought the bill, Luca handed his company credit card over with a flourish, making a point of not even opening the little black folder on its silver tray to look at the figures.

We headed back to the office and each grabbed an espresso. I cupped it in my hands, inhaling its bitter warmth, wishing it could tell me what to do; that it could somehow make this ok.

Luca's phone rang. He picked it up before the second ring. "*Pronto! … Si … Si … Certo.*" He hung up.

"Forensics are done. They have what they need. They'll be keeping everything apart from the ring, which you can pick up on your way to your hotel this evening. My jeweller has valued this ring at – are you ready for this? – €50,000. Even a copy would cost thousands to make and take two weeks apparently. We don't have that time. You're going to have to use the real thing for this."

Shit! This is it. We're both silently agreeing I'm going to propose.

I made that funny air-over-teeth noise normally reserved for builders when asked how much a roof repair might cost. That was one hell of a rock to hand over when I knew it had a dubious history and I wasn't sure I wanted to be part of its future.

"You'll have to give her the ring. Of course, it will be evidence in the trial, if that happens, so it will belong to the State at that point, but we'll cross that bridge if we come to it."

I hadn't thought of that. "There's no way I could afford to

replace that ring!"

"We'll have to get creative. Let's not worry about that just now, Christof. The main thing is to get it on her finger. Fast!"

"But I'm not sure I want to give her a tainted diamond to celebrate our marriage promise. You know as well as I do that Denucci won't have got this ring by honourable means. Who knows who used to own it, or how they gave it up. Could you imagine asking Daniela to wear it, knowing what its history might be? Or that it's being used for blackmail?"

"Do you want to protect Sophie?" I gave Luca a look that told him to stop asking stupid questions. "Then she's going to have to be seen wearing that ring. Get over it. Show him you're taking the bribe. It's your only option now."

He was right. I had to do this. I had to put this ring's past behind me so that Sophie and I could have a future.

"Do you think the police have got any chance of putting Denucci behind bars?"

"I'm not going to lie to you; this case was the first thing they've been able to pin on him in years and now we've got no evidence. We've been looking into money trails, but Isabella isn't making the progress we had hoped for with tracing Denucci or his inner circle, and the police are hitting more dead ends than a blindfolded man in a maze. It's not the kind of work we normally do. To be honest, I wish you were back here. I'm sure we'd be closer to answers by now. Isabella's heart isn't in it," I smiled inside, glad that she wasn't his Golden Girl any more. He jolted me back to reality. "That's why we've got to protect Sophie. We had used our usual contacts to put the word out that you had been reassigned, but it's clear that they didn't believe us."

We sat in silence for a while. Then Luca asked me, "What time is your flight tomorrow?"

"9 a.m." I replied.

"You need distracting. Come to my place for dinner and catch up with Daniela and the kids. They'd love to see you. And it looks like you need to get in some emergency training for married life."

I was really pissed off with Christof for cancelling on me this weekend. Mum and Dad had been looking forward to seeing him and I had barely seen them since he moved to London. Okay, so their ten-week cruise around the Caribbean this spring, celebrating Dad's retirement, meant they hadn't been around much, but we needed to put in a bit more effort.

I was pretty sure this weekend was going to be death-by-cruise-photos, but I had brought enough wine with me to survive even the most extended slide show. Jonathan and Delilah were going to be there with the precious grandchildren, so that should distract Mum and Dad a bit. To be honest, after Wednesday night's partying and Thursday night's focus group, I'd have been happy to spend the weekend catching up on sleep. The kids have as little interest in me as I have in them, so at least I wouldn't be subject to them bouncing on my bed, long before sunrise, screaming at the world with frustration because Aunty Sophie wouldn't get up to play with them.

What is it about kids that people love so much? They seem to spend the first three years pouring bodily fluids out of every orifice for someone else to clear up, then the next ten years demanding payment in recognition of their very existence by being given every toy, game and gadget they have ever seen in a TV ad, and then they turn into slouchy teenagers who want nothing to do with you for half a decade. Nowadays, according to the research, they then head off to uni, rack up mountains of debt, pick up a few well-chosen STDs and then end up living back at home until their parents finally find a way to chuck them out ... hopefully before they reach thirty.

Not for me. Thank goodness Christof isn't clucky.

I got the train to Shenfield after work and experienced the bliss of the Friday evening commute. Why do they give out free newspapers at London stations? What are we supposed to do with them? Rush hour commuters are packed into carriages with so little space that even a sardine would lodge a formal complaint. Then they think you're going to have the elbow room to read a newspaper? The guy next to me poked me in the eye with the corner of his *Evening Standard* – twice – in the first five minutes. Of course, I'm British, so *I* apologised to *him*.

I cricked my neck between the next few stations, trying to read the headlines on the newspaper of the person standing in front of me. They were about some celebrity who had taken a stand on a campaign that was important to them, but then it turned out they had their facts wrong. I wondered how much of that story was true.

My feet were killing me in my work shoes as I stood in the train carriage, so tightly crammed against my fellow travellers that I could probably have bent my knees and taken the weight off my toes without falling over. I had given a big presentation for our key client today. It had gone well, fuelled by caffeine and doughnuts to keep me awake. But that had meant wearing posh togs and high heels. It was an unwritten rule at work that presentations equalled heels for the women.

"They're not just buying your research results, Sophie," Jeff had told me, a few days before my first client pitch on behalf of the firm, "they're buying their perceived confidence in you. And that means you need to look the part: snappy suit; gorgeous heels

– not high enough to make you wobble, but enough to make an impression. I want the clients to be impressed by how you look. And no, I don't have a budget for that. That's why I pay you so much."

He doesn't. Not compared to the Creative Director, who wouldn't be able to produce his advertising campaigns without my research; who only shows up for a few hours a day because he needs to "rest his creative genius". But pay structures in tiny companies were never likely to be fair.

I longed for a seat to be able to take off these stupid shoes, even for a few minutes. I wouldn't have cared had people stared at me. I wished I had brought my headphones, then I could have listened to some music. Instead, I practised that deep breathing technique that Jem's yoga teacher had taught me. It helped. If nothing else, it passed the time. But I was sure I felt a bit more relaxed by the time we pulled in at Shenfield station.

The moment I was in Dad's car, the shoes were off. Relief. Joy. The simple things in life. I wished Christof were here. He is a genius at easing tension out of my tired feet, sitting on the sofa, chatting about our days while dinner cooks on the other side of his lounge. Ten minutes of his magic hands and I feel like I've had a full-body massage. I miss him. I realised that the only evening I had seen him in the past week was Tuesday. That wasn't great. And we had rowed about Jamie – again. I had been in the shower when my phone had bleeped with a text. It was next to Christof on the coffee table by the sofa, where he had been reading an Italian business magazine, and the preview of the message flashed up on the screen.

"Are you around later? Need to talk. J."

It was one of the few times I have ever seen Christof lose his cool. He had been angry about Jamie still hanging around when 'surely he knows we're living together?' He accused me of not having told him. I found myself defending my right to keep my old friends, even though I had already told Jamie to leave me alone.

"Mum's done macaroni cheese for dinner," Dad interrupted my thoughts. *Yay! My childhood favourite.* No one makes it quite like Mum does. I've tried to sneak the recipe from her, reverse-engineering it as I look over her shoulder, but I can never reproduce it at home. Her version involves half a mountain of cheese and just enough of the right kind of mustard. But even if I use what look like the exact same ingredients, mine is always a pale imitation.

Dinner was mouth-watering and I resigned myself to what was going to be inevitable – the interrogation over Christof.

Where was he? *Milan.* Why hadn't he come? *Emergency for work.* What was he doing in Milan? *Ditto.* Doesn't he know we haven't seen him for ages? *You've been on a cruise.* What is it he does? *I'm not really sure.* Don't you guys talk? *Yes, of course we do, but we've got more interesting things to talk about than work.* Are you sure you're happy dear? *Yes, of course we are...*

But would I tell them if I weren't? No. And are we really happy? I wasn't sure. This wasn't how I had imagined it would be. I guess I'd stupidly thought that every day would feel like the cherry festival, or Toulouse, or Christmas at his farm, wrapped up in our love – and lust – and hopes for the future: relaxed, happy, there for each other. Instead it feels like we're extras in a film, being shuffled from one set to another, wearing different characters' costumes ten times a week, waving at each other as we pass and occasionally chatting in the queue for the canteen lorry.

Saturday morning brought me a deliciously long lie-in until just after ten. If Christof had been here, we'd have been crammed into the tiny single bed from my teens, forced to hug each other all night, to stop ourselves from falling onto the floor, and we'd have sneaked in a silent quickie, before Mum could interrupt us with her deliberately loud stamping up the stairs, carrying a tray with two cups of tea we hadn't asked for. We'd have giggled. I missed him. It's weird how I miss him more now we are living together than I used to when we were living apart, back in October, when we only saw each other a few times a week.

Christof knows how busy I am and how much he travels. He really could put in a bit more effort. How on earth can I talk to him about that though, without causing his inner Italian to get defensive? I know I need to find a way.

The Big Cruise Slideshow was planned for after the kids were asleep. Part of me toyed with feeding them so much sugar that they wouldn't sleep until midnight, as a means of postponing the agony, but I was pretty sure Delilah would thwart those plans. I got to spend the day pottering, catching up on some work, nattering with Dad. Then at 2 p.m. my phone rang. International and unavailable. That would be Christof… on so many levels.

I excused myself from Dad's greenhouse tour and went back up to my room to take the call in private. After falling asleep on my own last night, I was feeling a bit frosty and Christof wasn't slow on picking that up.

"Is something wrong, Sophie?"

"I'm pissed off that you dumped us this weekend. Really, what was so important about your bloody precious work that it couldn't wait until next week?"

Silence. I hadn't wanted a row, but that was what we were going to get.

"Well?"

It's part of what makes me so good at my job, being like a terrier and never giving up, once I'm on the scent. I do the same with picking fights. I keep going until I get a rise. And woe betide anyone who stands calmly in the way of a good row.

"I'm so sorry I had to go away this weekend. I really miss you, Sophie. I miss you when we're at home too."

"Oh, so you want me to stop going out and quit my job? Would that make you happy?" I snapped. We both knew I was taking his comments to the extreme, but I wanted to get an emotional response from him. No, I didn't *want* it; I *needed* it. I needed him to show me some passion.

"Don't be silly, Sophie."

"Oh, so I'm silly now?" I was close to yelling, I was so cross with him. This felt good! Though I wouldn't have admitted that to him.

"Sophie," he sounded truly sad. I stopped. Something melted. The anger drained away. I wanted to cry.

"Sophie, I miss you so much. I just want to be with you, like we are whenever we go away, out of London. I want to find a way to bring that home. I don't know how."

My heart was swelling up, ready to burst. I wanted that too. I didn't answer.

"Sophie? Are you still there?"

Deep breath. "I miss you Christof."

I heard him sigh – relief – nearly a thousand miles away.

"I'm done here sooner than I had expected, so I can get an earlier flight in the morning. How about I meet your train at Liverpool Street at two tomorrow? I'd like to take you out for the afternoon. We could call it a date?"

My Inner Drama Queen didn't want to let him off so lightly. *What about your weekend bag? Doesn't he think about you carrying that all around London?* I told her I could dump it at work. *Doesn't he know you'll be tired?* Why would I be tired? I can sleep in again tomorrow and it's not like Death-By-Cruise-Slideshow is going to be taxing this evening. *He needs to know who's boss; make him pay for ditching you this weekend!* Oh, sod you, you've got a point.

"That would be lovely. But you dumped me this weekend and left me to the mercy of interrogation-by-parents at dinner last night about where you were, so you can bring me champagne to make up for it."

"That's a deal." I could hear him smiling again. I realised I hadn't seen him smile for a while. We had stopped making each other laugh. That had to change.

"I'll see you at two then. Will you be wearing a red carnation and carrying a copy of the *Financial Times* under your left arm?" I was only half-joking.

"It's not quite that long since we last saw each other, *carina*, though I can't wait to see you."

"You too."

"Sophie?" he hesitated.

"Yes?"

"I love you."

Wow. I hadn't heard those words for a while. Why had we stopped telling each other that? So soon. I love the way it makes me tingle when he says it. I could tell he really meant it today. *Oh shit, I'm talking to myself, not him. He'll be waiting for me to say something.* I could hear his disappointment in the silence.

"I love it when you say that." It was the best I could manage. I felt his smile fade at the other end of the phone. *Oh poop. Why do I pull on a full bodysuit of armour when I talk about my emotions with him? I don't have a problem with it, with the girls. Why can't I tell him how I feel?* I sensed I had about three nanoseconds to rescue this. Deep breath. I needed to mean this. Why was it so hard to tell the truth?

"Christof, I love you. I really do. And I miss you so much. I can't wait to see you tomorrow." I blurted it out as a single word and hoped he could decode it.

He was grinning from ear to ear. I could hear it in his reply. "I can't wait to see you tomorrow either." He meant it.

I was on a high and that made me invincible. There was nothing that Jonathan, Delilah, the kids, or the cruise photos, could throw at me that would get in the way of me looking forward to seeing Christof again tomorrow.

Today was the Big Day. I had to ask Sophie to spend the rest of her life with me, for all the wrong reasons. Or were they wrong? I wanted to protect her from Denucci's mob and this was the only way that Luca and I could think of doing it. We had reasonable intelligence that his team was prepared to carry out their threat from last summer of me 'not walking away' from the next attack. And they had made their target clear: Sophie would be first. I couldn't bear to see her hurt… because of me. I was going to follow Luca's advice and ask her to marry me.

Is this insane? Probably. Would I have done it anyway? Probably. Yes. Just not yet.

We were still ironing out the kinks from moving in together. I didn't think she was ready for this kind of commitment. She was so used to being independent.

Would she turn me down? It was a massive thing. If she wasn't ready to spend more time with me when we were already living together, why would she want to marry me? To promise to live together for the rest of our lives? But I couldn't risk her saying no.

I needed to make this proposal as romantic as I could, to

drum up the excitement to the level that would get this proposal sweeping her off her feet; so she would say yes. I hated lying to her. This felt manipulative. I needed to deal with that. I needed to get to the point where I wasn't lying to her. I needed to convince myself first, if I wanted to convince her.

I was due to be back in London late morning. I had to propose tonight, to give Sophie a few days to think it over, to make sure she would be wearing the ring in public by the end of the week. I needed a fail-safe proposal plan by the plane landed.

I boarded the plane and tried to relax my mind, to get into my creative zone. *What kinds of things does Sophie love doing? What have we not done since we've lived in London? What did she love most about the cherry festival? And Toulouse?*

The weather was forecast to be good today and this needed to be something I could organise at really short notice. I had called Sophie last night and let her know I wanted to meet her at Liverpool Street to take her out for the afternoon. By the time I got home, I had hatched a plan and made the phone calls. I had to pull in a few favours – and pay some hefty premiums – but I needed to make this convincing. I caught myself thinking that it was a pity work didn't have a budget to cover this, then I realised that was the wrong attitude to have about proposing to the woman I love!

I checked the time her train was due in and made sure I met her at the end of the platform, after the ticket barrier. She saw me from a distance and I noticed her pace quicken: a good sign. We hugged and kissed hello, then I took her bag from her shoulder.

"Will you let me carry it *this* time?" I asked, knowing she was thinking back to the time we'd met at the cherry festival, when she wouldn't let me carry her enormous rucksack, despite being exhausted from the heat, and unable to find her hotel. She laughed and kissed me again. I could feel she had let me back in. Her defences were down. We held hands as I walked her to the street entrance to the station.

"Aren't we using the Tube?" she asked.

I gestured towards the black limo waiting in the pick-up area.

"Your carriage, my lady."

She laughed, surprised to see a perfectly attired chauffeur holding the door open and smiling at her. She stepped into the back seat and the driver closed the door behind her. I put her bag in the boot and he opened the door for me on the other side. I turned to look at her, reminding myself how beautiful she is.

"How were your parents?"

"Oh, the usual. But I don't really want to talk about them. Where are you taking me?"

"You'll see."

We held hands on the air-conditioned back seat, watching the world go by as the driver took us towards the river, pulling up at a jetty with a small motor cruiser moored at it, gleaming brightly in the sunshine. I remembered going on one of these in Hong Kong once. The captain had called it a "junk". Far from it.

"Is this where we're going?" she asked, looking surprised. A quick flash of panic told me I had never taken her on a boat before. I had no idea if she had sea legs. But she was smiling, so I guessed we were okay.

Our driver opened Sophie's door and she got out. "My bag?" she asked.

"It's okay, we'll get it back later." She nodded in agreement.

The captain of the boat was waiting for us at the jetty. "Welcome to the *Prometheus*," he said, gesturing for us to walk up the gang plank, closing the gate behind us. The limo drove away.

"I'll be up top, doing the steering and stuff. Make yourselves at home. Yell if you need anything. But you should have everything you need here." He smiled and walked up the ladder to the top deck.

I guided Sophie round to the back of the boat and she laughed as she saw a blue-checked picnic blanket laid out for us, just like the one we had used at the festival (that had taken some finding this morning). There were two pizza boxes, napkins, champagne in its ice bucket, crystal flutes and little pots of deli treats.

"Does it remind you of anywhere?" I asked.

She pointed at the miniature vase in the middle of the blanket, plain and white with a single-stemmed red honeysuckle in it. "Where did you find that?" she asked.

I smiled. The magic was working. She was remembering the red honeysuckle that covered the gate to the Secret Garden, back at the cherry festival.

"And in the boxes…?"

"You guessed it. Piping hot pizza. The recipe might not be quite as good as in Italy, but it's the best London could provide. Open it; see if you remember the toppings."

She lifted each lid in turn, looked at me and grinned. Somehow, I had found somewhere that could replicate the exact toppings we had in the Secret Garden … or as close as a non-Italian pizzeria could manage. We sat down on the picnic blanket and kissed. It felt so good to be back with her.

"I don't want it to get cold. Let's eat!" I said, pouring us each a glass of champagne.

I handed her a glass and raised a toast. "To us!"

"To us!"

We ate and talked and kissed and drank champagne, talking about the good times we had spent together, our hopes for things we could do in the future; just enjoying being together. The passing London skyline was wasted on us.

"But what about the cherries? There aren't any cherries!" Sophie teased, once we had cleared the picnic blanket of its treats. I walked over to the fridge and opened the door, pulling out two china plates, each with a perfect cherry pavlova on it. She grinned a smile so radiant it made my heart skip a beat.

A second bottle of champagne was well on its way to being empty by the time we reached St Katharine Docks, where the boat moored, leaving us a short walk to our next stop – as planned.

"Did you enjoy your picnic?" asked the captain, as he came down to secure his boat.

"It was wonderful, thank you!" replied Sophie, meaning it. The captain grinned as he opened the gate for us and waved goodbye.

We were hand in hand, walking along the riverbank. "Where to now?" Sophie asked, with the look of excitement on her face telling me my plan was working – so far.

"We're going to find an oak tree," I replied, pointing at the picnic blanket, still under my arm. Sophie laughed and hugged me.

"Thank you." We kissed. Again. It had been a wonderful afternoon so far.

We walked for five minutes to a tiny park next to the Tower of London, the home of the Crown Jewels. Unlike the bigger parks, like St James and Hyde Park, it was fairly quiet, ignored by tourists and locals alike. It didn't take long to find a big, old shady London plane tree, with no one sitting under it. I reached inside the picnic blanket and pulled out a white sash, which I tied round the tree. Sophie looked confused. "Imagine I'm an oak tree," it said. She laughed. There were no oaks in this part of the city. She nodded her approval. I spread out the blanket and we lay back looking up at the blue sky: the same sky we had lost ourselves in at the cherry festival, yet different. I realised, as I remembered back, that that was when I had fallen in love with Sophie, when she was talking about how the London blue sky was so different from the Italian one.

"It's so long since we have taken time out, just for us. We're so busy. I miss that. I miss you." She glanced over at me, vaguely curious, tipsy on the champagne, wary of criticism and I could sense her bracing for a fight.

Shit, I'm doing it. "Sophie, there's something I need to ask you.

"Hmm... Yes?" she replied, pushing herself up on her elbows, distracted by family with a kite, ambitiously trying to fly it, despite the cramped space and lack of breeze.

Okay, let's build up to this.

"Do you think you could get some time off work in early July?"

I've got her attention now. That's a start! We were both sitting up now. She was facing me.

"Will you come with me for a week to Perugia, for the jazz festival? It's in early July. I know you'd love it and it would be incredible to get a whole week to ourselves. Do you think you could get the time off work?"

Her face lit up and she looked at me with a big grin. "Oh, I'm desperate for a holiday and I really would love to have some quiet time together." I didn't like to tell her that the Umbria Jazz was really very noisy and very busy. "I feel like London is always pulling me in so many directions. I don't have any client commitments until later in the month, so I'm sure I can sort something out with Jeff."

"That's wonderful," I said, really meaning it, thinking back to how I'd felt about being with her in Toulouse and realising how hungry I was for more of that.

"There's something else, though," I said, my heart starting to race. *This is it. Just do it, Christof.* She looked at me quizzically; those beautiful blue eyes shining and happy. "There's a special reason I want to take you to Perugia as soon as we can get away."

"Oh, what's that?"

Just. Do. It!

"I'm hoping it might be a special holiday; one we remember forever," I was starting to garble my words, trying to convince myself I meant this, which I knew I did, but I couldn't risk her saying no. "One to celebrate our engagement?"

She looked confused, surprised and then excited. I was down on one knee, ring box out of pocket.

"Sophie, will you marry me?"

Shit. Just. Done. It. Holding out the box. Lid is still down. Bugger. Am I supposed to show her the ring to help her with her decision? A big rock gets a yes; a small one gets a no? Should I have kept it in my pocket until she said yes? She's crying. No. That wasn't what was supposed to happen. She said something. I'm too busy talking to myself to hear it.

"Pardon?"

"For fuck's sake, Christof, at least listen to the reply if you're going to propose to me! I said yes!"

She was grinning and crying – joy in her eyes. We had connected again; defences down. I suddenly realised how much I wanted this – to be with her forever. A torrent of love and excitement was flooding through every cell in my body; fireworks were going off inside me.

People had stopped to watch and there was a round of applause. I guessed we were meant to hug. I stood up and swept her off her feet in a monster hug and a kiss, the ring box still in my hand, behind her back.

After a few moments we calmed down. The tension and

worry of the past few days melted with such suddenness that it threatened to make my knees give way. Sophie had said yes and now my little white lie would keep her safe. I was fully aware I should have been overflowing with happiness and joy, not just relief - the woman I loved had just agreed to marry me - which added a generous portion of guilt to the mix.

"Wasn't there a box you wanted to show me?" she asked, with a cheeky grin, knowing full well what would be inside it. I went back on one knee and opened the box lid, showing her the diamond. She gasped – a good reaction – and so did what was now a crowd. Phone cameras pretend-clicked and flashed. I sensed invisible digital zooms making the most of this moment and wondered whether we would go viral on social media. So much the better if we did... if it reached Denucci.

I took out the ring and slipped it onto her finger. She held her hand out to admire it.

"It's beautiful! Where did you get it from?"

I hated lying to her, but this one was a must. I had agreed that with Luca. She must never know the truth about this. No one but Luca and I ever would. I had carefully planned an answer that didn't involve a single *real* lie, but still covered the truth.

"It's why I went to Milan this weekend; to sort this. I know a jeweller who specialises in vintage jewellery; the kind of thing you just can't get from modern workshops. I knew it had to be the right ring for you. Do you like it?"

"I love it!"

We kissed again and the crowd sighed in unison.

Shouts of "congratulations" and "nice one, mate" echoed around us. One woman was crying with emotion. Another was pointing at Sophie's ring and then her own and saying something sharp to the man standing next to her, who was looking sheepish in his Armani suit.

"I think we ought to get out of here. What do you reckon?" I asked. She smiled back at me a smile I wanted to see every day for the rest of my life. I held her hand, noticing the unfamiliar glint of her diamond as we walked through the London evening sunshine, waving goodbye to our audience as we left.

Our limo was waiting for us where I had agreed to meet him, to take us home without the bustle of the Underground. Sophie kept staring at the ring and I couldn't help wondering if she preferred it to me. I wondered if seeing her love it so much would always make me feel guilty, or whether I would get used to it, over time. We got back to my flat and the driver opened the car door for her, handing me the rucksack and giving her back the picnic blanket. We waved him goodbye.

We were barely through the door of the flat when we got to do what we had wanted to do since we left the park. We make love for hours. We hadn't done that in ages. We fell asleep, exhausted, wrapped in each other's arms, as the birds started to sing, not caring that we had got to get up for work soon. It was wonderful. Perfect. Now it was sinking in, I knew I had never felt as happy in my life as I did in that moment.

As Sophie drifted off to sleep, she looked at the ring one more time, as though to check it was real and hadn't suffered from Cinderella's midnight curse. "It's a perfect fit!" she said. "How did you know?"

It hit me like one of Denucci's thugs' punches: how *did* they know?

June

Gifted

a month's salary
to be treasured forever
when given with love

"Show it to me then!" commanded Jem, almost before we had sat down at our red and white table outside her favourite brasserie.

I held out my hand to let the light catch my diamond. I had done that a lot in the last few days. Responses had ranged from simple, stunned silence to "Wow! He must be loaded!" and the slightly more appropriate, "Wow! He must really love you!"

It was funny how people judged a man by the size of the rock he gave his fiancée. Christof isn't normally flashy with money; his clothes take up a quarter of the space of mine in our bedroom and most of his kitchen equipment is older than him. He doesn't splash out. But, whatever his attitude towards money, this was one hell of a ring.

"This rock landed on your ring finger, out of the blue?" was Jem's considered response.

"How do you mean?"

"I mean, you weren't expecting him to propose?"

"No, actually, I wasn't. We've been going through a bit of a rough patch in the past month. You know, getting used to being a couple and living together. Things weren't *bad*, but they weren't *great*. But this," I wiggled my ring finger on my left hand, "proves he wants to make it work. It changes everything."

"Does it?"

"Of course!"

"In what way?"

I had to pause and think about this. Jem wasn't as excited as I had thought she would be. After all, marrying off her godchildren was something she saw as a key part of her godmotherly duties.

"I'm not sure about this," she said, waving an accusatory finger at the ring, "Do you love him?"

"Yes!"

"But getting married is such a big commitment."

"Look, I know things have been tough. He's been doing too much travelling and I've been working too hard; too many late nights with focus groups. We haven't been seeing each other much and he doesn't want to go out as much as I do, so I've been spending time with the girls on my own."

"How much time are you spending together ... as a couple?"

I thought back over the last few weeks. I hadn't realised how little it was.

"Maybe one or two evenings a week, and some time at weekends."

"That's not much; not in this early stage of living together."

"But he never wants to go out with me!"

"Has it occurred to you that he might be exhausted? New country? New job? Setting up a new team? Travelling to and from Italy? Living in a language that isn't his native tongue? That stresses your brain and wears you out, you know." Jem could see she was having the desired effect. "And maybe he's objecting to you going out so much because he really wants to spend time with you? Making the most of the honeymoon effect of moving in together? He might not want to go out with a big bunch of your girlfriends."

Cogs were visibly turning in my brain. I hadn't thought about this from Christof's point of view. And Jem knew it.

"How much effort are *you* actually putting into the relationship, *chica*?" she delivered this as a final blow to my already wincing ego. "When did you last *show* Christof how much he means to you, through your actions – *your* choices?"

The penny dropped. *You're right. Damn you.*

"What could you do, to prove to him – and to yourself – that you're putting your relationship at the top of your priority list, Sophie?"

She gave me time to mull it over. She ordered us a house cocktail each while we started to look through the menu for dinner. It flashed through my mind: should I be out with Jem tonight or at home with Christof? Then I remembered he had flown over to Italy for three days to support the end of the cherry festival and to sign the deal for selling the harvest. He'd got a much better offer this year without Signor Perillo lurking with his lies, and it had technically been wrapped up back in April, but tradition said he had to go to the festival to meet with the buyer, to show him the quality and shake hands on the final contract.

We had talked about whether I should go with him, but I was snowed under with work. And we both knew we'd just be trying to recapture the magic of last summer when we'd met at the festival. It wouldn't work. He was off for three nights and he would be back on Sunday. I was really missing him. We had been keeping in touch with messages and I knew this was important to him. Pietro had organised most of the festival work for him but, as the owner of the farm, he was expected to show up in person.

"I'm not trying to make you feel guilty," Jem interrupted my daydreaming, "but you've just agreed to spend the rest of your life with this guy and, so far, it doesn't look like you've been putting a huge amount of effort into the relationship. You need to turn this around now, if you want to still be happy when you're eighty."

I wrinkled my nose with involuntary disgust at the thought of Christof and me being *old*.

Jem laughed.

"Just have a think about it. How could you work with him to build a rock-solid foundation for this relationship, so that you're strong together, no matter what happens?"

My blank face told her I was clueless on this.

"What are you ordering?" I asked, in a blatant attempt to change the subject.

"We're both having the special," she replied. "I need to take one decision out of your life."

I didn't object. She called the waiter over and ordered. He collected the menus and brought us our water and a basket of straight-from-the-oven slices of baguette.

"Any ideas yet?"

I shook my head.

"It's really simple, Sophie; it's just about shifting your attitude. You've got to *mean* it. When you're at home, be present, not working on your laptop or thinking about other stuff. Make sure you connect – properly connect, not *distractedly* connect – every day. Make eye contact. Smile. Listen to him. Focus on the little things that show you love him. Involve him in your decisions on how you spend your time. It doesn't mean you have to become a hermit. But it does mean you're promising to consider how your choices might affect him. Otherwise you're living a lie, pretending to be a couple, whilst secretly still seeing yourself as single."

I winced at her accusation and returned with an attack. "Are you lecturing me? You're not exactly the queen of long-term relationships yourself!"

"You know I'm not lecturing you, Sophie. And I'm not surprised you're getting a bit defensive. I just want to help you to have a wonderful marriage. And that has to start with taking *actions* that show how much you care, not just day-dreaming your way through the years."

I retracted the cactus spines… a little. Humble-pie time?

Our dishes arrived: fresh pasta with red peppers, beans and courgettes, wrapped in a blue cheese and cream sauce, seasoned with just enough freshly ground black pepper. Making the most of the flavours bought me more thinking time.

"You're right, Jem. I haven't been putting in much effort. I've been treating Christof more like a flatmate than a boyfriend, but I need him to make changes too."

"Then you need to talk to him about that. The quickest way to damage a relationship is to store up resentments and expect the other person to second-guess what's wrong."

I carried on with the game of trying to get my tagliatelle to stay on my fork long enough to reach my mouth without redecorating my dark blue top.

"When do I need to get my new hat by?"

I gave her a blank look.

"Wedding? Date?"

"Oh, we haven't set a date yet."

Jem's left eyebrow lifted, implying she was waiting for an explanation.

"We talked about it and you know how wedding plans take over your life, once you've started?"

Jem nodded.

"Well, we decided to give ourselves the whole summer, just to enjoy being engaged. We'll start the wedding planning in the winter. If anyone tries to give us their *advice* – which has started already – we'll ask them to get back to us after Christmas. Mum isn't impressed, but I think she understands."

"Wise decision. Make the most of the two-of-you time, before everyone else starts interfering."

"And Jeff, my boss at work, has been a bit weird about it." Jem raised that eyebrow in her questioning way, waiting for me to continue. "He has been making a real fuss about how he doesn't want me getting distracted with wedding plans and honeymoon ideas. He hasn't even congratulated me yet."

Jem paused and sighed. "I'm guessing he's seen it happen before. Marriage and motherhood would cost his business dearly, when he relies on someone like you in a senior position. I know it's not fair." She hesitated and grinned. "Maybe he fancies you?"

I almost spat a French bean across the table as I half-choked on it, letting her know what a stupid idea I thought that was. "More likely he wants to fire me for being incompetent!"

Jem's expression let me know what she thought of that comment, but she refrained from contradicting me.

We finished our main course and the waiter cleared the plates, returning with a hopeful look and the dessert menus. Jem chose her favourite: sticky-toffee pudding with custard. I picked the obvious choice: sweet cherry pie with vanilla ice cream.

"What else is on your mind?" asked Jem. I was an open book to her.

I took a deliberately slow mouthful of the cherry pie. The pastry was crisp, with caramelised sugar sprinkled on top, and the cherries inside melted as I ate them, flooding my taste buds with the sweetness of summer. The vanilla ice cream was what Dad calls "proper vanilla". I could see the tiny black specs from the seeds of the vanilla pod; "None of that *vanilla essence* nonsense!" I heard him say in my head.

I took a deep breath and came clean with Jem.

"It's Jamie."

"Oh God, you're not still seeing him, are you? Can't you tell that Christof is a much better catch?"

"It's nothing like that. I had told him to leave me alone. I had blocked him on my phone and Facebook because I was sick of him messaging me. But he still shows up, like a bad smell."

"He's still in love with you."

"I'm not sure. He's not in with a chance and he knows it. But I can't believe it's coincidence that I just *happen* to bump into him as often as I do. He's being smarmy and flattering and it's driving me crazy." I bought myself time with another spoonful of a pie I was barely tasting. "The other night I went out for a drink after work with the team to celebrate getting engaged to Christof," I started.

"Shouldn't Christof have been invited?" interrupted Jem.

I paused. Yes, probably. She knew the answer.

"Anyway, we had just sat at the tables outside when somehow Jamie was there, sitting opposite me and being super-friendly, like long-lost soulmates. Seriously, if the team at work hadn't already met Christof, they'd think I was seeing Jamie. And showing him the ring made no difference. It didn't change his behaviour in any way."

"And how does Christof feel about your Old Flame hanging around?"

She knew I hadn't told him. "He doesn't know most of it. It makes him angry. So…" I was mumbling into my now-empty wine glass, "so I make up excuses and stuff."

"So you're lying to him?"

My cheeks went as red as the cherries had been, telling Jem her guess had hit the target. How did Christof feel about this? I wasn't sure I had given that much thought. I fiddled with my engagement ring to distract myself. It felt heavy and strange on my finger. I had been lying to the man I had just agreed to marry about hanging out with my ex. "He's not impressed." I admitted. "I think he's getting jealous. He says he wonders if Jamie spends more time with me than he does. It's ridiculous."

"Is it? Really? See it from his point of view. How much are

you talking about Jamie?"

"Not at all."

"Then how does he know you're spending time with him?"

"Because there were a couple of times over the past few months I was due to meet up with Christof and Jamie was there, hanging around like a skunk's farewell fragrance when Christof arrived."

"You need to get this sorted. You can't have Jamie spoiling what you and Christof have. I'm assuming you've told him to get lost? To leave you alone?" Yes, I had, but how much effort had I *really* made to get rid of him? "So … you're secretly flattered by the attention he's giving you, which you feel Christof isn't … but which Christof can't because you hardly ever see him?"

She had nailed it. I stared at my cherry pie, watching the melting ice cream turn the crisp pastry to soggy mush.

"Sophie, you have to make it clear to Jamie that you don't want to see him anymore. He's a shit. He's damaging your relationship with Christof and he isn't adding anything positive to your life. He needs to get his marching orders." I nodded. "Do you want me to get him *sorted*? I've got *people* who can help."

"No way! I can handle this!" I was only half-shocked. It wasn't the first time that Jem had offered to take *direct action* to fix messes I had found myself in.

"Well, at least let me look into things a bit for you. I've got a hunch that there's something going on with the guy. Let me do that to help?"

"Okay. But keep it subtle, please."

"*Moi*? Unsubtle? I don't know what you mean!" she retorted, feigning offence. We both laughed. It broke the tension. Eating out with Jem proved the old adage that there was no such thing as a free lunch. She made me work hard for my food. And I was grateful to her for it. I had plenty to think about, as I headed home to our empty flat and hugged Christof's pillow until I fell asleep.

It had taken a long time for Anna to forgive me for leaving her in the lurch over our flat-hunting, but we were back to being friends now. Tonight was only the second time I had seen her since I got engaged. When I met her after work a few days after the proposal, she wasn't very impressed by the ring. *Bling* she called it. She made it clear she thought I was making a massive mistake and did her best to pour cold water over my excitement. We didn't talk for a while. But she'd texted me today and said she had something she needed to ask me, so I popped round to her flat after work. Christof said he was cooking dinner, so I was going to go back home to eat, which annoyed Anna, because she had wanted to make an evening of it. It also annoyed Christof, because he knew I'd be back later than promised and too tired to chat with him. *As usual, Sophie upsets everyone.*

I arrived at Anna's place at six and she was less frosty than the last time I'd seen her, which was a relief. The kettle was already on and within minutes we were sitting on her sofa – my old bed – chatting away. We were talking about joint friends, Anna's work, my team and as much as I could legally tell her about my research clients, and even the weather. But there was a tension; something she wasn't saying. We had lost that easy-going, putting-the-world-to-rights vibe we used to have. I knew it was the engagement. She was worried it was going to change everything. And she was probably right.

Lucy had told me that when she and Sam got engaged one of her friends had been really grumpy with her, and when they set the date for the wedding the friend ditched her, because it was "too short notice", as though they had chosen the date to spite her. After that, she'd never spoken to Lucy again; she wouldn't return calls; she ignored messages; and she pretended to be out if Lucy went to her house. It broke Lucy's heart. She never found out what she had done wrong. Her old friend had liked Sam and it wasn't as though she thought he was a psychopath. Surely she should have been happy for them?

I didn't want that happening with Anna, so I was putting in the effort. But it was nearly seven and I had promised Christof I'd leave not long after that, so I had to go in with the "Didn't you say you had something to tell me?" prompt.

Anna's face darkened to match the atmosphere in her flat. She put her mug down on the table between us and looked me in the eyes.

"What is it, Anna?" I asked, starting to panic. "Is something wrong? Are you ill? Are you in trouble?"

"Oh no, nothing like that. I'm fine."

"Well, what did you call me over for?"

She hesitated, took a visibly deep breath and dived in. "That Italian woman Christof used to see... you know, the one who makes supermodels look ugly?"

"Isabella," I half-spat. I wasn't sure I wanted to hear what was coming next.

"Are you really sure that relationship is over?"

She might as well have stabbed me for the shock I felt at having my deepest fears spoken out loud by someone else. I pulled myself together. "Of course it is!" I insisted, far too light-heartedly. And Anna knew it. She could smell blood like a shark after a shipwreck and wanted to go in for the kill – the 'kill' being my relationship with Christof of course. Or perhaps my happiness, in general. *Bitch. Why is she doing this?* I sang 'la la la' to myself in my head, hoping to drown out whatever she was about to say. If I didn't give it my attention, then it wouldn't be real.

"What do you think he's *really* doing all those times he goes to Milan?"

"Working, of course! Or checking on the farm." I snapped back, with the ferocity of a terrier fighting for its favourite toy.

"But where is he staying?"

"In his flat!"

"Really? Who with?"

I didn't answer. Instead I let my Inner Pedant discuss whether she should have asked "with whom?"

"He could do those visits as day trips, you know … if he wanted to. I've checked the flight times."

Was she gathering evidence for a conspiracy plot? "This is crazy. What proof do you have? Why are you saying these things, Anna? Remember that night when you lied to me about him having phoned after I got back from Italy?" I wasn't sure if I had forgiven her for that yet, even though it was nearly a year ago now.

"I saw them."

Ice cold filled my stomach, seeping into my chest and freezing my thoughts. This couldn't be right. Christof wouldn't cheat on me, would he? But Anna wouldn't lie. Not about this?

"I saw them, on a Monday evening about three weeks ago, going into some posh restaurant I walked past on my way home from work. He had his arm round her. He was smiling at her. They looked happy, relaxed. Just the two of them."

I didn't have anything to say. My Inner Drama Queen was freaking out so much I couldn't actually hear what she was saying, despite her living in my head. Anna knew she had won. She was clever enough to let silence finish her work. Eventually, fighting back the tears and waves of rage, having unravelled the past few weeks' cluttered memories, I managed to speak.

"That was the night he came home smelling of perfume.

Something flowery. He told me he had gone out for dinner with work colleagues, to wrap up some meeting. I picked a fight – a big one. He promised me he was telling the truth. I believed him. I'm such an idiot."

Anna went to the fridge and brought back a bottle of wine with two glasses. A New Zealand Sauvignon Blanc, my favourite. She knew that. She must have had it ready, waiting for me to need it. She had planned all of this. *The cow.*

"Why are you only telling me this now? Why didn't you tell me before I agreed to marry him?" I knew I was projecting my rage – the betrayal – on Anna, but she was a good target.

"I didn't want to hurt you, Sophie. Then you were waving the bling- at me and I didn't think you would listen." She started to open the wine, ready to turn this into a session of man-bashing.

"No! I'm not staying." I was almost shouting. She looked hurt; angry. "I have to have this out with him."

I grabbed my bag and headed out of the door without even saying goodbye to her. That wasn't what she had expected. But I needed to find out the truth. Had Christof been lying to me? *The shit! Has he been having an affair with Isabella? Then why propose to me? But Anna saw them. And she was right, all those Milan trips could have been day trips, couldn't they?*

By the time I was back at the flat I was fired up to scream at him; to hurt him; to make him pay for what he had done.

I had had to go back to Italy last weekend to help with the final few days of the cherry festival. Sophie had been more understanding than I had expected. We had agreed there was no point in her coming with me. She'd have felt left out – it was all business – and we would have kept comparing it to the wonders of last year. I knew that wouldn't do us any good.

I stayed with Nonna at the farm on Saturday night before flying back to London on Sunday morning. It was good to see her and she was on a high, with us having got such a good price for the full harvest this year: the opposite of last year's stress. It meant much less work for her this summer. She was looking more frail than I had seen her before. Paler. Slower. I didn't want to think about what it might mean. She assured me she was fine. But I wasn't sure if I could trust her to tell me the truth. And things are still icy with Pietro. He's so angry at me living in England instead of Italy that I'm sure my leverage over him with Francesco is the only reason he's still managing the farm.

Sophie met me at the airport, which was a wonderful surprise. I got home to find she had prepared a "welcome home" late lunch, which was one of the few times she had ever cooked in what I still, in my head, think of as *my* flat, despite her stuff being everywhere. She seemed to be putting in more effort at the moment. I wasn't complaining. We spent the afternoon curled up on the sofa, snuggled under a blanket against an unseasonably cold, grey, drizzly June afternoon, pretending to watch an old black and white film, whilst thoroughly making up for not having seen each other for a few days.

Since then, we'd been so busy talking about the festival and her meet-up with Jem and our plans for our holiday in Perugia that Sophie hadn't asked me much about Nonna or Pietro or anyone, other than checking that they were well. I was relieved. I had realised on the plane back to London that I hadn't mentioned our engagement to any of them, which shocked me, and also made me wonder why.

I convinced myself that it was because they would get too

excited and want to force us to get planning the Big Day already. I didn't want to get into arguments about getting married in London or in Italy or – Sophie's parents' preference – in their village church just outside of Shenfield. It's a place they hadn't set foot in since Sophie's christening, but that didn't stop it from being the only permissible location for our wedding.

But in my heart I knew it wasn't about avoiding the excitement and stress for them. It was because *I'm* not excited. Yes, I know in my heart that I want to spend the rest of my life with Sophie and I know we can make this work. But I also know I proposed to her for the wrong reasons. I used what was probably a stolen ring and I was accepting a blackmail offer by giving it to her. It stabbed me with guilt and fear every time I saw it on her finger. Every time I see it, I feel like I'm lying to her – which I am.

I didn't tell Nonna or Pietro. Or Giovanni, when he asked me about *bella Sofia* from last year, though he beamed to hear we're still together. And he asked about the sister option again. I won't be telling Sophie I hadn't told them. She'd go mad at me. And she'd be right to.

I should be proud of the commitment that Sophie and I have made to each other. But it just doesn't feel right. Yet.

I read once that the energy with which you sign a contract is the energy that runs through that contract. If you sign a tenancy agreement to rent a flat, while feeling full of desperation and worry, that's how living there will feel.

How did that translate into proposing to the most wonderful woman I had ever met, when we had been rowing about her seeing her ex-boyfriend, when I was feeling guilty about not trusting her and I was only giving her the ring to stop her from being attacked by hardened criminals? What kind of energy would run through *that* marriage? Because surely the engagement ring was a contract?

I was really happy to be engaged to Sophie, but I hated the fact that Denucci had backed me into it, and that it was his illicit ring I had been forced to use. None of this felt right. And I was sure that Sophie could sense there was something off.

And then there was the photo I got at the flat today. Plain A4 envelope: self-sealing, so there was no DNA. Hand-delivered. A single photo. Black and white again.

It was Sophie. Looking happy, wearing her engagement ring, with a glass of chilled white wine in her hand, lifting it to her mouth. She really was beautiful. I knew who the photo was from before I turned it over and saw the handwritten message on the back:

"Hai scelto bene. Se cambi idea, le faremo una visita."

You made the right decision. Change your mind and she'll get a visit.

Relief and fear fought for pride of place on my inner podium. I felt such relief that Denucci had seen proof that I had accepted the deal. But I also knew he wasn't stupid. If he caught any sign of things changing, or me being back on the case, he had made it clear that Sophie's safety was at risk.

I was about to text Luca to let him know the latest when something made me turn the photo back over and look at it more carefully. Who was Sophie with? She was staring into someone's eyes, smiling. Who was it?

Jamie.

Anger raged inside of me, threatening to make me do something I would regret. Something *he* would regret. I now understood why duels were such a popular way of settling offences in the past.

We're engaged! She's got to stop hanging around with this guy.

How can she keep telling me sob stories about him stalking her when she looks so happy in his company?

After a few minutes of wanting to punch walls, I calmed down enough to be rational about this. I was going to have to talk to her about it tonight and I was dreading how she would react. But I needed to know what was going on. I had never mentioned to Sophie what I had seen back in the autumn, when she had been in that bar with Jamie. Maybe I had hoped it would just go away. Like a cold draught from a cellar door on a summer's day, I realised I didn't trust my fiancée.

I had been expecting her back an hour ago, but I knew how she could lose track of time when she was with Anna. I didn't want to come across as possessive, so I ate my share of dinner on my own and left hers in the oven, on low, for whenever she got back.

I was sitting on the sofa with a book when the front door opened and then slammed shut with enough force to trigger a minor avalanche in a small Alpine village a thousand miles away. My heart sank. I was tired of being in the firing line when Sophie had had a bad day. I didn't look up when she stamped into the room, hoping that keeping my nose in my book might mean I avoided some of her anger.

"Are you fucking Isabella?"

That got my attention. And it trumped my 'why are you lying to me about hanging around with Jamie?' I looked up and saw the venom she was firing at me. She was white. Her eyes were wide. She would probably have foamed at the mouth if she had been able to, she was so livid.

"What on earth gave you that idea?" I didn't see any point in denying it until I knew how she had got this one into her head.

"Are you or aren't you? Don't avoid the question!"

I sighed. I probably rolled my eyes as well. That didn't help. If it were possible, Sophie seemed to get even more angry.

"Well?" she screamed so loudly that I was waiting for pictures to jump off the wall and glasses to shatter.

"No, of course I'm not."

"Then why did you lie to me about being with her on that Monday night when you came home stinking of perfume?"

Fuck! I had thought we had been through that one. But she was right. I hadn't been entirely truthful.

"I didn't lie. I had a working dinner with some of the guys in our department and Isabella was over for the night. She got them to invite her along."

"Why didn't you tell me?"

"Why should I? It wasn't important. I didn't want to stress you out."

"Was it her perfume? That flowery shit I could smell on you."

"Possibly." *Definitely.*

"How did it get on you?"

"I don't know," except that I did. "She wears a lot of the stuff."

"You're still lying to me."

Please God, tell me she didn't have someone in the restaurant, watching what Isabella did while the guys were on their fag break.

"You were seen, walking into the restaurant together with your arm round her."

For a moment I was genuinely confused. I didn't have my arm round Isabella. I'd rather slow-dance with a hungry piranha than have physical contact with her.

"Who saw me and what, exactly, did they see?"

"Anna was over the road, going to the Tube after work. She saw you with your arm round her."

"I didn't have my arm round her. I might have had my arm behind her, but I promise you there was no physical contact. From Anna's viewpoint she wouldn't have been able to see the difference."

"So, you're not shagging her?"

"No, I'm not. And you know I'm not. And you can call the guys at work if you don't believe me," I said, holding out my phone to her, "they were the ones who invited her."

She was starting to deflate. But she still needed someone to be angry about. Rather than admitting that Anna was wrong – that she had been shit-stirring again – it had to get vented at me. I hate how insecure Sophie is about Isabella. I'd just proposed to her, for goodness' sake. Couldn't she take that as evidence that I wasn't interested in anyone else? But I knew I needed to let her calm down before I talked to her about the photos. Otherwise we'd be in for her using her €50,000 engagement ring for shot-put practice, trying to make holes in the walls with it.

I turned back to reading my book as she stamped to our room to change out of her work clothes. When she came back she had calmed down enough that I felt the courage to raise the Jamie issue.

"Sophie, there's something I need to talk to you about."

She stopped and looked at me. I wondered what was going through her head. I showed her the photograph, being careful not to let her see the writing on the back. She looked sheepish.

"Could you help me to understand this, please?"

The irony was not lost on either of us. She had heard a bit of worthless gossip from Anna about Isabella and had tried to destroy our relationship with it, screaming abuse and hatred at me. I had photographic evidence of her with her ex, someone she claimed she couldn't stand, after our engagement, and the atmosphere was still calm.

"He was waiting for me after work. I went out for a quick drink with the guys to celebrate our engagement. He tagged along. I was telling him to leave me alone – that I'm engaged. I will never be interested in him again."

"It's not a photo that exactly screams 'leave me alone', Sophie."

"You've got to believe me!"

Have I? I'm not convinced. For someone she claims is a stalker, she looks strangely happy to see him. I needed to calm down; to think; to work out how to move through this evening's mess. And she hadn't asked me how I got the photo. I wouldn't have had a credible answer for that. I was relying on her anger and indignation to protect me from awkward questions.

"Dinner's in the oven. I've eaten. You were late. You promised you wouldn't be. I'm going outside."

She walked to the kitchen area, seemed to pause and then turned on me, half-screaming, "Anyway, what the fuck are you doing with a photo of me like that? Have you hired a private detective?"

I should never have shown her the photo. That was a stupid mistake. I had been angry. Impulsive. Now I was going to have to lie – fast. "It was sent to me at work. The team have been practising low-key surveillance techniques for an investigation they're doing. It was someone's idea of a sick practical joke. I'm going to be having words with them tomorrow." A big, fat lie, to protect her from the truth.

I picked up the photograph and put it back in its envelope, taking it to our bedroom to hide it, so she couldn't translate Denucci's note on the back, then I walked back through the lounge to the garden for some thinking space.

It was so late it was nearly dark, despite being so close to the longest day. I loved how private it felt, sitting under my cherry tree, hidden by its drooping branches, heavy with a thick curtain of leaves and ripening cherries, as though the terrace houses around my flat had melted away.

I sat out there, thinking, for the long, slow time it took for Sophie to eat her dried-out dinner. I didn't want to argue with her, but she had to admit that the photo with Jamie was incriminating. And that stuff about him stalking her? It was just ridiculous. If he were and she didn't like it, why would she let him join her and her work colleagues for drinks? It struck me that I had only been out with them once. I wondered if they saw more of him than me.

But I had calmed down now. I needed to find a way to trust her on this, to believe that she wasn't lying to me, like I'd been lying to her. I didn't believe she was having an affair with Jamie. But I wished she would stay away from him.

I thought back to the photo and the message on the back of it. A threat. No doubt about that. I shivered. Denucci wasn't stupid. He would still be watching us. I still hadn't told Luca about the message. I'd told him about the photo, so he could relax a bit. But if I told him about Denucci's threat to Sophie he would tell me we had to split up, to protect her. I couldn't face that.

I can handle this. It's only a week until we go away and I know she'll be safe until then. There's no way Denucci will know where we are then, so I can relax for a few weeks. We had extended our Perugia trip to include some time in my favourite village in the Italian mountains. I put my sense of unease to the back of my mind, where I could ignore its persistent nagging.

I was about to get up and stretch, to go back inside and make my peace with Sophie, when I saw the light from the back door as it opened. Sophie was silhouetted in the doorway carrying two wine glasses. The light caught the deep red liquid as she edged her way cautiously down the steps. A peace offering.

She picked a path to the cherry tree, not benefiting from the night vision I had from sitting out here since just after sunset. I could smell the earthy richness of the soil under the cherry tree;

families cooking their evening dinner in the neighbouring terraces; the scent of the deep-scarlet rose that tumbled over the fence beside me.

"May I sit down?" she asked.

I paused a moment and then patted the ground next to me. She sat and handed me my glass.

"I'm sorry," she said. It was unusual for her to apologise first. She was really trying. "I feel really cross that you think there could be something between me and Jamie. He's an idiot. Really. And I feel angry that you won't believe he's been following me around. He feels like a stalker. I know I need to be firmer with him, maybe even threaten him with reporting him to the police, if he won't leave me alone."

"Thank you." I sipped the wine. It was a good one. Not too strong. Deep red. Fragrant. Singing songs of the land where the grapes grew.

"I was on such a high that evening, so happy that you had proposed, I guess I would have welcomed Saddam Hussein to the table, had he asked to join us." I didn't point out how difficult that would have been, given that we had all seen the video footage of the dictator's demise. "And I accept that you didn't go out for dinner with just Isabella; that there were other people from work there. It's just that she's so stunning, I always feel like you're comparing me with her. I hate the fact that you work together."

"I'm sorry Anna upset you with what she saw. I admit that, in isolation, it might have looked bad. But you have to stop comparing yourself to Isabella. I don't. You are the most beautiful creature in my world. Your smile makes my heart skip a beat. Your eyes melt me to the soul. And as for the rest of you," she giggled as my fingertips moved over her body to illustrate my point, "you leave me helpless to resist you."

She leaned her head against my shoulder and we both started to relax. We kissed. It felt good.

"Isabella is one of the most heartless people I have ever known. Her beauty means she expects the world to revolve around her. And she hates that, for me, it doesn't."

"But you went out with her for ages?"

"Yes, but that was years ago, before I knew her for who she really was. She opened my eyes to how cruel she can be. I might have forgiven her, but I'll never, ever trust her again."

"Can we stop talking about her?" Sophie asked, as she moved over to kiss me again, her hand wandering towards my groin, unbuckling my belt and unbuttoning my jeans. I didn't object. I blissed out as she gave me the best blow job I can ever remember, leaning back against my cherry tree. Why was it I felt like I had just been *bought?*

July

Fairytales

a lifetime's longing
for the partner of their dreams
but is 'yes' enough?

It was a couple of days before we were going on holiday and we had invited Jem round to the flat for dinner. It was the first time she had been here on her own. The last time she had visited had been with Mum and Dad and I had cooked a disaster of a Sunday lunch – one Mum would probably never allow me to forget.

So, to make sure I didn't poison her, Christof was cooking. Nonna had taught him well. He was so relaxed in the kitchen. Everything happened at just the right time, in the right order, perfectly done. Tonight's delicacy was homemade tagliatelle with asparagus carbonara. It was one of his favourite things to cook in early summer.

I was late home as usual, so the pasta was already made, hanging on its rack, drying, ready to be cooked. It would only take two minutes.

Christof had already made a fabulously colourful salad, including the very first of his tomatoes, an early variety called Latah, apparently, raised lovingly on a sunny windowsill. I didn't care, as long as they tasted good. We had rocket from the garden and also a red curly leafed lettuce. He apologised for having had to buy the peppers though. The English summer meant his wouldn't ripen until late August. He was trying to grow them, despite Nonna's misgivings. It was funny to hear him feeling guilty about not having grown the entire meal himself. My previous boyfriends would have been proud just to have managed to *make* a salad, let alone to have *grown* it.

The carbonara was meat-free, but used the same sauce. Somehow, by the magic of Christof, it all came together in under five minutes, once we were ready.

Jem and I laid the table and uncorked the wine. It was a red, perfectly matched to the dish, Christof told us. He'd managed to hunt down one from the area where we were going to on holiday, to give Jem a taste of what she was missing out on. "Not that you'd want me coming with you though?" she joked.

Dinner was divine. It was great to see Jem and Christof so relaxed around each other: my two favourite people. I probably shouldn't admit that to Mum.

We were clearing away the dinner plates when Christof's mobile rang. He ducked over to check who it was.

"It's Luca. I'm sorry. I need to take this," he apologised, picking up his phone and jabbering away in Italian, moving into our bedroom. Something must have been important for Luca to disturb him so late. I made a mental note, yet again, that I needed to put in more effort to learn his mother tongue. Or should I say *father tongue*, in his case?

Jem came straight over to me, the moment Christof had closed the door.

"I've got an update!" she whispered, conspiratorially.

"About Jamie?"

"Yes!"

"What have you found out?"

"He's heavily in debt. Very heavily. Gambling. Rash investing. About to lose his house."

"And the Jag?" I asked with a slight smirk, remembering the grief that car had caused me when we were together.

"Oh, that's long gone."

"What has all this got to do with me?"

"He's used up all of his capital. He's living beyond his means and he's got in with a bad crowd. Loan sharks. The posh version. And you're about to marry a wealthy landowner."

Was I? I hadn't thought about it that way. But yes, I guessed Christof owned a farm, a business, a flat in a prime area of Milan, a flat where they had the cherry festival and this place, minus the mortgage, in a good area of suburban London. Compared to Jamie that made him rolling in it. He was so low-key about it I hadn't noticed.

"Does he want money from me?"

"Probably not. My sources weren't clear on that one. He stopped hanging around for a while, over Christmas and New Year, didn't he?"

"Yes, how do you know?"

"He had found himself a posh girlfriend. One who would get him a title, as well as a gold mine."

"What happened?"

"He proposed. Her Daddy did his homework; checked his background. Jamie was out of the running before he could place a bet on himself."

I laughed. Not kind. But it was funny to think of Jamie imagining himself as set for life, only to be found out so easily. I was sure that Daddy had contacts who could easily tell him what he needed to know.

"Basically, Jamie is a total shit. And he's desperate. The fact that he's hanging around you like a fart after a dodgy kebab means he thinks you're useful to him. My advice is to get rid. Permanently."

She was right. I needed to get tough. No more sympathy. Jamie didn't like me. He saw me as one of his options for finding the money to clear his debts, so he could rack up more.

"Do you want me to have him *warned off*?"

There was deep code in those two words – 'warned off' – and I knew what Jem was hinting at. She could get it *sorted* for me. But I didn't want that kind of thing on my conscience, so I shook my head and smiled at her.

"Very kind of you to offer, but I'll handle this. Christof and I go away at the weekend. That should put him off the trail. Maybe he'll find someone else to stalk. I've told him to leave me alone, now I'm engaged, and if he doesn't maybe I'll threaten to call the police."

"Okay, as you wish. But remember, the offer's there if he doesn't take no for an answer."

Christof walked back through the door, oblivious to our discussion, with a forced-looking smile on his face.

"Everything okay?" I asked.

"Of course! Why wouldn't it be?" he asked, slightly too brightly.

We carried on with the evening, relaxed, but Jem and I knew we were all hiding something. Jem left late, full of smiles and good wishes for our holiday.

It was just past the longest day, so the evening was still light despite the hour, with a long, slow sunset turning the windows of the neighbouring terraces into orange and pink lights. We sat on a picnic blanket under the cherry tree and finished the night off with a cherry brandy. Christof told me it was some of the last batch his Dad had made. He was down to the last two bottles. He told me he wanted to save the final bottle to celebrate our wedding, whenever we decided that would be. I curled up close to him and wrapped my arms around him. He did the same. My head was resting in that comfy spot just below his shoulder, where I could hear his heart beating. I felt so contented. I wanted to stay like this forever.

The cherries were nearly ripe. I wondered if the birds would steal the harvest before we got back from Italy.

I'm pretty sure that Sophie would have insisted on walking, had she known how bumpy the landing would be. For those who are afraid of flying, there should be a warning on the plane ticket to Perugia: the hills at the end of the journey give you a decent dose of turbulence and the flight path to land at the airport does a viciously sharp turn as the plane descends, which could lead an unsuspecting, nervous passenger to start thinking they were down to their last few minutes. I held Sophie's hand for most of the flight, to help her stay calm, and I distracted her with sufficient in-flight, pre-lunch wine and enough inane conversation to take her mind off the journey, but she nearly freaked out at that final approach. As she carried her suitcase down the steps to the tarmac she looked so relieved I thought, for a moment, she was about to do a Pope John Paul II and kiss the ground.

Perugia airport is one of the tiniest international airports ever. By the time you make it through passport control, your luggage is already waiting for you on a bench, if you brought any. We headed outside into the baking July heat to take a taxi to our apartment, just twenty minutes away. Perugia comes in two parts: the old town and the new town. It's built on a hill and the new town, with its tower blocks and car parking, forms a moat-like ring at the bottom of the hill, hugging the old town, which is squeezed onto the hilltop. The old town's streets lend themselves to being pedestrianised, with ancient churches and halls, and it has hardly changed in hundreds of years.

Our bus took us to the bottom of the *minimetro*, in the old town. It's a funicular railway that connects the two parts of the town. Then we took the underground escalators through a ruined sixteenth century fortress, steeped in ancient history, to reach our apartment. I had found it online and I held my breath as I collected the key from a local shopkeeper, as instructed, hoping it would live up to its photos. It did.

There was no lift in the building so we had to lug our cases up four flights of stairs. After I unlocked the heavy door, I was immediately struck by how light it was compared to many of the hotel rooms in the city, where the buildings were so tightly packed together that the most likely view was that of the next hotel's wall.

We put down our cases and explored. There was a large bedroom with a welcoming, oversized double bed, plus a spacious, open-plan living and cooking area. I hoped this might help Sophie to understand why I loved that in our flat at home. She had never understood it, preferring a separate kitchen. Beyond the partly drawn curtains there was a generous balcony, with a table and two chairs, and the most incredible view of the valley. Sophie turned and grinned at me.

"You did well, my man!"

I took that as a thank you. We could see Assisi in the distance. I had always felt drawn to go there. But not this time. This time was just for me and Sophie. No 800-year-old monks were allowed to get in the way of this break.

We showered together and then unpacked, before heading into town for lunch.

Perugia was buzzing, crowded, excited, with professional jazz musicians on every corner, as part of the Umbria Jazz festival. A huge clown on stilts as tall as me made his way expertly though the masses, forcing people to stop and stare. Someone was juggling fire sticks on the corner of the main square. An artist was drawing a jumbo-sized rendition of Botticelli's *The Birth of*

Venus on the pavement in chalk, with a mesmerised crowd looking on. He didn't care that it would be walked over and washed away by bedtime.

Everywhere we went there was music. People were relaxed, meandering; stopping at cafés; just enjoying themselves, as though we had all made a deal with the jazz – you keep us entertained and we'll put life on hold for a few days.

We were going to have seven wonderful days to ourselves. Lazy mornings in bed. Coffee on our balcony. Long, hot showers. Late nights, tipsy on the local wines, enjoying being together. Just us.

Wine. Ice cream. Pizza. Pasta. Salads. Cherries, of course.

I needed to take my mind off things at home. The other night, when Luca phoned, he told me that the police wanted me to reconsider withdrawing my affidavit. That meant that there was a chance they hadn't deleted it from their system yet. It was vital that Denucci knew I had taken his bribe, so Luca was working hard to persuade the police to accept my decision. I was trying not to think about it, but I had started jumping at my own shadow again. I couldn't tell Sophie.

We sat in a bar on the top of a cliff drop, drinking chilled white wine and watching the birds fly over the valley. There was nothing to do; nothing important happening. I stroked Sophie's tourist-tired feet, as they rested on my lap, not caring what anyone might think. Our mobiles were switched off. We connected like we'd never connected before. The worries of London melted away.

I showed Sophie my favourite hidden spots and the streets, built like stone staircases, that went on forever. We laughed as we remembered the day we'd first met on one of those. I took her to just enough churches that she could feel she had *done* Perugia, but not so many that her smile faded.

I showed her my favourite street market, perching dangerously along a set of near-vertical steps, with people selling everything from kitchen brooms to hand-crafted jewellery. Sophie stopped at an artist's stand. His paintings were bright and colourful, radiating happiness. There was one that caught her eye. He could tell, so he no doubt mentally doubled the price. She didn't care.

"Christof, I want to buy that one," she said, pointing at a stylised view of the valley. The rolling hills were purple and green and golden brown, with the bluest sky. Assisi sat in the centre, understated, as though it couldn't work out what all the fuss is about. "It reminds me of the view from our balcony. I want to put it up in our flat – in the lounge. Would that be okay?"

Of course it was. I smiled and agreed. There was no point in haggling. The artist knew when the deal was done. He wrapped up the picture and we took it back to our apartment, tucking it safely into my suitcase, to protect its journey to its new home.

I love it when she says 'our flat'. It feels ike she's planning our future; like she feels that we belong together. Little things like that means more to me than her accepting a glitzy ring.

Our few days in Perugia passed quickly, with so much to do and yet so little need to hurry. It was as though the more we relaxed, the faster time flowed.

We headed out for our last evening before we were due to go to the Italian mountains, north-east of Milan. We were giving the cherry farm a miss this time, so I wouldn't get dragged back into the harvest work. Nonna was okay with that, having had me visit twice in June. The crowds were heaving as *Funk Off*, perhaps the most popular band in the festival, was loving every moment of being on stage. The group of over fifteen men were playing every size of saxophone available, plus a decent selection of brass instruments. Their marketing was great: they paraded through the town centre several times a day, playing as they walked, making sure everyone knew when their next stage concert was and selling T-shirts and CDs. They had become a bit of an institution for the festival.

Everyone's attention was absorbed by the genius they were co-creating, when Sophie leaned over to me, as we sat on the steps of the old town hall, with hundreds of others, watching the current concert.

"Everyone is here at the concert. Remember that alleyway we found near the water fountain earlier today?" I liked her thinking. She didn't need to say any more. I took her hand and pulled her through the crowds, just like we'd done at the cherry festival when we first met. The alleyway was empty. I was grateful to her for wearing a dress, not trousers, as I pulled off her pants and tucked them in my pocket. My fingers were exploring her. She was groaning and loving it. I could tell how much she wanted me. I felt the same.

She was unbuckling my belt and fumbling with the buttons on my jeans. I used my free hand to help. Neither of us wanted to wait a moment longer than we had to. She set me free from my boxers. She was leaning against the wall. I lifted her up to sit on my hips and carefully guided myself inside her. She groaned and smiled and closed her eyes, lost in the sensations. She opened them to look back at me, staring into my eyes with a look that told me she wanted this as much as I did.

We made love with a passion we hadn't shown each other in months. Kissing. Hard. Thrusting. Hands everywhere. This wouldn't take long. We both came at the same time and our excitement was drowned out by the jazz. Out of breath. Laughing. Exhausted. In love. *That. Was. Incredible.*

I vowed to myself that I would do whatever it took to get to spend the rest of my life with this wonderful woman.

We were standing in a thick ring of music lovers, late morning on our final day in Perugia, with the drumming of a percussion jazz band dictating the rhythm of our movements. They were from Austria: their twelve large bass-style drums, another twelve mid-sized drums and all manner of percussion noises, from cymbals to wooden blocks, created music like I had never heard before. It was incredible to watch them play together, all in perfect time, barely conducted by the band leader with a football referee's whistle. They knew their rhythms off by heart. Each song was unique.

I looked at my watch. "About an hour until we need to go," I said to Sophie, loving being here with her, with my arm wrapped round her waist, feeling closer than we'd ever been before. We had rekindled that early spark, getting out of the humdrum of London. I loved the way I kept catching her looking at her engagement ring, when she thought I wasn't looking, though it was always accompanied by a flash of worry, hoping that the ring wasn't a bad omen. Would that feeling ever wear off?

"Damn! I forgot to get a postcard for Mum and Dad. They'll go crazy if I don't send one. They act like WhatsApp was never invented."

"We've got to leave for our apartment to grab our bags soon, then we'll get our taxi to the station. There's a shop just over there. You've got plenty of time. I'll wait here." I replied, unwilling to tear myself away from the last few minutes of music.

She smiled at me and gave me a generous kiss, before spinning round in her long, white summer dress to disappear into a neighbouring shop. I noticed some of the men in the crowd giving me envious glances. They were right. She looked stunning and I felt proud to have her walking by my side.

I popped into the shop, having grabbed a random postcard from the rack by the door, fulfilling my daughterly duty.

"*Un francobollo per l'Inghilterra, per favore.*" A stamp for England, please, I asked at the till, as I handed over the postcard. I could write it on the train and post it from Milan where we would be picking up Christof's car to get to the mountains this evening. It would reach Mum and Dad faster from there.

The woman told me how much it was and my blank face made it clear that the number was beyond my current Italian. She pointed at the figures on the till. I smiled and handed her a note. She gave me my change, with my postcard and stamp in a little white bag.

"*Grazie!*" I tucked my change into my wallet, stuffing it and the postcard safely into my shoulder bag. I did up the zip and then slung the bag diagonally over my left shoulder and right side, "It means the pickpockets can't grab it as easily," Dad had told me, back in the days when going on holiday with your parents was still vaguely cool.

I headed out of the shop to cross the road back to the band and the sun momentarily blinded me, as I was scanning the crowd for signs of Christof. It must be time to go.

I was lost in the band's music when my mobile rang. I knew something was wrong the instant Luca's name flashed up on the display. My pulse quickened, even before he spoke.

He didn't bother with pleasantries, "Christof, the police have released your affidavit. First thing this morning. Whoever is feeding Denucci information from the police will have told him. He will think you have double-crossed him. You and Sophie need to get somewhere safe – invisible – while we try to fix this. You need to go! Now!"

I couldn't breathe. My thumb froze over the red circle that had ended the call. Luca hadn't needed an answer. I pushed down the dread and panic that were pounding my brain as though I were inside one of the band's big drums, stopping me from thinking straight. I scanned the crowd for signs of Sophie and started to run towards the shop where she had been buying the postcard.

I thought I had seen Christof running towards me; it must have taken me longer than I had realised to buy the stamp. I had started to cross the road when a white car pulled up in front of me, out of nowhere, nearly running me over. My heart pounded with shock. *I must pay more attention.* I had forgotten that this part of town wasn't pedestrianised.

A window wound down on the car – the back window, nearest to me. "*Scusi, signorina,*" said a friendly looking man in his fifties, wearing a white suit to match his car. He was wearing dark sunglasses and an old scar sloped down his right cheek.

I stopped instinctively. It's what I've been programmed to do when someone says 'excuse me'.

He opened the door and leaned out of the car, "*Scusi, signorina! Dov'è il Palazzo dei Priori?*"

He had just asked me where something was, but I didn't have

a clue which place he might mean. "I'm sorry, I don't speak Italian," I replied politely in English, and started to walk off.

But before I could turn away, I felt a push from behind and somehow I was bundled into the car. A man jumped in behind me, slamming the door.

"Christof!" I hear my voice screaming it. Over and over. I know he can't hear me. The jazz and the sound of the car engine pulling away drown out my words.

The man who pushed me into the car shoves a heavy hand over my mouth, to stop me from shouting.

What are they going to do with me?

I heard a car in the street pulling away so fast the tyres screeched – an unusual thing to do in an area where crowds could spill into the streets without warning. It set off alarm bells in my head. Where was Sophie?

I looked around in desperation, trying to spot her. She should have been out of the shop by now. I heard shouting from next to the shop. A man was trying to get help.

"*Hanno preso la donna!*" They took the woman.

A sudden knowing of which woman turned my stomach. I ran over to him.

"*Vestito bianco?*" White dress?

He nodded violently. "White car," he yelled and pointed in the direction the car had gone.

I'm running. I think I can see it in the distance. It's crazy – I'll never catch up, but I have to try! Why had I let her go? I thought we were safe.

The road is long and straight. I look up side streets, but they're tiny and packed with people. They can't have taken one of those. I keep sprinting straight ahead. They could be half a mile away by now. They could be on the motorway in minutes. This is crazy. But I don't know what else to do.

Pounding feet. Blind panic. Have to find her. They've got her.

My muscles scream the words my breathing stops my mouth from saying. Fire burning in my legs. Chest founding. A stitch in my side. I can't do this! I have to. I dodge through tourists, knocking them out of the way. I can't hear their abuse. They don't understand. I have to save Sophie. They could kill her. I don't want to think that. But past files flash across my mind. I know what Denucci can do. Revenge is important to him. They're going to hurt Sophie to punish me.

I hear knuckles crunch. My body tenses, too terrified to think about what might happen next.

He pins my arms to my sides, like a bodyguard trying to keep me in, not out. I can smell his sweat. His cigarettes. The beer he had last night, lingering on his breath and his clothes. The man in the white suit moves towards me. Screaming is no longer enough. I'm silent. Waiting. I don't even struggle. I know it will only make it worse. There is nothing I can do.

The man in white smiles at me, like a friendly old uncle, and says something in Italian.

"Vogliamo il nostro anello."

I don't know what that means. I don't know what he is going to do. I don't know where they are taking me. My bag is still across my body, digging into my back as I'm pressed against the seat. My phone is in there, but I'd be dead before I could call Christof and I can't remember the number for the Italian police. There is no way I could even unlock the keypad. My brain is screaming so loudly I can no longer hear my thoughts.

He's reaching towards me and he grabs my left hand, holding it firmly. With his other hand he pulls the ring off my finger. "No!" I'm crying. Is this just a robbery? I thought they were going to hurt me. "That's mine! Give it back!" I'm wriggling and kicking and struggling to get free.

The man shakes his head and smiles as though telling a tantruming child that their strop won't work. He pulls a small white envelope out of the inside pocket of his suit jacket, drops the ring into it, presses the seal closed and puts it back into his pocket. He is silent. So calm. Unmoved by my terror.

He reaches inside his suit pocket again. I start to panic. Is it going to be a knife? A gun? Are they going to attack me? My blood ignores the July heatwave and freezes in my veins. My heart is trying to escape from my ribcage. I feel numb.

He pulls out a small white card. A business card shape.

He reaches over to me. Instinctively I try to reach out my hand to take it from him. His bodyguard tightens his grip on me. The bare skin on my arms screams like school playground Chinese burns.

The man in the white suit reaches over towards my chest. I try to recoil, but that just brings me even closer to the bodyguard. I think I'm going to be sick.

The man in white reaches inside the top of my dress and finds my bra, starting to tuck the card inside it. I try to scream. To make him stop. My voice fails me. He brushes my breast with his fingertips, touching my nipple, lingering. I feel myself blanking everything out. I don't want to remember this. I don't know what's coming next. He's smiling. The shit is enjoying this. He pinches my nipple and I feel it harden under his touch. Involuntary reflex. I hate myself for it.

"Lucky boy," he says in English, as he brushes his fingertips over my chest, up to my chin, and touches my lips. Then he stops.

He nods at the bodyguard and says something to the driver. Where are they taking me? What are they going to do to me? They've stolen my ring, why won't they let me go?

I'm running on the road now. The pavements are too crowded. I can't go on much longer. But I force myself to keep moving. It's the only thing I can think of that might save her. This is all my fault.

Right ahead of me, there's a band walking through the streets, surrounded by a crowd of fans. The road is blocked. I can't breathe. There's a white car beeping its horn. People are shouting at it.

The car screeches to a halt. There's a crowd in front of us, blocking the street. We can't drive.

The man in white is yelling at his driver. The bodyguard is distracted. He has loosened his grip on me. I unfreeze and seize my chance.

I wrench myself free and turn around, screaming and yelling and banging on the car's rear windscreen. People are turning to look at us. The man in white has thrust his hand over my mouth. I bite him. He hits my face. My cheekbone. It hurts. He's yelling at the bodyguard.

The bodyguard opens the car door. He drags me out and dumps me on the pavement. I land hard. My body screams objections. He must have thrown me. I hear the door slam and the car reverses, beeping its horn, people yelling at it. Everything goes black.

The car has gone! Reversing back up the street and veering up a side road, as though it doesn't care who might be in the way. People are jumping onto the pavement. I hear screams. A band is playing in the distance, pretending the world is still normal. A crowd has formed, near to where the car was. A woman is yelling, "Una donna! Buttata fuori dalla macchina!" A woman! Thrown out of the car.

I push through them. They're crowded tightly around a mass of white cloth. The left side of her face is bleeding. What have they done to her? I throw myself onto my knees and scream her name, "Sophie!" Time stops as I wait, terrified, to see if she responds. Am I too late?

She doesn't respond. I lift her up in my arms. She's lifeless. Limp. But she still has colour in her cheeks.

She's not dead. Just unconscious.

My body tries to force me to rest as the relief floods through me. But we're only just getting started. We're not safe yet.

"Police! We need the police!" I hear people calling. No we don't. No, we really don't. We can't trust the police on this, after what happened this morning. We have to get to safety.

"I need a taxi!" I scream at the crowd, shaking Sophie, shouting her name. Someone must have heard me because a few moments later a car with the familiar yellow paintwork pulls over.

"Give me space!" I yell. The crowd parts. Someone has opened the back door of the taxi. I pick Sophie up, her bag still wrapped round her, and lift her onto the back seat.

I gave the taxi driver the address of our apartment. My arms were wrapped around Sophie. He drove quickly, sensing the obvious urgency. Had she just passed out? Did they attack her? Did they drug her?

We arrived at the apartment. I didn't want to, but I started to lay Sophie down on the back seat so that I could get our luggage. She stiffened, half-opening her eyes. "Don't leave me!" She really meant it. She was terrified. I gave the taxi driver our key and explained where he needed to leave it, once he had our bags. He was surprisingly willing to help, given how suspicious our situation must have looked to him.

I sat in the back of his car, holding Sophie. He was back after a few minutes. Our bags were in his boot.

"Where to?" We had to get to Milan. Then we would take my car into the mountains. We had to get there tonight.

We had tickets from Perugia station, but it would be a slow, stopping service to Florence, where we would change for the fast train to Milan. I couldn't put Sophie through that. And someone would call an ambulance. Or the police. There was nothing for it.

"Firenze, Santa Maria Novella, per favore." I replied, asking him to drive us all the way to the main train station in Florence. He shook his head, sucking air over teeth. He muttered about it being too far. I could see he didn't want to get involved. I didn't blame him. There was nothing for it. I reached for my emergency cash, a tight roll of hundred-euro notes I always carried hidden

on me, because I never knew when I might need them. Standard protocol. I pulled off a handful of them and gave them to him. That seemed to change his mind.

I pulled off another three. "These are for you if you get us there in under two hours." He nodded.

I didn't want to tell him which train we were getting or where we were going. I had no idea who might find him later.

He made good progress through the town and soon we were cruising the motorway towards Florence.

Sophie had gone into shock. She was icy cold. Shaking. Her teeth were chattering so much it sounded like she had brought the percussion jazz band with her. She couldn't talk. All I could do was wrap my jacket round her and hold her, stroking her hair, telling her she was safe.

Although the driver maxed out the speed limits, it was still the slowest two hours of my life. Sophie had fallen asleep, which was probably a good thing. But it meant she still hadn't told me anything about what had happened. Given that we had an audience, that was probably for the best.

I couldn't stop torturing myself about what they might have done to her, had that band not blocked the road. I had studied enough about the Camorra to know they would have hurt her to hurt me. Believing I had double-crossed them meant that negotiating wouldn't have been an option any more – they wouldn't have released her, no matter what I had promised. It would have been revenge: punishment for my betrayal; even though I was innocent. She could have been murdered because the police were so desperate to prove the fraud case against Denucci.

The driver edged his way through the tourist-packed streets of Florence, doing his best to earn his tip. He pulled up outside of the train station and opened the door for me. I had managed to wake Sophie up enough that I thought she could walk. I didn't want to draw even more attention to us. I hoped she would be able to pull her own suitcase. I would be supporting her weight and I couldn't do that as well as pull my own and hers.

I was on hyper-alert as we got out of the taxi, in case we had been followed. The driver put our suitcases next to us. I handed him his tip. He was in his car and had pulled away before I could even say *grazie*. I hoped my money had bought his silence. Sophie's kidnapping would be the talk of the festival.

I turned to her and realised there was no way she could pull a case, so I found a way to prop hers up on mine and I pulled both, as I supported her to walk through the noisy, crowded station.

Somehow, I managed to get us through the thousands of commuters to our platform. I had booked a first-class compartment and bought the extra seats, as a treat, so that we would have some space on our own for the journey. I hadn't planned to use it for this. I found the carriage and the porter helped with our suitcases. I almost carried Sophie up the steps. She was groggy. Only half there.

The porter asked if she was okay. I explained that she was really tired, that she had had too much wine for lunch and I thought she might have sunstroke. He fell for it.

I accepted his offer to bring us coffees.

They arrived quickly, which was highly unusual, hinting at his curiosity. I pulled down the blinds and locked the door to our compartment. I felt so tense I was almost holding my breath, waiting until our train pulled away. We would have nearly two hours undisturbed, until we got to Milan. We should be safe. For now.

Sophie was lying on the bench seat opposite me, wrapped in my jumper, my jacket and her shawl, which I had found in her bag. I would try to wake her soon and persuade her to drink the coffee. I needed to know what had happened.

But first I had a call to make. Luca. I couldn't hide this from him. He answered on the first ring, making it clear he had been waiting to hear from me.

I explained about the kidnapping, telling him where we were and keeping it brief, in case Sophie was listening. He agreed to arrange for my car to be waiting for us at Milano Centrale station. He would meet us at our B&B in the mountains. He asked if I was safe to drive. I was shaken and running on high alert, but I needed to feel like I was back in control of the situation, so I told him I would be fine.

I had done all I could practically, and suddenly the adrenalin stopped. It had kept me going for nearly three hours now. I felt myself deflating, like a balloon that got played with too roughly at a children's party.

I gently woke Sophie and helped her to sit up. She was still clinging to me, terror screaming silently in her eyes as she refused to let me go. I had turned up the temperature in the compartment when we'd got on the train, so she wouldn't be cold, but she was still icy.

She opened her eyes enough to see me properly. She started to cry. The floodgates were opening.

She held out her left hand. At first, I couldn't work out what she was trying to show me. "They took the ring!"

She was sobbing, showing me her empty finger. Why hadn't I noticed this before?

My worst fears were realised: Denucci believed I had taken the bribe and still agreed to testify.

"What happened? Tell me! What did they say to you?"

She shook her head.

"They must have said something?"

"*Vogliamo nostro nello.*" She mispronounced it, but I still understood. I pretended not to. I didn't want to have to explain it all to her. *Vogliamo il nostro anello.* "We want our ring."

They knew. They thought I had tried to bluff them. This was the worst possible news. Sophie wasn't safe. They had followed us to Perugia. They would follow us anywhere.

I fumbled in my bra, struggling to pull out the business card, as its sharp corner caught on lace. I shuddered at the memory of that man's touch as he put it there. I would never forget the look on his face as he enjoyed touching me.

I handed the card to Christof.

All colour drained from his face. "How did that get inside your bra?" he demanded. I didn't want to tell him.

"What does it say?" I hadn't seen the card yet. And even if I had, I was in no state to make out the curly red writing on it.

La prossima volta non mi comporterò così.

"What does that mean?" I spat the words like bullets from a machine gun.

"There's no direct equivalent, but it's like 'No more Mr Nice Guy', in English."

"What does *that* mean?" I was yelling now.

He didn't answer. Couldn't? Wouldn't? I couldn't tell.

"Did they say anything else to you, Sophie?" he asked. He sounded scared. That freaked me out. He was supposed to be my rock. I couldn't handle this if he was scared too.

I toyed with not telling him. I wanted to hurt him. Something told me this was his fault. But my need to understand was greater than my need to cause him pain, just now.

"Lucky boy." Christof looked confused.

"Just before we hit the crowed and they threw me out of the car, he said 'lucky boy', in English. It was the only thing he said to me in English. What did he mean? Who is he talking about? Did he know you?"

Christof hesitated. I could see him thinking. Processing. About to tell me a difficult truth? Or pulling together a lie?

Lucky boy. He'd said it in English. Deliberately. He wanted Sophie to tell me. He wanted me to have to tell her. He knew I had kept her in the dark on this.

I swerved her question. "Oh, he's probably just assuming you have a boyfriend and he's saying he's lucky."

Sophie gave me a look I had never seen on her face before. It chilled me. "You're lying," she said slowly, with venom. She was right. "Who the hell were they?"

"I'm so sorry. We need to get to Milan. Then we'll take my car to the mountains. We have to see Luca. I've arranged for him to meet us there. You're safe. You're with me now."

"They knew you!" she shrieked. I realised she hadn't guessed this before. Her face showed her brain processing this new information. "Is this your fault? And why did they take my ring?" I didn't answer. I couldn't. Not here.

The effort of talking had exhausted her. I was pumped with adrenalin again, at the shock of realising what this might do to our relationship; at the worry about getting us safely to the mountains, but I tried to stay calm. She reluctantly agreed to lean against me, for support and warmth, and she fell asleep, resentfully wrapped in my arms.

I didn't want to be near him. I knew this was his fault but I didn't understand why and I was too tired to move. And too cold. I wished I wasn't wearing my summer dress. I remembered the last time I had travelled from Florence to Milan, the day I first met Christof. I had worn my Italian-train-proof clothes to stop myself from freezing on the train, then I'd nearly died of heat as I lugged my bags to my hotel.

Part of me wished I had missed that train.

We arrived on time at Milano Centrale. Sophie was awake, but silent. I'd have given anything to know what she was thinking. She had shut me out. We thanked our porter as we said goodbye. I was grateful he had taken the hint and left us in peace for the journey. I stood on the platform, looking up at the huge iron arches of the station, with glass between the struts, which usually flooded it with light. Tonight, they were framing a sunset. It looked inappropriately poetic.

My car was waiting for us at the pick-up point. Our local driver from work handed me the keys, putting our bags in the boot. Sophie got in to the passenger seat and strapped herself in. I pulled away and navigated the familiar streets towards the SS36 motorway out of town.

Sophie watched silently as we drove past Lecco, keeping to the motorway with the occasional treat of exquisite views of Lake Como. You could see why people paid millions to live there. The final rays of light were mirrored on the ripples of the lake. It would have taken our breath away, had things been different. Maybe one day it still would.

I realised how hungry I was. We hadn't eaten since breakfast and it was now gone eight. I wished we could have stopped for dinner at one of the many restaurants that line the rocky edges of the lake, enjoying each other's company, drinking in the view.

After a couple of hours, we left the highway through the valley, not long after Sondrio, and took a zigzagging road up into the mountains. How I had missed them. I used to come up here to walk at weekends when I lived in Milan. My heart sang with a split second of joy at returning, but I had forgotten how heart-stopping some of these drops could be and I had to concentrate to keep us safe. I was feeling exhausted. Sophie was still silent. A local overtook us on a hairpin bend at high speed, with not a care in the world; certain of the road, its cambers, knowing its potholes. I wasn't certain about anything anymore.

We reached our village and wound our way to our guest house. The Palazzo. I had stayed here before, many times. In fact, it was where I used to stay whenever I wanted to lose myself in nature at the weekends, when I lived in Milan.

We were expected. And we were on time. Beatrice, the owner, met us at our car, gesturing that her assistant would take our bags to our room. She hugged us both, scolding me that it was too long since she had seen me and greeting Sophie like an old friend. Then she bypassed the usual offer of a glass of local grappa, made to her grandmother's recipe with local herbs collected from the mountains, and gestured for us to follow her. Luca must have briefed her – at least with as much as she needed to know.

There was no fuss. She took us to my favourite room, with breath-taking views of the Valtellina and the mountains behind the valley. I could just make out the slightest trace of their outline in the last light of the evening.

Sophie sat on the bed and curled up into a ball. I thought she might be about to cry.

"I'm so sorry, Sophie. You can't sleep yet. We need to talk with Luca." She gave me a look that told me exactly how she felt about that idea.

"He won't take long, I promise. We've got a bath with this room. As soon as we've talked to him, I'll run you a nice hot bath, full of bubbles. You can relax. It will all be okay. I promise." She gave me the look again, making it clear how little she trusted me promising her anything, ever again. Each time the thought of *the future* had crept into my mind today, I had swatted it away, like an irritatingly persistent fly. I had to stay in this moment, to fix what was here now, before I could allow myself to worry about what tomorrow might hold, let alone next month; whether Sophie would want anything to do with me, once she knew how little of the truth I had shared with her.

Beatrice knocked politely on the door. She was holding a tray with a pot of tea and a cold dinner: some local cheeses, today's fresh bread, tomatoes, homemade jams and butter. She put it down on the coffee table next to the sofa in our room.

"It's a tea with local herbs," she said, gesturing at the blue-and-white antique pot. "They're calming, soothing for the nerves."

Sophie managed half a smile, her British politeness still showing despite what she had been through today.

"Shall I help you to get changed, into something warmer?" Beatrice asked her. Sophie nodded, not making eye contact.

"I think it would be best if you went to see Luca," Beatrice said, ushering me out of the room. I felt a twinge of jealousy that Sophie would let Bea help her, but not me. Then I remembered that this was all my fault and felt glad that Sophie would even allow me to be in the same room.

I walked down the ancient stone steps with their 500 years of history and found Luca in the dining room. It was one of my favourite places ever. There was a retired grand piano in the corner, used as a sideboard for drinks and breakfast delicacies. And the walls were covered with intricately painted murals, depicting scenes from the lives of the family that had built this impressive old house all those years ago. You could spend hours looking at them. Some of the faces were much newer, where generations of owners had inserted themselves into the historical record.

Luca was waiting for me, grappa glasses ready. I told him all I knew. There wasn't much more than I had told him on the train. Apart from the ring. And the "lucky boy". He didn't mince his words.

"This is bad, Christof," he told me, as though I didn't already know, "really bad."

I took a sip of my brandy. It burned my throat as I swallowed. I was grateful for the sensation, having been numb for so much of the day. "What are we going to do, Luca?" I asked him, hoping he would have a plan.

"I have to be honest with you, Christof. I don't know. Not yet. But we need to start by talking with Sophie. We need to know everything she can tell us."

We walked back upstairs and I nervously knocked on the bedroom door. Bea told us to come in.

Sophie was sitting on the bed, wrapped up in blankets, nibbling on the food. She had slightly more colour. She was dressed for winter. In July.

"Sophie, this is Luca," I said, introducing him, immediately feeling stupid as I remembered they had already met when I took

Sophie to Milan after Christmas. She grunted a hello. He gave her a distracted smile. Pleasantries weren't high up on either of their lists.

"Sophie, I know this is hard of you, but I need you to tell me everything that happened. You too, Christof. Don't miss out a single detail: every face, every gesture, every word. It's the only way I'm going to be able to help you."

Sophie started to talk. Slowly. Quietly. Hating reliving her afternoon. She told us about the man in the white suit fondling her. I saw the look of disgust in her face. She cried. Rage rose up inside me, clenching my fists, ready to find the bastard who had hurt my love; the woman I adored; the woman I had put at risk; the woman I had lied to.

"I'm going to kill Denucci!" I announced. I meant it.

"It won't have been him!" Luca dived in, checking I wasn't making a grab for my car keys. He was right. I stood still. Still seething. But I knew Denucci wouldn't do his own dirty work. That wasn't the way things worked. I stared into Luca's eyes. He knew what was going through my head. He would have felt the same way, had someone kidnapped Daniela and molested her. And I knew how much worse it could have been; how different things could have been, had the road block not forced them to ditch Sophie, once she started to shout and attract attention to them, but how easy it would still be for them to do worse.

"Who the FUCK is Denucci?" We had almost forgotten Sophie was there.

Luca gave me a look that said more than 'oops'. There was no way we could keep pretending that this was a random attack. He sat down on the sofa again, leaving me to pace the room, and explained the bare minimum to Sophie. He knew I had never told her about those aspects of my work. I had convinced myself that I wasn't lying to her – I just hadn't told her the bits of the truth she didn't need to know.

She ranted. Shouted. Threw accusations of lying. Screamed about how she had trusted me. Told me our entire relationship was a fake. Luca had the decency to squirm as she got personal about it. She had every right to be furious with me. I was eternally grateful to Luca for not mentioning the ring or the proposal. That would always be our secret.

Eventually Sophie had enough answers to allow her rage to burn out. She was exhausted and the herbs had made her sleepy. Luca was staying in one of the other rooms, so he left us in peace.

I ran the bath I had promised Sophie and sat with her, stroking her hair, as she relaxed in the warm, scented water in silence. I helped her to dry off and to find clothes to use as pyjamas. Under any other circumstance those clothes wouldn't have stayed on for long, but something had changed. I couldn't tell if it was temporary or forever. She allowed me to lie next to her, holding her, breathing in the smell of her hair, wanting with all my heart and soul to wind back time and make this morning not have happened.

She fell asleep in my arms, wrapped in an unseasonably warm duvet on this humid night, still wearing my jumper. I looked down at my beautiful fiancée, the moonlight dancing in her hair, looking so peaceful, as though today had been a normal day of sight-seeing. My heart felt ready to burst. I loved her so much. I just wanted to protect her. But I didn't know how. I stared up at the ancient ceiling beams in our beautiful bedroom. Half a millennium they had been there. Twenty generations of dramas, of joys, of births, of deaths they had witnessed, without judgement, without sharing advice.

I couldn't sleep; my mind was racing. I couldn't risk Sophie getting hurt again. I wasn't going to testify against Denucci, even if it meant he got away with everything he had done. I remembered the first fraudster at our client's firm, who had ended up *disappearing*. And the Managing Director of the firm who had found out about it and then took a permanent swim in his pool – and the security guard who fell into the vat of sugar. Ice-cold shivers screamed up my spine. I felt sick. I knew that Denucci would stop at nothing to get revenge. He thought I had double-crossed him; broken the deal. I needed to seriously consider our options. But 'life as usual' didn't appear to be one of them. I had some decisions to make.

For now, I knew we were safe. But I was scared to fall asleep. I didn't know what tomorrow would hold.

***

It must have been the middle of the night. The room was darker than I had ever noticed a room being. There were no streetlights and it was close to the new moon. I wondered what the stars were like. It felt like being blindfolded. I felt Christof's arms around me and snuggled into his warmth.

Then I remembered.

"You bastard!" I yelled at him, jolting him awake as I pulled away and wrapped the duvet around myself, as though for protection. "You could have got me killed with your lies!" I felt rage forcing its way out of every pore. I fumbled for the switch for the bedside light.

Christof was pulling himself up to face me, obviously still half-asleep and squinting against the sudden brightness. "I know," he whispered, "and I'm sorry. So very sorry." He looked haggard; ten years older than yesterday morning. A sliver of sympathy threatened to soften the emotional armour I had been wearing. The rage was melting into just anger.

"Why did you do it? Why did you lie to me? Why did you put me at risk?"

He stared at the duvet cover and fidgeted with a loose thread. "I lied because I love you!" he said, not moving his head, but daring to look up at me, to check my reaction.

I leapt out of bed. "You what?" I screamed at near-banshee-level.

"I lied because I love you," he answered, his face full of confusion.

"And that makes it ok, does it? *You loved me*, so you lied to me! *You loved me*, so you got me mixed up in some mafia thing. *You loved me*, so you got me kidnapped. *You loved me*, so you nearly got me murdered! I don't need that kind of *love*!"

"I'm sorry."

"Is that all you've got to say for yourself?" I was pacing up and down the bedroom, feeling the coolness of the wooden floorboards, the duvet wrapped round me. Christof was huddled on the bed in just his boxers, looking as vulnerable as a child on its first day at school. But I wasn't going to weaken.

"Tell me everything. And I mean *everything*!" I demanded. I waited, still pacing. He sat in silence, unmoving. I wasn't feeling patient. "Ok, let's start with your work. What is it you *really* do and how did you get messed up with the Mafia?"

"The *Camorra*," he corrected me, quietly. "The Mafia is Sicily and the Camorra is Napoli – Naples. Mafia with a lower-case 'm' is the generic term."

"I don't give a flying *fuck* where they come from or how they feel about capital letters! I want to know why they wanted to kill me!" I could see that Christof was thinking, trying to work out what to tell me. Was he working out more lies? "I want the truth, the whole truth and nothing but the truth!" I shouted as I threw myself onto a 200-year-old armchair and hid my face in the duvet that was still swaddling me.

"I promise I'll tell you the truth. You deserve it."

I threw him a glare that did little to encourage him as he continued, telling me about his work as a consultant, about the 'special cases' they sometimes took on for clients, about how he had got mixed up in a Camorra fraud case, about how hard it is for the police to ever pin anything on a mafia boss.

I bit my tongue until I could almost taste blood, trying not to shout and interrupt him. I wanted to know everything. He explained how they had kidnapped me to try to persuade him not to testify.

"And what would they have done to me, had the crowd not blocked the road?" I asked, dreading the answer, but needing to know.

He hesitated, then looked at me with such fear in his eyes that I knew he was telling the truth, "I don't want to think about it, Sophie. I'm so sorry you got caught up in this."

"And what happens now? Are we safe? Am I on the run for the rest of time? Will I find a horse's head in the bed when I get home?"

Christof laughed. And then stopped himself, realising it wasn't the appropriate response. "No. They won't do that." I waited for more. "Luca is talking to his Camorra experts and he'll know more in the morning." I could tell he was holding back.

"Am I safe?" I yelled.

"For now, yes."

"What does that mean?" I watched him stare at the bed sheet and shake his head. "I don't know. I'm sorry, Sophie, I just don't know yet. I hope so."

I needed to change the subject. *I hope so* wasn't anywhere near good enough, but I knew he had nothing more to say.

"And this?" I asked, using my hands to gesture between the

two of us. "How much of *this* was lies?"

"None of it, Sophie! I promise you! I fell in love with you at the cherry festival and I have always been honest about how I feel about you. I did what I did to protect you. I promise you our relationship is real!"

"I don't think your promises count for much!" I spat at him, wanting to see him suffer. "I think you should sleep on the sofa."

I pulled an old blanket over myself and tried to get to sleep, but I couldn't. The horsehair in my sofa was like sleeping on cactus spikes. My mind was a torrent of 'what if' questions. I had hated not being able to reassure Sophie that she was safe. Part of me felt hurt that she hadn't once asked whether I was safe, but I suspected I deserved that response.

I felt guilty that I hadn't told her the *whole truth*, but I couldn't. I didn't tell her about the stake-out that went wrong after my night with Miss Italy. I didn't tell her about the real reason I was living in London. I didn't tell her about the ring. I knew our relationship would never survive knowing all of that. I convinced myself I wasn't lying; just protecting her - again.

I was staring out of the bedroom window, not long after dawn, mesmerised by the flight of the swallows that nested in the roof of this ancient building, when there was a gentle tapping at the door. Sophie was still sound asleep, so I opened it and Luca beckoned me to follow him downstairs. He looked tired, with dark rings under his eyes, and he had been smoking, which was unlike him.

"No, I haven't been to bed yet. You owe me one," he tried to joke, even though we both knew that it was the firm who owed *me*, since I had only taken the risk of the Denucci case so that they would earn the client's fee. "We have convinced the police to burn your affidavit and to put the word out with their contacts that releasing it had been a computer error. I had to tell them about the kidnapping to get them to agree to withdraw your evidence, and they wanted to interview Sophie, but I have been insistent that you don't want to press charges."

Luca looked serious. The playful smile that usually twinkled around his eyes was missing. "There's something you're not telling me, isn't there, Luca?" I asked, not sure if I wanted the answer. He nodded, silently. I raised my eyebrows, to tell him I was ready to hear it, even if it was bad news.

"Our Camorra experts believe that Sophie is safe. Now Denucci has his €50,000 ring back, once he knows your evidence had already been withdrawn, he'll leave you both in peace." Luca looked at me, seeing my face visibly relax with relief. "We are assuming that the same mole who told him your affidavit had been submitted will also get him the message that it had been a mistake. But we have to allow time for that to happen. It seems pretty certain that you weren't followed yesterday; that no one knows you are here. You're safe here for a few days. I'd suggest you stay here and get over what happened yesterday. It's far enough out of the way that no one will trace you, as long as you run cash-only and no mobile – just a precautionary measure. That will be sorted for you later this morning."

"So, it's going to be ok?" I almost whispered the words, scarcely daring to hope them, as I felt my knees buckle, landing me on the arm of the sofa behind me.

"I can't make you any promises, Christof," Luca said, his face looking calmer than I had seen in a while, "but I agree with our Camorra expert. It's likely that Denucci will leave you alone, once the *grapevine* has got the message to him. After all, he has won – he got you to withdraw your evidence, he got his ring back and he scared the hell out of you and your fiancée. But we need to wait until we have heard confirmation from the police through their agents in the Camorra loop. This kind of thing will be big gossip."

Relief wiped me out and I started to cry, letting go of a year full of fear and worry. Luca gave me a hug, not judging me; fully aware of what I had been through. I realised he had been through much of it, too. I dared to hope it might be over. We could move on with life, without the Denucci case hanging over us any more.

Luca had decided to go back to Milan, to be with his family, and to give Sophie and me peace and quiet while we waited for confirmation from the *grapevine*. We were the only guests at the Palazzo by the time Sophie woke up. She was still icy with anger, but she agreed to come down to breakfast with me.

As we picked at our food I explained what Luca had told me; what the Camorra expert had concluded – that we were safe and just staying here for a few more days, as a precautionary measure, until it was confirmed by the clan's gossip. At first it was clear she still didn't trust me, but then she looked relieved, and soon afterwards she took off my winter jumper and started to eat properly, for the first time since before the kidnapping. But something had changed; she was more distant – almost formal with me. It was clear how much work I would have to do, to have a chance of saving our relationship.

Sophie asked me to leave her alone for the morning, so I spent it helping Bea out with some marketing ideas for next season. It's not my area of expertise, but it felt good to get to talk about something that didn't trigger the emotions I was still denying from the past 24 hours.

When Sophie came down and asked me where we could get

lunch it felt like a major peace offering. Over the next hour in a nearby pizzeria, we did very little talking and even less eye contact, but it gave me the faintest chink of hope.

Bea suggested Sophie might like a massage at the home of a friend of hers in the afternoon. Bea explained quietly to me, in Italian, that the friend spoke no English and Sophie spoke little Italian, so there was no danger of them gossiping about what had happened. I felt guilty about feeling relieved.

Then in the evening Sophie agreed to come out for dinner with me, despite wanting to stay in our room with a tray of treats from Bea. We sat in a quiet corner of a near-empty hotel restaurant, far too early in the evening for its local clientele to want to eat. And we started to talk.

I answered question after question from Sophie, as best I could. But the foundations of our relationship were still as rickety as a plank-and-rope bridge over a ravine. I wanted to talk about how we could rebuild our trust – about how I didn't want to lose her. But I didn't dare.

Over the next few days we went for walks in the hills and even a picnic, but Sophie still wouldn't let me even hold her hand. We were sitting under a tree, looking at the view, lost in silence, when I decided I had had enough of being the bad guy. There were questions I hadn't asked Sophie over the last few months and it was time to remind her that she wasn't the only one who had lied.

I took a deep breath, aware that I had to take care with how I phrased my question. I had been thinking about it for days. Months? "Sophie, there's something I need to ask you." She didn't look up from the piece of grass she had been fiddling with.

"I remember the last time you said that!" she threw back at me, with fresh venom in her eyes. So did I. The afternoon I proposed. *Fuck!* Not the best of starts. I decided to continue.

"Is Jamie really *just* a friend?"

Daggers flew in my direction as she hissed, "And what do you mean by *that*?"

Ok, I got that one wrong, too. I carried on, knowing I now had to finish what I had started. "I mean, is he *really* a friend, after how he treated you? I just don't understand why you still see so much of him."

"I don't!" she snapped, but we both knew she was lying.

"I think we both know you do, Sophie." I said, as gently as I could manage. I refused to give in to the jealousy that had got in the way of me trusting her for so long.

"It's not like I *invite* him, you know!"

"No. But you don't turn him away, either, do you?" She stared at the blade of grass with the fascination of a scientist on the verge of a Nobel-prize-winning discovery. "Why do you lie to me about it?"

I knew it was a step too far, but after days of accusations and guilt, I had a desperate need to rebalance things; to make her see that she, too, hadn't been totally fair.

"I don't lie! Tell me one time I've lied!"

"The photo of you with your engagement ring?"

"That was a one-off! And you shouldn't have had your team snooping on me!"

I hadn't told her that had been yet another lie. I took a deep breath. I had one more example that I knew she couldn't deny. "What about last November when I was late for dinner at Andrea's?"

She flushed. "What are you talking about?"

"I went to meet you at the bar and saw the two of you together. I felt hurt. I didn't want to create a scene."

"So you lied and pretended you were late and told me to meet you at Andrea's instead?"

"I didn't want to know the truth, so close to leaving London."

"What you're saying is you don't really trust me?"

"I want to. Really, I do. But I find it hard when you keep telling me you don't like Jamie, but he always seems to be there."

Like a kettle running out of steam I saw the emotions pass over her face – anger and indignation; confusion; more anger; then acceptance. "Why did you lie to me, Sophie?"

She paused. I wished I could read her thoughts. "I lied because I loved you," she whispered, repeating my words from the night after the kidnapping. "I didn't want you getting jealous or worrying. It didn't seem important. I didn't want to hurt you."

"*Loved* me?" I searched her eyes for any hint that she might still love me; that using the past tense had been a subconscious thing. I waited for seconds that felt like days for her to answer.

"I do love you, Christof, but I don't know if I *trust* you."

I didn't know what to say. Telling her she could trust me would count for nothing. "How do we rebuild this, Sophie? I don't want to lose you."

After a long pause, she eased her way towards me and let me hug her as we sat and watched the sun set over the Valtellina mountains. And I dared to hope that we might have a future.

It was the morning of what was scheduled to be our final day at the Palazzo and Sophie and I returned from a walk in the valley to find Luca waiting for us in our room. The thunder in his face made it clear this wasn't a courtesy call.

"I've got good news," he started, the forced politeness ringing through his tone as he smiled at Sophie and ignored me, "the police have confirmed that the gossip in the Camorra clans is about how Denucci got one over on you, Christof. He's laughing at you, so there's no need for him to take further revenge. He knows there's no way you'll testify now, so we believe you're safe.

It's over."

Sophie leapt at him with a bear hug, which he returned. "I can't believe it! That's brilliant! Is it really true?" she gabbled.

"I wouldn't joke about something as serious as this, Sophie, don't worry!" he smiled back at her. Her relief was contagious.

"Thank you so much, Luca! Are we really going to be ok?"

"Yes, I believe you are."

Sophie grinned, hugging him again before bouncing through the door shouting that she had to tell Bea, who was in her office, downstairs.

"It's wonderful news that we're safe, Luca. Thank you for everything." I said, as I sank onto the sofa, scarcely daring to let go of the fear and worry that had been a constant soundtrack in my thoughts for so many months.

Luca closed the door and the laughter vanished from his face, replaced with a thunderous scowl. "Who the fuck did you tell about the ring?" he yelled, making no attempt to maintain dignity, knowing we couldn't be overheard through the Palazzo's 500-year-old, metre-thick walls. "The police are demanding we hand it over, as evidence of Denucci's bribery in the fraud case. How the hell did they know about it?"

"You must have let slip when you told them about the kidnapping!" I defended myself, feeling confused, sprinting through my memories in case there had been any time I might have said anything. But there wasn't.

"I told them Sophie had been kidnapped and then ditched when the crowd blocked the road. I said nothing about them molesting her or taking anything; they would have insisted on pressing charges. It wasn't me."

"It wasn't me!" I yelled back. We were glaring at each other, our faces just inches apart. I could smell espresso and stale cigarettes. I wasn't going to blink first.

"Then who the hell told them, Christof?"

"How should I know? Maybe you told someone at work? Or one of the people who saw the ring said something?"

"Not possible. The only information about it is in the encrypted part of my hard drive, to which I am the only one with a password. And I took the precaution of using external agencies for the forensics and the valuation of the ring, so there wouldn't be anyone internally who could connect it with any of our cases. It certainly wasn't me."

"Everything is hackable, Luca. Our work proves that! And it wasn't me. I mean, really? I could see his anger running out of steam. "Why would I risk Sophie ever finding out by telling anyone? That would be crazy!" He knew I was right.

"But somebody knew, Christof. And they told the police about it. It seems that mole is working two ways."

Luca wandered over to the window to admire the view, distracting himself from the implications of this news. We both knew that the Denucci case was now closed for us, work-wise. The client work was finished and I wasn't going to testify. So that should mean it was all over.

But someone out there had been feeding information they shouldn't have had access to, to Denucci and to the police. And we had no idea where in the chain they might be getting that information from. Maybe it was more than one person. And even if Sophie and I were now unofficially 'safe', I felt a deep and urgent need to find out who that mole was. I hated the idea of a stranger knowing so much about me and passing on half-truths that endangered my safety – Sophie's safety.

Then it hit me. We were physically safe, but what if the mole told Sophie about the ring, as some kind of revenge? She would never forgive me. We would be over. I couldn't take the risk of that happening. But I had no way of preventing it. That fear would give me something new to lie awake at night, worrying about. I could sense it risked becoming my new obsession. I pushed it to the back of my mind, letting it gnaw away in silence at the peace Luca's news had brought me just ten minutes before.

And I knew, deep down, that it was all my fault. I had agreed to take Denucci's bribe. And I would spend forever worrying that Sophie might find out.

Luca headed back to Milan and Christof and I took a picnic from Bea with us on a long walk through the hillside. It was our last chance to get some quiet time together, before we flew back to England the next morning. I was opening up to accept affection from Christof again, but we were far from being lovers. There was a gulf between us; one I didn't know if we could close. I wanted to trust him again, to let him back in, but I didn't feel like I could; not yet.

On our walks over the past few days, we talked about some of the things that had been straining our relationship, before we came away. I hadn't realised how stressed-out Christof had been about me bumping into Jamie. It hadn't seemed like such a big deal to me. But I promised to write and tell him to leave me alone.

In return, Christof promised not to keep his work or his worries from me. And I promised to stop stressing about him working with Isabella, as long as he was honest about when he saw her. We're not back to how we were yet, and I'm not sure we ever will be, but I'm holding on to hope that things will change.

Towards the end of this afternoon's walk, I plucked up the courage to ask Sophie about our future; about whether she still wanted us to live together. My knees nearly buckled with relief when she looked shocked and surprised. Yes, we would still be living together. Yes, she wanted to try to make this work. But neither of us had the courage to mention our engagement. It was still too early for that. And neither of us brought up the subject of the ring or replacing it. I couldn't face that discussion and I knew that Sophie was still traumatised by how she had lost it.

"You have to make me a promise, Christof," Sophie said, letting me put my arm around her shoulder, as we leaned against an old tree with a breath-taking view of the setting sun painting pictures in the clouds.

"Go on…" was all I could manage. I felt a new wariness in our relationship that tainted every discussion, every question, every touch, with a wash of worry and tension.

"Promise me: no more lies. No more not telling the whole truth. I need to know I can trust you, if we're going to make this work."

I kissed the top of her head, breathing in the fragrance of her hair, as I closed my eyes and sighed, drowning in how much I loved her. "I promise," I replied. But I knew I was already lying to her. I had no choice.

Get The First Two Chapters Of Book 3

www.clarejosa.com/firsttellnolies/club

Members Get Access To:

Exclusive deleted scenes
Interviews with the author
The first two chapters of book 3 in the series
Book 2 ½ in the Denucci Deception series

Join Free Now:
www.clarejosa.com/firsttellnolies/club

Message From The Author:

I really hope you enjoyed *First, Tell No Lies*. If you did, please could you leave a review wherever you bought it (or on Amazon) letting people know why you liked it? It helps more readers to find the book! And you can let my team know by emailing hello@clarejosa.com. I would love to hear from you.

www.ClareJosaAuthor.com

About Clare Josa

Clare Josa speaks and teaches internationally on how changing the world isn't about what you *do*, it's about who you allow yourself to *become*.

She originally trained as an engineer, but she is also an NLP Trainer (practical psychology) and a certified Meditation & Yoga teacher. She is famous for demystifying Ancient Wisdom into practical actions you can take to change your life in less time than it takes to boil a kettle. And it all comes with a bucket load of common sense and a generous dollop of humour.

First, Tell No Lies is her second novel, following on from the 'unputdownable' You Take Yourself With You.

When not changing the world or compulsively writing, she loves hanging out with her family, somewhere sunny, experimenting in her kitchen with fermented food, or losing herself in a good book.

Printed in Great Britain
by Amazon